The Rumour

Also by Elin Hilderbrand

Winter Street
The Matchmaker
Beautiful Day
Summerland
Silver Girl
The Island
The Castaways
A Summer Affair
Barefoot
The Love Season
The Blue Bistro
Summer People
Nantucket Nights
The Beach Club

About the author

The following rumours about Elin Hilderbrand are true: she writes her novels in longhand, she is a good cook and a terrible gardener, and she is fighting breast cancer. Everything else is up for speculation. *The Rumour* is her fifteenth novel.

You can visit Elin's website at www.elinhilderbrand.net, follow her on Twitter @elinhilderbrand or find out more on her Facebook page www.facebook.com/ElinHilderbrand.

The Rumour

Elin Hilderbrand

HODDER &
STOUGHTON

First published in the USA in 2015 by Little, Brown and Company
A division of Hachette Book Group, Inc.
First published in Great Britain in 2015 by Hodder & Stoughton
An Hachette UK company

1

A CIP catalogue record for this title is available from the British Library

Trade Paperback ISBN 978 1 473 61117 7
Ebook ISBN 978 1 473 61116 0

Printed and bound by CPI Group (UK) Ltd, Croydon, CR0 4YY

Hodder & Stoughton policy is to use papers that are natural,
renewable and recyclable products and made from wood grown in sustainable
forests. The logging and manufacturing processes are expected to conform
to the environmental regulations of the country of origin.

Hodder & Stoughton Ltd
Carmelite House
50 Victoria Embankment
London EC4Y 0DZ

www.hodder.co.uk

It is with the humblest gratitude that I dedicate this book to
Dr. Michelle Specht, for saving my life,
and to
Dr. Amy Colwell, for saving my body.
#mamastrong

NANTUCKET

We didn't like to gossip; we loved to gossip.

Did you hear?

Most of the time, living on Nantucket comforted us; we felt like Mother Ocean was holding us in the palm of her hand. But sometimes, the island made us restless and irritable. Winter was bad, but spring was worse, because except for a few short weeks, it was indistinguishable from winter.

What had T. S. Eliot written? *April is the cruellest month.*

Gossip was always the most rampant in the spring. It ran like water in a newly thawed brook; it circulated through the air like pollen. We could no sooner refrain from repeating what we'd heard than we could keep from rubbing our swollen, itchy eyes.

We weren't mean spirited or vindictive or cruel; we were simply bored, and after the long stretch without summer visitors, summer money, summer magic, our reservoirs were dry.

Besides which, we were human beings, saddled with our own curiosities and our own insecurities. We were aware of things happening in the wider world—human genomes being decoded on the MIT campus, tectonic plates shifting

in California, Putin waging war in Ukraine—but none of these events captured our interest like those taking place on the 105 square miles of our home island. We gossiped at the dentist, in the salon, in the produce section of the Stop & Shop, around the bar at the Boarding House; we gossiped over appetizers at the Anglers' Club on Friday nights, between the pews of five o'clock Mass on Saturday nights, and in line at the Hub as we waited to buy our *New York Times* on Sunday mornings.

Did you hear?

There was never any way to predict who would be our subject. But if someone had told us, in the frigid, steel-skied middle of April, that most of our summer would be spent whispering about Grace and Eddie Pancik...

...and Trevor Llewellyn and Madeline King...

...and about the renowned landscape architect Benton Coe...

...our mouths might have dropped open in shock.

No way.

Not possible.

They were some of the loveliest people we knew.

APRIL

MADELINE

The first two calls were from Marlo, Angie's assistant, but the third call was from Angie herself, and Madeline let it go straight to voice mail.

She knew what Angie was going to say because Marlo had been quite effective at hammering home the point: they needed catalog copy for the new novel by Friday, or Monday at the *very* latest. Theirs was a business of deadlines.

As Madeline listened to Angie's message, she held the phone several inches from her ear, as if the distance would soften the blow.

New novel. Friday. Monday at the very latest. As I'm sure you're aware, Madeline.

Madeline was at her kitchen counter, with her blank legal pad sitting in front of her. Her previous novel, *Islandia,* had come to her like cold syrup out of a glass bottle. The progress was slow—line by line, paragraph by paragraph—but the path it would take had always been clear to her. *Islandia* had been a dystopian tale of Nantucket four hundred years in the future; the island was being consumed by the Atlantic Ocean, thanks to global warming. Everyone was doomed except for

Madeline's teenage protagonists, second cousins Jack and Diane (so named after Madeline's favorite song growing up), who survived in a dinghy until the novel's end.

Madeline credited inspiration for this novel to the seven months she had spent nursing her father-in-law, Big T, before he died. His prostate cancer had metastasized to his brain and then his liver, and though this had crushed Madeline's spirit, it had been beneficial to her imagination. Her prevailing thoughts were ones of illness, the decay of the body, the decay of mankind. She had then read a fascinating article about global warming in *The New Yorker* (which she had started subscribing to at age nineteen, in order to better herself). The article said that if humankind didn't change its pattern of consumption, islands like Nantucket and Martha's Vineyard, and barrier islands like the Outer Banks, would be subsumed in less than four centuries.

Islandia was a departure from the autobiographical nature of her previous two novels, *The Easy Coast* and *Hotel Springford*. It had been warmly welcomed by her publishing house and deemed a "bigger" book. Madeline's agent, Redd Dreyfus, had negotiated a brilliant deal, a low-six-figure advance for two books. This was such an exciting and unexpected development that it had nearly set Madeline's curly blond hair on fire.

Now, however, most of the advance was gone in an investment with Eddie, and Madeline was on the hook to deliver at least an *idea* for a second novel. She was supposed to come up with a hundred-word description for the catalog that would go to the sales reps.

But Madeline didn't even have that much.

She was blocked.

She was disrupted from her anxiety by the rumble of the

UPS truck and the thump of a package on the front porch. She hurried out, hoping to find a box containing an idea for a brilliant new novel, but she was treated instead to the school portraits of her son, Brick.

Wow, gorgeous.

Madeline sat down on the front step of the porch, even though it was freezing and she didn't have a coat on. She was mesmerized by how the portrait contained both the little boy Brick used to be—with his thick blond hair and the deep dimple in his right cheek—and the man he was rapidly becoming. He would look like Trevor and Big T, but with Madeline's blue eyes and her smile (which showed a little too much gum, she'd always self-critically believed). She carried the portraits inside and pulled all of Brick's school photos from the secretary, lining them up on the rug, from kindergarten through high school.

Good-looking kid, she thought. She had desperately wanted another child, but after three miscarriages, she gave up.

She wondered if Grace had gotten the twins' portraits and if she was going through this exact same ritual at her house on Wauwinet Road. Madeline grabbed her phone, thinking only briefly of the awful, soul-shrinking message from Angie, and she called Grace.

No answer at the house. Maybe she was out with the chickens. Maybe she was in the garden. Maybe she had a migraine. Madeline used to keep track of Grace's migraines on a special calendar, until Trevor found the calendar and told Madeline that one of the reasons she might not be as productive with her writing as she wanted was that she allowed herself to worry about things like Grace's migraines. Madeline had thrown the calendar away.

Should she call Grace's cell? Grace never answered; she checked her texts every two or three weeks. Madeline would have better luck mailing Grace a letter.

She hung up without leaving a message and then collected the pictures of Brick. It was official: she could get *nothing done* in this house. The dishwasher called to her: *Empty me!* The laundry in the dryer called to her: *Fold me!* The counter-tops said: *Wipe me down!* There was always *something*— the house phone rang, the garbagemen came, there was dinner to plan, shop for, prepare—every single night! Brick needed to be dropped off or picked up; the car had to be inspected, the recycling sorted, the checkbook balanced, the bills paid. Other mothers commented on how nice it must be that Madeline was able to "work from home." But working from home was a constant battle between the work and the home.

Friday. Monday at the very latest.

The mudroom door opened and shut, and Madeline heard whistling, something from *Mary Poppins*. Was it that late already? Madeline's husband, Trevor, strolled in, wearing his very cute pilot's hat. *"Chim-chiminey, chim-chiminey, chim-chim-cheroo!"* Trevor fancied himself the second coming of Dick Van Dyke.

"Hey," he said. He gathered Madeline up in his arms, and she rested her face against the front of his shirt and airline-issued polyester tie. Trevor was a pilot for Scout Airlines, which flew from Nantucket to Hyannis, Boston, and Providence. "How was your day?"

Madeline started to cry. She couldn't believe it was five o'clock already. How was her day? *What* day? Her day had evaporated. She had exactly nothing to show for herself.

"I'm blocked," she said. "I don't have a single idea, and the wolves are at the door."

"I'm telling you," he said. "You should just..."

She shook her head to silence him. She knew what he was going to say. He was going to tell her to write a sequel to *Islandia*. It was a logical solution to her problem, but in her heart, Madeline felt this was a cop-out. She had ended *Islandia* with her characters heading safely into an unknown future; that, she felt, was the *right* ending. She didn't want to tell readers what happened next. If she wrote a sequel, she would be doing so only because she couldn't come up with new characters and a new plot.

She couldn't come up with new characters or a new plot.

So maybe Trevor was right. A sequel. Could she undo the end of the world?

She wiped her eyes and raised her face for a kiss. Trevor said, "What's for dinner?"

"Pizza?" she said. "Thai food?"

His expression fell. She hadn't gotten any writing done, but she hadn't shopped for or made dinner, either. How could she explain that trying to come up with an idea to write about was even more time consuming than writing itself?

"I'm sorry," she said.

He kissed her forehead. "It's okay," he said. "Let's get pizza from Sophie T's. Is Brick getting a ride home from practice?"

"Yes," Madeline said. "With Calgary."

Trevor loosened his tie and pulled a beer from the fridge. "Guess who was on my first flight this morning."

"Who?" Madeline said.

"Benton Coe," Trevor said.

"Really," Madeline said.

Benton Coe was the owner of Coe Designs, the island's most prestigious landscape architecture firm. He was the man who was turning Grace's three-acre property into the most dazzling yard and gardens on Nantucket Island and possibly in the Commonwealth of Massachusetts.

Benton Coe was back.

Well, that would explain why Grace hadn't answered the phone.

GRACE

She had started her transformation secretly, just after the first of the year, in anticipation of this very day.

Benton's return.

She had started taking spinning classes at the gym, and she had lost twenty-one pounds — most of it weight she had gained when the twins were born and that she'd never quite been able to shed. Now, she was down two dress sizes and in need of new jeans. She had also, finally, allowed her stylist, Ann, to get the gray out of her part and add some chestnut highlights to the front of her dark hair. And all of the time she'd spent outside getting the preliminary gardening done and dealing with the hens had given her face the glow of the season's first sun.

She felt better about herself than she had in years.

Madeline had commented on this on Saturday night, when they were out to dinner at American Seasons. She and Grace

had gone to the ladies' room together, and when Madeline caught sight of Grace in the mirror, she said, "You look *hot*, sister. Downright *gorgeous*."

Eddie had noticed the weight loss ("You look good, Gracie—skinny") but not the hair, and the girls had noticed the hair ("Highlights," Allegra had said, "—smart move") but not Grace's new, svelte figure. Grace wasn't surprised. Eddie was consumed with his spec houses, Hope with her studies and the flute, Allegra with her romance with Brick Llewellyn and her potential modeling career. To the three of them, Grace was wife, mother, cook, housekeeper. She was the raiser of chickens and purveyor of organic eggs, she was a hypochondriac with her "recurring migraines." She was Eddie's lover every Sunday morning and on certain random nights of the week. Grace knew that her family loved her, but she wasn't their focus the way she had been when she and Eddie were first married and the girls were small.

Did she feel taken for granted? Sure, a little. She supposed she was hardly the only wife and mother to feel this way.

At ten o'clock on the dot, Benton's big black truck pulled into the driveway, and the tops of Grace's ears started to buzz. They would be turning pink, a sure sign that she was nervous. She had a bit of a crush on Benton Coe, a harmless crush that was never going anywhere, because Benton had a girlfriend named McGuvvy, and Grace, of course, was married.

She watched him climb out of the truck. Did he look different? No, he looked the same. Tall, tall, tall—a full eight or nine inches taller than Eddie—and he had the shoulders of a

king or a conqueror. He had ginger-colored hair that curled up from under his red Ohio State Buckeyes hat, and laugh lines at his brown eyes. He was wearing his usual spring uniform of a navy-blue hooded sweatshirt with a four-leaf clover on the front—the logo for Coe Designs—jeans, and work boots. He was lightly tanned. He had spent the winter in Morocco.

They were *friends*. She had missed him. Grace ran to the door to greet him.

"Benton!" she said.

When he saw her, he did a double take that made Grace's heart sing.

"My God, Grace," he said. "You look...wow. Just wow. I'm speechless."

She stepped out onto the front porch and hugged him tightly. He was so strong, he picked her clear up off the ground. And then they both laughed and Benton set her down.

"Good to see you!" he said.

"And you!" she said.

They stared at each other. Grace couldn't tell if it was romantic or awkward. Awkward, she decided. They were friends; conversation was supposed to come easily. She couldn't work with the man all summer and achieve their goals if she was going to act like a thunderstruck thirteen-year-old girl. She had to snap out of it!

"Thank you for the postcards," she said.

"You got them?" he said. "You never know with foreign mail."

"I got four or five," Grace said, trying to keep her tone casual. Those postcards, numbering five and tucked safely

into her lingerie drawer, had fueled her little crush throughout the chilly, gray winter.

Benton Coe. His reputation preceded him: the most talented landscape architect on Nantucket, even though he was barely forty. He had been on the island five years by the time Grace had hired him, having been brought over originally by the Nantucket Historical Association to overhaul the grounds of their twenty-four properties. Before coming to Nantucket, Benton Coe had designed gardens in Savannah, Georgia, and Oxford, Mississippi—places so lush, he said, that he could hear the grass grow. He'd grown up in Youngstown, Ohio, and gone to college at Ohio State, where his work-study job had been with the grounds crew, fostering his love of landscaping. He did a semester abroad in Surrey, England; he was still partial to English gardens. Nothing like them, he told Grace. The British were good at world domination but even better with phlox, foxglove, boxwood, and the rose.

By the time Benton Coe had finished with the NHA properties—winning awards from every horticultural and historical preservation organization in New England—he was in high demand. He did gardens for the Amsters out in Dionis, and the Kepplings in Shimmo—work that Grace was lucky enough to see through her involvement with the Nantucket Garden Club.

When Eddie bought the house in Wauwinet, with its three undeveloped acres of surrounding land, Grace had her chance. She hired Benton Coe.

They had been in sync from the beginning. Last summer, they had planted grass and carved out beds; they dug, tiled, and filled the swimming pool, and they constructed a foot-bridge that spanned the creek. Benton supervised the building of the garden shed and the henhouse. There were fifty decisions a day. Normally with clients, Benton was given free rein. But, he admitted, he was enjoying collaborating with Grace. It was more fun than deciding everything himself, he said. It was stimulating to execute plans with someone whose sensibility dovetailed so nicely with his own.

Grace was charmed by Benton Coe's choice of words. *Sensibility:* Had anyone before ever appreciated Grace's *sensibility?* Her aesthetic? Her taste? Her instincts? No, she didn't think so. She had been a dutiful daughter and grand-daughter, a tolerant sister, a diligent student, a halfway-decent breakfast waitress, a devoted wife and mother, and an excep-tional friend. But had anyone — including Eddie, including Madeline — appreciated Grace's sensibility?

Dovetail: it was such a delicate word, such a sweet and tender way of describing how Grace and Benton matched up, how they fit together without gaps or leaks, without strife or collision.

It was *stimulating,* he said, a word too sexual for Grace to properly contemplate.

At the end of last summer, Benton confessed that coming to Grace's house out in Wauwinet had been the high point of each day. He said that the reason he had never brought along his manager, Donovan, was because Benton had wanted to keep this project for himself.

Grace understood. She had begun to feel a flutter in her chest every time his black pickup pulled into the driveway.

Benton stopped by at ten o'clock, Monday through Saturday, even when it wasn't required. Sometimes, he stayed only ten minutes, enough time for a quick tête-à-tête, another phrase of his that Grace relished. She imagined their foreheads touching. She imagined them kissing.

But... only imagined.

Fall arrived, as it always did, and they put the garden to bed. Then it was winter, and Benton embarked on his travels. The first postcard arrived from Casablanca, postmarked January 4, the day he arrived. Two weeks later, one came from Essaouira, on the coast; a week later, one from Agdz, in the desert; two weeks later, one from the Ourika Valley, in the Atlas Mountains. All of these were signed exactly the same way: *Look at this! XO, Benton*

Twenty days passed with no postcards, during which time Grace figured he'd forgotten about her; or possibly his girlfriend, McGuvvy, had flown over for a visit. But then a postcard arrived from Marrakech that said: *My favorite place by far. I wish you could see what I'm seeing. XO, B*

This card set Grace's "sensibility" ablaze; she read it a thousand times. She used it as a bookmark in the novel she was reading, *The Sheltering Sky,* by Paul Bowles, chosen because it was as close as she could get to wandering through the souks and traversing the sand dunes of northern Africa herself.

She thought endlessly about Benton's change of wording. *I wish you could see what I'm seeing.* The skeptic in Grace said that this was merely a variation on the old postcard message *Wish you were here.* But the blossoming romantic in her pictured a tête-à-tête, their heads together, their eyes seeing the same thing, their sensibilities dovetailing.

She loved that he had shortened Benton to *B.*

Grace had gathered all the postcards together and placed them in her top dresser drawer with her underwear, bras, and her black silk pajamas.

Grace said, "Can I get you anything to drink?"

Benton snapped his fingers. "Darn it. I got you a present while I was away, but I forgot it. I'll bring it tomorrow."

"You didn't have to get me anything," Grace said. A present from Morocco! Grace's mind raced. She thought of the gauzy harem pants that belly dancers wore. She thought of silver finger cymbals, tasseled silk pillows in deep, rich colors; she thought of burled wood boxes with secret compartments. She thought of a hookah pipe packed with strawberry tobacco. She thought of exotic oils and fragrant spices — threads of saffron, cinnamon sticks, cardamom pods. She thought of the belly dancer again. Benton had bought her a present!

"Did you bring back gifts for all your clients?" she asked.

"No," he said. "Only you."

Only her! She practically backflipped her way out to the garden.

They spent nearly an hour inspecting each section of Grace's property, discussing possible changes and enhancements. They started at the far edge, way out by the Adirondack chairs

that overlooked Polpis Harbor—the water still resembled a cold steel plate—and they meandered over the rolling, grassy knolls to the swimming pool and hot tub (both still covered, although Grace and Eddie had used the hot tub late one night back in January, when the spec houses were on schedule and Eddie was more relaxed). They lingered at the tulip bed—Benton's baby—and at the rosebushes, which over the winter had become a thorny, inhospitable tangle.

"Things are coming along," Benton said. He touched Grace's back lightly, and an electric current ran up her spine, to her neck. "I think this year is our year."

They had a shared goal: they wanted a photo shoot in a major media outlet. Benton was partial to *Classic Garden* magazine, but Grace was thinking of a spread in the home-and-garden section of the Sunday *Boston Globe*. She had convinced Eddie to hire a publicist, Hester Phan, to whom he was paying a small fortune—but it was the only way to get news of their collaboration out there.

"Let me see the shed," Benton said. "I've missed it."

Grace unlatched the door. Benton ushered Grace through the door first, then followed. The space was tight with both of them inside; Grace feared he would hear her heart pounding.

The garden shed had been modeled after a traditional Nantucket home: gray shingles with white trim. Inside, it featured a soapstone counter and a copper farmer's sink. The far wall was covered with pegboard, on which hung Grace's rakes, hoes, spades, trowels, and pruners. There was a potting bench, handcrafted from reclaimed pine barn board, and shelves that held Grace's collection of watering cans and her

decorative pots. A painted sign hung over the farmer's sink: *A garden is not a matter of life or death. It is far more important than that.* The shed had an annex off the side that held the riding lawn mower and the three weed whackers. Although Grace had hired Benton, she did all of the hands-on gardening herself—the mowing, the weeding, the mulching, the pruning and deadheading. Along with tending the hens and running her organic-egg business, it was a full-time job. It was her passion.

The shed was the crown jewel of the yard. A garden was a garden was a garden, but magazine editors loved bricks and mortar. They wanted an interior space that was crisp, organized, and as whimsical as Santa's workshop.

Grace and Benton stood facing each other, their hips leaning against the edge of the sink. Benton was so tall that the top of his head grazed the slanted ceiling. Grace's ears were bright pink; she could feel it.

Benton took an exaggerated breath. "I love how this place smells," he said. "Cut grass and potting soil."

Grace too loved how the garden shed smelled. She loved it better than almost anything in the world.

"Do you want to see the hens?" she asked. "You know they'll cluck themselves into a frenzy for you."

Benton laughed. His eyes crinkled. Grace's ears burned like glowing coals. He said, "I have to hit the road, I'm afraid. Things to do, people to see."

People to see. Even this innocent phrase made Grace jealous. Her face must have shown her disappointment, because Benton said, "Don't worry, Grace. We have all summer in front of us."

*   *   *

Grace was still in a daze—she had broken two of Hillary's eggs accidentally—when the twins walked in, home from school.

Hope entered first, carrying her flute case. Then Allegra, carrying only the twelve-hundred-dollar Stella McCartney hobo bag she had bullied Eddie into buying her when Eddie took her to Manhattan for the modeling interview. Not a book or paper in sight, which was why Allegra had straight C's. Eddie let her slide because he had graduated from New Bedford High School with C's, and look at how successful he was now! Grace shook off the residue of whatever inappropriate emotions she'd been having for Benton Coe and focused on her girls, her sun and moon. Allegra was the sun—bright and hot and shining. Hope was the moon—placid, serene, inscrutable. Grace was a little more in awe of Allegra because...well, because she was Allegra. And Grace was more protective of Hope because they had almost lost her at birth.

"Hello, lovelies," Grace said. She tried to scoop both girls up in an embrace, but they executed a perfectly synchronized bob-and-weave to avoid her—Allegra to the left, Hope to the right—and headed toward their bedrooms, where they would remain with the doors shut until dinner.

Which, tonight, would be quiche Lorraine and spinach salad. Eddie liked meat and potatoes, but since he'd taken on the spec houses, he appreciated the frugality of eating their own home-farmed eggs.

Grace tried not to take offense at the evasion—not a word of greeting, no thought to ask how *her* day had been. If Grace

were to be very honest, she might admit that lately her daughters made her feel more lonely instead of less so.

"How was school?" Grace called after them. But there was no response.

"We're having quiche for dinner!" Grace said. "Around six!" No response.

There had most certainly been days this past winter when being so thoroughly ignored had sent Grace into a fog of depression. She yearned to make the girls cups of hot tea and bake them chocolate chip cookies and sit around looking at fashion magazines while Allegra talked about her weekend plans with Brick and Hope pulled out her flute and played a few bars of a Mozart concerto. But even Grace realized this was unrealistic. They were, after all, *teenage girls* and could be counted on to think only of themselves.

Today, Grace didn't care. Today, Grace headed back to her master bathroom to paint her toenails.

Benton Coe had returned. This year was their year. They had all summer in front of them.

HOPE

Sometimes she wished her parents had never told her the story of her birth, and yet it had been part of her personal narrative since she was old enough to understand it. Hope—or baby number two, the smaller, weaker twin—had had her umbilical cord wrapped around her neck, a fact that escaped

the obstetrician's notice because Allegra had popped out healthy, whole, and hogging the entire room's attention for the first time of a million in her life. Once the doctor noticed that baby number two was in distress, Grace was raced to the operating room, where Hope was delivered by emergency C-section four minutes later. But she was nearly dead by the time they got her out. She was, her father liked to dramatically say, the color of a damson plum, and he had thought, *There's no chance.* But the doctor had resuscitated Hope, kept her alive on a ventilator, and she and Eddie had been taken in the MedFlight helicopter to Boston while Grace and Allegra stayed at Nantucket Cottage Hospital.

Hope had been in the NICU for a week before she was named. The name her parents *had* picked out was Allison — Allegra and Allison, for nauseating twin symmetry — but after all that transpired, they changed their minds and decided to call her Hope, no explanation needed.

She was a survivor, an underdog who had prevailed; she was the smaller, weaker twin, all but ignored while her sister took center stage; she was lucky just to be alive. The doctors had told her parents that Hope might be brain damaged or hindered in some other way.

"But," her mother said, "you are just as right as rain."

Hope had no idea what that meant, but she did wish her parents had kept the story of her birth to themselves. She wished it were secret history that nobody ever talked about, rather than being the event that defined her.

Smaller, weaker, lucky to be alive. Whereas Allegra was bigger and stronger, her easy life an apparent birthright. In the fourth-grade class play, Allegra had been cast as Alice in

Alice in Wonderland, and Hope as the Dormouse. Then, as now, this had pretty much summed up their differences.

Allegra was okay. At times. Not as smart as Hope, or at least not as book smart; in school, she put forth minimum effort. Hope had one class with Allegra: health, taught by the phys ed teacher, Ms. Norman. It was a layup, the easiest A in the world, because it was nutrition and exercise and personal hygiene, basic stuff everyone on earth already knew from being a human and being raised by other humans. And yet Allegra never handed in her homework, and when Ms. Norman called on her in class, asking her to name the most prevalent nutrient found in milk, Allegra gave a derisory laugh and said, "Um? Don't know?" She sounded like a moron, and Hope was embarrassed to have shared a womb with her. Anyone who had ever watched a cereal commercial knew the answer was calcium.

Out of the classroom, however, Allegra and her best friend, Hollis Brancato, ruled the school. They were the real twins, matched in their prettiness, their long, shiny hair (although Hollis's was blond to Allegra's brunette), the makeup right out of magazines, their carefully curated clothes. Who knew how many thousands of dollars Allegra had wheedled out of their father so that she could have "pieces" by Parker and Alice + Olivia and Dolce Vita. Allegra's one coup over Hollis was that she had been invited to New York City for a modeling interview. Allegra had told Hollis and everyone else at school that she was "still waiting to hear," meaning she might start her climb up to the ranks of Gisele and Kate any day. Only Hope knew that the woman at the modeling agency had declared Allegra three inches too short and too "standard issue" in the beauty department to ever get any work.

The other thing that only Hope knew was that, although Allegra had been dating Brick Llewellyn for the past two years, she was cheating on him with Ian Coburn, a rich kid who had graduated from Nantucket High School the year before and who was now a freshman at Boston College.

To Hope's knowledge, Allegra had seen Ian three of the past four weekends. Allegra was supposed to be flying over to the Cape every Saturday to take a fancy, expensive, guaranteed-to-get-results SAT prep course at the community college, but Allegra had ditched the class, and Ian picked her up in his red Camaro and they "drove around," whatever that meant. This past weekend, they had gone to the Cape Cod Mall, where Ian bought Allegra three Chanel lipsticks from the makeup counter at Macy's; then they enjoyed a long, boozy lunch at the Naked Oyster, Allegra using a fake ID saying that she was a twenty-seven-year-old resident of Grand Rapids, Michigan. Allegra had asked Hope to cover for her—both with Brick and with her parents. She had offered to *pay* Hope, or lend Hope the fake ID, even though Allegra and Hope both knew Hope would never need it.

Hope agreed, but not because she wanted the ID or the money.

She wanted Brick.

For two years, Hope had assumed there would be *no way* Brick would ever break up with her sister. They would be one of those couples who grew up together, made it work long distance through four years of college (if Allegra got into college, which at this point seemed doubtful), and then married, had children, and found themselves celebrating their fiftieth wedding anniversary. Although Brick might have shared this vision, what neither he nor Hope had considered was that

Allegra was Allegra, which meant not smart enough to know a good thing when she had it. Allegra was a seeker and a climber and an opportunist, and she had a short attention span. Allegra would get caught with Ian Coburn, and that would be the end of her and Brick. Hope just had to wait.

Hope and Brick texted each other regularly about their honors chemistry homework, a fact that Hope did not share with her sister, and she knew Brick didn't either. Allegra hadn't been selected to take honors chem; she was in regular chem with other underachievers like Hollis and their friend Bluto.

At five thirty, when Hope knew Brick would be home from baseball practice, she shot him a text: *Hot glass looks like cool glass.* This was how they started every conversation about their chem homework, an inside joke referring to the enormous sign hanging over the Smart Board in their classroom. Mr. Hence lived in mortal fear of one of his students picking up a beaker that had recently been over the Bunsen burner.

No response. Maybe Brick wasn't ready to tackle chem yet. Maybe he was taking a shower or hanging out with his parents. Brick liked to spend time with his parents — whereas Hope, and especially Allegra, avoided it like the plague — because Trevor and Madeline were so cool, and the three of them in their family were, like, friends.

Sometimes Hope thought that she might not want to date Brick as much as become his adopted sister.

She texted: *Have you looked at the questions on page 242? Inert gases?*

No response. Hope could send two unanswered texts but not three. That would make her look desperate and pushy.

A second later, her phone pinged.

Brick wrote, *Was your sister really at class on Saturday? Or did she ditch and go to the mall?*

Hope ogled her screen. Here it was, then, at a time she least expected it. Brick was on to Allegra. It was all Hope could do not to spill the beans.

She wrote: *Class, I think. Why?*

Brick wrote: *Someone said they saw her at the mall.*

Hope wrote: *Which someone?*

Brick wrote: *Someone.*

Hope wrote: *Come on. Who.*

Brick wrote: *Parker Marz. He said she was with some guy in a Boston College sweatshirt. Doesn't your cousin go to BC?*

Hope chewed her pencil eraser. Her cousins were all older, although one of them—the biggest, most pompous jerk of the bunch—*had* gone to BC, prompting Eddie to tell his favorite joke. *How do you know if someone goes to BC? They'll tell you.*

Hope wrote: *One of our cousins went to BC. A while ago.*

Brick wrote: *Oh. Okay.*

Hope wrote: *Did you ask Allegra about it?*

Brick wrote: *Nah. Not a big deal. Never mind.*

Burying his head in the sand, Hope thought. She couldn't blame him. The truth was too awful to contemplate.

Hope went to church every week with her mother. She was a spiritual person, she believed in God, she bought most of the tenets of the Catholic Church but not all of them. She did believe in prayer, and so she said a heartfelt one for Brick, and then she opened to page 242 and started learning about the inert gases.

EDDIE

He bounced up the cobblestone street in his Porsche Cayenne, wearing his lucky Panama hat, waving at everyone he saw. Grace liked to accuse him of what she called "indiscriminate waving."

"You didn't even *know* that person," she said once. "Why did you wave?"

The fact was, Eddie was a little nearsighted, and he feared not waving to the wrong person more than he feared waving to a complete stranger. A not-wave in the real-estate business could mean a killed deal or a lost rental; it could mean missing out on thousands of dollars of potential income.

Next to Eddie, on the passenger seat, were four bills from the spec houses on Eagle Wing Lane. Or, more correctly, four bills from 13 Eagle Wing Lane, because Eddie had been forced to stop construction on numbers 9 and 11. He simply didn't have the cash.

Getting four bills in one day should be illegal, Eddie thought. Three should be the maximum. But today's mail had brought four; his secretary, Eloise, had handed them over, pinched between her thumb and index finger, as if she were giving him someone's snotty handkerchief.

The first bill, for putting in the foundation, came in at twenty-two grand. Eddie blinked, then felt a rush of relief when he realized he had already paid that one. But a call to Gerry, the foundation guy, revealed that Eddie had paid for the foundations of numbers 9 and 11 but not for the foundation of number 13.

His Panama hat was not lucky. He would have taken it off

and thrown it into the way back, but he so believed in its powers that he feared taking it off in anger would cause him to crash the Porsche and die, leaving Grace and the girls in debt.

Before he'd left the office, he'd stopped by the desk of his sister, Barbie, who was the only other broker that worked with him, because she was, essentially, the only person on Nantucket that he trusted other than his wife and children.

He said, "What am I gonna do about money?"

Barbie looked up at him through her frosted bangs. She wasn't the most beautiful woman on the island, but she presented what she had to maximum advantage. She always wore a dress — she favored Diane von Furstenberg wrap dresses (Eddie had no clue, but Allegra had schooled him as to Aunt Barbie's tastes), always heels (Manolo Blahniks), always the perfume (he didn't know what it was called, but it was so distinctively *her* that it might as well have been called Barbie). She was wearing her signature piece of jewelry: a black pearl that was the same size as the jawbreakers they used to steal from the five-and-dime when they were kids.

They had grown up on Purchase Street in New Bedford, dirt poor. High school for Eddie had been two pairs of corduroy pants (gray and beige) and two pilled sweaters (gray and beige), two button-down shirts (white and red plaid), and a pair of zippy red-and-blue running shoes that his mother had found at Goodwill. The shoes had come to define him as he proceeded to break every sprinting record at New Bedford High School and other high schools across the Commonwealth, earning himself the nickname Fast Eddie.

Eddie was able to run away from his disadvantages, but

Barbie, eleven months his junior, had been forced to face them. She had been teased mercilessly about her clothes, her shoes, her hair, her smell—and she had gotten into fights and was suspended three times before she graduated from high school. In Barbie's mind, he knew, there could never be enough money.

"I have a novel idea," she said. "Try selling a house."

"Funny," he said. The market was a frozen tundra.

"Well," Barbie said, checking her desk calendar, "that guy is coming with his group to Low Beach Road next week."

"What guy?"

"You know what guy," Barbie said. "The guy who asked."

The guy who asked: Eddie wished he didn't know what his sister was talking about, but he did. She was referring to Ronan Last-Name-Withheld.

One of the perennial aces in Eddie's hand was the house at 10 Low Beach Road. This was a showcase house right on the Atlantic Ocean with six—count them, six—master suites, an infinity-edge pool, two gourmet kitchens (one indoor, one outdoor), a grass tennis court, a five-thousand-square-foot basement with a movie theater, an arcade filled with vintage pinball machines, a gym that was exactly like the one the New England Patriots worked out in during the off-season, a sauna, a mahogany-paneled billiards room, and a walk-in cigar humidor. Also, there was a stucco-walled wine cellar with a table that had originally been built for William of Orange. The house rented for fifty thousand dollars a week, and Eddie had the exclusive listing. The owner was a thirty-year-old graduate of Nantucket High School who had gone to Cal Tech, where he invented a computer chip that was used

in every ATM in America. The owner had married a super-model and lived out in L.A. The owner and supermodel came to Nantucket for two weeks every August; the rest of the season, the house was Eddie's to rent.

The year before, Eddie had rented the house to a group of businessmen from Las Vegas. They were a gaming operation called DeepWell that had chosen Nantucket for their annual retreat. The leader of the group, Ronan Last-Name-Withheld, had arrived at the house before Eddie's team of five Russian housecleaners were quite finished, and Ronan LNW said, "Any chance these girls could come back later and entertain the guys?"

"Entertain?" Eddie had asked. He knew what Ronan LNW was getting at — or he *thought* he did, anyway. He squinted quizzically at Ronan. "They don't juggle, and I'm pretty sure they don't sing."

Ronan said, "Ten grand extra in it for you. Per night."

Ten grand per night. Eddie had felt dizzy.

He wasn't going to lie: for a moment, he had considered it. He would pay the girls a thousand dollars apiece per night, and he and Barbie would split the other five — per night.

But then his good sense took over, his moral compass spun and landed on true north, and Eddie said, in a self-righteous tone of voice he didn't even *recognize,* "No, I'm sorry, I don't think that will work out."

Ronan LNW had backed off immediately. "Okay, man, no problem, no problem. I was only asking."

*   *   *

But now, as Eddie drove out of town, toward his house on the Wauwinet Road—where, it was certainly possible, more bills awaited—he thought, *Ten grand per night.* Over the course of a week, his cut would be seventeen-five. *Could* he ask the girls? Would they *understand?* It would be a lot of money for them, possibly too much money to turn down. It was illegal, of course, so there was the risk of getting caught.

When Eddie had posed this question to Barbie, she had snorted and said, "It's the world's oldest profession, Eddie. You hardly invented it."

He gave her a look.

She said, "It couldn't hurt to ask, you know. Just call them and ask. They love you. They would eat fire for you."

The pile of bills on the passenger seat seemed to smolder, and at the same time, Eddie's heartburn started, even though he had eaten only a bread-and-butter sandwich for lunch.

Fifty-eight large. There was nowhere else to get the money short of taking a third mortgage out on his house. He could probably squeeze another forty or fifty in equity there. The two commercial properties he owned were leveraged to the hilt. He was sinking. There was no other way to look at it. He, Edward Pancik, Fast Eddie, the savviest real-estate agent on this island, was going under.

There wasn't really room in his life right now for a moral compass.

He decided to do some exploratory work. First, a call to Ronan LNW.

"Hey, man," Eddie said. "It's Eddie, Eddie Pancik, Fast Eddie, Nantucket."

"Fast Eddie!" Ronan LNW said. People loved his nickname, men especially. Eddie wasn't quite sure why.

"Hey, do you remember asking me about those Russian girls last year?"

"Yeah, man," Ronan said. "Why? Have you rethought the idea? Possibly landed in a different square?"

"Possibly," Eddie said.

Next, the more challenging conversation. Eddie called Nadia, the spokesperson for the five Russian girls, as her English was the best.

He explained the indecent proposal as delicately as he could. *Group of American businessmen checking into the house next week... Would you be willing to get all dolled up and go over around ten o'clock at night and have drinks with the gentlemen?*

It would mean a thousand dollars, cash, for each of you.

But... it's probably not just drinks, Nadia. You girls would have to do whatever they asked.

And you can't tell anyone — or you'll be fired and then deported.

Nadia was silent for a second, and Eddie thought, *Oh boy.* Nadia and the girls were illegal, so they had no recourse against him for asking, but still, he felt like a heel. If they quit, he would have to replace them, probably at a higher wage.

But then Nadia started babbling away in Russian, presumably to Elise or Tonya. The girls squealed with what sounded like... joy? Excitement?

"Yes," Nadia said to Eddie. "Yes, we do it."

It sounded to Eddie like the girls were *crazy* about the idea. Could he be misunderstanding their tone? A thousand dollars a night *was* an assload of money. Besides which, these men weren't losers picked off Times Square; nor were they thick-necked Russian thugs. These were cultured, refined, rich business executives.

Fair to say, three of the five probably had delusions of a marriage proposal somewhere down the road. They sounded as excited as girls going to the prom.

Elise took the phone away from Nadia. Elise was the smallest of the bunch, the runt of the litter. She said, "Eddie, you are best, thank you, Eddie!"

Eddie hung up the phone feeling weirdly proud of himself. Almost as if he had, indeed, invented it.

MAY

MADELINE

Redd Dreyfus, Madeline's agent, called to say he'd bought her two more weeks with the catalog copy.

"And when I say bought, I mean *bought*," he said. "I cashed in a favor that Angie Turner has owed me for eight years, a favor I have been saving and polishing like a diamond. And I am using it on your behalf. Don't make me sorry, Madeline. Come up with something great."

This should have made Madeline feel better—she had two more weeks—but instead, the mounting pressure made her head ache.

She meant to spend her first day of reprieve *really brainstorming*...but when she went in search of her favorite pen, it turned into an hour of organizing the junk drawer. In her defense, that drawer *really* needed to be cleaned out. Madeline found half a petrified peanut butter sandwich in there, along with broken scissors, an empty tin of ground pepper, four lanyards from Scout Air, a campaign pin from 2006 for a selectman who no longer lived on Nantucket, three bottles of dried-up nail polish (when was the last time Madeline had worn nail polish?), as well as rubber bands, paper

clips, expired coupons, safety pins, screws, nails, picture hooks, bottle caps, Elmer's glue, a baby's pacifier, and, yes, thankfully, her favorite pen — bright pink, for breast-cancer awareness.

The second hour Madeline spent on eBay, looking for drawer organizers. She had a crazy idea that if she cleaned the clutter from the junk drawer, she would clean the clutter from her brain.

Drawer organizers ordered: $21.99 with shipping.

Then, shockingly, it was three o'clock in the afternoon and time for her to go to Brick's baseball game.

In the bleachers, Madeline sat with Rachel McMann, Calgary's mother. Rachel was a nice woman, if a touch overbearing and a bit rah-rah for Madeline's taste. Rachel always wore her Nantucket Whalers apparel to games, and she carried a navy-and-white pom-pom, which she shook at every possible opportunity. Rachel had gone to the University of Delaware, where, she liked to tell people, she had been social director of her sorority, Kappa Alpha Theta.

Rachel worked as a real-estate agent for Bayberry Properties, which was the rival of Eddie's agency, Island Fog Realty. For this reason, Eddie and Grace did not care for Rachel.

Plus, there was the thing that had happened between Grace and Eddie's daughter Hope and Rachel's son, Calgary, at Christmas. If Grace knew Madeline was voluntarily sitting with Rachel McMann, she would strongly disapprove.

But Madeline believed that the parents of her child's friends and teammates were a necessary part of her personal

community. Brick and Calgary had been friends since pre-school. Madeline and Rachel had been attending sporting events together since the kids were five years old, playing T-ball. And today, Madeline could use a dose of Rachel's optimism.

Madeline had actually brought her legal pad to the game, just in case inspiration struck between the second and third innings or during a trip to the concession stands for sun-flower seeds.

Rachel eyed the notebook with her usual sunny enthusiasm. She said, "How's the writing going?"

Madeline couldn't help but be truthful; it was her nature. She said, "Working from home is killing me. Today, I organized the junk drawer and spent an hour on eBay."

Rachel said, "You need a writing studio."

Madeline said, "You got that right."

Rachel said, "I'm serious. Like Virginia Woolf said, every woman writer needs five hundred pounds a year and a room of one's own."

Madeline blinked. She was impressed that Rachel McMann had just quoted Virginia Woolf. Even Grace might have been won over by that.

Rachel leaned in. She said, "Seriously, Madeline, I have just the place."

Madeline should have stopped Rachel then and there. She should have said that, while a writing studio would have been nice, it was a pipe dream, because she and Trevor couldn't afford such an extravagance. Some months, their mortgage was a stretch—not to mention utilities, insurance, groceries, cell phone bills, gas, car repairs, Saturday nights out, Brick's college fund, and a large leftover hospital bill

from when Big T died. *Life is expensive*, Madeline should have said. *Virginia Woolf will have to wait.*

But instead, Madeline said, "Really?"

Rachel said, "Yes, really! A one-bedroom unit in the blue Victorian on the corner of Centre and India. The last time one of those units became available was in 2004."

And Madeline said, "Wow."

Much to Madeline's relief, Rachel had let the subject drop there. She resumed watching the game and shaking the pom-pom, and Madeline held her blank legal pad protectively on her lap.

The next day, as Madeline was trying to brainstorm but was also chopping onions, potatoes, and carrots for a pot roast — because she couldn't let dinner slide once again — Rachel called and said, "What time can you come look at the unit on Centre Street?"

Madeline had stammered before finally saying, "You... mean today?"

"Today," Rachel said. "It will go today, or tomorrow at the latest. It's exactly what you're looking for, Madeline, I promise."

Madeline stared at the mess of onion skins, potato peels, and carrot tops on her cutting board. The pot roast would go in the slow cooker, but all of this would have to be cleaned up, and she had to run to the store for more beef broth. How did other women get *anything* done?

I need to get out of this house, she thought.

"I'll come right now," Madeline said.

The apartment *was* ideal, in its simplicity and location. Madeline had hoped the price would be outrageous, way beyond her means, so that she could automatically dismiss it. But it was far less than Madeline had expected. And Rachel was willing to give her a six-month lease...because she was a friend.

"Let me call Trevor," Madeline said.

"Naturally," Rachel said.

Madeline listened to the ringing of Trevor's phone. If he didn't answer, she would have an excuse to back out.

"Hello?" Trevor said.

She explained the situation sotto voce: looking at a writing studio, in town, not a bad price, six-month lease. Should she try it out, like an office where she could go to write?

"Hell yes," he said. "It's *exactly* what you need."

It *was* exactly what she needed. But it was money out the door, the last of her advance.

She said, "I'm just worried...I mean, we promised Brick a car, and we still have six installments due to the hospital for your dad..."

"You have to spend money to make money," Trevor said. "We can buy Brick a car when your next royalty check comes, and we're on a payment plan with the hospital. You shouldn't have to give up a dream situation because of bills my father left behind. This is an investment in your next book."

Madeline took a deep breath. The only way she could describe this moment was as one where she decided to jump off a cliff, or out of an airplane.

She said, "I'm going to take it."

Trevor said, "Good girl."

*   *   *

Madeline hung up. She said to Rachel, "I'm going to take it."

Rachel said, "You are the luckiest woman in the world to have a husband like Trevor. Andy would never let me do this. He would think it looked bad."

She squinted at Rachel. "Do *you* think it looks bad?" she asked. "That I got my own place?"

"No!" Rachel exclaimed. "You have a *reason*. You're an *artist. A novelist.*"

An artist. A novelist. Madeline basked in the warmth of those words.

Virginia Woolf. A room of one's own.

Rachel handed Madeline the keys and gave her a squeeze. "Congratulations," she said.

The next morning, Madeline packed up her legal pad, her pens, the novel she was reading — *Family Happiness*, by Laurie Colwin, for the fortieth time — and her own brown-bag lunch. Down the road, she would stock the apartment with groceries, but not today. Today, she was going to write write write write write.

The apartment was part of an old whaling captain's home. It had been built in 1873, refurbished in 1927 and then again in 2002, when it was subdivided into apartments. Rachel said that the woman who had been living in the unit before Madeline had moved to the Virgin Islands because she

couldn't handle another Nantucket winter. It included a parking spot—that alone, Madeline thought, made the place worth the rent. Across the street was Madeline's favorite breakfast restaurant, Black-Eyed Susan's. It wasn't open for the season yet, but soon enough Madeline would be able to pop over and get a veggie scramble and a latte to go. City living!

Madeline fit her key into the lock and stepped into…her apartment!

It was *so exciting*—although, in truth, the space was nothing special. The walls were painted flat eggshell white. The previous renter had, thankfully, left behind some basic pieces of furniture: a sofa and two armchairs covered in beige linen slipcovers, a plush area rug in squares of varying aquas and blues, a round blond wood dining table with four chairs, and—the only thing of interest—a wooden box with fifteen compartments, covered with a thin sheet of glass. In each compartment lay a bird's egg nestled in straw—plover, eastern gray gull, black-backed gull, long-tailed duck, oystercatcher, least tern.

Rachel had apologized about the box with the bird eggs and had offered to dispose of it, but Madeline wanted to keep it.

There was a small galley kitchen with particleboard cabinets, a tiny bathroom with a fiberglass stall shower, and a bedroom containing nothing but a full-size box spring and mattress, bare of linens.

The apartment wasn't remarkable in any aspect—except that it was hers.

So here was something she'd missed out on all her life: a place of her own. Madeline wanted to walk down the street

to Flowers on Chestnut and buy a fresh bouquet, she wanted a selection of herbal teas, she wanted colorful throw pillows and a soft chenille blanket, she wanted beeswax taper candles that she would light when the sun started to go down, she wanted a wireless speaker so she could listen to Mozart and Brahms.

No time to dream about that now. Madeline needed to write! She turned her cell phone off. Nothing was a natural predator of productive fiction writing like the cell phone. Ditto the laptop. As she had well learned, the laptop could destroy a day.

Madeline took her legal pads, her pens, and the Laurie Colwin book out of her backpack and set up a "desk" at the round dining table.

Candles would be nice.

And Mozart.

But for now, she would have to go without.

Madeline had wanted to be a writer since she was old enough to hold a pencil. The desire was coded in her genes, but it was also a result of how she had been raised, or not raised. She had grown up in the help quarters of the Hotel del Coronado near San Diego, where her mother worked as a banquet waitress. In the long nights of her mother's absence—every night potentially terrifying, as the Hotel del was *known* to be haunted by the ghost of Kate Morgan—Madeline would keep her imagination occupied by writing stories about a girl hero named Gretchen Green. Gretchen Green was the oldest of seven sisters, she had two glamorous parents, she lived in a

beach mansion in La Jolla, and she was followed everywhere by her dachshund, Walter Mondale. Madeline had lost all of her Gretchen Green stories, but if she were to come across them now, she knew she would find blatant documentation of every single element that had been missing from her own childhood. Sisters. Parents. A home. A pet. A sense that she, Madeline, was special.

The passion for writing lasted into college. Madeline attended San Diego State, where she studied with a female writer who was so fabulous and inspiring that Madeline was terrified to disappoint her and therefore had handed in only incomplete stories. *It's not quite finished* had been Madeline's standard excuse. Since none of her pieces was ever truly done, they could not be criticized for imperfections.

The writing professor was encouraging, nonetheless. "You have a way with language," she told Madeline. "Your pieces have a lot of surface energy. I would be interested in seeing you delve deeper. You should try and finish at least one of these stories. You seem to have an issue with resolution."

In her senior year, Madeline applied to four MFA programs, but she was accepted at only one, her last choice, Bellini University in Florida—otherwise known as Bikini University.

Depression ensued. Madeline had had her heart *set* on the University of Iowa. When the rejection letter came, she burst into tears. If it wasn't going to be Iowa, then she wanted Columbia, but that didn't happen either (the applicant pool, the letter said, was especially strong that year); nor did she

get into the University of Michigan. It looked like it would be Bellini or nothing.

At that time, Madeline was dating a former USC football player named Geoffrey, who worked as a bouncer at the Coaster Saloon, on Mission Beach. She knew Geoffrey had strong feelings for her, but he was a loser. Mission Beach was seedy, and Geoffrey sold drugs on the side. When Madeline told Geoffrey that she was applying to graduate school, he panicked about her moving away and said he would go with her. When Madeline expressed skepticism about this plan, he got a tattoo of her name on the soft underside of his forearm. *MAD,* the tattoo said, because this was what he called her.

Geoffrey was excited to move to Florida and get something going there, which meant getting a job at a bar and finding people to sell drugs to.

No, Madeline decided. She wasn't going to Florida. She would not settle for Bikini University, and she would not settle for Geoffrey. Late one night, after his shift, she broke up with him.

What transpired next was the worst thing that had ever happened to Madeline. On a night shortly after the breakup, Geoffrey went on a bender of tequila and cocaine, and he showed up at Madeline's dorm room at three o'clock in the morning, when both Madeline and her roommate were fast asleep, and he carried Madeline out of the building. He loaded her into the back of a panel van he had stolen from the parking lot of the Coaster Saloon and bound her wrists and ankles with plastic zip ties. He gagged her with a bandanna and took her to a motel in Encanto, where he kept her for fifty-two hours, until he finally ran out of cocaine and passed

out cold. Madeline was able to make enough noise banging her elbows against the flimsy hotel wall that a Hispanic cleaning lady heard her, opened the door, and called the police.

After Madeline testified and after Geoffrey was sent to jail, she wanted to get as far away from Southern California as she possibly could. With the help of her former San Diego State professor, Madeline found a bed for the summer in a "writer's retreat" on Nantucket Island. The "writer's retreat" ended up being a bunch of Chi O girls from the University of North Carolina who had majored in English and liked to host poetry slams. But the room was cheap, and Madeline found a job busing tables at 21 Federal, leaving her days free to write.

By the end of summer, she had finished her first piece of writing ever—a novel entitled *The Easy Coast,* about a young woman who is brutally kidnapped by her loser drug-dealing boyfriend.

With further help from her former San Diego State professor, Madeline sent *The Easy Coast* to three agents in New York, and within a week, all three had called saying they wanted to represent her. Madeline flew from Nantucket to New York to meet with these agents, and this was how she met Trevor.

He had been her pilot.

Trevor liked to describe the way Madeline looked when he first met her: she was a beautiful blond from Southern California on the day her greatest dream was about to come true.

That year, in Madeline's memory, was a giant starburst, an explosion of heat and light. Her book found an agent—Redd Dreyfus—and shortly thereafter, a thirty-thousand-dollar

advance from an up-and-coming editor named Angie Turner at the publishing house Final Word. *And* Madeline met Trevor Llewellyn, and the two of them fell in love. Nine months into the relationship, they were engaged. By that time, Madeline's book had received two starred prepublication reviews, from the notoriously cranky *Kirkus* and from *Publishers Weekly,* both announcing the emergence of a startling new talent.

"Startling new talent." Madeline turned that phrase over and over in her mind as she stared now at her blank legal pad.

The Easy Coast hadn't been a *huge* commercial success—it sold around fifteen thousand copies in hardcover—but it did well enough that Angie offered her a contract for a second novel.

Madeline's next book, *Hotel Springford,* had been about a girl growing up in a grand old storied and haunted hotel with her banquet-waitress mother. It hadn't sold as well as *The Easy Coast*, but Madeline had written it when Brick was a baby and she was too consumed with changing diapers and pureeing squash to worry about book sales.

After *Hotel Springford,* Madeline was surprised to feel the urge to write subside, for the first time in her life, supplanted by the joys and exhaustion of motherhood. She decided to take a hiatus from writing and just enjoy being a mom for a while. She loved life with Brick; it made the bumps in the road—her three lost pregnancies, Big T's illness and death—bearable.

When Brick entered middle school and Madeline's hopes for another child were pretty much dashed, she got back to writing fiction on her own timetable. The result was *Islandia,*

which earned her the six-figure, two-book deal and ultimately landed her in her current predicament.

It had seemed like *so much money* last year, but after Redd's cut and taxes, what was left was enough to pay off their backed-up credit cards, invest the fifty thousand dollars with Eddie, who seemed to make money in his sleep...and rent the apartment.

Madeline stared at the blank page. Would scented candles help? It was quiet in the apartment, but Madeline could hear voices and passing traffic out on the street. Mozart or Brahms would block that out. Writing a novel on deadline was hard work, especially when she was so preoccupied.

She gazed out the window, down onto Centre Street. Back in the whaling days, Centre Street was known as Petticoat Row, because the men had all gone off on whaling expeditions, leaving behind the women to run the businesses.

Petticoat Row wasn't a bad title, but Angie was allergic to historical novels. They didn't sell unless your name was Philippa Gregory.

The streetscape wasn't as inspiring as Madeline had hoped.

A favor as cherished as a diamond had been cashed in on her behalf. Redd Dreyfus was an old-fashioned New York literary agent. He was rotund, he drank Scotch, he smoked cigars and took editors to lunch at the Grill Room at the Four Seasons, where he ordered the sirloin bloody rare. For some reason, Angie owed him. Angie Turner was whippet thin; she wore pencil skirts and slingbacks. She drank chardonnay and picked at salads. Madeline wondered about the favor. She imagined it involved another author, someone deeply respected and badly behaved. She imagined it involved sex, drugs, or

money, though more likely it had to do with foreign rights or a publicity gaffe.

She would have liked to have parsed the particulars of her emotions with Trevor, but Trevor would be in the air. People thought that being a pilot was hard, but once one knew how to fly, it was actually pretty much the same as driving a bus, but with more sex appeal. Because of the sunglasses, Madeline liked to say.

She picked up the display box of bird eggs. They were all delicate and perfect in their eggness, each nestled in a cushy bed of straw in its compartment. Alternately speckled, smooth, and cobbled, with the subtlest variance of colors: white, cream, ivory, porcelain, tint of blue, tint of green. Was the woman who had moved to the Virgin Islands an ornithologist? Madeline had once given a magazine interview in which she said *Every life contains a novel*. Could she reasonably write a novel about a female ornithologist who moves from Nantucket to the Virgin Islands?

She knew nothing about the Virgin Islands.

A knock at the door startled Madeline so badly that she nearly tossed the box of eggs into the air.

Who...?

Madeline was terrified, despite the fact that it was broad daylight and she was smack dab in the middle of town. She still suffered from a lingering case of PTSD, even now, more than twenty years after her kidnapping. She was terrified of sudden noises, and she would *never* have been able to write an S&M novel like *Fifty Shades*. Ropes and blindfolds and gags made her hyperventilate to the point of passing out.

Who was at the door?

Madeline waited, holding her breath, hoping whoever it was would retreat.

Another knock. Steady, insistent. Madeline's car was in the driveway. Any one of a thousand people would have recognized her car.

Madeline tiptoed over to the door, not wanting her footsteps to be heard.

A familiar male voice said, "Madeline, I know you're in there. Open up, it's me."

Me? Madeline thought. The voice was *so* familiar, and yet in her panic, she couldn't identify it.

She unlocked the door and cracked it open.

Eddie.

Madeline exhaled. "Jesus," she said. "You scared me."

He was wearing a white linen shirt and khaki linen pants and a Panama hat and the tan Versace loafers he loved so much. This was his summer uniform, and Madeline thought he was pushing the season a little bit. It was "warm" today, at sixty-two degrees, but it was still far from summer, and here was Eddie, dressed like a pimp in Havana circa 1955. And yet, the look worked for him. Fast Eddie. He could list a house at ten a.m., show it twice, and have it sold at ten percent above the asking price by afternoon. People *loved* the Panama hat, which came not from Panama, as people would likely think, but from someplace in Peru or Ecuador.

Every year, someone on Nantucket went as Fast Eddie for Halloween.

"Can I come in?" he said. "Please?"

Madeline ushered him inside. Her pride at having her own place was pretty much quashed once Eddie dragged his assessing eye around the digs.

"How did you know I was here?" Madeline asked. "I haven't even told Grace about this yet."

"How do I know anything?" Eddie said. "I heard it on the street. So, what are you paying?"

"Um..." Madeline thought about lying, but he would find out the truth. He probably already knew the truth; asking was just a pretense. "Two thousand a month."

"Ha!" One short, derisory laugh.

Madeline waited for the follow-up.

He said, "I could have gotten it for you for fifteen hundred, maybe twelve."

He's bluffing, Madeline thought.

"Oh?" she said.

"But you went with Rachel."

"I did," Madeline said. "She was sort of pushy when I mentioned it. And I didn't want to bother you with it."

"You wouldn't have *bothered* me," Eddie said. "This is a quiet time of year for me. I could have gotten you this place, and I would have done you better on the rent. Frankly, I'm surprised you decided to use Rachel. After what Calgary did to Hope..."

Madeline thought, *Calgary didn't do anything to Hope except for break up with her a week before the Christmas formal.* And, supposedly, he gave the sea-glass pendant necklace—which probably cost all of thirty dollars—to another girl, Kylie Eckers. But hadn't teenagers been doing this kind of thing since the beginning of time? Why should *Rachel* be punished?

"What are you doing here, Eddie?" Madeline asked.

"Once I heard you got a 'writing studio,'" Eddie said, "I had to come see it for myself."

She didn't like the way he said *writing studio.* It made this decision sound fanciful and absurd, like she had bought a unicorn.

"I'm working," Madeline said, nodding at her blank legal pad.

"Are you?"

"Trying."

"I still haven't read your last book," Eddie said. "But everyone else loved it."

Madeline knew that Eddie had never and would never read any of her work. The last book Eddie had even bothered to crack open was *Dune,* in the tenth grade.

Eddie gave himself a tour of the apartment, his interest in her writing evaporating like a bad smell. In the kitchen, he opened the cabinets, then the creaky door to the outdated dishwasher. In the bathroom, he turned on the water in the sink. And in the bedroom, he emitted a dissatisfied *hmmmpf.*

Madeline rolled her eyes. Really, what did Eddie Pancik care about a piddly one-bedroom apartment that rented for two thousand dollars a month? The only rental he handled was the famous fifty-thousand-dollar-a-week house on Low Beach Road, from which he took a whopping weekly commission.

Eddie popped out of the bedroom and readjusted his Panama hat in that way he had, giving Madeline a glimpse of his shaved head. Madeline had known him so long, she remembered his curls.

"What does Trevor think of this place?" he asked.

"He was very supportive," Madeline said.

"Of course he was," Eddie said. "You deserve your own

time and your own space, Maddie. There's no reason to feel guilty about it."

"I don't feel guilty," Madeline said.

"Except you're paying too much," Eddie said.

"Speaking of money...," Madeline said. She couldn't believe she was going to bring this up, but there were so few times when she and Eddie were alone together that she felt compelled to at least *ask*. "Is there any way Trevor and I might see our investment back from you sooner rather than later? I'm not going to lie to you, Eddie. Taking this apartment was kind of a stretch. And Brick wants a car. I would honestly be okay with not making a dime in profit if you could just return the fifty grand to us."

"I'm confused," Eddie said. "Why did you invest with me if you didn't care about *profit?*"

Why *had* she invested? Greed, she supposed, and hubris. Eddie had come to her and Trevor with the opportunity to double their money, and Madeline had been tantalized by the prospect. She and Trevor had been struggling financially for so long—while Grace and Eddie bought a huge house on three acres, bought a brand-new Range Rover and a Porsche Cayenne; while they let the twins shop online at Saks and Neiman Marcus—that Madeline had been determined to invest with Eddie because she finally *could*.

However, she didn't want to admit this to Eddie. She had outkicked her coverage.

"Is there any way we could get it back, say, next month?" she asked.

"Next month?" Eddie said. He raised his eyebrows and gave her a devilish smile, one of his facial expressions that Madeline found attractive. "You do understand what I'm in

the middle of, right? I'm building spec houses. I'm going to build them and then sell them, and we will all see our profit when I sell them. Right now, I'm just trying to get them finished."

"Are you close?" Madeline said.

There was a long silence, long enough that Madeline thought perhaps Eddie hadn't heard her, and she was about to ask again when he said, "No, Maddie, not really. I'm not really close at all."

"But we're still thinking June for a return, right?" she said. "June, or at the latest August. That's what you told us back in January, Eddie."

"Yes, Maddie, I know that's what I told you, but things have changed since January. You have to take into account market variations."

Madeline tried not to panic. Eddie was such a canny businessman that she hadn't worried about investing with him for one second. Trevor had warned Madeline that financial deals—loans, investments, what have you—were exactly the kind of thing that ruined friendships. But Madeline had insisted.

"Market variations," she said. She didn't know what that meant, exactly, but she figured it meant her money was tied up for the time being.

"Yes," Eddie said.

He was giving her his sensitive expression now, which she also liked. Eddie did have a sweetness to him, although it appeared only rarely, and mostly when he was dealing with his daughters.

"I should go," he said. "Leave you to work your magic. We'll see you tomorrow night for dinner. Grace is making shrimp tacos."

Madeline exhaled. One small blessing, dinner at the Pancik house. Trevor and Brick wouldn't have to eat pizza again. Grace was a phenomenal cook.

"Don't tell her about this place," Madeline said. "I want to surprise her."

"Will do," Eddie said. He suddenly looked keen to leave, pronto.

Madeline saw Eddie to the door. "See ya, Eddie," she said. "Thanks for stopping by."

After Eddie was gone, she flopped onto the sofa. *Market variations?* They *would* get their money back, though, right? There was a signed paper somewhere. But Madeline was worried. If she wanted money, she would have to get to work, write this book, make it something special. The mere thought was overwhelming.

She needed a nap.

NANTUCKET

Sultan Nash, who had been hired to repaint the outside trim on Black-Eyed Susan's, watched Madeline King park her car in one of the three spots of the blue Victorian across the street.

Sultan knew Madeline because he had grown up on the

island with her husband, Trevor, playing football at the Boys & Girls Club. He noticed Madeline's turquoise Mini Cooper in the parking spot because he'd tried to park his pickup truck in that same spot the week before, and he'd narrowly escaped being towed. Sultan Nash had been irate about this. He knew it was private property, but he also held tight to the belief that anyone who had been born and raised on the island should be able to park wherever they wanted, whenever they wanted. He had appeared at town meeting for a string of ten years running and aired this opinion.

He waved at Madeline and said, "I wouldn't park there if I were you."

She grinned. "I'm renting one of the apartments in this building."

Renting one of the apartments? Sultan thought. Had the unimaginable happened? Had Trevor and Madeline *split?* Sultan had seen them both at a wedding the previous fall, and he had noted how deliriously in love they seemed, like newlyweds themselves. At the end of the night, Trevor had done a soft-shoe dance for Madeline — he was actually pretty good — and when he was done, Madeline had laid a kiss on him that made Sultan blush. He would have given his right arm for a marriage like that.

About half an hour after Sultan saw Madeline enter the Victorian, he noticed Eddie Pancik knocking on the door. Madeline opened the door, and Eddie disappeared inside.

Sultan mentioned this to Darlene Lanta, a waitress at the Downyflake, which was where Sultan ate lunch every day in an as-yet-unsuccessful attempt to date Darlene Lanta.

Darlene said, "So let me get this straight: Madeline King

got an *apartment in town* and Eddie Pancik stopped by to *visit?*"

Sultan nodded and took a bite of his BLT.

Rachel McMann told her husband, Andy (or Dr. Andy, as he was known to his dental patients), that she had rented Madeline "a room of her own." Which Dr. Andy—who was a habitual half listener, due to the fact that the people he was most often conversing with had their mouths wide open and at least one metal tool inside and therefore were unintelligible anyway—construed to mean "a place of her own." He had never read Virginia Woolf.

Rachel also said, "I basically lucked into the rental, right place at the right time, as I keep telling you, sweetheart. I can't believe Madeline didn't go with Eddie Pancik."

Dr. Andy wondered if Madeline and Trevor had split. He didn't care to surmise. But he accidentally mentioned what Rachel had told him to Janice, his hygienist, the next morning. Janice was married to a title examiner named Alicia, so she frequently lent a different perspective to the dramas that Dr. Andy told her about, all of which he heard from Rachel.

Janice said, "Madeline King moved out? That doesn't make any sense. Are you sure that's what Rachel told you?"

Dr. Andy was sure, or pretty sure. He said, "I guess Rachel expected her to go with Eddie Pancik."

Janice, being a hygienist, was also something of a half listener. She heard this as *Rachel expected that Madeline would get together with Eddie Pancik.*

"Really?" Janice said. "That doesn't seem likely, does it? Eddie Pancik? Isn't she best friends with his wife?"

Dr. Andy said, "I suppose anything is possible, Janice. But we shouldn't say anything one way or another about Eddie Pancik. He's our landlord. We could easily find ourselves out on the street."

Janice said, "I've always thought that Madeline King should write a novel about a dentist's office."

Dr. Andy agreed that she should, then walked off to scrub up for his nine a.m. root canal, leaving Janice to ask her next patient, Phoenix Hernandez, whom Janice counted as one of her many trusted confidantes, whether she thought Madeline King should get together with Eddie Pancik now that Madeline had her own place in town.

GRACE

Grace's perennials were starting to sprout, her spring bulbs were in blossom—narcissus, hyacinths, tulips—and her Japanese cherry trees had thousands of nascent buds. Two more weeks and those trees would be in full-on luscious pink bloom, just like Grace's heart.

Benton came to the house every day at ten.

The gift Benton brought her from Morocco was an elaborately cast silver pot for brewing mint tea, and two etched crystal glasses. When Benton first showed Grace the teapot,

her spirits fell. A teapot was neither sexy nor romantic. He might as well have brought her a tagine pot.

But going through the ritual—harvesting the most robust spearmint leaves from Grace's indoor herb garden, then boiling water and adding just the right amount of sugar into the curvy silver pot, then pouring the elixir into the etched crystal glasses and sipping—turned out to be a sensual shared experience.

"Do you like it?" Benton asked.

"I've never tasted anything so pure," Grace admitted. "It tastes like the color green."

Relief and, Grace thought, tenderness mingled on his face.

They brewed mint tea every day and drank it as they discussed their plans for the yard. They decided to put in a long, narrow bed of daylilies off the front of the deck.

Benton said, "I haven't had much experience with daylilies."

"Well then," Grace said, "this is where I will teach *you*."

Grace's grandmother Sabine, a woman Grace had worshipped for her refined tastes, had raised daylilies in her garden, and as a child, Grace had become entranced not so much with the flowers themselves as with their poetic names: 'Jock Randall,' 'Ice Carnival,' 'Ginger Creek,' 'Maude's Valentine.'

She and Benton sat side by side at Grace's kitchen table and pored over the catalog.

"I think we need some masculine varieties," Benton said.

"How about 'Rocket Booster'? Or 'Piano Man'? Or 'Freedom's Highway'?"

" 'Wolf Eyes,' " Grace said.

" 'Apple Jack,' " Benton said. His fingers grazed hers as he turned the page, and her ears started to buzz.

"I'm partial to sweeter names," Grace said. "We should get some 'Baby Darling.' "

"Please," Benton said. "Please don't make me plant a flower called 'Baby Darling.' "

Grace laughed. "What about 'Butter Cream'?" she said.

"I'll give you 'Butter Cream,' " Benton said, "if you give me 'Broadway Starfish.' "

"Look at this one," Grace said. " 'Bullfrog Kisses.' " She pointed to the photo in the catalog.

"That is not a particularly attractive flower," Benton said. "Then again, who would want to be kissed by a bullfrog?"

Grace turned the page. She picked out the best-looking flower on the page and said its name before she thought to stop herself. " 'Blue Desire.' "

" 'Blue Desire,' " he said. "I like it." He raised his head, and their eyes locked. Grace knew the tips of her ears must be flaming red.

He's going to kiss me, she thought. He moved in. Their lips were just about to touch. Grace sucked in her breath, and the soft sound this made seemed to send a jolt through Benton. He backed away.

"Whoa," he said. "I'm so sorry, Grace. I think the names of these flowers are getting me riled up."

"Don't be sorry!" she said quickly. She was devastated that he'd stopped. She wanted to go back to where they'd been a moment before, the fun intimacy of selecting flowers,

but the magic of that had passed. She closed the catalog and decided to ask him the question she'd been wanting to ask for the past two weeks. "Did McGuvvy go with you to Morocco?"

"She didn't," Benton said. "She got a job teaching sailing out in San Diego. We broke up."

As this news settled over Grace, he drummed his fingers on the table nervously.

She said, "So you're a free man."

"*I'm* free, yes," Benton said.

"Benton..."

"You're married, Grace," he said. "To Eddie, who pays my bills."

"I..."

"Don't say it," Benton said. He let out a long exhale and stared into his tea. "You have a house, you have children, you have a whole life with Eddie." Benton took a sip of his tea. "I'm your gardener."

"You're a lot more than my gardener," Grace said. "This winter, when I got your postcards..."

"Don't say it."

"I realized how much you meant to me," Grace said. "My...friendship with you. This garden, this yard, what we're trying to create here, means something to me."

Benton said, "You have to stop."

"Stop what?" Grace said. "Stop how I feel? Stop how you feel?"

"You don't *know* how I feel," Benton said.

This clammed her up. She thought, *Oh God, it's one sided.* Unrequited. The loneliest word in the English language.

"How do you feel?" Grace asked.

"Confused," he said.

She sat with that in silence.

"I am not *that guy,*" Benton said. "I never have been. And it's not like you're just some random married woman I met at a bar. You're my client."

"I know," Grace said.

"I am *not* that guy," he said. He backed his chair away from the table. "I need to shift my focus."

"Away from me," Grace said.

"Away from you."

"But you do like me," Grace said.

"Oh, Grace," he said. "I more than like you."

The next morning, Benton showed up twenty minutes later than usual, and for those twenty minutes, Grace thought he might not be coming at all. She thought, *He's going to drop me as a client. He's going to* fire *me.* He "more than liked" her, but because of this, they would have to stop working together.

When Benton's truck did finally pull into the driveway, Grace felt faint with relief. She hurried out to the backyard, and in order to seem like she hadn't been standing around, waiting for him to show up, she started pulling nonexistent weeds in the tulip bed.

"Hey, Grace," Benton said as he rounded the house. He held out a brown box from Petticoat Row Bakery. "I brought you something."

His tone was light. Normalcy had been restored. Grace was relieved but also crushed. She said, "Should I pick some mint?"

"Hell yes!" he said.

In the kitchen, Benton made the tea while Grace washed her hands and tried to calm her nerves. Then, together, they took their established places at Grace's kitchen table.

Benton opened the brown pastry box to reveal four pale-green *macaron*s with pale-pink filling.

"I became partial to *macaron*s from a French bakery in Marrakech," he said. "But I think these are just as good." He held one out to her.

Grace accepted the cookie and took a bite. She couldn't help herself; she groaned with pleasure.

He said, "Try it with the tea."

With a sip of the tea, yes. It was a taste explosion.

He said, "Do you like it?"

"Nirvana," she said.

He held her eyes and smiled at her, and her heart fell to the bottom of her stomach. He set down his glass of tea. He shook his head at her like she had done something wrong. He said, very softly, "Oh boy."

And then he cupped her chin, and he kissed her.

MADELINE

Brick didn't want to go to the Pancik house for dinner.

"Honey," Madeline said, "why not?"

Brick shrugged. He had come home from baseball practice and collapsed on the sofa; now, his eyes were glued to the TV — ESPN, *The Sports Reporters.*

Madeline sat down carefully next to him. "Honey?" she said.

"Don't feel like it."

This was a first. Brick normally chomped at the bit to get over to the Panciks' whenever Grace invited them for dinner. It was the only time he was allowed to hang out with Allegra in her bedroom — with the door open, of course.

"Honey, is everything okay with Allegra?" Madeline asked.

He shrugged. "Dunno."

Madeline stared at her hands. Sixteen years she had raised this child, but she had never quite mastered the art of getting him to confide in her. Trevor was much better at it. She waited, literally biting her tongue until she tasted the metallic tang of blood.

She was rewarded. He said, "I'm not sure what's going on. She's been acting weird. I thought maybe it was a bad time of the month for her or whatever, but now I'm thinking she's probably sick of me."

Would it be awful of Madeline to say that she wasn't surprised? Allegra had positive qualities, chief among them her beauty, her composure, her confidence. What sixteen-year-old girl had such confidence? She could also be quite

funny; she did a dead-on impression of the kids' English teacher, Mrs. Kraft. But there had been something about Allegra since she was young, something superior and entitled and not quite nice that she mostly saved for her mother. She brought Grace to tears on a regular basis, and, as Grace's best friend, Madeline had always been there to listen. *Yes, that was a horrifying thing for your daughter to say. Yes, that was a selfish and thoughtless action. But she's young, she'll grow out of it.*

Allegra made Madeline feel relieved that she'd never had a daughter herself.

"Sick of you, honey?" Madeline said. "How could anyone ever be sick of you?"

Weak smile.

Madeline didn't let her true opinions of Allegra surface very often, because Allegra was Brick's girlfriend; he was besotted. At the beginning of the romance, there had been so much kissing and hands everywhere, too, that Madeline had asked them to please stop. She was far from a prude, but all of that newly discovered desire on display was embarrassing. Allegra's blue eyes had flashed silver with her triumph. She had converted Brick to the Church of Allegra. He worshipped her.

Allegra made Brick happy, and it was more than sex; when he heard her voice, his face lit up.

Madeline and Grace had made a promise when the kids started dating. *We won't get involved.* They would let Allegra and Brick work out their differences. Madeline had always wondered what would happen if they broke up. She had hoped it would be a mutual decision made when they both headed off to separate colleges.

"Please," Madeline said. "Please come to dinner. You and Allegra can talk things over in person."

"No," Brick said. "Just tell everyone I don't feel well." He swallowed. "It's not a lie. My heart hurts."

Madeline smoothed the hair from Brick's forehead. "Oh, honey."

"Please, Mom. I would really rather hang here alone. You and Dad go."

"What about something to eat? I can make you a grilled cheese?"

"Mom, I'm *fine*."

Trevor entered the living room, wearing his green striped good-luck party shirt. His golden hair glinted, and it looked like he had gotten sun on his face—the start of his summer tan. By August, he would be deep brown and his hair three shades lighter. He looked just as Californian as Madeline, if not more so.

"What's going on?" Trevor asked.

"Brick wants to stay home," Madeline said. "Maybe we should all cancel. Maybe we should stay home and order pizza instead."

"Nonsense," Trevor said. "Grace went to a lot of trouble— you know she did, she always does—and we're going." He offered Brick a hand. "All of us."

"I brought that Malbec you like," Madeline said, setting the wine down on Grace's gorgeous blue Bahia granite—or, as Eddie liked to call it, the sexiest countertop in the world.

Grace was busy pushing onions and peppers around in the

skillet; her head was engulfed in fragrant steam. "You're the best friend evah," she said, imitating what they both called her "Barbie New Bedfahd" accent. "Let's have us some."

Outside the glass doors, Madeline watched Eddie hand Trevor a beer and Brick a Coke. Brick settled into one of the rattan deck chairs with canvas-covered cushions. One of the twins came into sight, all long brown hair and long legs in jeans. Madeline hoped it was Allegra; she hoped Allegra would give Brick a kiss from the old days and make Trevor and Eddie blush and cringe respectfully. But it wasn't Allegra; it was Hope. She wore her hair parted down the middle and tucked behind her ears. Her face was a tick off the glorious beauty of her sister's; her eyes were squintier, her cheeks fuller. But what Hope lacked in glamour, she made up for in grace. She had a quiet, serious soul and an easy elegance, the likes of which Madeline had witnessed before only in women like Jacqueline Onassis and Audrey Hepburn.

Of the two girls, Madeline preferred Hope. She rarely let herself admit this.

"The garden is looking good," Madeline said. This was an understatement: the yard and garden dazzled, as always. The rest of Nantucket was still gloomy gray, the grass brown, the trees bare, and the daffodils that lined Milestone Road drooped from weeks of punishing wind and rain. But Grace's yard was green and lush, as though these three acres had received sunshine by special order. The flower beds had sharp, precise edges; it looked like elves had trimmed the grass with manicure scissors. Everything was sprouted and ready to burst. There was an oval bed of tulips that would have made a Dutchman cry. It contained seven hundred bulbs

in flame orange, snow white, cherry red, amethyst, and three luscious shades of pink—powder, shell, and deep fuchsia. The tulip bed alone was enough to make Madeline believe in God. All of the stonework had been scrubbed, as had Grace's antique cast-iron planters and her five-foot statue of the angel Gabriel, bought from a church in Lourdes, which was where Grace had done a semester abroad when she was at Mount Holyoke. There was a park bench salvaged from the Tuileries said to date back to the era of Claude Monet and Auguste Renoir. Voluptuous ferns lined the bench in the exact places where Claude and Auguste would have set their butts. At the edge of the property sat the garden shed and the henhouse. The doors to the henhouse were closed tight; the chickens were asleep.

Madeline let her eyes linger on the wooden footbridge that spanned the brook, then the handcrafted birdhouses, then the Adirondack chairs, artfully arranged to overlook Polpis Harbor. The swimming pool, a dark-tiled rectangle surrounded by old paving stones and the same cobblestones they used on Main Street downtown, was still covered, as was the hot tub. Everything about the Pancik property was paradisaical. Madeline had been to the house thousands of times, and every time the sumptuous beauty of the place stole her breath away. She couldn't imagine what it would be like to live with this yard, to see it every second of every day.

Madeline's "yard" was patches of brown dirt, sand, and crabgrass and, at the border of the property, a mess of scrubby trees, pricker bushes, and weeds. She had one hydrangea, which grew sickly purple flowers. Grace's hydrangeas— numbering twenty-two—were all pageant winners. They bloomed in blue, purple, pink, white, and green. Madeline

hadn't even known green hydrangeas existed, but yes, they were called 'Limelight' hydrangeas, and Grace's were divine.

"Benton has been here," Grace said.

"Yes, I can tell," Madeline said. "Because I only hear from you once every three days."

Grace's expression was hard to read. It was half apologetic smile, half something else. "Wine, please," she sang out. "I'd love some wine."

Madeline pulled two of Grace's Baccarat goblets out of the cabinet. Grace liked to use the goblets on Wednesday nights, even though they were fragile and each one cost as much as a night's stay in the penthouse at the Four Seasons. Madeline had broken one goblet, Grace had broken one, and Eddie had broken two in consecutive weeks. Madeline poured two lavish glasses of the plummy Malbec and brought one to Grace at the stove. "I have some news," she said.

"You and me both," Grace said. She took a swill of her wine, then set the goblet down on the sexy granite. "But mine is going to have to wait until later. What's yours?"

Madeline sucked in a preparatory breath. She worried that Grace would be mad that she had rented the apartment from Rachel McMann, and possibly also that she'd taken the apartment without showing Grace first.

She said, "I rented an apartment in town."

"What?" Grace yelped.

"It's not what it sounds like," Madeline said. "I'm going to use it as a writing studio."

Grace's face lit up, and she imitated the patrician accent of her grandmother Sabine. "Splendid, my darling! Where in town?"

"In the blue Victorian on the corner of India and Centre."

"I've always loved that building," Grace said. She turned down the heat under the onions and peppers and came over to give Madeline a hug. "So you're a real working girl now, with office space of your own. I'm so *jealous!* But you deserve it."

Madeline said, "That's what everyone keeps saying, but I'm not sure it's true. It was pretty expensive."

"How much?" Grace asked.

"Two thousand a month."

"Eh," Grace said, shrugging. She returned to the stove and picked up her wine. "That seems reasonable for town in summer."

Right, Madeline thought. It would seem reasonable to Grace because Grace had never worried about money a day in her life. Grace had been raised in an old Puritan family, the Harpers of Salem, Massachusetts; Grace's ninth-great grandfather had been the attorney who defended Bridget Bishop, one of the women accused of being a witch. (*I am no witch. I am innocent. I know nothing of it.* Hanged June 10, 1692.) Grace had three older brothers, the Harper boys, all of them now civil rights attorneys in Boston. Grace and her brothers had been forced to dress for dinner every night growing up in their majestic brick mansion on Essex Street. On the maternal side of the family was Grandmother Sabine, who owned a three-hundred-acre estate in Wayland that Grace used to visit every Sunday. These afternoons included games of croquet in the summer and sleigh rides in the winter. Madeline had always loved hearing details of Grace's upbringing; she savored them like petit fours. But she couldn't expect Grace to understand what feeling financially strapped was like.

"And, listen," Madeline said, wanting to be truthful,

because that was her nature. "I heard about the apartment through Rachel McMann."

"Ugh," Grace said.

"Eddie is all bent out of shape about it, I think. He stopped by to see the place, and he seemed unhappy I'd gone through Rachel. But it happened by accident. I opened my big mouth, and you know Rachel..."

"Pushy," Grace said.

"She seized the moment," Madeline said. "If I'd taken time to collect my wits...if I'd been, you know, *hunting* for a place, I would have called Eddie. You know I would have."

Grace waved her hand dismissively. "Eddie will get over it," she said.

Madeline felt nearly dizzy with relief. She hadn't expected Grace to take the news on such an even keel. Grace was wound pretty tightly most days, and news like this could catapult her into unreasonable territory. But tonight, Grace was in an exceptional mood. Madeline couldn't remember the last time she'd seen her friend so...playful...so relaxed. She was practically glowing.

"Go outside with the boys," Grace said. "I'm almost finished up here."

"Madeline!" Eddie said. He kissed her cheek. "Long time, *no see!*"

"Eddie," she said. Air kiss, and the expected waft of Eternity by Calvin Klein, which he had started wearing right out of high school. He smiled at Madeline crookedly, then hovered a hand above the grill to see if it was ready.

Eddie said to Trevor, "So...what do you think about your girl's new digs?"

"I think it's great," Trevor said. He swatted Madeline on the butt. "No more excuses about not getting anything done. Now, she should be writing a book a year, or two books a year, like that other Nantucket novelist."

"Two books a year!" Eddie said. "Then you could not only invest in my spec houses, you could buy one."

Madeline tightened her fingers around the delicate stem of the Baccarat wineglass. Hearing Eddie bring up the spec houses made her tense enough to snap it.

Madeline took Trevor's arm. "Let's walk to the bridge."

They strolled across the wide swath of soft, emerald lawn, toward the footbridge that crossed the brook. The sound the water made when it ran over the rocks was musical, like chimes. Madeline closed her eyes briefly and tried to savor the sound. It was the type of rocks Benton Coe had used, or the way he'd positioned them.

"Listen," she said. "I asked Eddie for our fifty grand back."

"You did?" Trevor said. "When?"

"Yesterday," she said. "He stopped by the apartment."

"He *did?*" Trevor said. "I don't know how I feel about you entertaining strange men in that place. After all, I haven't even seen it yet." His tone was jokey, but Madeline sensed he was a little miffed.

"He came by to tell me how mad he was that I'd rented from Rachel," Madeline said.

"Oh," Trevor said, and she felt him ease up. "That sounds like our friend Fast Eddie."

"Just tell me it's going to be okay," Madeline said. "I'm going to write another book, and we're going to get our money back."

Trevor kissed her, then took both of her hands in his. "It's going to be okay."

Madeline turned around. Eddie, Hope, and Brick were all unabashedly staring at them. And Grace, too, from inside the kitchen.

Eddie called out, "Whaddya doin' over there? Proposing marriage?"

They walked back to the patio, where Grace had laid out her standard appetizer spread: smoked bluefish pâté, rosemary flat breads, farmhouse cheddar, fig jam, roasted peppers, Marcona almonds, Armenian string cheese, and a stick of herbed salami with two kinds of mustard. There were Bremner wafers and soft unsalted butter for Eddie, which he ate for his heartburn, and there were Triscuits and Cheez Whiz for Brick, because it was his favorite snack and Grace always kept it on hand for him. Brick didn't seemed cheered by the fresh can of Cheez Whiz, however.

There was still no sign of Allegra.

Eddie raised his glass of wine. "Here's to Madeline's new apartment," he said. "Congratulations."

HOPE

Allegra didn't come down to dinner until the very last minute. Their mother had called up to her three times, and then Eddie called up to her. Eddie was the only person who held sway over Allegra because he was the one who paid her credit card bill.

Allegra came out onto the deck, her eyes glued to her phone, her thumbs flying.

Hope said, "Who are you texting?"

Everyone else grew quiet—not because anyone else (except for Brick) cared whom Allegra was texting, but because Hope rarely spoke, and so when she did, everyone made a point to listen.

"Nobody," Allegra said. She finished up and slid the phone into the front pocket of her sleek leather jacket. She was wearing her skinny Citizens, black ballet flats, a black lace blouse from Dolce Vita, and the soft caramel leather jacket. She looked like she'd just climbed off the back of some guy's Ducati on the Italian Riviera.

She beamed at the assembled families, as if shocked and delighted to find them all there, as if she hadn't heard them from upstairs in her bedroom for the past half hour.

"Hey, everyone!" she said. "Hey, Brick!"

Brick made an eighth of a turn in his chair, then waved in her general direction. "Hey."

It was strained—but did he know about Ian Coburn? No, Hope didn't think so. Allegra had managed to keep her mouth shut about Ian. She hadn't even told her sworn bestie, Hollis. *Hollis doesn't need to know,* Allegra had said on one occasion. And then, on a second occasion, she said, *If I told Hollis, the entire school would know before we finished saying the Pledge. I love that girl, but she* cannot *keep a secret.* The only person she had told about Ian Coburn was Hope.

Ian Coburn was taking his final exams at BC. He would be back on Nantucket the following week.

"What are you going to do then?" Hope had asked her sister.

"What do you think I'm going to do?" Allegra said.

Hope had no idea. She could see Allegra breaking up with Brick, and she could also see Allegra breaking up with Ian Coburn. And, she could *easily* see Allegra having the ego to try to juggle both boys over the summer.

Hope had said, "You're going to play it by ear? Wait and see how it goes?"

"Exactly," Allegra said.

Of course this was her sister's answer. Allegra believed in nothing so strongly as her own good fortune, and in things working out in her own best interest.

But she would blow it.

Allegra put a hand on Brick's shoulder and then bent over and kissed the top of his head like she was his mother. Hope felt a pang for Brick. Was it not *totally obvious* that Allegra's reservoir of sexy, romantic feelings for him had run dry and that she was preoccupied by her phone, which they could all hear vibrating away in her jacket pocket?

"Who's texting you?" Brick asked.

"Texting me?" Allegra said. She smiled innocently, as though she couldn't feel the persistent vibration of Ian Coburn's messages against her left breast. She plucked her phone from her pocket and checked the display. "Oh, it's Hollis. She's asking about math."

She was a born liar, Hope thought. It was incredible. She should skip the modeling career and go straight to politics.

"I don't believe you," Brick said. "Show me the text!" He reached out to grab Allegra's phone, but in the process, he hit

Madeline's glass of red wine — which shattered and sent a Malbecian spray all over Allegra's Italian leather jacket.

Allegra shrieked.

Madeline said, "Oh, Brick, no!"

Trevor said, "Honey, it was an accident."

Madeline set about picking up pieces of the wineglass while Allegra whipped off her leather jacket, taking her phone out of her pocket first and setting it on the dry part of the table, right where both Hope and Brick could see it, when Ian Coburn texted yet again.

"Ian Coburn?" Brick said. "Since when do you get texts from Ian Coburn?"

"Jesus, Brick!" Allegra said. "This jacket cost me a fortune!"

Eddie cleared his throat. "*Me* a fortune," he said. "Is it ruined?"

Allegra wiped at it with napkins, but the wine had left a shower of dark stains that looked like splattered blood.

"It's an Italian jacket, right?" Hope said. "You'd think they would make them wine resistant."

"I can't *believe* this!" Allegra said.

Grace got a sponge for the wine, and Madeline threw the shards of glass into the trash. Grace said, "Do you want the sponge for your coat, honey?"

"You can't put *water* on it, Mother," Allegra said.

"Tone," Eddie warned.

Allegra's phone continued to buzz.

Her family was so predictable, Hope thought. Possibly they believed that she, too, was predictable — but nobody knew that in a month, maybe two, she would be dating Brick.

Brick said, "Ian Coburn sure has a lot to say to you."

Allegra snatched up her phone. "It's none of your business who texts me."

"Really?" he said.

"I'm putting the shrimp on," Eddie said.

"I think maybe we should go home," Madeline said.

Grace handed Eddie a large platter of shrimp and jalapeño skewers. When he laid the first one on the hot grill, there was an angry hiss.

Grace said, "You should *not* go home. It's just a glass and a little spill. But, Eddie, you need to apologize to Madeline for giving her a hard time about Rachel McMann."

Rachel McMann, Hope thought. *Ew.*

Rachel was the mother of Hope's sworn enemy, Calgary McMann. Hope had dated Calgary for four weeks before she finally allowed him to get to third base, but he broke up with her right after, making Hope feel like there was something wrong with her. When Calgary and his friends saw Hope in the hallway, they made a strange hand motion that Hope didn't understand, and there was no one she could ask, but she knew it wasn't good. In response, she flipped them off, which made them laugh. Calgary had left Hope without a date for the Christmas formal; the red velvet cocktail dress that she and Grace had bought at Hepburn went unworn. Calgary had asked Kylie Eckers to the formal, but Kylie got so drunk at the preparty that the principal and superintendent stopped her at the door and called her parents to come pick her up. When Hope heard that news from Allegra the next morning, she felt somewhat vindicated, but now, five months later, her hatred of both Kylie and Calgary had become indelible, like a fossil in rock.

"Rachel McMann wasn't worthy of your commission," Eddie said. "That was my only point."

"I don't think she took a commission," Madeline said.

"Oh, believe me, she took a commission," Eddie said.

Just the name Rachel McMann made Hope feel sick. She couldn't stand another second of this conversation.

"Mom?" she said. "I'm not hungry."

"I'm not hungry either," Brick said. He looked at Madeline. "Can we go home, Mom, please?"

"Yes," Madeline said. "I think we should."

That was the last thing Hope heard before she marched upstairs, except for the buzzing of Allegra's phone.

MADELINE

You can't *go!*" Grace said. "We haven't eaten yet! I made fresh pineapple salsa. I made mango *panna cotta*."

"I don't feel well," Brick said.

"Can you hang on a little while longer, buddy?" Trevor asked. "We'll eat and then we'll go."

Madeline was all for trying to set things right. She felt awful that Brick had broken another one of the five-hundred-dollar wine goblets, but this led to annoyance that Grace insisted on using such expensive crystal for casual family dinners in the first place. Madeline felt like she should offer to pay for the glass, or for Allegra's jacket, even though she didn't

have the money. Although clearly she *did* have the money, because she was blowing two grand a month on the rent for a room of her own!

Madeline collapsed in a rattan chair, defeated. Then she popped back up. She wanted more wine; she would drink it from a juice glass.

Grace followed her into the kitchen. "I don't want you to leave until you and I have a chance to talk in private. We'll go upstairs after dinner. This isn't something I can discuss on the phone."

"Oh," Madeline said. "Okay."

"Dinner's ready!" Eddie called.

Conversation at dinner was interrupted by the insistent buzzing of Allegra's phone.

Eddie finally said, "Allegra, turn it off or take it inside."

"Ian Coburn must really want to talk to you," Brick said.

Allegra said, "We're friends, okay? Is that not allowed?"

Trevor said, "The salsa is delicious."

"Thank you," Grace said.

Eddie, Madeline noticed, hadn't touched his food. He was still picking Bremner wafers off the appetizer plate.

"It's allowed," Brick said. "Of course it's allowed. As long as you're only friends. As long as that's all it is."

"Of *course* that's *all it is*," Allegra said. She threw her embroidered napkin on top of her taco mess. Grace, Madeline knew, laundered and ironed each napkin before these dinners. "How dare you suggest otherwise!"

Otherwise, Madeline thought. Something was going on

between Allegra and Ian Coburn. She felt a hot, pulsing anger. Then she remembered her vow with Grace. *We won't get involved.*

"Allegra—" Brick said.

But Allegra was up and out of her chair, her phone tucked into the pocket of her ruined jacket.

She said, "Save it, Brick." And disappeared into the kitchen.

Brick looked like he wanted to chase after her, but he stayed put.

Madeline finished her glass of wine. She stood up to refill her glass, but Grace said, "It's gone. Do you want Eddie to grab another bottle from the cellar?"

No, Madeline thought. They should go. Poor Brick had been humiliated enough for one night. But Grace had something to tell her that couldn't be discussed over the phone, and Madeline was intrigued.

"Yes," she said.

Eddie brought up two bottles of Screaming Eagle cabernet, and Madeline blinked. Was she seeing things? He'd always said he was saving those bottles for his deathbed.

Madeline said, "Edward, what are you doing?"

He said, "I want to pour this tonight. I'm not sure why— it's just a gut feeling."

"That's as good a reason as any," Trevor said. "I can't wait to taste it."

Grace went into the kitchen to bring everyone a fresh Baccarat wine goblet.

Brick said, "You're having more *wine?* I thought you said we could go. Dad?"

Trevor said, "This is the best wine any of us are likely to taste. Eddie spent... how long on the wait list?"

"Eight years and seven months," Eddie said proudly.

"I don't care," Brick said. "Sorry, Mr. Pancik. I just want to go."

They should go, Madeline thought. Brick never complained. They should save the Screaming Eagle for a night when there was something to celebrate. Such as the spec houses selling and a major return on her and Trevor's investment coming in.

But Eddie pulled the cork and started pouring the adults wine. They all touched glasses in a moment of peace.

Allegra poked her head out of her bedroom window and called down to the deck. "Brick, would you come up here, please?"

Madeline watched indecision cross her son's face.

"Please, Brick?" Allegra said.

Brick stood up and went inside.

"Good," Grace whispered. "They'll work things out."

Ian Coburn, Madeline thought. He was a very good-looking kid who had graduated from Nantucket High School the year before. His father was a private-equity guy who commuted back and forth to New York City. His mother was shrill and oblivious to everything but her son's charms. Ian Coburn had been one of the kids who had been allowed to have parties and serve alcohol with his parents' blessing. He was, Madeline thought, bad news.

We won't get involved.

"Keep the door open!" Eddie called out.

Grace refilled her and Madeline's glasses while Eddie watched how much of his precious wine left the bottle. Grace said, "I have something I want to show Madeline upstairs. Will you boys be all right out here by yourselves?"

"Cigars," Eddie said to Trevor.

"I hear ya," Trevor said.

"Oh, look," Eddie said. "I have two Cohibas right here in my pocket."

Madeline followed Grace inside, through the kitchen, and up the grand, sweeping staircase. One could fit three or four of the Llewellyns' house inside the Pancik house, but Madeline had given up on envy long ago. It was fruitless.

They entered Grace's study, which was a near-exact replica of her grandmother Sabine's study at the estate in Wayland. The room was too dark and formal for Madeline's sunny tastes, although it was elegant. There were hunting prints on the taupe walls, built-in walnut bookshelves, and thick brocade drapes. Grace had inherited the enormous, ornately carved mahogany desk from Sabine, along with the thick Persian rug—hundreds of thousands of silk knots in burgundy and navy and cream. Madeline inhaled. She did love the way the room smelled—like sandalwood and old books. Grace had been a French-literature major at Mount Holyoke, so her shelves were lined with Victor Hugo and Voltaire, Colette and Proust, Émile Zola, Dumas, Camus. She had a collection of twenty-four Ted Muehling candlesticks, which held an

assortment of slender white, ivory, and dove-gray candles. She had an antique ink pot and a quill pen that actually worked. A banjo clock ticked on the wall and announced the passing of every fifteen minutes in a brassy tenor.

Grace shut and locked the heavy door and dimmed the lights on the huge pewter chandelier that hung from the ceiling. If Madeline had a study with a door that locked, she thought, then she wouldn't have needed to spend twelve thousand dollars on the apartment.

But Madeline was too good a friend to begrudge Grace her study. It wasn't merely an excuse for interior decorating: Grace had gardening issues to take care of, and she ran the business of raising Araucana chickens and selling organic eggs.

Madeline sat in the green leather armchair and draped a thick, cream-colored chenille blanket over her lap. Grace collapsed across the crushed-velvet sofa. She propped her chin up on a golden brocade pillow and stared into her goblet of Screaming Eagle, which she held with both hands.

"Grace," Madeline said, "what is it?"

"Do you remember when I told you that I had a crush on Benton Coe?" she said.

"Yes," Madeline said. "Obviously." It had been at the end of last summer. She and Grace had been plunked at the waterline at Steps Beach, drinking homemade watermelon margaritas that Grace was serving from a thermos. Tequila had long been truth serum for Grace, and so somewhere in the middle of the warm, drowsy afternoon, she'd reached over to touch Madeline's arm—waking Madeline from a nap—and she'd said, "I have a crush on Benton Coe."

Madeline had still been half or three-quarters asleep, but she said, "No, Grace, you don't."

"Yes," Grace had said. "Yes, I do. You must know what I mean. You must have had a silly, harmless crush on someone over the course of your marriage."

Madeline shook her head. "No."

"Really?" Grace said. "You guys have *always* been Dick Van Dyke and Mary Tyler Moore?"

"Always," Madeline said.

The conversation had ended there, but Madeline hadn't forgotten it.

Now, Grace said, "Something has started between us."

Madeline had had so much wine, she couldn't even form the appropriate expression on her face. And what would the appropriate expression *be?* Shock? Horror? Disapproval? Madeline had never been one to judge; the spectrum of human experience was simply too vast to believe in absolute right or absolute wrong.

"What *kind* of something?" Madeline asked.

"He brought me pistachio *macaron*s from the bakery," Grace said. "And then he kissed me."

"*Kissed* you?" Madeline said. "Was it just one time?"

"It was just once at first," Grace said. "But then it happened again in the garden shed. And it happened a third time while we were putting up the hammock." She swirled the wine in her goblet with such abandon that Madeline feared she would spill it all over the golden pillow. Grace was

pretty drunk. Possibly she was blowing the "kissing" out of proportion.

"Now," she said, "it happens every day."

"Every day?" Madeline said. "What kind of kissing is it?"

"The best kind," Grace said. "The kind of kissing that makes me dizzy. You know what that feels like, right?"

"Right," Madeline said. Her and Trevor, the summer of 1993.

"Or maybe it's desire particular to a forty-year-old woman who has been ignored for so long."

"Does Eddie ignore you in *bed?*" Madeline asked.

Grace shrugged—meaning what, Madeline wasn't sure. "It's been so long since I was his primary focus," she said. "How long, do you think?"

"A long time," Madeline admitted. For pretty much as long as Madeline had known Eddie—close to twenty years—he had taken Grace for granted. Grace had complained about it in the past, but she also said she understood that Eddie was busy. Their lifestyle took an enormous amount of money to sustain, and Grace brought in three hundred dollars a week selling eggs, which was just enough to fill her Range Rover with gas and pay the girls' cell-phone bills. The leather jacket Allegra had been wearing tonight had probably cost more than what Madeline spent on groceries in a month. Eddie had a lot of pressure on his five-foot-eight frame, hence his constant case of heartburn.

"I'm lonely," Grace said. "I've been lonely for years."

"Are you going to *sleep* with him?" Madeline asked. She was whispering now. She could not *believe* Grace was involved with Benton Coe.

"I don't know," Grace said. "I haven't decided yet."

"I would try getting back to just being friends," Madeline said.

"That's easier said than done," Grace said. "I feel like I'm in a race car and there's no reverse."

"How do you see this ending?" Madeline asked. "I'll point out, Grace, because I'm your best friend and it's my job, that no good can come of this."

"I know," Grace said. "Do you remember the séance?"

Rhetorical question.

The séance had been held in Grace and Eddie's basement on Mischief Night the previous October. Eddie's sister, Barbie Pancik, was known for having certain prescient powers. When she was in her twenties, she had purchased a crystal ball at a flea market in Brimfield, and it had made its way around the party circuit on Nantucket, back when Barbie used to do the party circuit. Somehow Grace and Eddie had convinced Barbie to bring it over on Mischief Night—the twins and Brick safely ensconced at a party at Hannah Dromanian's house. Barbie had not only said okay; she had dressed up as a full-on gypsy, in a long black dress, with her frosted hair wrapped up in an Hermès scarf.

She had sat for a long time, staring, so long that Eddie and Grace and Madeline and Trevor began to fidget like school-children, and then, when Barbie took a breath, they all tensed.

She said, in the world's most uncomfortable voice, making everyone at the table believe that she was *absolutely telling the truth:* "Two of the women at this table will betray the person on their left."

Eddie was to Grace's left, Grace to Madeline's left, Trevor to Barbie's left.

Now, Grace said, "Barbie predicted I would betray Eddie."

"The séance was idiotic," Madeline said. "You didn't *believe* what Barbie said?"

"I think about it," Grace said.

"If you believe what Barbie said, then that means that either Barbie is going to betray Trevor—which doesn't seem likely—or I'm going to betray you, which is even less likely, since you're my best friend."

"Yes," Grace said. "Thank you."

"The séance wasn't real, Grace."

Grace set her wine safely on the side table and sat up to face Madeline. "What I can't get over is how suddenly my life has changed. Everything *was* normal and boring. And now... now, my life is a novel."

NANTUCKET

On Saturday night, Damon, the bartender at the Pearl, heard the rumor from the hostess, Phoenix Hernandez, who had been to the dentist earlier in the week.

It was all over town by noon on Sunday. This was partially because Damon's housemate, Blue Sky, worked as the bartender upstairs at Ventuno, and Blue Sky's mother, Alice, was the elementary-school secretary, and Blue Sky's aunt Margaret worked at the Nantucket RMV. Blue Sky, Alice, and Margaret

met for breakfast every Sunday morning at the Fog Island Café, where Blue Sky told her aunt and mother the notable stories from her weekend.

Part of the rumor was substantiated when Rachel McMann, an enthusiastic user of social media, posted a picture of the outside of the blue Victorian in a tweet that said, *Just rented space to a Nantucket author! #nantucket #bayberryproperties #islandia.* This was retweeted by Jacinda Morgan, the office manager at Bayberry Properties, who was required to retweet anything using the hashtag #bayberryproperties to all ten thousand of their followers. It was also retweeted by Madeline's publisher, Final Word, who was required to retweet anything that used the hashtag of any one of their thirteen hundred titles to their 1.1 million followers.

Did you hear?

EDDIE

Saturday night at eight o'clock, Eddie went to the old Cumberland Farms to buy some cherry Tums. The old Cumberland Farms was run down and catered to a questionable clientele—teenagers on skateboards, heroin addicts, petty criminals, pretty much the bottom of the Nantucket barrel—but it was the only place on the island that sold cherry Tums, and Eddie was in dire need.

At nine thirty, he was due at Low Beach Road to meet with Ronan LNW. And at ten o'clock, the girls would arrive.

Grace normally liked to pin Eddie down to a date night on Saturdays, but this week the topic had — blessedly — not come up, and Eddie hadn't looked a gift horse in the mouth. Grace had made lobster stew and baked fresh baguettes, and shortly after cleaning up from dinner, just as Eddie was wondering how he was going to break the news that he had to go to work, she retreated to her study, saying she had some garden planning she wanted to do.

Hope was driving Allegra into town, then she was coming home to practice the flute. Allegra hadn't made the honor roll and hence hadn't earned the privilege of driving the four-door Jeep Sahara that Eddie had given both twins for their sixteenth birthday. Allegra had said she would get a ride home, and Eddie asked, *From whom?* And Allegra had said, *I don't know, Daddy, from* someone. The girl had five thousand friends, and, although Eddie was pretty sure she drank and probably also smoked, she had never gotten into *trouble* trouble. Of course, for the past two years, she had spent most of her free time with Brick — but recently, her plans had become vague. *Going into town to hang out on the Strip, maybe catch a movie.*

Eddie said, *Call me if you need a ride. I'll come get you, no matter what time.*

Allegra had hugged him and said, *Thank you, Daddy,* while Hope looked at him like he was the world's easiest mark.

To Hope, Eddie said, "I have to go check on a rental. I should be home by ten thirty, eleven at the latest."

Hope had shrugged.

Now, at the old Cumberland Farms, Eddie picked two bottles of cherry Tums off the shelf and brought them to the counter.

A voice behind him said, "Hey there, Eddie."

Eddie turned around. It took Eddie a second to recognize the man because he wasn't in uniform. Ed Kapenash, the chief of police, was wearing a white shirt, jeans, and a blazer.

"Hey, Chief," Eddie said, and he shook Ed's hand. Eddie paid for his Tums, took his change, accepted the bag, then turned around to smile at the Chief.

The Chief said, "Wait for me by the door for a second, would you?"

"Sure thing," Eddie said. His heart felt like it was being fed to a pack of feral dogs. While he waited, he popped open the Tums and chewed up a small handful. What would the Chief want with Eddie? Only the very worst came to mind.

The Chief was buying a gallon of milk. He held it up. "Much cheaper here," he said.

Eddie smiled. "Don't I know it."

"Eggs are cheaper, too—but then, I guess you don't buy eggs anymore."

"Grace's hens have spoiled me rotten," Eddie said. "I'll never go back."

The Chief opened the door and walked with Eddie out to the parking lot. His cruiser was parked next to Eddie's Cayenne. Thank God Eddie had gotten the thing inspected!

Eddie hesitated before heading to his car. Did the Chief want to talk to him?

The Chief said, "So, how are things with you, Eddie?"

"Oh," Eddie said, "can't complain, I guess."

"You're building those houses on Eagle Wing Lane?"

"I'm trying," Eddie said.

"And are you still taking on that high-roller rental on Low Beach Road?" the Chief asked.

Eddie wanted to look the Chief in the eye, but he couldn't. He stared at the chipped shingles on the side of the building.

"I am," Eddie said.

"All of those guys are big spenders, huh?" the Chief said. "Fifty grand a week." He whistled.

Eddie's heart was in red, raging turmoil. He nodded.

The Chief clapped Eddie on the back. "Well, nobody deserves to rake in the spoils more than you, my friend. You've been in the business a long time. You hustle faster than anyone I know."

These sounded like words of encouragement. But were they?

"What you did when we sold the MacAvoy house was incredibly generous. I'll never forget it, and neither will Andrea. And neither will Chloe or Finn."

"Well," Eddie said, "it was the least I could do." He held up his bag of Tums in a kind of salute, then headed for his car.

"Have a good night," the Chief said.

"And you," Eddie said. "Enjoy that milk."

Eddie waited in his Cayenne for the Chief to drive away before pulling out his phone.

He wanted to call Ronan LNW and cancel. Running into the *chief of police* only moments before doing the worst thing he had ever done or hoped to do? It meant there was trouble. The police were watching the house. Possibly Ronan LNW was an informant for the FBI. Possibly, Eddie was being *set up* by Glenn Daley, who was Rachel McMann's boss at Bayberry

Properties and who would like nothing more than to see Eddie and Barbie go belly up.

But then Eddie calmed himself. Ronan worked at Deep-Well in Las Vegas. It was a legitimate company; Eddie had googled it. Prostitution was legal in parts of Nevada, so that was probably what Ronan LNW was used to. To him, it was no big deal.

Okay, man, no problem, no problem. I was only asking.

Cancel? Half of Eddie's conscience and half of his good sense said yes.

But it was so much money. And he was on the verge of drowning. Chapter 11 — or worse.

But... money would do him no good in jail.

He popped three more Tums.

He had two daughters and a very sweet wife at home. If Grace knew he was doing this, she would kill him, then die of shame herself. She would tell Eddie that she was relieved her grandmother Sabine hadn't lived to meet Eddie, because he would in no way have passed muster. She'd told him this once before in anger, and the hurt had stuck with him. Why wasn't he good enough? Because he'd grown up in an apartment over Ramos Dry Cleaners on Purchase Street in New Bedford, where both his parents worked sixteen hours a day? Because he'd lost his track scholarship to Plymouth State after failing English senior year and then failing last-chance summer school? Because, instead of going to college, he'd come to Nantucket Island and gotten a job washing dishes at the Straight Wharf, then became a buser, then a waiter, then waited on the right person, a man named Winthrop Bing, now dead, who liked the way Eddie hustled and asked if he wanted a chance to get into real estate?

You hustle faster than anyone I know. That was what the Chief had said.

The Chief liked Eddie because six years earlier, when the Chief's best friend, Greg MacAvoy, and his wife, Tess, were killed in a sailing accident, the Chief, who was the executor of the will, had to sell the house. Eddie came up with a buyer in three days at full asking price—and he'd waived his commission. It was the one and only time in his career that he'd ever waived a commission. He did it because everyone else in the community was reaching out to help Chloe and Finn, the orphaned twins, so Eddie joined in, forgoing the twenty-one thousand dollars due to him, despite his natural Machiavellian proclivities.

And look! The Chief still remembered his generosity. The Chief thought he was a good guy. Well, he *was* a good guy. What he was about to do was illegal, yes, but he wasn't actually *hurting* anyone.

It was legal in parts of Nevada.

Legal in Amsterdam. Were the Dutch bad people?

Cancel?

The bald truth was, he needed the money. On top of everything else, Madeline wanted her fifty grand back! *That* had been an uncomfortable conversation.

Eddie decided to call Barbie. He wasn't sure if she would be at home or if she was away. As close as they were, she rarely shared her weekend plans. On the company calendar, she used the shorthand *P,* for *personal*—which meant anything that wasn't Island Fog Realty business. Her desk was littered with pens and notepads from fancy hotels—the Plaza and Waldorf, the Drake in Chicago, the Four Seasons in Santa Barbara—but if Eddie asked if she had *stayed* at the Four

Seasons in Santa Barbara, she would tell him it was "P." Barbie didn't believe in social networking or sharing her whereabouts or being part of a community, real or virtual. She existed to please herself.

She answered on the first ring. She was reliable that way.

"Sorry to bother you," Eddie said.

Silence. She wouldn't even say if he was bothering her or not.

"What's up?" she said.

"I'm having second thoughts about sending the girls," he said. "I just saw the chief of police."

"At the *house?*" she said.

"No, at Cumberland Farms. He was buying milk."

"Do you think he was following you?"

"No," Eddie said, though the thought had never occurred to him. "Not following me. I'm pretty sure he got there first."

"I don't understand," Barbie said. "What's the problem, then?"

"It's illegal."

"You just figured that out?"

"You don't have a gut feeling on this, do you?" he asked. Barbie's instincts were *uncanny*. She could see certain things before they happened.

"My gut feeling is that it will be just fine," Barbie said. "Not to mention very lucrative. I suggested it, remember? If it makes you feel better, just tell yourself it was all my idea."

"All your idea, but it will be me going to jail."

"That's not going to happen, Ed."

"You're sure?"

"I'm sure."

"What if I get in trouble? Are you even on island?"

Silence. Then, "Yes, actually, I am, if you must know."

"Okay, good," Eddie said.

"Text me when you have the cash," she said.

"Will do," he said, and he hung up. They were going to do this, then. He and Barbie were going to become de facto pimp and madam of a Russian prostitution ring down on Low Beach Road.

One more phone call, he thought. To the girls, to make sure they knew what they were getting into.

Nadia answered the phone.

Eddie said, "Are you ladies ready?"

"Yes, we ready," Nadia said. "We all go to salon to get manicure, pedicure, Eddie, with our own money, because there is more, bigger money coming tonight."

"Nice," Eddie said. "I'm sure you look very pretty."

"Who cares about pretty?" Nadia said. "Hands will be ruined tomorrow anyway, with the cleaning."

"Okay, Cinderella," Eddie said. "I'll see you shortly."

He popped two more Tums. They weren't working. His heartburn was so bad that he really needed prescription-strength medication, but who had time to go to the doctor?

Eddie pulled up in front of the house and sat in the dark car, waiting for Nadia and the other girls. Then he realized he should go down to the house and meet Ronan LNW and get the money part squared away so that the money and the girls weren't connected. This was Eddie's logic, but he wished he had some guidelines. Surely some depraved soul

on the Internet had written a manual on how to run a prostitution ring without getting caught?

The front door to the house was standing wide open, and in the background, Eddie could hear Eric Clapton singing *"Cocaine."*

"Knock, knock!" Eddie said, stepping into the foyer. "Hello, hello!" He didn't feel bad about his intrusion. Technically, while the owner was in L.A., this house was Eddie's responsibility.

He nearly collided with Ronan LNW, who was rushing down the stairs, holding a mirror crisscrossed with lines of cocaine, like a white, powdery tic-tac-toe board. Ronan was in bare feet, wearing jeans and an unbuttoned white shirt.

"Fast Eddie!" he said. His nostrils were pink and twitchy as a rabbit's, and his pupils had been swallowed up by green iris; Eddie had the unsettling thought that he was dealing with a zombie. And Ronan was sweating profusely. "Are the girls here? You probably want your money. Here, hold this."

He handed Eddie the mirror, and Eddie gazed down at his reflection, cut through by lines of coke. He was simply not comfortable with any of this.

Ronan appeared with a regular brown paper bag from the Stop & Shop. "Here you go, man. They'll come every night this week, right? And I'm paying half now and half at the end?"

Eddie nodded, afraid to give verbal confirmation, lest there was a wiretap somewhere in the house. He was anxious to get the drugs out of his hands. Back in the late 1980s, when Eddie arrived on Nantucket, everyone he knew had done drugs. When Eddie worked at the Straight Wharf, cocaine

had practically been served at the staff meal. But Eddie had steered clear of the stuff. Back then, he'd still been a runner, and he feared contaminating his body. Besides which, he knew drugs were bad; he'd seen them undo half his high school class in New Bedford.

He handed Ronan back the mirror and accepted the paper bag, then peered inside. Cash. For one glorious moment, Eddie's heart felt like a helium balloon.

Ronan nodded down at the mirror. "You wanna do a line, man?"

Eddie held up a palm. "No, thanks. Not my scene. I'm a father."

Ronan stared at him.

Eddie thought, *And I'm a pimp.*

Ronan said, "You know, I like that hat." He took Eddie's Panama hat off his head and placed it on his own.

Eddie wanted to reach out and reclaim it. He was willing to do just about anything to make this transaction go smoothly, but giving up his Panama hat wasn't one of them. He always kept a stable of three hats, *just in case,* so he did have two others just like it at home—but each hat cost $375 and took six weeks to replace.

"I get them specially made in Montecristi, Ecuador," Eddie said.

"Cool," Ronan LNW said. His eyes were spinning spirals, like in the cartoons. Eddie was afraid to touch him or even ask for the hat back. If Ronan LNW was dealing in prostitutes and drugs, then he probably had a gun, too. Eddie could not *believe* how nefarious this situation was turning out to be.

Just then, the girls walked in, though Eddie barely recognized them. During the day, when they were cleaning, they wore sweatpants and kept their hair tied up in bandannas. But tonight, they were wearing tight, shiny dresses and high heels, and their hair had been teased and sprayed. They had apparently bought one eye-shadow sampler, and each had chosen a color — Nadia blue, Julia green, Tonya violet, Gabrielle a lurid yellow, and tiny Elise shimmery brown.

"Eddie, Eddie, Eddie!" they cried out. They all stopped to double-cheek kiss him, even though they had never done anything but put their hands out for money before.

Eddie held the wrist of Nadia while the other girls followed Ronan, in Eddie's Panama hat, and the ersatz tic-tac-toe board up the stairs.

Eddie said, "You're clear on what's happening here, right, Nadia? Nobody but us can know. Otherwise, it'll be back to Russia for the five of you."

"Kyrgyzstan," Nadia said.

"Exactly," Eddie said.

Nadia patted Eddie's cheek. "Do not worry, Eddie. We understand. It just business."

Eddie walked back toward his car with the shopping bag, smarting about his lost hat. He told himself that he had two others just like it at home. He told himself to focus on the bigger picture.

After all, Barbie had been right. Things had gone just fine.

HOPE

Allegra texted Hope at ten thirty on Saturday night. *Please come pick me up.*

Hope was thrown by the word *please*. Allegra never, ever used *please, thank you,* or *excuse me* when communicating with Hope.

Where are you? Hope texted back. She had dropped Allegra in front of the Dreamland Theatre, but she knew Allegra had had no intention of seeing a movie. Now, she worried something was wrong.

At Calgary's house, Allegra texted. *Please come get me.*

NFW, Hope texted. *Find another ride.*

Pls! Allegra texted.

Three uses of the word *please*. Something definitely wrong. Hope waited.

PLS HOPE!

Hope waited.

PLS PLS PLS PLS!!!! I'll owe you.

You already owe me already! For covering for you! Hope texted, but she put on her sandals. She had practiced the flute for two hours, until her tongue and lips hurt, then she had looked at her chemistry homework. She was pretty sure Allegra was out with Ian Coburn, which meant Brick might be home and willing to text with her about acids and bases. But if she texted *Hot glass looks like cool glass* and Brick was out having fun the way teenagers were supposed to on Saturday nights, then Hope would feel like the biggest loser on earth.

When she set her chemistry book down, she was officially out of options for her Saturday night.

She did NOT want to go to Calgary's house, the same house where she had allowed him to get to third base while lying on his bed last December.

Calgary had asked Hope to the Christmas formal the week before Thanksgiving, and she had said yes, even though she realized she was a date of convenience—Calgary was Brick's best friend, and Brick was taking Allegra. Right after Hope said yes, Calgary started paying all kinds of boyfriend-like attention to her. He invited her to his basketball games, where a seat was reserved for her in the family section. Hope sat and made awkward conversation with Rachel McMann and Dr. Andy (who had been Hope's dentist until Rachel got her real-estate license and joined a rival agency, when Eddie moved the whole family to Dr. Torre).

Calgary started walking Hope to class and walking her to the bus. He asked her to the movies one night, and after the movies there was some mad kissing on the front step of Jack Wills, which was shuttered and closed for the season. Then Christmas Stroll weekend arrived, and Calgary and Hope walked around holding hands. They waited for Santa to arrive in his fire engine, they listened to the Victorian carolers, they got chowder and cocoa from the food tent. At one point, Calgary stepped into Stephanie's, the gift shop, alone, because he said he wanted to get a present for Hope. Hope sat on a bench with her eyes closed until he emerged with a small bag that contained a tiny box. Jewelry. Something special, something binding. This was turning into a relationship.

Hope couldn't believe it. Calgary was popular and good looking; he was a three-sport athlete and president of the Japanese club, which might have been really dorky except that Calgary was so cool, he made the Japanese club cool, and lots

of people joined, most of whom couldn't speak a word of Japanese. Calgary could speak Japanese fluently; his parents, in a burst of foresight, had hired a Japanese au pair when he was small, and when her visa expired, they paid one of the sushi chefs at Lola to be his tutor. Calgary wanted to go to the University of Pennsylvania, major in Japanese and business, and proceed to become more successful than any man they knew.

The Saturday night of Stroll, Hope let Calgary feel her breasts and put his mouth on them. He called them exquisite, and Hope ran her hands through Calgary's hair, because this was something she had seen actresses do in the movies. Calgary had nice brown curls that smelled like pinecones. Touching his hair while he kissed her breasts made her fall in love a little, which she suspected was a bad development.

The weekend after Christmas Stroll, Calgary's parents went off island to a Marriage Encounter weekend in Fall River, and Calgary invited Hope over to hang out. This was a setup, she thought, for them to both lose their virginity, and she deliberated for several hours before accepting. She wasn't sure she wanted to lose her virginity to Calgary McMann—because, although he was good looking and spoke fluent Japanese and sank 88 percent of his free throws, and although she'd felt something when she touched his hair and he explored her breasts with his mouth, it wasn't the big, all-consuming fireball of TRUE LOVE she'd been expecting. But, she realized, she might not meet that person for another twenty years, and did she really want to be a virgin when she was thirty-six? Wasn't it a rite of passage to get it out of the way? Calgary wasn't a bad choice.

Hope agreed to go.

They went up to Calgary's bedroom. He had lit candles and had music playing—John Mayer. Hope wondered if Calgary had consulted Brick about these details. Allegra *loved* John Mayer and had intimated that she and Brick had sex while listening to "Your Body is a Wonderland" all the time. Hope decided that the candles and music were nice, the empty house was nice, and Calgary had made his bed and plumped the pillows.

All systems go, then—kissing, Hope's shirt off, Calgary's shirt off, Hope's bra unhooked, Calgary's mouth on her breasts, Hope's hands in his hair. Eventually Calgary began fiddling with the button of her jeans. She helped him unbutton and unzip, then sucked in her breath to create room for him to slip his hands down inside her underwear (lacy thong, borrowed from Allegra, for the occasion).

This was where, somehow, things went wrong. Hope didn't even have the vocabulary to describe it. Calgary was rough. He poked where he should have rubbed, he stabbed where he should have gently explored. Hope cried out, wriggled in pain, tried to pull her jeans off even farther so he could see what he was doing. He said, "Oh yeah, you like that, you like that, baby," in some desperate and nearly violent tone she didn't recognize. She did *not* like it, not at all, but she was afraid to say so. She was aware that most teenage boys found the female anatomy perplexing, but Calgary was treating her delicate parts like something he needed to tame.

"Stop," Hope finally said, when his fingernail scraped inside of her. "Be gentle."

"Gentle?" Calgary said, as if this were the last word that

might apply to the sex act. He pulled his finger out and delivered it straight to his mouth, where he sucked it clean. "You taste...," he said. "I don't know."

Hope lay on his bed with her jeans and the lace thong binding her midthigh. "You don't know what?"

He said something in Japanese; it sounded like he was ordering sushi.

Hope stared at the ceiling. "You don't know *what,* Calgary?"

"I think you should leave," Calgary said.

Embarrassment, humiliation, shame, anger, a sense of gullible stupidity all collided. Hope's feelings for Calgary had immediately changed from the blandly positive to the blackest negative.

He'd driven Hope home in silence. She tried to turn the radio on, but he snapped it off. As she got out of the car in her driveway, she said, "Is it over, then?"

"Oh yes," Calgary said. "I'm asking someone else to the Christmas formal."

"Wow," Hope said. "Okay."

"You can think I'm a jerk," he said. "I don't care."

"I don't think that," Hope said. She absolutely *did* think that, but the bigger question was: what had gone wrong back at Calgary's house? She hadn't liked the way he was touching her, and maybe he didn't like what he was touching — or tasting. The mortification was enough to make her want to vaporize.

"Whatever, Hope," he said. "See you around."

She was being dismissed. Okay, fine. It happened between teenagers, she supposed, all the time, every day.

Now here she was, retracing her steps of that awful night, to pick up her sister. And why? Allegra was capable of finding a ride home, but she had asked and then begged Hope, and, as perverse as it was, Hope enjoyed being called upon to save the day. Hope herself had very lame social credentials; her only entrée to the cool people was through her sister.

She pulled up in front of the McMann house and honked. There was no way she was going inside.

She waited in the dark car, playing Cage the Elephant at ten thousand decibels. She wanted to seem like she'd arrived here from a different party, a party with college kids, where the music was better and the conversation was elevated.

Nobody appeared.

Hope texted Allegra. *I'm out front. Hurry.*

Still nothing. Hope laid on the horn.

Finally, the front door opened, and out came — Brick. Hope swallowed. He stumbled down the front steps and over to her car. He opened the passenger door and climbed in.

Hope said, "Where's Allegra?"

"She's not coming."

"She's not?"

"No," he said. His head fell forward on his neck like a wilting flower. "I was the one who texted you. I stole her phone."

"You...okay. Wow," Hope said.

"Ian Coburn showed up here, and Allegra was so excited

to see him that she left her phone on the coffee table. And I texted you."

That explained use of the word *please.* Hope focused on backing out of the driveway with caution. Reverse wasn't her strong suit.

Ian Coburn, she thought. Then she spied the red Camaro parked down the street.

Hope didn't know what to say. She took one last look at the gray shingles and white trim of Calgary's house, which was almost as nice as the house Hope and Allegra lived in. Dr. Andy made a lot of money as a dentist. "So, Ian showed up. Who else was there?"

"Calgary, obviously, Bluto was there, Hannah, Hollis, Kylie Eckers…"

"Ew," Hope said. "How is Allegra getting home?"

Brick shrugged. "I think we both know the answer to that."

"Maybe you should stay?" Hope suggested.

"I hate Ian Coburn. If Allegra wants to be friends with him, fine. Maybe she thinks he's cool because he's older or because he goes to BC or because he buys her beer. Whatever, fine, I'm not going to stop her. I can't. But I'm not staying. I can't stand Bluto or Hollis. Hannah is okay because she plays hockey, so at least she has an interest other than *Us* magazine, movie stars, and what they're wearing. Kylie Eckers is … geez, I can't even speak my true feelings about Kylie."

"No," Hope said. "Me either."

"You're smart to stay away from that scene."

Well, it wasn't exactly Hope being *smart.* She wasn't welcome with Allegra's crowd. They tolerated Hope to be polite, and they were nice to her corresponding to when Allegra

was nice to her. There were times when Allegra seemed to think it was cool to have a nerdy twin sister, someone who was everything she was not. Allegra had once told Hope that together, they were like one huge, awesome, complete person, and Hope had replied that she, Hope, was a complete person on her own. Hope had her own group of friends, the very smart kids in her honors math class—Evan, Henry, Anya. They rarely ventured out socially, but they were good people to eat lunch with.

"I'll take you home, then?" Hope said.

"Do you mind? I'm sorry, Hope. My parents promised to buy me a car, but...my mom got that new apartment for writing, so now there isn't enough money."

"That sucks," Hope said. "I'm sorry." She drove toward the Llewellyns' house, which was on the other side of the world as far as Nantucket was concerned.

Brick said, "When you texted back saying you've been covering for Allegra, what did that mean?"

Hope wasn't sure what to say. She was a terrible liar. "With my parents."

"Your parents?" he said. "Does it have anything to do with Ian Coburn? Anything at all?"

"No," Hope said.

"Have you ever heard Allegra talk about Ian? Does she mention him at home?"

Hope shrugged. "I guess."

"You guess?"

"A little," Hope said. "They're friends, like you said. She's allowed to have friends, Brick." Hope wasn't sure why she was defending Allegra. Allegra had no moral compass. She had lost it in the woods during their first Girl Scout camping trip,

when she had decided to sneak out with Hollis Brancato and smoke cigarettes over a pile of dead leaves. At eleven years old, she had nearly set the Hidden Forest on fire.

"Tell me the *truth!*" Brick shouted. "Is she seeing Ian Coburn?"

Hope was so alarmed by the question—even though she had been anticipating it for weeks—that she temporarily forgot she was operating a motor vehicle and she swerved into the oncoming lane. There was no one coming from either direction, but Hope's heart jumped into her throat and stayed there. If she crashed the car, her parents would *kill* her.

"Tell me, Hope!" Brick said. "Is she *screwing* him?"

"I have no idea!" Hope said. "Ask *her!*"

Brick made a strange choking noise, and Hope, fearing he was going to puke, pulled over onto the shoulder. Brick slumped against the passenger door. He was drunk. There had been nothing for him to do, she supposed, other than to try to drink away the fact that Allegra didn't love him anymore.

"Brick," Hope said.

But she was interrupted by blue and red lights in her rear-view mirror and one short burst of police siren, which was enough to cause Hope to cry out.

"Straighten up!" she barked at Brick. "And don't *say* anything!"

She turned the car off and pulled out her license and the Jeep's registration. She put down her window as a flashlight came

poking into the interior of the car. Hope looked up. It was either the best- or the worst-case scenario. The police officer was Curren Brancato, older brother of Hollis. Curren Brancato, Hope knew, had *just* joined the Nantucket police force. He was only six years older than Hope and Brick.

"What have we here?" Curren said. *"Allegra?"*

"No," Hope said. "I'm Hope. Allegra's sister."

"Oh, right," he said. "The good twin." He accepted her license and registration. "I see you at church with your mom."

Hope exhaled. "Yes."

"Have you been drinking, Hope?" Curren asked.

"Me?" Hope said. "No. I don't drink."

"Do you have a good explanation for why you crossed the centerline and then nearly drove off the road?"

Hope vaguely remembered Curren Brancato when he was in high school. He had been a football star — his nickname was Blue Thunder — but in the final games of his senior year, he had been declared ineligible because he was failing Spanish. Hope had only been in sixth grade — back then, Hope and Allegra had shared all of their friends, including Hollis — but Hope remembered the outrage caused by Curren's academic ineligibility. The Whalers had had a shot at the Massachusetts Super Bowl, but not without Curren Brancato. Although the Boosters made a fuss, Curren wasn't allowed to play. Hope had taken the episode as a big fat cautionary tale on squandered talent.

Curren had pulled a phoenix, however, and risen from the ashes. He attended a military college in Vermont, then the Boston Police Academy. Then he returned to Nantucket, where he was hailed as a homegrown hero.

"I know I crossed the centerline," Hope said. "I'm sorry."

"But why?" Curren said. "And then you nearly drove into the trees."

"Um . . . ?" Hope said.

Curren Brancato—Officer Brancato—poked his head into the Jeep and studied Brick. "Is *he* drunk?"

"Affirmative," Brick said.

Hope sighed. She had hoped Brick would pretend to be asleep.

"You have a junior license, Hope," Officer Brancato said. "Which means that you're breaking curfew right now. And your erratic driving? I could see to it that you don't drive again until your eighteenth birthday."

Great, Hope thought. A lot of good going to church had done her.

She said, "My sister needed a ride home from a party. She's with Hollis." Hope paused, wondering if mention of Curren's sister would help her cause. "But then Allegra decided she wanted to stay, and Brick was ready to go, so I'm taking him home. I'm sorry I was all over the road. I was changing the radio station, and I got distracted."

"Your radio isn't even on," Curren said.

"I know," Hope said. "I turned it off when you pulled me over."

Curren studied Brick for a second and then Hope for a longer second. Finally, he said, "Hollis is bad news."

Hope stared at the steering wheel, afraid to agree or disagree.

"Is your *sister* bad news?" Curren asked. He kind of sounded like he hoped Allegra *was* bad news. If he had pulled

Allegra over and she had been alone, Hope was pretty sure she knew what would have happened.

"Yes," Brick said.

This made Curren—Officer Brancato—laugh. He said, "I'm going to let you go with just a verbal warning."

Hope exhaled. "Thank you."

"You're welcome," Curren said. His voice was half-kind and half-congratulatory of his own magnanimity. "Be good, be smart, stay out of trouble, go to college."

Hope nodded solemnly, as though this were good, original advice.

Curren handed back her license and registration. "Okay, Hope. See you in church."

Hope drove home at the cautious speed of twenty-five miles per hour, feeling the giddy lightness of someone who has been let off the hook. Brick fell asleep. When Hope pulled up to the Llewellyn house, Hope nudged him, and, like a robot, he climbed out of the car and lurched for the front door. Hope thought to warn him not to *tell* anyone— especially not his parents, especially not Allegra—that she'd been pulled over. But she doubted he would remember it, anyway.

Allegra shook Hope awake in the middle of the night. It took a minute for Hope to figure out what, exactly, was happening,

but then she saw her sister's face twisted in anger. Allegra's lip was curled, and her hair tickled Hope's face, which was effective torture.

Hope pushed Allegra away. "Get *off* me," she said. "What are you *doing?*"

"You and Brick got pulled over," she said. "Curren texted Hollis right away. He said something was going *on* between the two of you."

"What?" Hope said.

"He said you were driving *all over the road*. Which says to me that the two of you were fooling around."

"What?" Hope said.

"Don't play dumb with me, Hope. I don't believe the naive act. I know you nearly had sex with Calgary. I know you know what you're doing with boys. You had your hands on Brick tonight, or you let him put his hands on you."

"I did *not,*" Hope said. "Now get away from me, please. Get out of my room."

"You went after my boyfriend," Allegra said. "I know you like him, Mopey Hopey. I know you want him."

"Do *not* call me that," Hope said. *Mopey Hopey:* the insidious nickname that Allegra had invented the day they started middle school. "Really, what do you care? You've been cheating on Brick left and right with Ian Coburn, including tonight, right in front of his face. I'm sure you're *glad* I took Brick home so you didn't have to *deal* with him."

"He *stole* my phone to text you!" Allegra said. "The two of you have something going on."

"We do *not,*" Hope said. "Don't be a douche waffle."

From out of the dark air came a hard, stinging slap. Hope gasped. It hurt enough for her to cry, but she wouldn't give

Allegra the satisfaction. Hope pulled her duvet over her head and said, "I'm not going to sink to your level, Allegra. Now, get out of my room."

"I'm going to tell everyone what a slut you are," Allegra said. "Stealing your twin sister's boyfriend."

"What a slut *I* am?" Hope said. "That's rich. I could just as easily call Hollis tomorrow and tell her about you and Ian Coburn. Or I'll tell Brick. Or I'll tell them both. Brick has pretty much figured it out, anyway. He was asking me what I knew, and I was so freaked out that I crossed the centerline. *Because I was worried you were going to get caught. I was worried for you, Allegra.* Now, good night."

NANTUCKET

Did you hear?

Hope Pancik had slept with Brick Llewellyn. Sergeant Curren Brancato, whom many of us still thought of as Blue Thunder #33, had found them parked on a dirt lane off Shimmo Pond Road, buck naked, Hope's bare feet pressed up against the steamed window, a pile of clothes strewn across the backseat of the Panciks' Jeep.

Certain details corroborated this story. Allegra wasn't walking with Brick between classes anymore. Instead, Allegra walked with Hollis Brancato and Bluto, while Brick hung out with Parker Marz. Parker was the shortest, smallest player on the Whaler varsity baseball team, the weakest link, but he had

gumption and spirit, and he had jumped at the chance to be Brick's sidekick.

Hope and Allegra didn't speak to each other during the school day, but they had never spoken much before. Hope sat with her smart math friends at lunch in what seemed like a subdued state, and she left lunch early to head to the band room to practice the flute. When she passed through the cafeteria, someone let go a wolf whistle, to which she did not respond.

Allegra Pancik refused to discuss the matter of the betrayal with any of her friends, including Hollis Brancato. This made everyone in the high school believe that Allegra was taking the situation very, very seriously—perhaps more seriously than she had taken anything in her sixteen years.

GRACE

The week started with a beautiful, sunny, and *warm* day— an expected high of *seventy-eight* degrees!—and Grace put on a jean skirt she hadn't worn since before the twins were born.

When Benton arrived, he whistled at her from across the yard. "At last," he called out, "I get to see those bare legs."

Grace was standing out by the Adirondack chairs, drinking coffee as she overlooked Polpis Harbor. Finally, there were some boats in the water. Summer was on its way.

She watched Benton stride out to her. He was wearing a T-shirt and jeans, his Buckeyes hat, and his wraparound Oakley sunglasses with the lenses that reflected the spring sky. She couldn't get over how much she desired the man. When he reached her, she locked her arms around his neck, and they started kissing. Grace ran her fingers over his face, she tugged on the ginger curls that stuck out beneath his hat. Benton's hands grabbed her ass in her skirt, which was a new, surprising move for him, and then he lifted her up clear off the ground, and she wrapped her legs around him.

He groaned. She thought, *This is it. It's going to happen.* He was so hard that she could feel him poking through his jeans. She tightened her legs.

"Please," she said.

"I can't," he said. He bit her bottom lip and looked her in the eyes. "Damn it. I can't resist you. I'm going to make love to you right here in the grass, right here in the sun. Are you okay with that?"

She was in such a state of delirium, every inch of her body yearning for him, that she couldn't even answer. She set her feet back on the ground and was about to lie back when she heard a distinctive squeaking noise. She whipped around to see Hope settling into the hammock with a book.

"Oh no!" Grace whispered. What was *Hope* doing home? Then Grace remembered that both girls had taken the SAT that morning, and when they were done with the test, they were done for the day.

Benton also turned and saw Hope. He looked at Grace. *Shit!* he mouthed. *Did she see?*

"I don't know," Grace whispered. "I don't think so?"

The hammock was a hundred yards away, but it faced in the direction of the Adirondack chairs and the harbor, so how could Hope *not* have seen her mother with her legs wrapped around Benton Coe's waist, the two of them madly kissing? And yet, Hope hadn't screamed and fled for the house; nor had she called Grace out and demanded an explanation. She hadn't so much as cleared her throat. So maybe she hadn't seen.

"Act normal," Grace said.

"Normal?" Benton said, as if he didn't know what the word meant. He was visibly shaken. Grace reached for his hand and gave it a discreet squeeze.

"Come say hi," she said. "If you scurry off, it will really look suspicious."

"Let's talk about gardening," Benton said.

"The rose bed," Grace said. "Lecture me."

Benton raised his voice a little as they walked toward the hammock. "You need to cut them back if you want to force a more lavish bloom," he said. "I know it sounds counterintuitive. And you should wipe down each leaf with a mixture of two parts water and one part lemon juice."

Grace nodded, then pretended to notice Hope in the hammock. "Darling!" she said. "You're home! How was the test?"

Hope gazed at Grace and Benton over the top of her book. Her expression was impossible to gauge. "Fine," she said.

"Fine," Grace repeated. "What does that mean, *fine?*"

"It means the test was fine, Mother," Hope said. "And Allegra wanted me to tell you she went to the beach."

"How did Allegra do on the test?" Grace asked.

Hope said, "I have no idea." She gave Benton a smile that seemed friendly and sincere. "Hey, Benton."

"Hey, Hope," Benton said. "It's good to see you! What are you reading?"

Hope held up her book: *Love in the Time of Cholera,* by García Márquez. "It's for honors English," she said.

"García Márquez is one of my favorite writers," Benton said. "Are you enjoying it?"

"I haven't really gotten into it yet," Hope said.

"Have you ever read Nabokov?" Benton asked. "*Lolita*? You have to read *Lolita*. You basically shouldn't be allowed to claim personhood until you've read *Lolita*."

Hope shook her head, and Grace gave Benton's arm a playful swat. "She's only sixteen," Grace said. "I'm not sure she's ready for *Lolita*."

"One is never too young for fine literature," Benton said. "I'm so used to telling my clients which perennials to plant in the shade...but reading is my secret passion. Have you ever heard of *Goodbye, Columbus* by Philip Roth? That's my favorite book of all time. You will love it."

Hope shook her head.

"Any Salinger?"

"*Catcher in the Rye,*" Hope said. "For English. But I didn't like it."

"It's hard to understand the subtext, I think," Benton said. "Holden is all messed up because his brother died. You should try *Franny and Zooey*."

"Okay," Hope said.

"Have you read the Cheever stories?" Benton asked.

"I loved the Cheever stories," Grace said. She gazed up at Benton. "How do you know so much about books?"

"I was a literature major," Benton said.

"So was I," Grace said. "French literature."

Benton turned his attention back to Hope. "Have you read any Hemingway? *The Sun Also Rises*? Andre Dubus the father? God, now *that* man was a genius. Have you read any Updike?"

"No," said Hope.

Benton rubbed his hands together. "I'm being a typical white male and forgetting the women. Have you read Edith Wharton? *The Age of Innocence*? *The House of Mirth*?"

"No."

"I'm actually *jealous* of you!" Benton said. "I wish I was sixteen again and had the first reading of all those books ahead of me. Have you read John O'Hara's *An Appointment in Samarra*? That's another one of my favorites."

Hope shook her head. Grace couldn't believe how *amazing* it was to listen to Benton talk about books. Eddie had street smarts, but his reading material started and ended with purchase-and-sales agreements and the *Nantucket Standard* on Thursdays.

"Truman Capote, *Breakfast at Tiffany's*? Richard Russo? Peter Taylor, *The Old Forest*? Carson McCullers? What about any of the Russians? Tolstoy? Chekhov? Kafka? Isaac Babel?"

"You have to stop," Hope said. "I'm one of the smartest kids in my grade, and you're making me feel totally illiterate."

Benton laughed. "Listen, I'm going to make you a list of a hundred books. You can probably make it halfway through the list in a year."

"I would like that," Hope said. "Really."

"It's a deal," Benton said. He reached down and toggled

Hope's foot in her sneaker. "I've got to shove off. Good to see you, Hope."

"And you," Hope said.

"I'll walk you out," Grace said to Benton.

In the driveway, they stood at the driver's side of Benton's truck.

"Bullet dodged," Grace said. "She didn't see."

"Yeah, I know," Benton said. "But still...that was too close for comfort for me."

"And me," Grace said. "We'll have to be more careful next time."

"Grace," Benton said.

She didn't like the tone of his voice. "What?"

He took a breath. "She's *such* a great kid. And I'm sure Allegra is just as wonderful. You have a *family,* Grace. It doesn't make me feel good about what we're doing, and I'm sure it doesn't make you feel too terrific either."

"The girls have their own lives," Grace said. "And Eddie..."

"I think it would be best if I stopped coming for a while," Benton said.

"What?" Grace said.

"The yard is in good shape," Benton said. "If you have any questions, you can call me. My phone is always on."

"Benton?" she said. She swallowed. He was right. What, what, *what* would Grace have done if Hope *had* seen them? That would have been a completely different level of awful. "Okay, but you'll come back, right? I mean, you're not leaving me forever, are you?"

"No, Grace," he said. "I'm not leaving you forever." He touched her cheek, and then he climbed into his truck and drove off.

When Grace went back into the kitchen, Hope was at the counter, making a list on the notepad that Grace used for groceries. Hope said, "What was the book called that Benton said was his favorite?"

Grace looked at Hope. "I don't know?" she said, and she headed up to her study. She needed to talk to Madeline.

Benton didn't come the next morning, nor the next. *I think it would be best if I stopped coming for a while.* How long was a while? A week? Two weeks? A month? If he stayed away for a month, she would perish.

A vicious migraine descended on Wednesday afternoon, only it was a migraine of the heart, not the head. It was the worst emotional pain Grace had sustained since she couldn't remember when. Nothing mattered. She didn't care that it was a mild, sunny day filled with possibility. Grace could tend to the hens, collect eggs, spend a couple of good hours in the garden. Cooking usually made her feel better. She could make something complicated for dinner—an asparagus soufflé, a strawberry-rhubarb pie.

Instead, she went overboard with her Fioricet. She took two at four o'clock, when it became clear to her that Benton

wasn't going to stop by that day, and then a third and fourth at six o'clock, when she should have been making dinner. Grace locked herself in her study. Eddie and the girls would have to fend for themselves, if anyone was even home. No one had come up to check on her.

You have a family, *Grace.*

She couldn't fault Benton, and she certainly couldn't hate him. He was right! He had pulled the plug right before they crossed a line. Grace should be grateful. She had stood on the altar at the First Church in Salem and had vowed to love Edward Pancik, forsaking all others—but from the moment Benton Coe had brought her the Moroccan mint tea and shared that first pistachio *macaron,* Grace had been gob-smacked. And, truthfully, she had fallen for Benton before that. She had fallen for him the first time she ever saw him, the previous spring. He had been standing on the highest mud hill in her then-undeveloped yard. She had, she remembered, turned the enormous diamond of her wedding ring inward, so that it chewed at her palm. She had wished she were single.

He made her *so happy.* Even before the kissing, back when they were "just friends," seeing Benton had given her days meaning.

She took two more pills. The sixth pill sent Grace into a kaleidoscopic stratosphere—an *Alice in Wonderland* tea party in a field of poppies with Toto and Timothy Leary.

She pulled the shades down in her study and lay on the crushed-velvet sofa, marveling at how comfortable it was. She wondered that she had never thought to sleep there before.

*   *   *

In the morning, Grace awoke with a sensation of having been buried alive. She was parched, her eyes burned, her nostrils stung. She experienced a moment of profound befuddlement. Where was she? *Who* was she?

Grace Harper Pancik, she thought. In the study of her house on the Wauwinet Road. And there was someone knocking on her front door.

Grace staggered through the house, trying to bring herself back to reality; she might have been Rip Van Winkle, asleep for twenty years. She might have been just back from a journey on a time machine. It was Thursday. The clock said ten minutes after ten. Eddie would be at work, the girls at school.

On the kitchen counter sat an open pizza box, displaying one cold, congealed piece of mushroom-and-green-pepper pizza from Sophie T's. That explained what her family had eaten for dinner. There were dishes in the sink, and there was one of the Baccarat wineglasses holding the residue of red wine. Next to it, an empty bottle of the Screaming Eagle.

Eddie had clearly thought nothing of drinking his precious, prized wine without her. He hadn't managed to get the dishes into the dishwasher, nor the pizza box into the recycling bin. He had decided to wait for Grace to wake up and do it.

Still, the knocking.

Who would it be? Grace wondered. UPS and FedEx knew to just drop off.

Then, Grace thought: *Benton?* She hurried for the door. Normally, he just walked around the side of the house, into the yard, but he might not feel comfortable doing that under present circumstances.

But when Grace opened their massive front door—it was made of oak and was heavy enough to withstand a battering ram—the person she found standing before her was Madeline.

"Thank God you're alive," Madeline said. "Eddie called me. He said you'd locked yourself in your study and spent the *night* there?"

Grace opened the door so that Madeline could enter. She was getting a rebound headache, which was nearly as bad as a migraine and would require Excedrin and strong coffee to combat.

"I'm alive," Grace said. "But barely."

"It's a beautiful day," Madeline said. "I think we should go to lunch, sit outside, share a bottle of wine."

Grace peered out at the bright, warm day. It hurt her eyes to look at the sun.

"Don't you have to write in your apartment today?" When Grace had talked to Madeline on Monday, Madeline said something about a deadline she had to meet for the new book.

"I'm taking today off," Madeline said. "I'm devoting myself to you."

Grace felt stupidly grateful. She would take a shower, put on a dress, and go to lunch with Madeline.

She didn't know how any woman anywhere conducted an affair without having the ear of a best friend.

*   *   *

They went to the Great Harbor Yacht Club for lunch, since it had just opened for the season. The summer people had yet to arrive, so they would have the place virtually to themselves for confidential conversation. It was a stunner of a day, the kind of day that promised more days exactly like it, for months to come. The hostess led Grace and Madeline across the grass to the premium outdoor table for two, with an uninterrupted view of the harbor and the huge summer homes in Monomoy. The waitress handed them menus, and Grace said, "We'll have a very cold bottle of Sancerre, if you have it."

Madeline regarded her menu. "Definitely worth giving up work for," she said. "I love it here. You are so lucky."

Grace knew she was lucky. She and Eddie had languished on the wait list at the Nantucket Yacht Club for years before Grace realized that they would never get in. She supposed Eddie had pissed too many people off, or possibly the old Nantucket families who belonged there didn't want a man nicknamed Fast Eddie to join their ranks. But then the Great Harbor Yacht Club opened, and Eddie jumped at the opportunity; he was one of the first people to write a check for the six-figure initiation fee.

Grace studied the menu—oysters on the half shell, grilled Caesar salad with creamy Roquefort dressing, lobster club sandwich with shoestring fries—and tried to make herself feel hungry.

The waitress came with the wine, which Grace tasted and approved. The waitress poured two glasses, then set the bottle in a bucket of ice. Grace and Madeline touched glasses, and Grace said, "Thank you for making me do this."

Madeline said, "Thank you for buying lunch."

They laughed, but a short moment later, the waitress came back with an uneasy expression on her face. She leaned over to Grace and said, "I'm sorry to interrupt your drinks, but I just found out from our general manager that Accounting hasn't received your check for this year's dues? So, technically, I'm not allowed to serve you?"

"What?" Grace said. She reached for her phone to text Eddie. He handled all their bills. But cell phones were verboten at Great Harbor. She smiled at the waitress. "I have two ideas. One is, I could just pay you cash for lunch, and then we can clear up the missing dues check later? I'm sure my husband sent it, or he meant to send it. But he's got a lot going on at the moment with his business." Grace wondered if the invoice for the yacht club had gotten mixed up with some of the bills for the spec houses. Or, possibly, he had left the bill for Eloise to pay, and she had forgotten. She was getting older and tended to let things slip. Grace had encouraged him to replace her, but, as Eddie pointed out, she was related to half the island. He couldn't just fire her.

"I'm sorry," the waitress said. "I can't accept any cash."

"Okay," Grace said. "How about if I write you the check for the dues right now, and then, if you find my husband's check, or if it comes in the mail, you can tear it up."

"I'll ask the manager about that?" the waitress said.

She left to do so, and Grace pulled her checkbook out. She rolled her eyes at Madeline. "I can't believe Eddie," she said. "I'm totally mortified."

"Please," Madeline said. "I'm your best friend. I wish I could help."

The waitress reappeared. "Our manager said that would be fine."

"Okay," Grace said. "Good. How much is it?"

"Fifteen thousand dollars," the waitress said.

Grace wrote the check out, feeling Madeline's eyes on her. Fifteen thousand dollars. Back when Grace and Eddie had just met Madeline and Trevor, they would go for dinner on Saturday nights and split the bill. Madeline later admitted to Grace that the cost of the meal weighed on her mind every second, to the point where she almost couldn't enjoy her food. What had they ordered? How much had the wine cost? (Eddie always chose it.) Did they have enough cash, or would they have to pile it onto their credit cards, which were already sagging like a rained-on roof?

Oh! Grace had said. She'd had *no idea* Madeline felt that way. If she'd known, she would have encouraged Eddie to pay each and every time. But Eddie wouldn't have liked that. He was a naturally frugal person, a result of having grown up dirt poor, living over a dry cleaner's in downtown New Bedford.

If he paid every time, he might argue, what would happen to the Llewellyns' pride?

Now Grace wondered what Madeline was thinking. Thankfully, the waitress vanished with the check, and the issue was over.

Madeline said, "What's going on with Benton?"

Grace didn't have anything to describe except her longing. *No, Grace, I'm not leaving you forever.* But what if he was? What if he got back in touch with McGuvvy, called her up in San Diego and convinced her somehow to come back to Nantucket? Grace had stood at her window and waited for Benton's truck to appear in her driveway every morning. She took care of the chickens because they would starve with-

out her, but the rest of the garden she'd ignored, because she just couldn't make herself cut back the roses or wipe their leaves with lemon water. She couldn't deadhead the perennial bed. She couldn't even mow the lawn, and that was her favorite task.

She said, "The morning it happened, he started talking to Hope about the books he'd read that he thought she would enjoy. And it *killed* me. He became this other person. There I was, standing in front of my daughter—and with every book he mentioned, I fell more and more in love."

"Grace," Madeline said. "You are *not* in love. I know you think you are. But you're in love with Eddie and your girls."

Grace sipped her wine and looked out over the flat, blue surface of Nantucket Sound. "You're right," she said.

But Madeline wasn't right.

Three glasses of wine had turned Grace's attitude around. When she and Madeline parted ways in the parking lot, Grace said, "Thank you for listening."

Madeline said, "That's what I'm here for."

Madeline pulled out of the parking lot toward home, toward her perfect marriage to Trevor and their shared adoration of Brick. Grace decided to call Eddie and let him know about the yacht-club dues, but she was shuttled right to his voice mail, and when Grace called the office—which she was loath to do, because she really didn't want to talk to Eloise or Barbie, and those two screened Eddie's calls like he was the CEO of Microsoft—she got the recording.

She stared at her phone. The wine was coursing through her veins. She imagined it taking her good sense with it. *My phone is always on.*

As she texted Benton, the tops of her ears started to buzz. *Will you come tomorrow and have lunch? Just friends, promise. Noon?*

She decided she would not move from the yacht-club parking lot until he texted back. If she was there at midnight, so be it. But he texted back right away.

I'll be there.

She was in the gardening shed, scrubbing the copper farmer's sink, when Benton came strolling around the house.

"Hey!" she called out. "I'm in here."

Benton stepped through door and said, "You're a sight for sore eyes."

Grace laughed. "It's only been four days."

He walked over to her, and his hands went immediately on her hips. Because it was so hot, she was wearing only a bikini top and a pair of shorts.

"Are the girls at school?" he asked.

She grinned. "Safely at school."

"And Eddie?"

"Work," she said.

His mouth met her mouth, his tongue met her tongue, which made Grace feel as if she were going to faint, or die. The kissing was sweet at first and then incendiary. The gardening shed was hot hot hot to begin with, but once she was kissing Benton, they were both sweating and pulsing with

insane desire. He closed and locked the door and then lifted Grace up onto the lip of the sink. With a couple of deft movements, he untied her bikini top and pulled off her shorts, and then he knelt before her.

Later, they ate lunch.

Grace served a cold roast chicken, a fresh head of butter lettuce, a crock of herbed farmer's cheese, and fat, rosy radishes pulled from the garden. She cut thick slices of bread from a seeded multigrain loaf with a nice chewy crust, then she went back into the fridge and pulled out sweet butter, a jar of baby gherkins, a stick of summer sausage, and some whole-grain mustard.

"A ploughman's lunch!" Benton said. "Like the ones I used to have in Surrey."

"I'm glad you like it," Grace said.

"I like everything about you," he said.

You are not *in love.*

Benton helped Grace carry everything to the teak table outside, and they sat down with their feast, within full sight of the garden.

Together, they dug in, piecing together bites for each other: radish, sweet butter, and mustard. A slice of bread spread thick with farmer's cheese and topped with sausage.

Grace's hands were shaking as she fed him. He nibbled at the tips of her fingers.

He said, "Do you know the song 'Loving Cup' by the Rolling Stones?" He started to sing. *"I'm the ploughman in the valley with a face full of mud."*

Did she? She said, "I think so?"

"Here," he said. "I'll play it." He plugged his phone into the outdoor speaker, and music filled the backyard.

Benton took Grace's hand and pulled her to her feet. They started to slow dance to the song right there on the deck, Benton's arms around Grace, Grace's face resting on Benton's chest. She hadn't even known such happiness existed. *What a beautiful buzz, what a beautiful buzz.*

When Benton left, Grace ran up to her study.

She needed to call Madeline.

MADELINE

The apartment, which had seemed so *freeing* to Madeline initially, now felt like a jail cell. Madeline had to drag herself there, and when she walked in, she experienced something like panic. She had paid twelve thousand dollars for the place, and now she needed to make it earn its keep.

Pressure.

She couldn't write a word under such pressure.

She had no ideas for another novel. Not one.

She was plagued with all kinds of upsetting thoughts. They were running out of money, she had promised more than she could deliver, they should never have invested the

fifty thousand with Eddie. Trevor would have to ask for it back, since Madeline's plea had done no good.

She was past her deadline, the deadline Redd Dreyfus had extended for her. Redd had called her cell phone and left two exasperated messages, and both Angie and Angie's assistant, Marlo, e-mailed and then called. They needed the copy; otherwise she would be bumped from the list and there would be "financial repercussions."

Madeline capitulated. She had no choice. She would write a sequel to *Islandia*.

But when Madeline sat down with her legal pad and began an outline, the book she described wasn't a sequel to *Islandia*. The book she described was a hot, steamy love affair between a stay-at-home mother of two and her contractor.

I am not writing this, Madeline thought. *I am not writing this.* But she *was* writing it. The words were flowing out of her like something she spilled on the page.

Grace had said it herself: *Everything* was *normal and boring. And now . . . now, my life is a novel.*

Madeline didn't even commit to giving her two lovers names. She called them B and G.

The male protagonist, "B," is the project manager of the female protagonist's home renovation. The female protagonist, "G," is a stay-at-home mother of two girls—Irish twins, born eleven months apart. B and G start conferring every day on the renovation. Did G want an undermounted porcelain sink in the kitchen or a double stainless steel? What kind of countertops— granite, limestone, Corian? Backsplash of decorative tile or plain drywall? What kind of hardwood flooring—maple, cherry, antique knotty pine? What style for the cabinets? What kind of cabinet pulls?

B and G end up kissing for the first time in the first-floor powder room, during a discussion of fixtures for the sink. The quarters are tight—and dark, as the electrician has yet to come hang the lights. G is in the powder room when B walks in, and they accidentally bump hips. The next thing either of them knows, they are passionately kissing.

B starts bringing G Moroccan mint tea every day, as well as a box of four pistachio macarons from the local bakery, which they would share.

Madeline didn't even bother changing the kind of cookie. She supposed she could have made them white-chocolate melt-aways or peanut-butter truffles. She could have changed the Moroccan mint tea to an iced vanilla latte.

I am not writing this. I am not writing this. She couldn't turn this in. Grace would sue her. Or kill her. Or both.

But it was good. Madeline could see that it was good. It was spare and compelling. Grace's affair with Benton Coe did contain all the elements of good fiction: loneliness, desire, sex, betrayal.

B and G fall deeper and deeper in love as work on the house progresses. G's husband, a real-estate attorney named Ren, short for Renfrew, pays all the bills, including the astronomical bill for B's services, without complaint. He tells people he's happy that his wife is happy.

Madeline wrote one sample scene, and that was the scene of the two lovers eating a ploughman's lunch on the sunny deck. They feed each other; B nibbles on G's fingertips. And then they slow dance to "Loving Cup" by the Rolling Stones. Madeline couldn't even bring herself to change the song—"Loving Cup" was too perfect.

She could *not* write this novel. But she had nothing else, and so she typed up the outline and added the sample scene and e-mailed them to Redd Dreyfus with the subject line I TRIED.

EDDIE

He had a love-hate relationship with Memorial Day weekend. On the one hand, he couldn't wait for it to arrive, announcing, as it did, the start of summer.

Eddie loved the summer as much as anyone on Nantucket. He loved it not because the shops and restaurants opened, not because the lifeguards in their red tank suits and trunks patrolled the beaches, not because the lilacs were blooming and the weather was finally warm enough for barbecues and Wiffle ball games and outdoor showers. No...Eddie loved summer because summer meant the steamship was low in the water, the martini-and-oyster-seeking crowds milled outside of Cru, a line formed at the Chicken Box to hear the band Maxxtone, the parking lot of the Stop & Shop was filled to capacity, with people illegally parked in the handicapped spots, and the traffic on Orange Street made the year-rounders shout profanities at their dashboards.

Summer on Nantucket meant people. And people meant money—the buying and selling of houses, the renting of vacation weeks.

However, Memorial Day on Nantucket also meant Figawi, a Nantucket tradition that only grew bigger and more obnoxious every year. It was, ostensibly, a sailing race from Hyannis to Nantucket and back again. The genesis of the name was everyone's favorite fact about the weekend. One year, while sailing in dense fog, some old salt called out, "Hey, where the figawi?" And in this way, the race was named. Because, really—who doesn't love sanctioned profanity?

Figawi Weekend had morphed in recent years from a sailing race to a drinking race. It was a contest of who could drink the most, who could drink the fastest, who could stay up drinking the latest, who could get up the earliest and start drinking, who could act like the biggest jerk (this was the nicest term Eddie could come up with, although he had dozens at his disposal) while drinking. Figawi was popular with the postcollegiate crowd—kids who had just graduated from Hamilton or Bowdoin or Middlebury or, Eddie's least favorite, Boston College. ("How do you know if somebody went to BC?" he liked to quip. "They'll tell you.") These kids now had jobs in Manhattan or Boston as editorial assistants or Wall Street grunts or preschool teachers, or they were in law school at NYU or medical school at Harvard. They lived in apartments in the West Village or the Back Bay that their parents still paid for, but in general, they were trying to be adults. They met for drinks after work on Newbury Street or in Soho, they skipped church on Sundays and brunched instead, and on summer weekends they "went away."

Figawi Weekend on Nantucket was made for them. The men wore their faded red shorts from Murray's; they tied cable-knit sweaters around their necks, they wore sunglasses inside because they were so dreadfully hungover. The girls—

or, rather, *women*—paraded around in patio dresses without underwear. They all thought they were Diane von Fursten-berg by the Beverly Hills Hotel pool in 1973. And they all carried handbags that seemed to contain as much crap as a thirty-gallon Hefty bag. Eddie wanted to tell them that they could go on *Let's Make a Deal* with all the stuff they had in their purses—but they would have had no idea what he was talking about! Certain women, however, wore outfits that looked like they'd been stolen from the trailer-park clothesline—cutoff jean shorts and tight T-shirts that said SORRY FOR PARTYING.

The women irked Eddie more than the men, probably because he had daughters.

If the weather was sunny, the Figawians—truly their own nation—funneled down Hummock Pond Road in their rental Jeeps with cases of Bud Light in the back. The beaches were patrolled by rent-a-cops on ATVs who had a field day issuing tickets for public consumption and littering. The red-suited lifeguards pulled people out of the ocean left and right because the riptide was notoriously bad in May, and no matter how educated these young bucks were (*bucks* substituted for dozens of other terms Eddie had at his disposal), they didn't seem to know that the way to get out of the rip was to swim parallel to shore until the grip of the waves let them go.

But this year, there was rain.

Rain on Figawi weekend was a thousand times worse than sun on Figawi because the activities of beaching and drinking were replaced by drinking and drinking. The epicenter of Figawi drinking was always the Straight Wharf—specifically, the Tavern, the Gazebo, the eponymous Straight Wharf Res-taurant, and Cru. These restaurants were bursting at their

seersucker and madras seams with screaming, laughing, swearing, hiccupping, posturing nouveau adults who were only just learning how to appreciate a good Bloody Mary and suck down an oyster without dripping onto their Brooks Brothers.

Eddie wasn't sure what made him decide to head down to Cru at two o'clock on Saturday afternoon; he realized it was going to be a blender (this was the nicest word he could come up with, though he had dozens of others at his disposal). Barbie refused to leave her house during Figawi Weekend. She never told Eddie exactly what she did at home, but if he had to guess, he would say that when it was sunny, she sat on her back deck and drank prickly-pear margaritas. And if it rained, she indulged her lifelong crush on James Garner and watched old episodes of *The Rockford Files.*

Eddie supposed if he had to name what truly motivated him, he would say he wanted to be where the action was. Some day, these Figawians would grow up to be attorneys and surgeons, college presidents, NFL coaches, and, of course, hedge-fund managers. In five years, many of these Figawians would be married with a toddler on the ground and a baby on the way, and looking for a rental—one week, then two weeks, then the month of July, then the summer. In ten years, these Figawians would be ready to buy.

So basically, Eddie thought, the drink he was about to have was an investment in his pre-retirement years.

He bypassed the Gazebo, even though a rumor was circulating that two defensemen from the Boston Bruins were snuggled up against the bar in the midst of that dense black hole of humanity.

How do people breathe in there? he wondered. How did

they find room to bring their drinks to their mouths without elbowing someone in the jaw?

He bypassed the Straight Wharf Restaurant, although he liked it there. They served excellent bluefish pâté, and the restaurant attached to the bar was some of the finest dining on Nantucket. But Eddie wouldn't touch it with a ten-thousand-foot pole this weekend. Even as he passed, he saw two young bucks holding a girl in a white strapless sundress by her ankles over the side of the balcony.

She was screaming, "Put me down! Damn it it, Leo, put me *down!* I'm going to puke! I'm going to...*puke!*"

Eddie slowed down to see if the young lady would, in fact, puke, or, better still, if her breasts would pop out of her dress, or if the young bucks would lose their grip on her ankles and drop her headfirst into the bushes.

"I see London, I see France," one of the bucks said, looking down the girl's skirt.

"I'm going to *puke*, Leo!" she screamed. And a split second later, she did, and Eddie checked his watch. Five minutes after two, and the puking had begun.

Eddie headed down to Cru. Cru was upscale; the crowd was marginally older and more monied. Three years earlier, Eddie had happened across the owner of 10 Low Beach Road at the back bar at Cru, and that was where the deal for Eddie to rent the house had been struck.

Do you think you can get fifty K? the owner had asked.

I don't think *I can,* Eddie had said. *I* know *I can.*

I like the confidence of that statement, the owner had said.

In the back of his mind, Eddie was hoping for similar luck from this outing. He needed something big. Something *legal.* Financially, he didn't feel that much different from the girl

hanging upside down — desperate, about to lose every shred of dignity.

The deal with DeepWell had gone so smoothly that Barbie had volunteered to call certain other groups renting Low Beach Road and offer the same scenario — five beautiful Russian women, ten thousand per night. Eddie couldn't believe how ballsy his sister was — he would be terrified to propose the idea to anyone — but he realized that the arrangement sounded better coming from a woman. Eddie had overheard Barbie in action on the phone. She was equal parts Barbara Eden from *I Dream of Jeannie* — granting these men their wildest wishes — and Israeli special-ops soldier, a person *not to be messed with.* To Eddie, she said, "If they turn me down, they turn me down. I pretend I never mentioned it."

But, so far, *nobody* had turned her down. Every corporate group wanted in. That very evening, a mining concern from West Virginia was checking in, and they were gung-ho for the girls.

And the girls — well, the girls were ecstatic.

Eddie was grateful for the cash, but there was a trade-off. He had chronic heartburn, and it was difficult to sleep at night. He constantly worried that someone was watching him.

But he needed the money. Grace had written a fifteen-thousand-dollar check to the Great Harbor Yacht Club, which had bounced.

"Bounced?" Grace had said when he told her. "What is going *on,* Eddie? I thought maybe it was Eloise's fault. I thought it was an administrative glitch."

He said, "The spec houses are taking all my spare funds, Grace. We might have to take a hiatus year from the yacht club, until I sell them."

Grace gave him an incredulous look. "You're telling me we don't have fifteen grand for the yacht club?"

"That's what I'm telling you."

"But when you say the check *bounced,* it makes it sound like we don't even have fifteen thousand in our account."

Eddie cleared his throat. He was not enjoying this conversation one bit. "We do not, presently, have fifteen thousand dollars in our account."

"How is that possible?" Grace said.

"The spec houses are eating me alive," Eddie said.

"Can't you just sell one unfinished?" Grace asked.

"That's a possibility," Eddie said. "Or we can be patient and wait until I sell a house."

"Do you have any irons in the fire?" Grace asked.

He smiled. "Always."

"Okay," Grace said. She took a deep breath. "I can survive the summer without the yacht club."

Eddie was relieved. Occasionally, in anger, he accused Grace of being spoiled because she had grown up with so much money. But the truth was, Grace was as levelheaded a woman as he had ever met. "Thank you for being understanding."

Grace said, "You still have money to pay Benton, though, right? And Hester Phan?"

"Right," Eddie said, uncertainly. Hester was the publicist who was supposed to get their garden into a magazine. The only reason Eddie had agreed to sponsor that effort was because he thought the potential article might reflect well on him as a real-estate agent.

The spec houses were in danger. Eddie had taken his cash from DeepWell and paid his plumber and Gerry for half the foundation of number 13.

As for Madeline and Trevor's money—well, he didn't know how to handle that situation.

He needed to sell a house.

The beautiful brunette owner of Cru was standing at the podium when Eddie walked in. Eddie had known her since she landed on the island, straight out of the University of Richmond. She greeted him with a nice hug and said, "You're not going to believe this, Eddie, but I have one stool available at the back bar. Are you alone?"

"I'm alone," he said, then wondered if he should feel embarrassed by this. *Nobody* celebrated Figawi alone; it went against the very nature of Figawi, which was all about getting shit-faced en masse and living out stories that no one could ever quite remember but that could be fudged and embellished for years to come. To venture out on Figawi weekend *alone* screamed loserdom, or so Eddie worried.

The bartender, a young woman who used to babysit for Eddie's twins, said, "Hey, Eddie, what can I get you?"

He couldn't remember his former babysitter's name. It was in the Elisa/Alyssa/Alicia vein, but he wasn't sure exactly which. Grace would know—Grace would also probably know the girl's middle name—but if Eddie texted her to ask, he would receive a response sometime next month, because Grace never checked her cell phone. He was disappointed in himself. He was a real-estate agent; it was his business to remember names.

"I'll have a..." He wasn't sure what he wanted. Around him, the drink of choice seemed to be the Bloody Mary. But

drinking a Bloody would immediately give Eddie heartburn; he was getting heartburn just *looking* at the Bloody belonging to the man next to him. "I'll have a Triple Eight martini, straight up with a twist, please."

"You know who invented the twist, right?" asked the man next to him. "It was John D. Rockefeller. He was a germophobe, and citrus was a natural disinfectant, so Rockefeller always asked his bartenders to run a lemon peel around the rim of his glass."

Eddie turned to the man. "I did *not* know that," he said, but such nuggets of trivia were always of great use to him. He would use that tidbit the next time he took a client out for drinks. As soon as that thought formed, Eddie realized that the man next to him was not just a man—it was Ed Kapenash, the chief of police. "Whoa! Chief!"

"How you doing, Eddie?" the Chief said with a smile. He and Eddie shook hands, and when Elisa/Alyssa/Alicia set down Eddie's martini, they touched glasses with great camaraderie. The Chief was here at Cru! Eddie could not have been more surprised if he'd bumped into the Chief in some foreign location—a bar in Hong Kong or a café in Amsterdam. He wondered if the Chief was following him. But again, the Chief had been here first. This was merely a coincidence.

"What are *you* doing here?" Eddie asked. The Chief was deeply incognito. He was wearing a navy polo shirt, a pair of khaki shorts, and the red Mount Gay Rum Figawi baseball hat that announced one's participation in the festivities. Eddie lowered his voice. "Are you undercover?"

The Chief threw his head back and laughed, which, in turn, made Eddie laugh. The Chief sucked down what was

left of his Bloody Mary and ordered another from their bartender, whom he called Eliza.

Eliza!

"I came down to check on the guys, see how they're doing, even though I'm off duty today," the Chief said. "Everyone assumes I hate this weekend, but everyone is wrong. I'm a sailor myself. I enjoy the energy."

Eddie nodded and laid into his drink, which had been perfectly made by his former babysitter Eliza.

Immediately, his mood improved.

"I don't mind it either," Eddie said. "And I enjoyed that story about Rockefeller. History always was my best subject."

"Oh yeah?" the Chief said. "Mine, too. I've done a bunch of reading about Rockefeller, Vanderbilt, Mellon — all the big industrialists."

Eddie said, "I wonder what future generations will say about us. I'm pretty sure they'll call us the Cell Phone Era." At that very moment, Eddie's cell phone rang — his ring tone was "Smoke on the Water" by Deep Purple, which made the Chief chuckle.

"That right there is the first and only song I ever learned to play on the guitar," he said.

Eddie checked his display: it was Nadia calling, probably to find out what time the girls should be at the house tonight. Eddie's skin grew hot and prickly. He silenced his phone, slipped it into his pocket, and took another swill of his drink.

"I forgot you were a sailor," Eddie said. He would call Nadia on his way back to the office. He *obviously* couldn't say one word to her while he was sitting next to the chief of police.

"I haven't sailed in six years," the Chief said. "Since Greg and Tess MacAvoy..."

"Oh God," Eddie said. "Right. I'm so sorry. I wasn't thinking..."

The Chief picked up his Bloody and rattled the ice, then added a shot of Tabasco, squeezed the lemon wedge, and stirred it up with his celery stick. "It's okay," the Chief said. "Greg and I used to sail Figawi every year. It was a tradition for us. I guess the real reason I come down here is to honor those memories. We always came here for a drink when we were done, back when it was the Rope Walk. Bloody Marys and a dozen littlenecks apiece."

Eddie finished off his drink and signaled Eliza for another. Eddie wasn't sure how they had landed on such a maudlin topic, but he felt it was his fault, and he wanted to make it right. When Eliza delivered his second martini, he held it up. "To Greg MacAvoy," he said.

The Chief nodded solemnly as he and Eddie clinked glasses again, but the Chief seemed too overcome for words. The Chief, Eddie realized in that moment, was just a human being, like the rest of them. He wasn't here to sting Eddie; he was a guy who had lost his best friend and was still mourning. "Greg had his flaws," the Chief finally said. "But I loved him like a brother. It's six years later, and I still can't believe he's gone. Sometimes, when it's just me in the cruiser and I'm out late either on rounds or headed for home, I can hear him laughing."

"I'm going to tell you something pathetic," Eddie said. "I've never had a friend like that."

"You're friends with Trevor Llewellyn," the Chief said. "Right? You guys do stuff together all the time."

"That's not really the same thing," Eddie said. And it wasn't. Eddie and Trevor got along great, they had fun

together, they occasionally had what Eddie thought of as "real" conversations, but almost always these conversations concerned their wives or children. There was no lasting bond between Eddie and Trevor. Eddie hadn't seen Trevor since dinner a couple of weeks earlier, and it was no big deal to Eddie, just as Eddie was sure it was no big deal to Trevor. Trevor was flying his planes, going about his daily business, just as Eddie was. "Trevor and I hang out, drink, smoke cigars. But honestly, that friendship is primarily powered by our wives. I would say the friendship you had with Greg was probably pretty rare."

"I'll agree with that," the Chief said. "Where did you grow up, Eddie?"

"New Bedford," Eddie said. "Downtown."

"Mean streets," the Chief said. "At least, as I understand it."

"I guess so," Eddie said. "My parents did the best they could, then my old man died of emphysema when I was fourteen, then my mother three years later, of lung cancer. They both smoked like chimneys, and Barbie, too. I never touched cigarettes because I ran track."

"That's right," the Chief said.

"Running kept me out of trouble," Eddie said. "I still hold the Commonwealth record for the four hundred."

"You don't say!" The Chief ordered another drink, and Eddie felt pleased by this. It was as if the three hundred other people in the bar had ceased to exist. He was hanging out and drinking and engaging in meaningful conversation with the chief of police. Maybe because Eddie had grown up in New Bedford, or maybe because Eddie's business had, for so many years, seemed so easy as to be illegal, or maybe because Eddie's conscience was aching, or maybe because he, Eddie, just like

everyone else in the world, needed authentic human connection, his present circumstances seemed monumental.

"Would you like to order a couple dozen littlenecks?" Eddie asked. "I know I'm not Greg MacAvoy, but I'm happy to help you eat them."

"Yes," the chief said. "I'd like that. I'd like that very much."

Eddie flagged Eliza and ordered up the clams.

"Thank you," the Chief said. "You're a good guy, Eddie. A really good guy."

At five o'clock, Eddie walked out of Cru feeling like a changed man — upright, clean, worthy, respectable. The Chief had left fifteen minutes earlier to get home to his wife and the MacAvoy twins, Chloe and Finn, whom he was now raising. The Chief had actually hugged Eddie good-bye and pounded him on the back, and they had exchanged cell-phone numbers, the Chief giving Eddie his supersecret number, which he was sure to answer any time of the day or night.

"If you ever need a hand or want to grab a drink," the Chief said, "just call me."

"I'll do that," Eddie said, and then he laughed. Too loudly? Too eagerly? The four vodka martinis had him by the shoulders; the Chief had had just as many drinks as Eddie, if not more, but he was a man who was unaffected by alcohol.

"I'll call you sometime to go fishing," the Chief said. "I bought a boat last year, a twenty-six-foot Whaler with a brand new two-fifty. Do you like to fish?"

"I love to fish," Eddie said, although this was a lie. He hated to fish. It was too much sit-around-and-wait for Eddie;

he would rather be in the office making money. But if the Chief wanted to go fishing, Eddie would go fishing. Trevor loved to fish and had belonged to the Anglers' Club since he was eighteen. It occurred to Eddie that Trevor might be a better choice as a friend for the Chief—but now Eddie was starting to sound like Grace.

"Great," the Chief said. "Take care, and enjoy the rest of your weekend."

"Okay, Chief," he said. He felt sorrowful at the Chief's departure. "I would definitely like to go fishing. Call me."

The Chief pointed at Eddie in a way that could have meant anything, and then he sliced his way through the intoxicated crowd, who all stepped aside for him because, even if they didn't know he was the police chief, they sensed his authority.

Now, out on the Straight Wharf by himself, Eddie saw Figawians stumbling and swaying, he saw potential fistfights brewing, he saw women losing their shoes and their hair ties and control of their bra straps. Walking back past the Straight Wharf Restaurant, Eddie spied the girl in the white strapless sundress sitting on the railing, drinking a Corona. She had puked and rallied. Good for her.

She saw him staring and waved at him. He walked quickly away. He was not going to lose this glow of virtue by flirting with someone half his age.

But he was going to lose the glow of virtue—yes, he was. He thought of the paper bag full of cash. He thought about how everyone on the staff at the Great Harbor Yacht Club now knew Eddie was in financial trouble. Soon, other mem-

bers would hear the rumor, and then there would be blood in the water. Glenn Daley, Eddie's archenemy, belonged to Great Harbor.

He needed to sell a house.

But until then, he had the girls.

MADELINE

Angie called, screaming. At first, Madeline thought it was angry screaming, but then she realized it was happy, joyful, excited screaming.

"I love it!" she said. "I absolutely fucking love it!"

Madeline was confused. "You love what?"

"Your new book!" Angie said.

"Wait a minute," Madeline said. "How did *you* get it?"

"Redd sent it to me," Angie said. "I read the sample scene. There is something in the writing that is so immediate, so electrifying, it nearly burned my fingers as I turned the page. Your characters have such hot chemistry. We're going to market it as 'the Playboy Channel meets HGTV.' After all, what woman *doesn't* want to sleep with her contractor?"

Madeline was stunned silent. She had sent the outline and sample scene to Redd because she'd wanted him to know that he hadn't cashed in his diamond-quality favor for her in vain. She had made a good-faith effort to come up with something else. She hadn't expected Redd to forward it to Angie, and she certainly hadn't anticipated this kind of enthusiasm.

The Playboy Channel meets HGTV?

"I want you to start writing as fast as you can," Angie said. "I want to bump this up to the winter list, and I think we can sell first serial to *Redbook*. The morning shows are going to love it! Gayle King is going to go nuts! She and Norah will fight over it."

Madeline swallowed. She tried to imagine herself going on *CBS This Morning* with Gayle King, Norah O'Donnell, and Charlie Rose to discuss a novel she had written...about Grace and Benton Coe.

"The thing is?" Madeline said. "There would be a lot I'd have to change, because the stuff I have in there now hits a little close to home."

"Do you know someone who has gone through this?" Angie asked. She gasped. *"You?"*

"No, not me!" Madeline said. Although if it *had* been her going through it, she surely wouldn't want her best friend writing a novel about it.

"It's okay if it *is* you," Angie said. "Did I ever tell you about the guy who tiled my master bathroom? He was *edible*. I wanted to *eat* him."

Madeline closed her eyes. She could not believe she had started this ball rolling. All across America, women would be admitting to having impure thoughts about their electricians and their plaster guys.

"I definitely have to change the mint tea," Madeline said. "And the pistachio *macaron*s. And the ploughman's lunch and them dancing to the song 'Loving Cup.'"

"Normally, I would say go right ahead, replace those details with equally vivid details—but in this case, Madeline, you really nailed it. Those details belong in there. You *can't*

take out the mint tea! You can't take out the ploughman's lunch, the way you describe the radishes and him feeding her—it's all too good to cut. It would be like Hemingway without the bullfights or Cheever without the six twenty-four to New Canaan."

"Yes, but...," Madeline said.

"Just keep it as it is," Angie said. "If we absolutely, positively have to change stuff later, we will."

"Okay," Madeline said uneasily.

"And have you thought of an ending?" Angie asked.

"An ending?"

"I know you have issues with resolution," Angie said. "But what I'd really like to see happen here is for...B and G to end up together." Madeline heard Angie slam a pen down on her desk. "I'm sick of women at the end of these novels doing the right thing, sticking with their husbands, pandering to 'family values.' Even *Fifty Shades of Grey* played it safe." She huffed. "I want an ending where the woman is happy instead of good."

"Okay," Madeline said. "I can do that." She was marginally more comfortable now that they were talking about the ending. Grace and Benton were still carrying on, so anything Madeline wrote would be wholly fictional.

"Great," Angie said. "This book is going to be a huge hit. I can feel it in my tooth fillings."

"Thanks?" Madeline said.

"We need to come up with a title," Angie said. "You don't have any ideas, do you?"

"I...I really haven't gotten that far," Madeline said. "I kind of wrote it as a lark? Or maybe more like a practice exercise?"

"A practice exercise? That's classic, it really is. This *practice exercise* is going right to the top of the *New York Times* bestseller list!" Angie said. "Don't worry about the title. I have people in house for that. We'll brainstorm."

"Okay?" Madeline said.

"I'll keep you in the loop," Angie said. "We won't give your book a title without running it past you."

"Right," Madeline said.

"What are you doing on the phone with me?" Angie said. "Get writing!"

Madeline hung up.

What had she *done?*

It was fiction, she reminded herself. Deep breath in, deep breath out.

It.

Was.

Fiction.

Brick wanted a car, there were bills to pay; she had rented this stupid apartment for twelve grand. College was on the horizon. Trevor was two thousand feet in the air. He was, technically, not even on the planet with her. She couldn't discuss any of this with Trevor anyway—unless she told him Grace's secret.

Two of the women at this table will betray the person on their left.

Eddie had been to Grace's left. Grace had been to Madeline's left. So here it was, then...her betrayal of Grace.

No, Madeline wouldn't do it.

But if Madeline pissed off Angie, Angie might nail her on breach of contract. Madeline might be forced by law to return the advance, most of which she'd already spent.

As Madeline saw it, she had two options. She could write the novel about Grace and Benton. Or she could default on her contract and return her advance money—and write another novel down the road, when she was ready.

The morning shows were tempting...but no.

She called Eddie again, to ask for her fifty thousand dollars back.

NANTUCKET

Thornton Bayle, the paving king of Nantucket, who was resurfacing the parking lot of the Nantucket Yacht Club, overheard Eddie Pancik on his cell phone. The Nantucket Yacht Club was right across the street from the office of Island Fog Realty, and pretty much everyone in town knew that when Eddie was having a conversation he didn't want anyone else to hear, he headed across the street to the yacht-club parking lot.

What Thornton Bayle overheard, late in the afternoon of Memorial Day, went something like this: *Madeline, yes, I understand your dilemma. I understand, Madeline! I told you*

June, and if not June then August. Madeline, if I could I would, but I just can't right now. You have to be patient. I need you to hang in there. I need you to believe in me. There were two parties involved from the get-go . . . you knew there was risk. Yes, you did. Madeline, please, I need you to cut me some slack. I will make everything right, but I can't do it today. You have to give me time, Madeline. Please, just give me time.

Well, he thought. *That's interesting.*

JUNE

HOPE

She weathered the rumor about her screwing Brick by holding her head high and not saying one word on the topic. Allegra was back to walking with Brick between classes, making him late for everything, because they stopped in front of every water fountain to kiss.

Hope couldn't watch them without wanting to barf.

Meanwhile, Allegra was still seeing Ian Coburn. She would tell Brick she was going to "stay home and cram for finals" and tell her parents that she was going to wait at the end of the driveway for Hollis to pick her up for a "study group," but instead it would be Ian Coburn in his red Camaro, whisking her away to study the fine art of giving a blow job while watching the sun go down from a remote stretch of beach in Madequecham.

Hope should have just told Brick while she had the chance: Yes, Allegra is seeing Ian. Yes, Allegra is screwing Ian.

Indeed, Hope was certain the reason the rumor about Hope and Brick died so quickly was because Allegra put her foot down and stomped it out. She knew Hope was capable of telling everyone about her and Ian Coburn.

A less nourishing thought was that the rumor about Hope and Brick had fizzled because nobody in their right mind could imagine Brick wanting to have sex with Hope.

Hope resumed believing that Allegra would blow it; she couldn't two-time all summer on this tiny island without getting caught. All Hope had to do was wait.

But waiting was tedious. The school year was drawing to a close, and the weather had warmed up. By the end of the first week of June, Hope had aced all her exams. There was nothing left to study for and no reason, even, to practice the flute. Her job at the rectory of St. Mary's Church would start right after school ended, but that would be a quiet, antisocial snooze. She would help Mrs. Aguiar file, and she would do some research for Father Declan's homilies. She would answer the phone and inform an endless string of visitors that Masses were held Saturday at 5:00 p.m. and Sunday at 8:30, 10:00, and 11:30, there was weekday Mass at 7:30 a.m., and there was a Spanish Mass at 7:00 p.m. on Sunday.

For now, when Hope came home from school, she would lie in the hammock strung tightly between two elms overlooking Polpis Harbor, and she would read. Allegra was already heading to the beach with her friends every afternoon to drink the beer that Bluto's older sister bought for them and then pass out in the sand. Allegra never invited Hope to go, and Hope's friends were home reading in their own hammocks or getting a jump on their college application essays. Hope comforted herself with the knowledge that next spring she, Hope, would be getting into the University of Virginia and Vanderbilt, and maybe even Duke, while Allegra would be waitlisted at North Podunk Junior College.

Still, it was lonely.

*   *   *

The only bright spot in Hope's life was her talks with Benton about books. She had started with *Goodbye, Columbus*, although it had struck her as old fashioned and macho. She had liked *Appointment in Samarra* much better. Benton had seemed really tickled that she was following his suggestions, and when he saw her, he made a point to ask her where she was in each book and how she was liking it.

The conversations never lasted as long as Hope wanted because Hope's mother always interrupted—calling Benton over to the henhouse or needing his help with the lawn mower. Some days, Grace made Benton elaborate lunches—seared-tuna Caesar salads or frisée *aux lardons* topped with poached eggs. And there was always a basket of crusty rolls and a small wooden cutting board with cheese, crackers, sausage, mustard, butter, and Marcona almonds.

Hope longed to be invited to join in these lunches, and she told her mother so.

"This is an important time for Benton and me to talk," Grace said. "I'm sorry, darling. Would you like me to make you a ham sandwich?"

"A ham sandwich?" Hope asked.

"On a baguette with sweet butter and fig jam?" Grace said. "You can eat it in the hammock while you read."

That did sound enticing, but not quite as enticing as sitting down at the table with her mother and Benton.

"I'd rather have salad with you guys," Hope said.

"I'm sorry, darling," Grace said. "We have gardening issues to discuss."

Gardening issues? Was her mother *serious?* She wasn't willing to include Hope in these lunches, despite her

near-constant pleas that both Hope and Allegra spend more time with her?

"Fine," Hope said. "A ham sandwich is fine."

Allegra's end-of-the-year grades were piss poor: low C's in chemistry, trig, and American history and a D in English, but a 79 in chorus—which, she pointed out, was nearly a B (the grade in chorus was impressive, Hope thought, since Allegra couldn't carry a tune to save her life). In an uncharacteristic display of backbone, Eddie informed Allegra that she would not have driving privileges for the summer. This was okay when she was out with Ian Coburn in the red Camaro, but to see Brick she either needed to take the shuttle (which came out to the Polpis Road only three times daily) or she had to beg Hope for a ride.

Hope agreed to chauffeur more than she might have, if only to see Brick. Brick seemed miserable. He was working part time at Nantucket Bank as an "information assistant," which, he announced, was the dullest of indoor jobs. He greeted people, he directed them either left, toward the tellers, or right, toward the loan officers; he was also in charge of showing people how to use the Penny Arcade, which sorted and counted change and spat out a receipt that customers could trade in for paper money. Brick looked bloated and pale; he had lost the luster and verve he'd possessed only a few weeks earlier.

There was a full week of graduation parties, and Allegra and Brick were invited to all of them. Hope wasn't invited

to any, although whenever they pulled in the driveway, Brick would say, "Why don't you come in for a while, Hope?"

"No, thank you," Hope said.

At more than one of the parties, Ian Coburn's red Camaro was already parked out front, and Hope thought, *How does she pull this off on a nightly basis?*

One day, when Benton was working in the rose bed, Hope ostentatiously threw herself across the hammock, brandishing the copy of *Lolita* that she had recently purchased.

She opened the book with a loud sigh, hoping Benton would notice her, but for a long time, he was consumed with cutting back the roses.

"Ow!" Benton said. He'd hit a thorn.

"Are you okay?" Hope asked. She was up and out of the hammock in a flash. "Do you want me to get you a Band-Aid?"

"Oh, Hope!" Benton said. "I didn't see you there. You're quiet as a mouse." He then noticed Hope's book. "Hey! You're reading *Lolita*!"

Hope blushed. "Yep."

Benton stepped out of the rose bed and wiped at his forehead with an orange bandanna. "I keep promising to get you that list of a hundred books, but I've been so busy."

"You have clients other than Mom, right?" Hope said.

"Right," Benton said. "I work on six projects at a time."

"You have five other clients?" Hope asked. "It feels like you're always here."

"Well," he said, gazing back at the house, "this one is my personal favorite. And I have a manager and ten college kids working for me."

"I don't understand why you're a gardener if you were a literature major," Hope said.

Benton laughed. "Life happens, Hope. I was on a work-study scholarship at Ohio State, and they put me on the grounds crew. I liked it. When I graduated, it was more appealing to me to work outside with yards and gardens, parks, green spaces. It's not that I don't dream of being an English teacher someday — I sort of do. But I guess I just prefer this kind of work."

"Did you read all the time when you were a teenager?" Hope asked.

"I read secretly," Benton said. "Late at night. During the day, I did regular teenage stuff. I played rugby, I drank beer in the woods with my bozo friends."

"You were sort of a combination of me and Allegra," Hope said.

"Maybe?" Benton said. "I don't really know your sister."

Hope felt happy about this. Most people liked Allegra better because she was outgoing, like Eddie. She could converse, tease, flirt, and make instant friends. If Benton met Allegra, he would prefer Allegra, or so Hope feared.

But maybe not. Allegra wouldn't tolerate a long discussion about books.

"She's nothing like me," Hope said. "She's beautiful and shallow."

Benton didn't flinch at this assessment. "*You're* beautiful," he said.

Hope shrugged. She could tell when someone was saying this just to be nice. "She's more beautiful. She and her best friend, Hollis, are the most popular girls in the school. Allegra has been dating Brick Llewellyn since the start of sophomore year, but now she's bored with him, but instead of just breaking up with him, she's been hanging out with this kid named Ian who goes to BC."

"BC," Benton said. "Good school."

Clearly, Benton hadn't heard Eddie's joke.

"She's not *cheating* on him," Hope said quickly. As much as she was aching for Allegra to get her comeuppance, she couldn't seem to be the one to turn her in. "But she isn't being very nice."

"And that bothers you?" Benton said.

"I want her to act like a decent human being," Hope said. She wished all this sounded less like an episode of *Degrassi* and more like painful, complicated real life. "Do you have any advice?"

"Actually," Benton said, "I do."

At that moment, Grace poked her head out the back sliding door. She seemed delighted to see Hope and Benton talking. "Benton," she said, "lunch is ready." To Hope, she said, "Honey? Would you like a ham sandwich?"

Hope shrugged. As always, her mother ruined everything. "I guess," she said.

GRACE

Just when she thought life couldn't get any better, she received a phone call from Hester Phan.

"I have exciting news," Hester said. Hester was a serious Vietnamese American woman with a deadpan voice. She sounded as if she were calling to tell Grace that there was a sale on rubber gloves at the Stop & Shop.

"You do?" Grace said.

"The home-and-garden editor of the *Boston Globe* loved the photos. They want to do a feature in the Sunday paper."

Grace shrieked. "When?" she said.

"They're sending a writer and photographer on July twenty-first," Hester said, "to run five days later on Sunday the twenty-sixth."

They had less than a month to get ready!

"Whoo-hoo!" Grace said. "Thank you, Hester, thank you!"

"That's my job," Hester said. "I'll call closer to the date with the exact details. And I'll send Eddie my final bill."

Grace hung up. She didn't know whether to call Eddie or Benton first. The right thing to do was to call Eddie. This was his house, and he was paying Hester's fee. Besides, she wanted to tell Benton in person.

She said, "You're not going to believe this! The *Boston Globe* said yes! The Sunday *Boston Globe!*"

"Yes to what?" Eddie said.

"Yes to the gardening feature!" Grace said.

"Oh, right, right," Eddie said. "Does this mean I can stop paying Hester?"

"After the final bill," Grace said. "Which, I think we agreed, includes a success bonus."

"Why should she get a bonus for success?" Eddie said. "It's her job. She should succeed as a matter of course, not get a bonus for it." He sounded like he was in some kind of cavern. His voice was reverberating, and Grace could hear his footsteps.

"Where are you?" she said.

"Number thirteen Eagle Wing Lane," he said.

"It sounds empty," Grace said. "Aren't there supposed to be guys working?"

"Yes," Eddie said. "There are supposed to be guys working."

She couldn't decipher the tone of his voice. Was he being sarcastic?

She didn't care. She was too excited about the Sunday *Boston Globe*. She said, "Honey, aren't you happy for me?"

"Thrilled," Eddie said.

Grace hung up. Eddie didn't sound thrilled—but what had she expected?

She wished the girls were home, but Hope had started her job at the church rectory, and Allegra was off island at her new SAT-prep course. Instead of once a week for six weeks, this class met every day for a week, including Saturday. Allegra needed yet another prep class because the other class had resulted in only a thirty-point increase in her critical-reading score, and her math score had stayed the same. Neither score was very high.

Eddie wasn't happy about spending money on another class, in addition to the cost of flying her back and forth.

Grace said that some people just didn't test well.

Eddie said she wasn't trying. Had Grace ever seen her studying?

No, Grace had not seen Allegra studying, and, furthermore, Allegra was out every single night.

Grace would tell the girls about the Sunday *Boston Globe* that evening at dinner.

Would they care?

Grace wanted to call Madeline, but Madeline had been very busy writing her new novel at the apartment, and Grace didn't want to interrupt her. However, she was too excited to keep the news to herself, and it was still half an hour until Benton would arrive.

Grace sent Madeline a text: *Sunday* Boston Globe *featuring my garden July 26!*

Madeline texted back: *Great!*

Grace tried not to feel deflated. *Great!* was an appropriate response. She couldn't expect anyone to understand how far beyond *Great!* this was.

Grace pulled the cork from a bottle of vintage Veuve Clicquot that she had found down in Eddie's wine fridge just as Benton rounded the corner of the house.

"Champagne?" he said. "What happened to mint tea?"

Grace poured two glasses but left them on the table. She said, "Hester Phan called."

He said, "Break it to me gently."

She said, "On Sunday, July twenty-sixth, we are going to be featured in the...*Boston Globe*!"

Benton swung her in a circle and let out a cowboy rodeo whoop.

This was the reaction Grace had been craving. As Benton took her face in his hands and started to kiss her, she marveled at how it felt to have someone in her life who shared her passion for this yard and who was just as over the moon about this feature as she was. A partner. A friend.

And more.

Benton pulled Grace by the hand toward the garden shed, leaving their champagne in the sun.

The following day, Grace received an invitation to the Nantucket Garden Club's Sunset Soiree. This year's soiree was being held at Jean Burton's home, which Grace had always thought of as the House of a Thousand Koi Ponds (really only five, but for Grace that was five too many). Jean was president of the Nantucket Garden Club; she had taken over for Grace when Grace's term ended. Jean was a native Texan, filled with charm and hospitality. She continued to call Grace for advice and help with logistics, and she kept Grace in the loop, even though Grace had become consumed with her own project.

Grace had been president for six years and had hosted the Sunset Soiree in her own yard years earlier at their old house, on Dover Street. The Sunset Soiree was a fabulous event, and for all the years Grace was involved, she had brought Madeline as her date.

But this year, she thought, she would take Benton.

She called Madeline to see what she thought.

"What if I took Benton to the Sunset Soiree?" Grace asked. "Would you be mad?"

Madeline was silent, but in the background, Grace could hear the sound of her pen scratching against paper, as well as the hum of her laptop.

"I won't be mad," Madeline said. "I like the Sunset Soiree just fine. The gardens are pretty, the food is good—but it's really your thing."

"I just don't want you to think I'm ditching you for Benton," Grace said.

"That's not the problem," Madeline said. "The problem is you being seen in public with Benton."

Yes, Grace had considered this. And yet, she really wanted to venture out in the wider world with Benton. The island was four miles wide by thirteen miles long; they couldn't exactly go to dinner at the Ship's Inn or walk the Sconset bluff hand in hand. The Sunset Soiree was a garden-club function, Benton was her landscape architect, and they had something to jointly brag about. Grace couldn't *wait* to tell Jean Burton and Susan Prendergast and Monica Delray about the Sunday *Boston Globe*! The Sunset Soiree would be a safe and appropriate place for her and Benton to go together.

"I'll ask Eddie's permission," Grace said. "I'm sure he'll say yes."

"I'm sure he *will* say yes," Madeline said. She sighed. "But you know how those women talk, Grace. Remember how Blond Sharon made such a big deal when Monica showed up in the mismatched Chanel flats? She accused Monica of being

drunk when she got dressed, and three days later, everyone had her checking in to Betty Ford. Those women are vipers. They're ruthless. If you go with Benton, they'll have a field day with it."

"Blond Sharon can kiss my ass," Grace said.

"You can do what you want," Madeline said. "But, as your best friend, I have to tell you, I would feel much better about you going with Benton if the two of you weren't..."

"I know," Grace said. And she did know. But she didn't care. She wanted to go to the Sunset Soiree with Benton. She wanted to have fun.

That night, she broached the topic with Eddie.

"You don't care if I go to the Sunset Soiree with Benton, do you?"

"What's the Sunset Soiree?" Eddie asked.

"The garden-club thing."

He waved a hand. "Have at it," he said. "As long as I don't have to go." He ran a Bremner wafer through butter. His heartburn had been so bad recently, he'd told Grace, that he could barely eat anything else.

Grace asked Benton the following morning. "Would you go as my date to the Sunset Soiree?"

His face lit up. "I'd love to," he said.

"It's at Jean Burton's house," Grace said.

"Koi ponds," Benton said.

Grace kissed him and grinned. She could not believe how *in sync* they were.

He said, "I've gone before, you know, four or five years ago, when it was at Jody Rouisse's house? Marla Amster took me, back when I was designing her gardens."

"You went with Marla Amster?" Grace said. "Now I'm jealous." She tried to remember that year. Jody Rouisse lived out in Shimmo. Yes, Grace remembered going with Madeline. She remembered the garden. In Grace's opinion, it had been lackluster: a lot of decorative grasses, with only one flower bed, and perennials that had been grouped by color; Grace had felt as if she were looking at a paint-by-numbers. But she didn't remember seeing Benton. She couldn't believe she had overlooked him. Now, he was all she could see.

"You don't need to be jealous," Benton said. "I wasn't in love with Marla Amster."

In love! In love! In love in love in love!

As soon as Benton left, Grace ran upstairs to call Madeline.

There was only one dark spot in Grace's week. On a late-night run to the Stop & Shop to get more butter lettuce and farmer's cheese and other lunch provisions, Grace saw a red sports car in the parking lot—with a girl inside who looked a lot like Allegra. The girl was kissing the blond boy in the driver's seat.

Grace nearly knocked on the window. *Allegra?* But then she thought better of it. If she were wrong, it would be bad, but if she were right, it would be even worse. Grace hurried into the store.

EDDIE

The last week of June, Eddie had a group from Kasper Snacks renting 10 Low Beach Road. Kenny Kasper had been referred to Eddie by Ronan LNW, and he had asked about having the girls come by over the course of the week. Eddie had said, "Let me see if I can make that magic happen."

The girls were basically working nonstop, and they had started to spend their money. Nadia had bought a barely used lime-green Jeep out of the classifieds for cash. Eddie said, "You don't want to flash the money around, Nadia, or people will start to ask questions."

He couldn't let anything mess up their situation. He was too dependent on the cash. At this point, it was his only steady source of income. He had one rather underwhelming list-ing on High Street in town that he had shown to the same couple four times—but in the end, they had passed, instead buying a significantly nicer home on upper Main Street from none other than Glenn Daley. Eddie had shown a seven-million-dollar house on Eel Point Road to a gay couple who had made an offer of five-five—but the owner had flat-out refused to even counter, and the couple wouldn't go any higher, saying that Nantucket was outrageously priced and they were going to look on Martha's Vineyard and Block Island instead. And two sisters who owned a four-million-dollar parcel of land on Hulbert Avenue—that Eddie had not one but two potential buyers interested in—had just pulled it off the market.

Eddie couldn't believe his rotten luck. He was trying to pay off the bills for number 13, but there were also his six

collective mortgage payments, groceries, Allegra's class, Benton Coe and the damn publicist with her "success bonus." And Madeline kept asking for her fifty thousand dollars back. She had actually surpassed asking and moved on to begging; in the last phone call, she had been vaguely threatening, making it sound like if Eddie didn't pay, something would happen that Eddie wouldn't like.

He understood Madeline was frustrated and possibly even frightened. Eddie had posed the loan of fifty thousand dollars to Trevor and Madeline as an "investment opportunity," and that was exactly what it would have been if Eddie had sufficient funds to finish the houses or if the market would start cooperating and produce buyers. What Eddie really needed were 2005-era buyers; back then, the economy had been booming, and houses were going for 30 percent above market within twelve hours of being listed.

He hadn't sold a house since October, a fact that depressed him. He was in a slump, like a baseball player. He had been struggling, then sinking, and now he was drowning. He had approached the Llewellyns at the start of the sinking period because he was tapped out at the banks and nobody else liked him or believed in him enough to lend him the kind of money he needed. He knew Madeline had just gotten a big advance, he knew she would persuade Trevor to say yes. What Eddie had not predicted was how irresponsible Madeline would be with her sudden windfall. She had rented an apartment she didn't need, and there went twelve grand of her after-tax dollars.

Eddie knew he should feel guilty about what he and Barbie were doing...but he had no choice. He sent Barbie a text about Kasper Snacks, even though she was sitting at her desk

on the other side of the office. Barbie was having modest success this year, but she was queen of the small listing—the $359,000 condo out by the airport, the $595,000 three-bedroom, two-bath mid-island home with an unfurnished basement—whereas Eddie dealt only with seven-figure, or preferably eight-figure, properties.

His hubris was his downfall, he supposed. But he was proud of his success—him, a boy from Purchase Street in New Bedford.

The text he sent Barbie said: *Girls at TLBR tomorrow night. Kasper Snacks.*

I didn't talk to Kasper Snacks, she texted. *How did they know?*

Referred by Ronan LNW, Eddie texted.

Trustworthy? Barbie texted.

Seemed to be.

Did you check out the company online? Barbie texted.

It's Kasper Snacks, Eddie texted. *Creator of the Donut Chip?*

Barbie texted, *???????*

Eddie texted, *Everyone eats them but you.*

Barbie flashed Eddie a look. *My gut is bothering me on this one,* she texted. *Count me out.*

Really? Eddie texted. *Barb, this is no different from any other time. Standard operating procedure.*

I'm out, Barbie texted. *Take my cut.*

You're serious? Eddie texted.

Very, Barbie texted.

He would have argued, but he was too titillated by the thought of an extra seventeen-five a week.

If you insist, Eddie texted. *Delete.*

Deleted, Barbie texted.

*   *   *

His office manager, Eloise, had been acting strangely the past two or three days, paying all kinds of extra-sweet attention to Eddie, when before she never paid him *any* attention. Eddie suspected she was going to ask for a raise—which he couldn't afford to give her, but neither could he afford to lose her. Eloise had brought him a potted snapdragon from Bartlett's Farm, saying he needed something to brighten up his desk. When he asked if he was going to have to water or deadhead it, she said she would take responsibility for the plant's care and maintenance.

She said, "I'll be your own personal gardener."

He said, "Well, my wife has one; why shouldn't I?"

Eloise stared at him, and Eddie said, "Benton Coe. Ever heard of him, Eloise?"

"Oh yes," Eloise said. "He did the rose beds in the back of the Eighteen Hundred House, and he designed the gardens at Greater Light, which are exquisite, I must say."

"I'm paying him like he's the Bill Gates of gardening," Eddie said. He gazed at the vaguely menacing fuchsia jaws of the snapdragon blossoms. "Anyway, this was a very thoughtful gift. Thank you, Eloise."

"Oh my goodness," Eloise said. "I nearly forgot."

"What?" Eddie said. He put on his Panama hat. He needed to get home to the girls. Eddie caught an occasional glimpse of Hope, but he hadn't set eyes on Allegra in more than three days. Grace had mentioned something about seeing Allegra, or someone who looked like Allegra, with a young man in a red Camaro, and Eddie wondered what *that* was all about. He would hate it if Allegra and Brick broke up, but maybe this

guy with the red Camaro had money and could take care of the expensive habits of Allegra's lifestyle. The modeling thing wasn't going to pan out for her, and yet she continued to dress like it might.

"A call came in for you while you were out, and I forgot to give you the message," Eloise said. She held out a pink slip, and Eddie's heart seized like an engine block without any oil. He needed an antacid, but they were in the console of his car—another reason he needed to leave. He feared the message was from Nadia, even though Eddie had made it clear she was never to call the office phone. Or it was Kenny Kasper. Maybe Barbie was right, and Kenny Kasper wasn't really Kenny Kasper; maybe he was Special Agent Kasper from the FBI.

Eloise made the announcement before Eddie could snatch up the slip and read it. "The police chief called," she said. "He wants you to go fishing with him tomorrow morning."

Eddie felt as excited as a girl who has been asked on her first date. The Chief had mentioned something about fishing, but men threw out offers like that all the time and never followed up. The Chief had actually gone to the trouble of seeking Eddie out.

Eddie called the Chief back. They decided to meet on the North Wharf at five thirty the next morning and stay out until one or two in the afternoon. The Chief would bring sandwiches and beer and the rods. All Eddie had to do was show up.

Eddie raced home to tell Grace and both girls the news. Both girls were home for dinner.

"I'm fishing with the police chief in the morning," Eddie said.

"Cool," Allegra said.

Hope shrugged and nibbled a piece of asparagus from between her fingers, a habit Eddie found unseemly but that was sanctioned by Grace, who said Grandmother Sabine used to eat her asparagus that way.

Grace said, "Don't forget that I'm going out Thursday night."

"You are?" Eddie said.

"The Sunset Soiree, remember?" Grace said. "Garden club?"

"Right," Eddie said. He didn't exactly remember, but anything involving the garden club meant he was mercifully excused. "I just think it was nice of the Chief to invite *me* fishing. Of all people."

"You hate to fish," Hope said.

"No, I don't," Eddie said. "Not really."

"Maybe it will be like that scene in *The Sopranos*," Allegra said, "where they invite the guy fishing because they want to kill him, then throw him overboard."

Eddie pushed his plate away. He had been enjoying his steak, mashed potatoes, and asparagus right up until Allegra said that. Indeed, the invitation was so unlikely that a part of Eddie believed it might be a planned sting. He would drink only one beer, he decided. He would take one when it was offered and nurse it all damn day; that way, he would be sure not to say anything stupid.

*   *   *

He awoke at four o'clock without help of an alarm; he was keyed up with nerves and excitement. He wore khaki shorts and white tennis shoes and a long-sleeved T-shirt from Santos Rubbish Removal, and he donned his Panama hat because he didn't feel like himself without it. He bought a coffee from the Hub as soon as it opened, then stopped by his office to use the john and check his voice mails. He had been so addled by the fishing invitation that he had forgotten to call Nadia and tell her about Kasper Snacks that night.

He had time now. He wasn't due on the wharf for thirty minutes. But he couldn't start his day by calling Nadia and then segue right into fishing with the police chief. He would call Nadia later, he decided. He had to. The fishing invitation, while magical in its way, had not made Eddie's financial problems go away.

The Chief had brought along his son, Eric, who was a student at Cornell's medical school, to serve as first mate. The men all shook hands, and then they strolled down the creaking dock as the sun came up behind them, spangling the water gold and silver. There were other men climbing onto other boats and getting things ready—ropes, engines, ice chests, poles and reels and lines—but the dock was serene and picturesque to Eddie. It was another world, life on the water, apart from the hustle and bustle and commerce and traffic and errands and meals and shopping and cell-phone conversations on land.

The Chief's boat was called *The Castaways*—this was a reference to Greg and Tess MacAvoy and Addison Wheeler and some of the Chief's other friends, but Eddie didn't want to broach the topic. He needed to grapple with the fact that he didn't know the first thing about fishing. He had been fishing a couple of years earlier with clients, but that had been a drinking trip more than a fishing trip; there had been twelve guys and three mates on that boat, and Eddie had cast only twice, holding the rod for all of six or seven minutes.

The night before, Eddie had googled *how to cast,* and he watched an instructional video on YouTube—pull back the bale, hold the line with index finger, gently bring pole over right shoulder, then cast, and when the line hit its arc, let the line go. Then replace bale and reel in.

Anyone could do it.

Eddie said, "What can I do to help?"

The Chief handed him the cooler. "Stick this in the galley, would you? Eric and I will take care of getting the lines set. We're going to troll on our way out, see if we can catch some bass off the bottom."

Eddie carried the cooler to the galley. At least he knew the galley was the kitchen. He was so nervous about his lack of experience that he opened the cooler and plucked a Stella out of the ice. Eddie's favorite. He flipped the top off, then wondered if he was being rude. Would Grandmother Sabine find him rude? Yes, undoubtedly. Eddie realized he should have waited for the beer to be offered, but, sorry, he couldn't wait. He needed something to take the edge off right now.

He said to the Chief, "Hope you don't mind, but I opened one of your beers."

The Chief waved a hand. "Help yourself." He and Eric were moving around the boat with skilled, precise movements, getting this thing ready and that thing ready. The Chief dealt mostly with the motor and the computer screen and the ropes and the hatches, while Eric handled the rods. There were big rods in holders and smaller rods that Eric was stringing with deft fingers.

The Chief finally started the engine, and Eric unlooped the ropes from the dock and stood out on the bow as the Chief backed the boat out of its slip. Eddie sat on the cushioned bench in front of the console and thought what a crime it was that he had lived on this island for so long and hadn't learned a single thing about the sea.

Forty minutes later, they were fishing the cross rip off the tip of Great Point. The lighthouse was rosy in the soft morning light. Great Point marked the far north of Nantucket; it was pristine in its natural beauty, and yet Eddie hadn't driven up the beach in years and years, since the girls were small. The water was the bluest Eddie had ever seen. It was amazing, this water, and there weren't any other boats fishing the rip that morning. In the very far distance, Eddie could make out the faint smudge of Monomoy Point on Cape Cod. Seagulls sang out, circling overhead.

Eric and the Chief checked the fish finder and decided to anchor and cast some lines. They had been trolling since they left the harbor, but they hadn't had any bites. The Chief dropped the anchor, and Eddie headed into the galley for a second beer, despite his vow to himself.

Eric said, "Eddie, you ready to throw a line?"

Eddie took a deep breath. *Was* he ready to throw a line? He stepped out onto the deck, set his beer bottle in one of the holders, and accepted the rod, which had a neon-orange lure shimmying like a showgirl on the end, from Eric.

"I'm ready," Eddie said.

He held the rod over the side of the boat so that the lure dangled a few feet from the surface of the water. The sea was calm; gentle waves slapped the bow.

Eric said, "Would you like me to cast that for you?"

Eddie was just about to say, *Yes, please!* with a sigh of massive relief, when the Chief barked out, "Eddie can cast his own line, can't you, Eddie?"

"Oh," Eddie said. "Sure thing." He looked at the reel and tried to play the video again in his mind. Something had to be moved one way or the other while he held the line. It was the bale, he remembered, and he flipped it over. He was to bring the rod gently back over his right shoulder and then fling the line way out into the water. At the arc, he was to let his finger go. There would be a satisfying whizzing noise, the sound of a skilled angler who had cast lines thousands of times and not merely looked it up online twelve hours earlier. Eddie was *not* a skilled angler, but he had always been good at faking it—faking it had been his surest strategy for success—and so he brought the rod back over his shoulder and flung the line. Out it went in a beautiful arc with the exact fluid motion he had dreamed he was capable of.

"Good cast!" the Chief called out.

Eddie beamed. He had never been prone to sentimentality, but he wished his father could have seen him. Edward

Pancik from Purchase Street in New Bedford could cast a deep-sea fishing line with the best of them.

"Now, reel it in!" Eric said.

Yes, yes, Eddie had forgotten that part. He wasn't sure how he expected to catch anything without reeling the line in.

The day only got better when Eddie caught his first fish. An insistent tug when he started to reel in his line told him there was definitely a FISH ON. He was on light tackle, which worked to Eddie's advantage, as Eddie was left handed and his forearms proved to be stronger than he thought. Still, he had to fight the bugger, bending toward the water when he reeled in and easing up when the fish wanted to run; then, when the fish got tired, Eddie would reel in again. Eddie wanted to say he had the natural instincts for this, but, in fact, Eric was standing at his side, coaching him when to reel in and when to relax. Once Eddie got the fish close enough to the boat—when he could see the iridescent scales shining from just beneath the surface, Eric instructed Eddie to pull up gently while Eric leaned down with the gaff, speared the fish, and brought it aboard.

It was a striped bass, a beauty of a fish, shining and muscular as it twisted in the sun.

The Chief was delighted. "That's good eating," he said. "Grace will be happy with you tonight, bringing home dinner."

Grace *would* be happy, Eddie thought. She loved freshly caught fish. But then he thought she might not even believe he had caught it.

"Would you take a picture of me and this beast?" Eddie said. He handed his phone to the Chief and grabbed the tail of the fish, which was still struggling for its life. But at that second, his phone started to ring.

"Call for you," the Chief said. "Should I...?" He was staring at the screen with an inscrutable expression.

"I can't believe you get reception out here," Eric said. "That's the thing I like best about fishing. No phones."

Eddie did his best not to snatch the phone out of the Chief's hand. It might be Nadia, or possibly one of the other girls. He should have shut off his phone before he got on the boat.

Eddie accepted the phone, then saw that the caller was Madeline.

"Jesus," he said. He declined the call and closed his eyes for a second, trying to maintain his peace of mind. If he started thinking about business and money and his loan to Madeline and Trevor, his day would be ruined.

I caught a thirty-seven-inch striped bass, he thought. *I caught dinner.*

He gave the Chief a weak smile. "I should have left my phone on shore."

"Maybe," the Chief said.

The phone call from Madeline did *not* affect Eddie's fishing karma—he immediately caught two bluefish. Then the Chief caught a striped bass a little smaller than Eddie's, then Eric caught a false albacore, which was exciting because they were

elusive. They pulled anchor and motored for the six-can buoy, where they stayed for nearly an hour without a bite.

"This is *beat*," Eric said. His voice was impatient, and Eddie was surprised. Weren't all anglers blessed with an infinite capacity for waiting it out? Eddie feared that Eric would want to give up and go home, and that was the last thing Eddie wanted. He could stay out on this boat forever.

Beer number three, then beer number four. Then Eddie stood up and took a leak off the stern. He had a buzz going; some food was probably in order.

As if reading his mind, the Chief said, "Let's motor over toward Sankaty Head and have some lunch and try our luck there."

"Good idea," Eddie said. He flipped the top off a fifth beer and settled back on the cushioned bench, basking in the sun. He had caught dinner. He loved that idea.

He must have dozed off, because he woke up a while later as both the Chief and Eric were reeling in fish. Two striped bass—and the one on the Chief's line put Eddie's to shame. Eddie stood up to see if he could help, but he was afraid he would only be in the way, so he sat back down again, then realized he had to pee again, so he went back to the stern, and by the time he returned, both fish were up on the deck, and Eric was cutting them off the line.

"This is it," the Chief said. "We're done. Let's have some lunch, and then we'll head back."

Eddie nodded, but his heart was heavy. The bluffs of

Sankaty were right in front of him. This was the island where he had lived for more than half his life, but for the past six hours, he felt like he'd been lucky enough to escape to another planet.

The Chief had made Italian subs with salami, ham, *capicola,* hot *soppressata,* provolone, olives, and cherry peppers. Eddie was so hungry, he devoured the whole sandwich without thinking—the peppers and the *soppressata* stung his lips and tongue, but he put out the fire with cold beer.

"So, how'd you like it?" the Chief asked.

"Great stuff," Eddie said. "I couldn't imagine a day better than this."

The Chief packed up the lunch trash and finally cracked open a beer for himself. Eric was now snoozing on the cushioned bench, and so the Chief pulled the anchor, then said to Eddie, "Come sit with me as we motor back, would you? There's something I want to talk to you about."

Eddie felt as if his heart were pumping a mixture of habanero sauce and snake venom. Here it was, then: the real reason for the invitation to fish. It had nothing to do with a budding friendship, nothing to do with Eddie being a good guy or the kind gesture of ordering littlenecks with the Chief at Cru because his longtime buddy was dead. Eddie grabbed a bottle of water from the cooler. He needed to sober up, pronto. Predictably, the *capicola* and *soppressata* repeated on him, and his heartburn started its low smolder.

He had come out on the fishing expedition without any Tums.

"Sure thing," Eddie said, his voice higher than normal. The Chief was at the wheel, and Eddie took a seat next to him. "What's up?"

The Chief was silent, his eyes unreadable behind his sunglasses. Another boat passed them—someone the Chief seemed to know, because he waved—and Eddie, although he didn't know the person, waved as well. He was so flustered that he had defaulted to indiscriminate waving. The Chief stood up and peered over the console. Eddie realized he was checking to make sure Eric was still asleep.

The Chief settled back down behind the wheel. "I'm only telling you this because I like you, Eddie. I think you're a hell of a guy."

Telling me what? Eddie thought, but he couldn't eke the words out.

"And I'm sure you think that because I'm the chief of police, I believe myself to be morally superior, but I do *not* think that, and I do not judge. I deal with people who make mistakes every hour of my working day—some of them are big, ugly mistakes—but most people, I find, are decent. Scared, lonely, bored, and misdirected at times, maybe—but decent."

Eddie sucked down half the bottle of water. He would basically trade his big toe for a handful of cherry Tums. "What is it you want to tell me, Ed?"

"People talk on this island," the Chief said. "You can't fathom the way people talk. The gossip, the rumors—it's absolutely insidious, and most of it I ignore. None of my business, I don't care, ninety-five percent of it is not even true." The Chief throttled up, and the boat jumped over waves and slapped the surface of the water with a force that rattled

Eddie's teeth, jaw, and skull. It was almost as if the Chief were trying to physically punish him. "But then I saw that phone call come in, and so I thought I'd better speak up."

"Phone call?" Eddie said. He couldn't even remember whom the phone call had been from. All he cared about was that it hadn't been Nadia. It had been...

Before the Chief could respond, the wind lifted Eddie's Panama hat off his head. By the time Eddie realized what had happened, his precious Panama hat was whipped away. It danced across their wake, fifty, then a hundred, yards behind them. Gone.

He turned to the Chief, wondering what kind of absurd request it would be for the Chief to swing the boat around so Eddie could fish for his hat—it would mean another $375 dollars and six weeks to replace—but the Chief's eyes were focused straight ahead on the blue, watery road between them and Nantucket Harbor.

The Chief had to raise his voice in order to be heard over the motor. "There's a rumor going around," he said. "I've heard it three times now."

"Rumor?" Eddie said. His second hat. Goner than gone.

"A rumor that you're having an affair," the Chief said. "With Madeline King."

Eddie shook hands with the Chief and with Eric and stumbled off the North Wharf holding a sturdy gallon ziplock bag containing five pounds of striped-bass fillets.

The Chief had said he believed him, but Eddie was dubious.

At first, Eddie had laughed. He found the idea *genuinely funny*. "Me?" he said. "Me and *Madeline?* Oh my God, no, no, *no!*" Eddie wasn't sure how to successfully get his point across. "No, I'm sorry for laughing right in your face, but that is simply *not* true."

The Chief said, "Eddie, I told you, I don't judge."

"Well, in this case, there is no *reason* to judge," Eddie said. "Because it's not true. I don't cheat on my wife. I've never been unfaithful, not once."

The Chief's face was blank. Eddie was probably saying too much. That was the problem with situations like this: if you said too little, people assumed you were guilty, and if you said too much, it sounded like you were overexplaining because you were guilty. Eddie wanted to ask the Chief where he had heard the rumor about him and Madeline— who were the three sources? Maybe Eddie could contact those sources and try and quash the gossip. But those, most likely, weren't the original sources. Gossip was like a virus that split and multiplied thousands upon thousands of times. If the Chief had heard the rumor three times, then it was everywhere.

Eddie nearly said, *The reason Madeline called is because she lent me money and she wants it back.*

That would, no doubt, explain the whole thing away, but the last thing Eddie Pancik wanted anyone on Nantucket to know was that he'd borrowed money from his best friends, who were by no means loaded themselves. For a real-estate agent, financial troubles were the *kiss of death*. If people thought he was a failure, then he would become a failure. No one was going to seek out a real-estate agent who was sinking.

"It's not true," Eddie said, in as humble and plaintive a voice as he could muster.

"Okay, Eddie," the Chief had said. "Okay."

The subject had dropped there, but even as Eric carved up the bass with the precision of the surgeon he would someday become, Eddie felt the conversation fouling the air. On top of everything else, Eddie had heartburn and the start of a hangover. There were Tums in his car and in his desk drawer at work. Suddenly, Eddie couldn't wait to get away.

With the handshake, the Chief had said, "Thanks for coming today, Eddie. I enjoyed hanging out. Let's do it again."

"The pleasure was mine," Eddie said. That had been true, until the very end. "Thank you for inviting me. I'd love to join you again sometime."

But as Eddie walked away, he was sure there wouldn't be another time. Or maybe there would be. The Chief *said* he didn't judge.

Eddie pulled out his phone. There was only the one missed call from Madeline — no texts, no new business. Should Eddie call Madeline back and tell her about this rumor? Maybe if they both worked to combat it, it would go away? Or would their joint effort have the opposite effect?

He decided not to call Madeline. He decided not to give the absurd idea any energy. He sure as hell couldn't have Grace finding out.

Instead, he dialed Nadia. He said, "You need to be at the house at ten o'clock tonight."

"We on it, Eddie," Nadia said. "Today, we all go to salon for hair, and to the dentist."

Dentist? Eddie thought. He felt virtuous for five or ten seconds; this side job was encouraging the girls to take care of themselves. He doubted any of them had ever visited a dentist before in their lives. He prayed they'd gone to Dr. Torre and not that clown McMann.

The sun beat down on the top of Eddie's bald head. He couldn't *believe* he'd lost another hat!

Tums, he thought. He needed Tums.

Eddie headed in the back door of his office and stuck the bag filled with fish fillets in the kitchen fridge, which also held three bottles of Dom Pérignon, kept handy to celebrate big closings, and a couple of cartons of Greek yogurt, which was what Eloise liked to eat for lunch.

He popped out to the main room. Barbie was on the phone, Eloise was on the computer.

"Hello, all," Eddie said.

"Eddie," Eloise said. "How was the fishing?"

"I can't complain," Eddie said. "A day on the water is better than a day anywhere else."

"I didn't even know you liked the water," Eloise said.

"No," Eddie said. "Me either."

"Well," Eloise said, "I brought you some Boston cream doughnuts from the Bake Shop, just in case you didn't catch any fish." She held out a box of doughnuts — eight left, which meant Eloise must have eaten four herself, because Barbie wouldn't touch doughnuts.

"I did catch fish," Eddie said. "But I can't resist." He plucked a doughnut out of the box.

"Oh, I know," Eloise said. "I know all your favorite things."

The phone rang, and Eloise hurried to answer it. *Please,* Eddie thought, *let that be a twenty-million-dollar listing.*

Eddie carried the box of doughnuts over to Barbie's desk and sat down at the chair next to it, meant for the buyers and sellers.

She said into the phone, "Listen, I have to call you back later. Bye-bye." And she hung up.

"Who was that?" Eddie asked.

"P," Barbie said.

P for *personal.* Eddie was aware that Barbie had men, lovers, dates, whatever, but he had no idea who they were and no clue whom to ask. Barbie knew everyone on this island, but she didn't have any close friends. For holidays, she celebrated with Eddie and Grace and the twins—or else she went away, presumably with the men she knew. Were any of the men wealthy? He wondered. Manolos were expensive, and Barbie drove a 1974 Alfa Romeo that required near-constant upkeep. But Barbie had bought her house in Fishers Landing outright in 1999, and she had no children. Her life was blissfully simple.

Eddie wished he could be more like Barbie. No one was out on the street gossiping about Barbie.

Eddie said, "Why is Eloise being so nice to me?" Sometimes Eloise buttered up Eddie after she'd had a fight with Barbie.

"No idea."

"You didn't lose your temper?"

"No, I didn't," Barbie said. "How goes your bromance with the Chief?"

"Funny," Eddie said. "It's not a *bromance.* It was two guys

fishing, Barb. I caught a striped bass. I have some to share, if you want a pound or two."

"No, thanks," Barbie said.

"Do you still have that bad feeling about the other thing?"

Barbie nodded. "I could be wrong. I'll probably regret not going in. I could use the money."

So maybe the men Barbie dates aren't wealthy, Eddie thought. Maybe she dated Chris, the mechanic who fixed her Alfa Romeo.

"That makes two of us."

"This market had better pick up," Barbie said. She stared listlessly at her computer screen.

"Have you heard any rumors about me?" Eddie asked.

"Rumors?" Barbie said.

"No?"

"No."

Eddie nodded and stood up, taking the box of doughnuts with him. He could not resist Boston cream. He devoured the doughnut in three bites.

MADELINE

The annual Nantucket–Martha's Vineyard all-star baseball game was normally one of Madeline's favorite days of the summer. But this year, Madeline was distracted by her writing.

Write as fast as you can, Angie had said.

Madeline had spoken to Eddie three times and left him as many messages, but it had become clear that she and Trevor weren't getting their money back anytime soon. Madeline had gone so far as to drive by the spec houses on Eagle Wing Lane to check on their progress, but all three were boarded up and silent. *Nobody* was working on them!

She had called Trevor. "There aren't any trucks out front, no workers, no action, no *nothing!*"

Trevor said, "Maybe Eddie is taking a hiatus for the summer. Maybe he has other things going on."

"He said *June!*" Madeline said. "It's practically July now. He said August at the latest. But there is no way these houses are going to be finished by August. They might not be finished by *next* August."

"Why are you so keen for the money?" Trevor said.

"We have bills, Trev. We promised Brick a car!" she said. "I know it was my idea to invest the money with Eddie..."

"A hundred percent your idea," Trevor confirmed.

"I'm kicking myself now," Madeline said.

"Madeline," Trevor said. "You *need* to *breathe.*" This was his standard line when he thought she was being hysterical and he wanted to calm her down—but today, it only served to agitate her further.

"I *am* breathing!" she screamed, and then she hung up.

Maybe Eddie has other things going on. Eddie had more going on than he even knew! Grace was *in love* with Benton Coe! She was excited to *take things to the next level* by going with Benton to the Sunset Soiree.

Listening to Grace was an addiction. Madeline could *NOT* wait for the next installment of the story. Madeline knew she should advise Grace to *turn the car around*. But instead, she was Grace's steadfast sounding board, and not only that — she was using everything Grace told her in her novel. Her characters "B" and "G" were moving full steam ahead. Madeline could *not* stop writing; nothing had *ever* come to her this easily. It was black magic, like the séance with Barbie.

Two of the women at this table will betray the person on their left.

But in a way, writing the novel felt natural and organic, as if Madeline were giving birth — this novel, somehow, was like the second child Madeline had never managed to have.

She couldn't stop. Could not pull the plug or abort the mission. She would write the novel and then, later, go back in and change everything so that nothing was recognizable except to Madeline herself.

For years, Madeline had been in charge of the potluck barbecue lunch between the games of the doubleheader with the Vineyard. Last week, she had managed to get the e-mail out, and the usual people signed up to bring the usual things. Cathleen Rook was bringing her pepperoni bread, which all the boys and coaches fought over, and Rachel had overvolunteered as usual and was bringing her potato-and-egg salad, pesto pasta, and a seven-layer Mexican dip. Madeline was in charge of condiments, paper products, Gatorade, bottled water, and ice — but she had spaced on the ice, so she had to stop at the airport gas station, where five bags of ice ran her twenty-five bucks.

She set out the hamburgers and hot dogs, rolls, paper plates and napkins, ketchup, mustard, and relish. The propane gas tanks on the grills were both full. When it came time to watch the actual game, Madeline found a shady spot in the bleachers, pulled out her legal pad, and started to write.

Diana Marz, Parker's mother, was the first to comment.

"Is that your new novel?" she asked.

Madeline smiled in what she hoped was a cryptic way. She had always wanted people to think of her as a novelist, but now, the less she said about her work, the better. She realized it might have been smarter to have left her legal pad at home, but she couldn't fight the urge to finish this one particular scene: B and G taking things to the next level by venturing out together in public—in this fictional case, to the Summer House pool, where they couldn't keep their hands off each other, both under the table and then later, splashing around in the pool. Madeline was currently writing a scene about some clandestine underwater fooling-around between B and G. Angie, she knew, would love it.

Every once in a while, Madeline raised her head from her work to take in a few seconds of the baseball game. Brick was playing first base, smacking his glove, trying to get Calgary McMann, who was pitching, to pick off the Vineyard base runner. Rachel was a few feet to Madeline's right, wearing a navy-and-white-striped sundress with a giant navy *N* on the front, which it seemed Rachel had applied herself with an iron. Rachel had brought her pom-pom. She cheered away, stopping every so often to apply SPF 50 to her face, even though she was wearing a large-brimmed straw hat.

Despite her keen interest in the game, Rachel, too, noticed Madeline writing.

"Look at you, scribbling away!" she sang out. "I see 'A Room of One's Own' has worked! You're a writing machine! I fully expect a mention on the acknowledgments page now."

Madeline nodded while finishing her sentence. It was the top of the seventh inning; she needed to head back over to the picnic area. But just then, her cell phone rang, and Madeline climbed down from the bleachers to answer it, believing that it might be Eddie, calling her back.

It was Redd Dreyfus.

He said, "You got the e-mail from Angie, yes?"

"From when?" Madeline asked.

"This morning."

"No," Madeline said. "I've got something else going on today, and I'm not near my computer." Normally, Redd liked to hear vignettes about "island life," and Madeline might have launched into a description of the Nantucket–Martha's Vineyard all-star baseball game, but right now, he sounded all business.

"Well," he said, "it appears the editorial board of Final Word made an executive decision on the title of your new novel."

"Oh God," Madeline said. "But wait a minute, I thought…"

"They've gone completely mad," Redd said. "Or completely postmodern."

"What's the title?" Madeline asked. From the stands, there was enthusiastic cheering, indicating the end of the game. Madeline plugged her ear.

"They're calling it *B/G,*" Redd said. "How would one even refer to that in spoken language, I wonder? 'B slash G'? It's reminiscent of what Prince did with that ludicrous symbol."

"*B/G?*" Madeline said. "No. We can't use that."

"It's been decided, I'm afraid," Redd said.

"Angie *said* she would run it past me first!" Madeline said. "She said I would have final approval."

"Welcome to the wonderful world of publishing," Redd said. "Angie and her superiors are in the business of selling books. They seem to think this absurd title will break new ground or, at the very least, create interest from a publicity standpoint."

"They can't use those initials!" Madeline said. "We have to change the initials. I don't care what to. Any other two letters will work."

"But those are the names of your characters," Redd said.

"For now!" Madeline said. "This book still needs a lot of editing!" She watched the crowd rise from the stands and make their way en masse toward the picnic tables. "Ask them to change the initials, Redd, please!"

"They think it's evocative of 'boy meets girl.' I don't think they'll look fondly upon changing the initials. Their company isn't called *Final Word* for no reason, Madeline."

"Listen, Redd, I have to go," Madeline said. "Please...do everything you can!" She hung up. *B/G?* They might as well have decided to call it *Benton and Grace*!

Madeline raced to the concession stand to get the Gatorades and waters on ice. Soon, Cathleen Rook showed up and began pulling side dishes out of the big cooler.

"Where's Rachel?" Madeline said. "Did she bring serving spoons for the potato salad or the pasta?"

"She's still in the stands," Cathleen said. "She started reading your book, and she said she couldn't put it down."

"*What?*" Madeline dropped a bag of ice in the grass and

darted through the hungry and expectant crowd until she reached the bleachers.

Sure enough, there was Rachel McMann, bent over Madeline's legal pad, eagerly reading.

Madeline all but ripped the pages from Rachel's hands. "What are you *doing?* This is my *work!*"

Rachel beamed. "I can't get over how *good* this is!" she said. "It's sexy stuff, Madeline, but smart sexy, seductive sexy. Look at me, I'm *flushed!*"

"*Rachel!*" Madeline said. "This is *not* for public consumption."

"I'm not the public, silly," Rachel said. "I'm your friend."

Madeline was so angry and embarrassed that she couldn't even meet Rachel's eyes. Instead, she focused on the *N* ironed on the front of Rachel's dress. *N* for *nosy!*

"This is going to *fly off the shelves!*" Rachel said.

Madeline hugged the notebook to her chest. "We *are* friends, Rachel, and for that reason I know I can trust you to please not tell anyone what the book is about…or that you even read it." She swallowed. "It's in the very early stages. Probably, everything you just read is going to change."

"If I were you I wouldn't change a word," Rachel said. "But don't worry, your secret is safe with me. I won't tell a soul."

Madeline had learned her lesson: she wasn't going to write *anywhere* but in her apartment. She wasn't even going to bring her legal pad home at night. It was going to stay in the apartment, tucked under the sofa cushions or hidden in the microwave oven.

Madeline was pretty sure Rachel had a duplicate key to her apartment, and at this point, Madeline wasn't sure she was beyond using it.

The next day, Madeline e-mailed Angie about changing the title. Madeline had suggested an alternate title: *Heaven Knows.*

Angie wrote back, saying, *We're going with* B/G. *Besides, when I hear* Heaven Knows, *I think of that bad Donna Summer song.*

Madeline then called Angie—three times—and three times she was greeted by Angie's voice mail. She couldn't even get Marlo, Angie's assistant, on the phone.

At five o'clock in the evening, there was a knock on her door.

Eddie, she thought. With her check.

She raced to open it.

Trevor was standing there, holding his very cute pilot's hat, looking grim.

"Hey, babe," she said. "This is a surprise. I thought maybe you would be Eddie." She kissed Trevor on the lips, but he didn't respond. In fact, he flinched a little.

"What's wrong?" she said.

"I heard a rumor today, from Pamela at the Island Air desk."

"Oh shit," Madeline said. It was about Grace and Benton

Coe; it had to be. This was so *bad* that Madeline felt sick. Pamela at the Island Air desk was one of the worst gossips on Nantucket—her, Blond Sharon, Janice the dental hygienist, and Rachel McMann.

Madeline pulled Trevor into the apartment and closed and locked the door behind him.

He collapsed on the sofa.

"What is it?" she said.

"You thought maybe I would be *Eddie?*" Trevor said. "Why would you think that? Does Eddie visit you here often?"

"No!" Madeline said. "He hasn't been here since the day I first rented it."

"Okay," Trevor said. "Because the rumor I heard...what Pamela told me she'd heard from at least *six other people*...is that you're having an affair with Eddie Pancik."

"Good God," Madeline said.

Trevor was quiet.

"It's not *true*," Madeline said. "Obviously. Where do people come up with this shit?"

"Oh, any one of a dozen places," Trevor said. "You got your own apartment, and Eddie stopped by to see you on the first day, and someone saw him. Then, someone else overheard him on the phone with you."

"I told you I called him," Madeline said, "because I want our money back. Life is expensive, and right now that fifty grand is the difference."

"What is so urgent all of a sudden?" Trevor asked. "Do you have gambling debts I don't know about?"

Madeline sat gently on the sofa next to her husband. "I'm having a hard time with the next novel," she said. "Like, a

really hard time. And I'm afraid I might have to pay my advance back."

"You're having a hard time with the new novel?" Trevor said. "That's not what I heard. I heard your new novel is all about this couple who is having some superhot extramarital affair."

"Who told you *that?*" Madeline said. "Did *Pamela* tell you that?"

"It doesn't really matter who told me that," Trevor said. "The rumor is out there, Madeline. People are saying that you and Eddie are having an affair and that this is the fuel for your supersexy new novel."

"You can't possibly believe this," Madeline said. "You know I would never be unfaithful."

Trevor picked her legal pad up. "Is this the new novel?"

Madeline tried to snatch it from his hands, but he hung on, and Madeline feared that between them, they would rip the pages. She fell back against the sofa cushions and tried to breathe. "It *is* my new novel, but I'm not ready for you to read it yet."

"Is it about a couple having a superhot extramarital affair?"

"Sort of," Madeline said.

Trevor threw the legal pad onto the coffee table. "Great."

"It's fiction!" Madeline said. "I write fiction. The problem is that nobody *wants* fiction anymore! They want memoir! They want 'based on a true story.' Everyone should be reading Mary Karr and Erik Larson! But that"—Madeline pointed at the legal pad—"is *made up!* It is the purest of fiction! I *made up* a story to entertain my readers!"

"*The Easy Coast* wasn't pure fiction," Trevor said. "It was

based on your real life. It was about Geoffrey. And *Hotel Springford* was about your relationship with your mother. So that means the only *pure* piece of fiction you've written was *Islandia* — and that was more like science fiction. I encouraged you to write a sequel. But no — apparently, you were compelled to write this garbage."

"It isn't garbage," Madeline said.

"You're right," Trevor said. "As angry and as embarrassed as I am, I respect you too much to call your work garbage."

"Maybe it is garbage," Madeline said. "I can't tell. It's nowhere close to finished." She stared at her husband's handsome profile. Meeting Trevor had been life's way of making amends for all the ways Madeline had been gypped earlier in life — the feeble parenting of her mother, the dangerous relationship with Geoffrey. With Trevor's love, she had essentially become Gretchen Green, girl hero. She had become the woman she wanted to be. Or nearly. She reached out to hug him.

Trevor didn't exactly push Madeline away, but he didn't embrace her either. He stiffened, and then he stood up.

"I need you to *help* me!" Madeline said. "I need you to *support* me. You're my husband."

"And you're my wife," Trevor said. His tone was marginally kinder, and Madeline felt a wash of relief. But then he said, "I think maybe you need space. Or I do."

"Space?" Madeline said. "What do you mean by *space?*"

"I think you should stay here for a few days," Trevor said. "While I try and process this."

"I don't *want* to stay here!" Madeline said. "What a horrible suggestion."

"If you let me read what you've written, I'll change my mind," Trevor said. "But I know you pretty damn well, Madeline King, and my gut tells me you're hiding something."

"I'm not *hiding* anything!" Madeline said. But her tone of voice wasn't convincing even to herself, and it would never fool Trevor. "I'm just a writer trying to protect my work."

"Madeline," he said.

She nearly blurted it out: *Grace is having an affair with Benton Coe, and I'm secretly using it as fodder for my new book. But it wasn't my fault! I got backed into a corner. Or I painted myself into one.*

"I don't want you to read it," she said. "Later you can, but not right now."

"Fair enough," he said. He stood up and moved for the door.

"You're serious," she said. "You're leaving?"

"Yes."

"How long is 'a few days'?" she asked. She worried that Trevor was saying *a few days* but actually meant *forever.*

"I don't know, Madeline," Trevor said. "A few days. If you need a firm number, I'd say a week."

"A *week?*"

"I need to simmer down," Trevor said.

That night, Madeline slept on the uncomfortable double bed in the apartment. She tried to think of it as fun, an adventure, but the mattress was stiff and unforgiving, and the sheets that she'd found in the bathroom closet smelled funny. There was one window in the bedroom that faced an alley which people

coming out of the Boarding House and Ventuno cut through to get home. Madeline could hear their footsteps and their voices, buoyant and slurred with alcohol. She should have had a glass of wine before bed herself, but she didn't want anyone to see her buying wine at Murray's and then heading back to her apartment with it.

She didn't have the desire or the money to take herself out to dinner—and how would that look, anyway? Madeline King, out to dinner alone, possibly waiting for her lover to show up.

She made herself a peanut-butter-and-banana sandwich for dinner.

She thought she might sleep better on the sofa, so she moved to the living room with her blanket and her pillow, but the front windows had no shades, no treatments at all, and light pollution from Centre Street poured in. Madeline sat up and stared at the box of bird eggs and wondered about the previous owner of this apartment, now living on a cliff somewhere in St. John.

How could she fix this? Should she have *Eddie* call Trevor and assuage his worries? That sounded like a good idea—maybe? Or it could backfire and make things way worse.

What if Trevor divorced her? The mere thought was preposterous. Or it had been until today. She and Trevor had spent the majority of their marriage on a path paved with rainbows. They were the Dick Van Dyke and Mary Tyler Moore of Nantucket!

But maybe that was why this idiotic rumor had spread—because people were jealous and they wanted the "happy couple" to be revealed as anything but.

*   *   *

When Madeline finally did fall asleep, she had a nightmare about Geoffrey. In real life, Geoffrey had had a shaved head and an elaborate tattoo of Prometheus on his back. But in Madeline's dream, Geoffrey was Rachel McMann's husband, Dr. Andy, only Dr. Andy had a mouthful of black teeth. When he secured the plastic zip ties to Madeline's wrists and ankles, he showed her his teeth, and she screamed, and the scream woke her up.

Madeline lay facedown on the sofa, her face buried in the cushion, and she thought, *What have I done?*

My gut tells me you're hiding something. Trevor would never have thought that if he hadn't heard the blasted rumor from Pamela.

Madeline stood up and paced the apartment, stopping at the dark window to shout at the street.

Mind!

Your!

Own!

Business!

Stop!

Gossiping!

She pictured women lunching at the Galley, talking about Madeline; she envisioned Janice, the hygienist at Dr. Andy's office, spreading the rumor to all of her patients. *Did you hear?* She pictured Pamela at Island Air telling Barry, the bartender at the airport restaurant, who in turn would tell his wife, Candace, who was the receptionist at the RJ Miller

Salon. Once it got into places like the dentists' offices and the salons, there would be no stopping it. Blond Sharon would tell her friends at the yacht club as they sailed and played tennis and ate Cobb salad. Then, of course, the brokers would get hold of it. It would be whispered about during an open house for an eleven-million-dollar listing in Monomoy. From there, it would travel out to Sconset—to the post office and the Summer House pool. People at the Wauwinet gatehouse would gossip about it as they let the air out of their tires before heading up to Great Point. Madeline knew she wasn't really the target; Eddie was the target. A lot of people hated Eddie. The librarians at the Atheneum would be talking about it, and the men who loaded cars onto the steamship, and the scuppers who had their boats serviced at Madaket Marine, and the cast of *Pygmalion,* put on by Theatre Workshop of Nantucket.

Did you hear? Madeline King and Eddie Pancik.

And she's writing a novel about it!

Madeline was so disgusted, so humiliated and embarrassed and horrified, and so *ashamed*—because she knew she had *opened herself up to this*—that she picked up the box of delicate bird eggs and brought it down over her bent knee so that the glass shattered and the eggs cracked and debris scattered all over the floor.

There, she thought. She had ruined the only authentic and interesting thing in this apartment.

In the morning, Madeline awoke to a text from Rachel McMann. It said: *Hey, there. Brick told Calgary that you've*

moved out for a while? Imagine you could use a friend? How about drinks on Wednesday night?

Madeline stared at the screen. Brick told Calgary! And now Rachel McMann knew that Madeline was staying at the apartment for a few days—which was, Madeline would have liked to point out, a whole lot different from "moving out"—and Rachel was also the one who had told the world about Madeline's new novel. She was the only one—other than Redd and Angie and the staff at Final Word, all of whom lived in Manhattan, which was basically another galaxy—who had read it!

Madeline wanted to text back: *Fuck you, Rachel.*

But instead, she deleted the text and got to work.

JULY

GRACE

The second they walked through Jean Burton's trellised arbor, Grace felt the eyes of fifty jealous women upon her.

She was on Benton's arm.

Jean, ever the gracious hostess, approached as soon as Grace and Benton entered the yard.

"Grace!" Jean said. "I am so happy to see you. And, Benton…" She moved in to give him a juicy smooch on the cheek. It would go this way all evening, Grace knew. The upstanding ladies of the Nantucket Garden Club would all fall over themselves for Benton's attention. Some of the women might even out-and-out proposition him.

But he belonged to Grace.

In years past, Grace had donned what Eddie called a "Mary, Mary, quite contrary" outfit for this event—a white blouse and long skirt, as well as her Peter Beaton straw hat. But tonight, she was wearing a brand-new black halter dress, a pearl choker, and a pair of black thong sandals that she had taken from Allegra's closet. She had decided to wear her hair down and loose, because that was how Benton liked it best.

Even Eddie did a double take when he saw her. "Wow," he said. "You look *great*. Where are you going again?"

"The Sunset Soiree," Grace said, trying not to show her frustration. The man didn't remember a thing she told him. "Nantucket Garden Club."

"Oh, right," Eddie said.

Grace nearly reminded him that she was attending with Benton and that Eddie had given his okay. But then she thought, *Why stir the pot?* She kissed Eddie and Hope good-bye. Allegra was out.

Grace had picked Benton up at his complex off Old South Road, out by the airport. Benton rented two large barnlike buildings that housed his fleet of work trucks and all of the trailers, mowers, and backhoes. He lived in an apartment on the top floor of one of the two buildings with his manager, Donovan, and Donovan's girlfriend, Leslie, who ran one of Benton's landscaping crews. When Benton socialized, he did so with Leslie and Donovan. They went to beach barbecues and art openings and listened to live music at the Lobster Trap. This was the extent of what Grace knew about Benton's life apart from her on Nantucket.

But now, she was seeing his space. It was dusty and indus-trial. There wasn't a blade of grass in sight. The driveway was gravel; the "yard" asphalt.

The cobbler's son has no shoes, Grace thought. Still, she liked seeing all of the small pickups lined up with the four-leaf clovers painted on the sides. This was Benton Coe's head-quarters, his mission control, his domain.

She honked the horn, a practice her grandmother Sabine would have frowned upon. An extramarital affair was one thing—certainly they had been prevalent in the 1940s and

'50s, when Sabine was Grace's age—but honking the car horn instead of walking to the front door was nigh unforgivable. But Grace didn't want this to seem like a "date." She didn't want to meet Donovan or Leslie, and she didn't want any of Benton's workers—some of whom lived in an apartment on the top floor of the other building—to see a woman in a black dress knocking on their boss's door.

But when Benton had come strolling out of the house in stone-white pants, a turquoise-blue button-down shirt, a navy blazer, and loafers, Grace swooned. She had to put her Range Rover in park and take a few metered breaths. The man was... so gorgeous. She had never seen him in anything other than jeans, a T-shirt, and his hooded sweatshirt.

He had climbed into the car and said, "Damn, Grace. You are so beautiful it blows my mind."

Smile and say thank you, she thought. But his words had left her tongue-tied. The tops of her ears buzzed.

Grace, never one to show up at a party empty handed, gave Jean a carton of pale blue eggs. "These are from Hillary and the other Araucanas," she said. "My best producers."

"I'm partial to Ladybird's speckled eggs," Benton said.

Jean accepted the carton and said, "I'll treat them like gold." Then she dramatically swept a hand, presenting her yard—manicured in its every aspect—and the mandolin player and the caterers passing hors d'oeuvres and also, Grace supposed, the sun, which was dutifully casting a golden, syrupy glow over the party. Immediately, Grace noticed *la grande table,* half of which served as a bar and half of which was a

groaning board of cheeses, grapes, strawberries, apricots, nuts, salami, marinated vegetables, crackers, baguette slices, quince paste, olives, and dips. Grace had invented *la grande table* three years earlier—it was just a ploughman's lunch on a bigger scale—and Jean had continued the tradition.

"Look at this!" Benton said. "Jean, you outdid yourself."

Jean beamed. "I learned everything I know from this breathtaking creature right here," she said, squeezing Grace's biceps. "I swear, Grace, when you walked in, I thought you were one of your daughters. You are positively glowing. You're not pregnant, are you?"

At this, Grace hooted as if she'd been goosed. "God no!" she said.

The other women at the soiree were all dressed in flowered sundresses and linen shifts; there was an abundance of Jack Rogers sandals and Lilly Pulitzer prints. They looked like extras in a Merchant Ivory film, but that was the point. Of all the cocktail parties on Nantucket all summer, this was the most elegant and genteel.

"Let's get a drink," Grace said.

"I'll get you one," Benton said. "What would you like?"

"I'll have a sauvignon blanc," Grace said. "A Sancerre, if they have it."

Benton headed off to the bar, and women descended on Grace like buzzards on roadkill—Jody Rouisse, Susan Prendergast, Monica Delray.

Monica said, "You lucky duck! You brought Benton!"

"He's dreamy," Jody said.

"And he sure cleans up well," Susan said.

"What happened to Madeline?" Monica asked. "Did the two of you have a *falling out?*"

"Falling out?" Grace said. She honestly couldn't remember the last time she and Madeline had even been cross with each other. "She's been really busy writing."

"Oh yes," Jody said. "We've heard."

"So I decided to bring Benton," Grace said. "He's been consulting with me on my garden since last summer."

"We know," Jody said. "We are *dying* to see your yard."

"We thought *you* might host the soiree this year," Susan said.

"It's not quite soiree worthy," Grace said, though of course it was, and then some. Jean had actually asked Grace, back in November, if she would be willing to host. But even then, Grace had been thinking of a gardening feature, and she hadn't wanted a hundred people walking across her grass and terrorizing the chickens.

"Oh, stop," Jody said. "You enjoy keeping it for yourself. Grace's secret garden."

Benton appeared by Grace's side and handed her a flute of champagne. "They only had chardonnay," he said. "So I thought you'd prefer this."

Grace accepted the flute and smiled at him. "I would, thank you."

"Ladies," Benton said. "Thank you for allowing a boor like me into your party. I can see my gender is greatly outnumbered, but I like it that way."

The assembled ladies giggled.

Jody said, "Grace was just telling us that you've been consulting with her."

"I'm there every day," Benton said. "It's my pet project."

"It's Benton's design, his brainchild," Grace said. "I take no credit. I am merely a worker bee."

"Have you told them the news?" Benton asked.

"What news?" Monica said.

"Are the two of you running away together?" Susan said. She put her hand on Benton's arm. "Don't take her, take me."

Benton laughed. He said, "It's Grace's news to tell."

Grace blinked. The conversation was getting away from her. When Benton had said her yard was his *pet project,* what did the other women think? Had they thought...? And what was that comment about Benton and Grace running away together?

Madeline had been right. These women were vipers.

"Your news, Grace?" Jody prompted.

She almost didn't want to tell them. Let them be surprised on July 26 when they opened the newspaper.

But Grace couldn't help herself. She said, "My garden is going to be featured in the *Boston Globe.* It'll be in the Sunday home-and-garden section."

There were some gasps and nods, a jealous eye roll from Jody Rouisse—no surprise there. She was the one who had called Benton dreamy, and she was going through a divorce. She would probably like nothing better than to sink her teeth into Benton's strong shoulder.

"That's great!" Susan Prendergast said. "You must be thrilled."

"I heard Eddie hired a publicist," Jody said. "Is that how this came about?"

"It is," Grace admitted. "Hester Phan. She sent out photographs and a full description in a press release, and the *Boston Globe* was the first to bite." The way she said this made it sound like there might have been more than one publication that wanted to shine its spotlight on Grace's garden.

"I was hoping for *Classic Garden*," Benton said. "I did a project in Savannah years ago that was featured in that magazine. They do a spectacular job."

"I do love *Classic Garden*," Susan said.

Grace wondered if she should have waited for *Classic Garden* to say yes before she agreed to the *Boston Globe;* that way, Benton would have had his first choice.

She sipped her champagne. The other women were looking at her with envy, yes, but also with a certain amount of disdain, or so she suspected. Her husband had hired a publicist, and now Grace's yard would be featured in the *Boston Globe*.

What was it, really, but a colossal display of vanity?

Before Grace could gauge how egregious getting a publicist for her garden might seem to these women, her thoughts were interrupted.

"Grace, hi!" a loud female voice said. "Hi, hi, hi, *hi!* I can't believe you two are *here*."

Grace turned to see Sharon Rhodes, otherwise known as Blond Sharon. Sharon Rhodes was nearly six feet tall, and she had aggressively dyed blond hair. She had a wide mouth with crowded teeth and a big, hearty, infectious laugh, which was her best feature. She was the loudest person in any room and was therefore always the center of attention. Tonight she stood out, as usual, in a poppy-red strapless blouse, tight white pants, and five-inch stiletto heels that were going to decimate Jean Burton's gorgeous lawn.

Flats, Grace thought. One wore flats to the Sunset Soiree for this very reason.

"Hi, Sharon," Grace said. She leaned in for an air kiss. "It's nice to see you."

Blond Sharon regarded Benton with undisguised interest. "I don't think we've ever been formally introduced," she said, offering her hand. "I'm Sharon Rhodes."

"Nice to meet you, Sharon Rhodes," Benton said, taking her hand.

"I've heard about your work, of course," Blond Sharon said. "And didn't you used to live with Katharine McGovern?"

"McGuvvy," Benton said. "Yes. Great girl. We've parted ways, but I hear she's very happy…"

"In San Diego!" Blond Sharon said. "She taught my children sailing at the yacht club last summer." Blond Sharon winked at Benton. "I think she was hoping you two would get married."

"It didn't work out that way, unfortunately," Benton said. "Wasn't in the cards."

Blond Sharon nodded, then looked between Grace and Benton as if trying to make sense of what she was seeing.

"Benton is consulting with me on my garden," Grace said. "He's got the magic touch. You should see my roses."

"I would like to see your roses," Blond Sharon said, "but you never invite me."

Grace smiled. She felt like she was the only person left on earth who cared about manners. God bless her grandmother Sabine and the Sundays Grace spent learning how to properly butter her bread. "You're invited any time," she told Blond Sharon.

Blond Sharon laughed as if this were the funniest thing she'd ever heard. It was pretty funny. If Blond Sharon showed up at Grace's house unannounced to take a gander at Grace's roses, Grace would pretend to be down with a migraine. She

would be grateful for the massive oak door separating her from Blond Sharon's curiosity. Her home was a fortress, and Blond Sharon wasn't welcome. Grace didn't think Blond Sharon was a bad person. She was just too obvious for Grace. Her clothes were too flashy, her heels too high; her laugh was too loud. Madeline felt the same way. If Madeline were here, they would talk about Blond Sharon the instant she stepped away.

As if reading her mind, Blond Sharon said, "So, Grace, have you heard about Madeline's new book? I guess Rachel McMann got to read some of it the other day."

"I know she's been hard at work," Grace said. She smiled at Benton. "Shall we repair to the garden?"

"Yes," Benton said in his Surrey accent. "Let's repair."

"You should ask Madeline about it!" Blond Sharon sang out.

"I'll do that," Grace agreed. She linked her arm through Benton's. "Good to see you."

Grace and Benton strolled along, admiring Jean Burton's beds, all of which were bordered with impatiens.

"Oh, impatiens," Benton whispered.

Grace squeezed his arm. She and Benton held the same opinion about impatiens. Tired and overdone.

They walked over to the first koi pond and watched the orange fish swim in lazy circles. Grace felt the same way about koi in ponds as she felt about tigers and lions in cages at the zoo.

"So, McGuvvy wanted to marry you?" Grace said.

"Oh, I don't know about that," Benton said. He stared at the surface of the water.

"You can tell me," Grace said. "I won't get jealous." This was a lie. Grace was already feeling jealous. The instant Blond Sharon said the name Katharine McGovern, the hair on her arms stood on end and her heart grew spikes. Grace knew that Benton and McGuvvy had lived together the previous summer. Grace had even *met* McGuvvy once, when she and Eddie and Madeline and Trevor were out to dinner at Le Languedoc. The Panciks and Llewellyns had been devouring their cheeseburgers and garlic fries at the bistro downstairs when Benton had walked in with a young woman. Grace had remembered feeling *extremely interested.* She wanted to get a gander at this curiously named woman.

My girlfriend, McGuvvy, was how Benton had referred to her last summer.

McGuvvy: it was the name of an elf, or a gremlin.

Benton had brought McGuvvy over to the table and introduced her. "Everyone, this is McGuvvy."

McGuvvy was what people meant when they used the phrase "girl next door." Her hair was auburn, she had freckles and glasses with black frames. She wore a white blouse with black embroidery over white pants, and black Jack Rogers sandals. Toenails painted turquoise. Was she pretty? Grace couldn't decide. She was pretty enough, and she was young. She seemed spirited, gung ho, ready for anything. She was probably lots of fun to be with. Grace knew only two things about her: she taught sailing at the Nantucket Yacht Club, and she did *not* care for gardening at all. When Grace had asked how that was working out, Benton said, "Fine, fine. We have different interests, no biggie."

Now, of course, Grace and Benton were lovers, and so any mention of McGuvvy was newly loaded.

"She wanted to get married and have kids," Benton said. He shrugged. "Can't really blame her. That's what women her age want."

"And you didn't want…which part?" Grace asked. "You didn't want to get married? Or you didn't want kids?" Grace had never considered the possibility of Benton wanting children. She thought of Jean Burton asking Grace if she was *pregnant.* Grace was forty-two years old; she was the mother of teenagers. She hadn't given any thought to being pregnant in years. She had felt Madeline was nuts to keep trying for another child after thirty-five, after Brick was in middle school.

But now, she wondered…if things progressed and Grace left Eddie and married Benton, would she consider having another child?

"I don't know, Grace. I guess I didn't want any of it with McGuvvy," Benton said.

Grace sipped her wine. She and Benton walked slowly around the other koi ponds, and then they followed a flagstone path that led to a hidden koi pond, one nearly encircled by white 'Annabelle' hydrangea bushes.

"*Six* koi ponds!" Benton said gleefully.

There was a stone bench by this pond, and none of the other partygoers had discovered it, so Grace sat. She wanted to finish the conversation.

"Do you want to get married?" Grace asked. "Do you want to have children?"

Benton regarded her and sighed. "That's a confusing question for me to answer right now."

Grace knew what he meant. The whole topic was fraught. She and Benton were having a love affair, which was hot and immediate. And, Grace had thought, evanescent. *How do you see things ending?* Madeline had asked. The answer, at that time, was that Grace had expected the whole thing to pop like a soap bubble. She had expected to wake up one day and feel back to her normal self, in love with her husband and her girls and her chickens. But now that she was deeper into it, now that she was, most certainly, *falling in love,* Grace couldn't bear to think of an ending. And so—if not an ending, a future. And if a future—then the answers to these questions were important.

"Forget marriage for a second," she said. "Do you want children?"

"Yes," he said. "I've always wanted children."

Grace sipped her wine. Tears sprang to her eyes for no reason. Despite the complications with Hope's birth, Grace could still have children. But she was old. Benton deserved someone younger, someone like McGuvvy.

He wiped the tear from her cheek. "Grace, please. Let's not have this conversation here. It's not a good idea."

"Yes, well," Grace said. "I wasn't the one who brought up McGuvvy."

"I didn't bring her up either," Benton said. "Your friend did."

"God," Grace said. "That woman is *not* my friend." She stood up from the bench and finished her champagne. She was suddenly angry, though she couldn't say why. She and Benton were having a tête-à-tête, as usual, but it had ventured into uncomfortable territory, and their sensibilities were no

longer dovetailing so nicely. Grace should never have exposed their tender new love to the outside world.

Benton pulled a handkerchief out of his pocket and handed it to Grace so she could dry her tears.

"My grandmother would have loved you," Grace said.

"You think?" Benton said. He held one of Grace's hands and gazed down at her with that look he had. She thought, *He's going to . . .*

But at that moment, Blond Sharon came clomping down the flagstone path with Jody Rouisse in tow.

"Oh, there you are!" Blond Sharon said. "We were wondering what became of the two of you."

Jody said, "Are you okay, Grace? Have you been *crying?*"

"I'm fine," Grace said, sniffing, shoring herself up to smile.

"We're going to hit *la grande table,*" Benton said. "I'm starving."

"I love the stinky cheese!" Blond Sharon said.

As Grace and Benton strolled out of the hidden koi pond, Grace said, "I want to get out of here."

"You read my mind," Benton said. "That woman *is* stinky cheese."

"They all are," Grace said. Suddenly, Grace felt like Eleanor must have when Grace introduced her to the henhouse. Hillary and Dolly had nearly pecked her half to death.

Grace found Jean Burton and made their excuses.

"I can't believe you're leaving so soon," Jean Burton said. "I haven't made my speech yet."

"I'll send a check," Grace said, giving Jean a hug. She hated to go, but she couldn't stay another second.

As soon as they were out on the street, Benton said, "Where to...?" The sun had finally set, and darkness was closing in.

"Should we go for a drink?" Grace said.

"We could," Benton said. "Or we could drive to the beach?"

"That seems risky," Grace said. They climbed into Grace's Range Rover, and Grace started the engine. She didn't want the evening to end—she never wanted it to end—but neither did she want to get caught in a compromising situation. She turned off Fair Street, onto Lucretia Mott Lane. The only reasonable thing to do was to take Benton home.

"Stop the car," Benton said.

"What?" Grace said.

"Stop the car."

Grace did as she was told. Her headlights shone down the length of the narrow lane. Nobody was around. Benton got out of the car.

"Where are you going?" Grace asked.

"Come with me, please. Shut off the headlights."

"I can't just block the road," Grace said.

"Nobody uses this road," Benton said.

Grace switched off the lights and got out of the car. It was dark now, and Lucretia Mott Lane was lined with ancient, leafy trees, trees that had known the Wampanoag Indians, and the Quakers, and the whaling widows.

Benton gathered Grace up in his arms and kissed her right in the middle of the street. It was thrilling but terrifying.

She said, "Someone is going to see us."

He said, "I don't care. I don't care who sees us. I love you, Grace. I love you."

She stared at him; tears stood in her eyes, making everything sharp and clear. "Yes," she said. "I love you, too. I have never loved anyone the way that I love you."

Grace drove Benton home, and when he told her that Donovan and Leslie were off island, seeing Lyle Lovett at the Cape Cod Melody Tent, Grace followed him upstairs to his apartment.

How do you see this ending?

She didn't.

Love the way she experienced it with Benton Coe was dramatic and urgent and all consuming. It was LOVE in capital letters, boldfaced, underlined. It made what she felt for Eddie seem like some other emotion entirely. She liked Eddie and had been charmed by him. He made her laugh and offered her what she so desperately needed: a way out of her house with her stifling parents and overbearing brothers. Eddie had presented her with an opportunity to create a home and raise children the way *she* wanted. He had let her be the boss and run the show. He had provided her with every material thing she could ask for. She was grateful to

Eddie for that, but she did not love him the way that she loved Benton.

When Grace got home, the house was dark and quiet — everyone was either out or asleep — and she was grateful.

She ran right up to her study, to call Madeline.

EDDIE

Grace went to her little garden-club party, and Allegra was out as always, leaving just Eddie and Hope at home. Grace hadn't made any dinner, which was unusual; she was too consumed with her dress and hair and makeup, Eddie supposed. She looked so beautiful that Eddie almost wished he were going with her. But the garden club...no. He'd rather stick his hand in a nest of killer bees.

What was he supposed to eat? He could scramble some eggs, he supposed. There were five fresh cartons on the counter.

But he could do better than eggs, he thought as Grace drove off in the Range Rover. He knocked on the closed door of Hope's room.

She swung the door open. "What?"

"Are you hungry?" Eddie asked.

She shrugged. She and Allegra shrugged in exactly the same way; it irritated him.

"Get dressed up," he said. "I'm taking you out for dinner."

Thirty minutes later found Eddie and Hope walking up a cobblestone path between two garden cottages, toward the grand front porch of the Summer House. Wafts of good smells came from inside, as well as the sound of the piano, and glasses clinking, conversation and laughter. Eddie's spirits lifted. He took Hope's arm. She looked lovely in a white sundress, with her hair in a French braid. She looked like a girl, whereas Allegra always looked scarily like a woman.

Eddie and Hope were seated at a table by one of the front windows. The Summer House had uneven wooden floors and the rustic, genteel feel of a summer house from the 1940s. The piano player favored Cole Porter. Eddie ordered a martini with a twist, and Hope got a Coke.

When the drinks came, Eddie raised his glass and said, "Cheers, Big Ears."

Hope said, "This is nice. Thanks, Dad."

Eddie nearly teared up. He worked his ass off, he hustled like no one else, and yet the three women in his life remained unimpressed. Eddie didn't need a parade, but it was nice to hear a thank-you every once in a while, an acknowledgment that he was more than just an ATM.

"You're very welcome."

Hope ordered the clam chowder and the Caesar salad, and Eddie splurged on the foie gras and the lamb chops. He

ordered a good bottle of pinot noir from the Willamette Valley, and then he leaned back in his chair and he said, "So, what's going on with your sister?"

"I have no idea," Hope said.

"Really?" Eddie said.

Hope said, "Please tell me you didn't invite me out to dinner on a recon mission about Allegra. If you want to know about Allegra, Daddy, ask Allegra."

"I'm sorry, you're right," Eddie said. "I have you here, and I care about you. What's going on with you?"

Hope shrugged.

"Do you like your job at the rectory?"

"It's fine."

"Father Declan isn't inappropriate with you, is he?" '

"Dad!" Hope said. "No! Please shut up."

"A father has to ask," Eddie said.

"I like Father Declan," Hope said. "He's smart. I'm reading John O'Hara's novel *An Appointment in Samarra,* and Father Declan said it was one of his favorite books in college."

The conversation had just gone over Eddie's head. He liked to tell people he hadn't read a book since *Dune* in the tenth grade, but he hadn't even read *Dune* all the way through. The last book Eddie had finished was *Stuart Little.*

"Is it a Catholic novel?" Eddie asked.

"No," Hope said. "Father Declan is a priest, Dad, but he's also a person. Not everything he does has to be 'Catholic.' "

"I know," Eddie said. He dug into his foie gras. He loved foie gras, but Grace wouldn't let him order it. She didn't approve of the way they force-fed the geese. As a raiser of chickens, she was offended by any type of fowl abuse. But Grace wasn't here now; she was at a garden party.

"I wonder if Mom is having fun at her garden party," he said.

Hope said, "Don't you think it's weird that she took Benton as her date?"

"She took who?"

"Benton Coe? The gardening guy?"

"Oh, that's *right,*" Eddie said. "She told me, but I forgot."

"Don't you think it's weird?" Hope said.

Did Eddie think it was weird? Well, it made him a little edgy, maybe, that Grace had dolled herself up into such a knockout for an evening with the gardener. But, although Benton was as big and tall as a Hun, Eddie didn't find him particularly threatening. He was a man who dealt with roses and tulips. Eddie didn't think he was gay, but he was definitely emotionally attuned toward the feminine — and this was exactly what Grace needed. She needed someone to talk to about her garden. Grace felt about the garden the way Barbie felt about privacy and the way Putin felt about Russian supremacy. Eddie had never been particularly passionate about anything except making money and running. But the running had been more of a God-given natural talent, which wasn't quite the same thing.

"No, I don't think it's weird," Eddie said. "Benton is the gardener, and they went to a garden-club event. Maybe I'm crazy, but that makes perfect sense to me. He can teach your mother the names of all the flowers."

"Mom already knows the names of the flowers," Hope said.

"Exactly," Eddie said. He finished the luscious lusciousness that was his foie gras, and then he waved over the waiter to pour his wine. Then a ghastly thought crossed his mind:

maybe Grace had heard the rumor about Eddie and Madeline and had orchestrated this "date" with Benton Coe in order to get back at him? But no—if Grace had heard the rumor, Eddie would have had a knife to his balls immediately. He didn't want to think about Grace and Benton Coe, and he sure as hell didn't want to think about the rumor about him and Madeline. He just wanted to enjoy dinner with his daughter; it had been so long since he'd been out.

Hope was finishing up her molten-chocolate lava cake, and Eddie was paying the bill—the lamb chops had cost forty-six dollars! How had he not noticed that before he ordered them?—when the chief of police approached the table.

"Eddie!" the Chief said.

Eddie jumped out of his chair. "Chief, how are you?" The two men shook hands, and Eddie presented Hope. "My daughter Hope. Hope, you know Chief Kapenash?"

Hope smiled shyly, whereas Eddie knew Allegra would have been up out of her chair, shaking his hand, eager to impress. But Eddie would not compare.

"You're having a father-daughter dinner?" the Chief asked.

"We are," Eddie said. How fortuitous that the Chief could witness this moment of excellent parenting. He was not by himself and *not* with Madeline or any other woman. He was with his daughter. It was the best P.R. Eddie could have asked for—and it was happening organically. "Her mother and sister are out, so we're taking advantage."

"Nice," the Chief said. "I'm just about to sit down and have a romantic dinner with my wife. Good to see you, Eddie."

"Good to see *you,* Chief," Eddie said. He remained standing until the Chief wandered away. The piano player launched into "Some Enchanted Evening." Eddie beamed at Hope.

She said, "Okay, I'm finished. Can we go?"

"We can go," Eddie said. He ushered Hope in front of him and walked out of the restaurant, indiscriminately waving to everyone he saw.

HOPE

A phone call came to the house in the middle of the night. Hope rolled over. She felt sick to her stomach; the food at the Summer House had been rich, and when Eddie had gotten up to go to the men's room, Hope had sneaked a sip of his martini, just to find out what it tasted like.

It had tasted like lemon-flavored lighter fluid. Hope nearly spat it out, but she didn't want to call attention to herself, and so she swallowed it.

Alcohol was disgusting.

The ringing of the phone stopped. Hope's stomach gurgled. She really hoped she didn't puke; she tried not to think about the martini. It had been so clear and innocuous looking that Hope had thought it would taste like water.

Suddenly, she heard her parents' voices in the hallway. Her mother was hitting what Hope thought of as her hysterical register. She heard them open the door to Allegra's

bedroom, which elicited more hysteria from Grace. So Allegra was still out. Hope checked her phone. It was ten after three.

Wow, Hope thought. Their curfew was eleven thirty. Allegra had shattered her previous broken curfew record of one forty-five.

Grace started to cry, and Eddie was trying to comfort her, but he started sounding a little shaky himself, and suddenly Hope wondered if maybe there was something *really wrong*— like maybe Allegra was hurt.

Or...?

Hope made it to her trash can in the nick of time. *Oh God,* she thought. The damned martini, never again, and never again clam chowder or Caesar salad, which was too bad, because they were her favorites, but, ugh, ick, vomiting ruined everything. She heaved and spat, and then, trembling, she collapsed on her bed until she had a rush of that thank-God-I-got-it-out feeling. Then she managed to stand and open her door.

"Dad?" she said. "Mom? What's going on?"

"Your sister is in trouble," Eddie said. "I'm headed to the police station. You go back to bed, please."

"What kind of trouble?" Hope asked. The police station wasn't good, but it was better than the hospital. "Is she hurt?"

"Not yet," Eddie said. "At least not until I get a hold of her."

Oh boy, Hope thought.

Grace said, "You're such a good girl, sweetheart. But your sister..."

Hope didn't want to hear it. She retreated to the safety of her bedroom and closed the door before Grace could finish her sentence.

*   *   *

Hope was such a good girl, but Allegra was…not. Nope, not at all. She and Ian Coburn had been caught out in Ram's Pasture, sitting on the hood of Ian's Camaro in just their underwear, drinking Wild Turkey and smoking weed. Further search of the car by police turned up a quarter ounce of cocaine, enough to arrest Ian, who was nineteen.

The police officer who found them was Curren Brancato, although it had been the chief of police who had called the house, as a courtesy to Eddie.

More interesting than what happened to Allegra was how Hope found out about it. At five thirty in the morning, she was awoken (with a funky mouth and the stench of vomit in her room) by a text from Brick Llewellyn.

It said: *I saw the photo. Your sister was cheating and you knew and you didn't tell me.*

And Hope thought: *What photo?*

Hope responded: *??????????*

Brick texted: *Hollis sent me a photo of Allegra and Ian in their underwear sitting on Ian's Camaro. They got caught smoking dope and drinking by our friend Officer Brancato. Ian = cocaine dealer = going to jail.*

As Hope was processing this, there was a knock on her door.

"Come in," Hope croaked.

Allegra tiptoed in, closing and locking the door behind her. She slipped into bed next to Hope.

"Whoa," Hope said. This kind of physical proximity to her sister was extremely unexpected. Allegra and Hope used to do things like snuggle in bed together and flip each other over in cheerleading moves, but it had been years and years since

Allegra had voluntarily touched Hope. Hope thought she might welcome Allegra's return to the bubble of their twin-hood, but she merely felt disgusted.

A second text came into Hope's phone, and as Allegra shook and wept into Hope's pillow, Hope checked it. There was the picture of Allegra and Ian. Ian was in just a pair of navy-blue boxer briefs, with a bottle of Wild Turkey between his legs. Allegra was in her pale-pink bra and panties—for a second Hope thought she was nude—and she was pinching a joint at her lips. Her eyes were closed on the inhale. This photographic evidence was so damning that Hope immediately deleted it, even while realizing that this didn't make the picture go away. Who had *taken* it? Hope wondered. Then, she realized, it must have been Officer Brancato. With his own personal phone. And he texted it to Hollis. This must have been some kind of professional breach of ethics, right? It hardly mattered, because, as the old adage went, a picture was worth a thousand words, and all thousand of these words said that Allegra was doing drugs, drinking, and cheating.

For the first time in years and years, Hope felt bad for her sister. She patted Allegra's hair and rubbed her back in circles.

"Sorry I don't smell that good," Hope said. "I puked."

"I don't care," Allegra said. "I probably don't smell like flowers either."

True, Hope thought. Marijuana, booze, cigarettes—or, as Mrs. Aguiar in the rectory office would say, the odors of hell and damnation.

"What are you the most upset about?" Hope asked.

This question was met with an extended bout of tears.

Hope continued to rub her sister's bony back. Allegra barely ate; possibly, she was still holding out for that modeling contract. Or she was so thin because she snorted cocaine with Ian Coburn off the dashboard of the red Camaro. Nothing, at this point, was beyond the realm of possibility.

"Ian going to jail?" Allegra said. "Brick hating my guts? Hollis telling everyone I'm a slut? Curren Brancato busted us. He took a picture. I thought he would be *cool* about it. I thought he would just let us *go*. But he was out to prove himself, or whatever. Big man on the Nantucket police force. As soon as he got back to his squad car, he texted the picture to Hollis. And Hollis, my own best friend, my soul sister, texted it to the rest of the universe."

Hope tried to think up some words of comfort. Hollis had sent the picture out. She and the rest of Allegra's friends were a gang of backstabbing opportunists.

"Mom and Dad are pissed," Allegra said. "Dad grounded me."

"Wow," Hope said. Eddie never grounded Allegra, but apparently being called in the middle of the night by the chief of police had done the trick.

"And he took my phone," Allegra said.

"Oh boy," Hope said.

"Can I use yours, please?" Allegra asked. "I need to text Brick."

"Just call him from the landline," Hope said.

"Let me use your phone."

"No," Hope said. "I'm not comfortable with that."

"Not *comfortable*?" Allegra said.

"Sorry," Hope said.

Allegra's face took on an expression that Hope thought of

as Standard Operating Bitch, but then, perhaps realizing that wouldn't get her what she wanted, she dissolved into tears. "What should I do, Hope?"

"Probably," Hope said, feeling a surge of tenderness for her sister, "you should try and sleep."

Later, when Allegra was in fact asleep and snoring softly in Hope's bed, Hope texted Brick.

She said: *You should probably forgive her.*

No way, he texted back. *Never.*

EDDIE

Eddie was still half-asleep when he arrived at the police station to pick up Allegra. The Chief had been the one to call Eddie, and when Eddie heard the Chief's voice, he turned into quivering jelly. He thought, *Barbie was right.* He thought, *The girls have been caught with Kasper Snacks out at Ten Low Beach Road.* Eddie wasn't going to lie. When the Chief said he was calling because Allegra had been caught drinking in Ram's Pasture, Eddie had felt *nearly giddy with relief.* Then the appropriate emotions caught up with him, and he said, "For God's sake, Ed, you're *kidding.*"

"I wish I were," the Chief said. "I'm sorry, Eddie. She's at the station. You'll have to go get her."

Eddie said, "I guess I took the wrong daughter out for dinner."

The Chief said, "They're teenagers, Eddie. What can you do?"

The Coburn kid's parents were at the station, the father a hothead all up in arms, yelling at the staff officer, the mother blond and silently uptight. Eddie didn't know either of them well enough to say hello. He would have liked to have told them what a bad influence and corrupting reprobate their son was, but Eddie focused on collecting Allegra and getting her home.

Once in the car, Eddie grounded Allegra for the rest of her life. Then he took her phone. He said, *Do you know what it feels like to have the chief of police call in the middle of the night? Your mother and I thought you were dead! But no, you're just a druggie boozehound sitting out in public in your underwear with some guy who isn't even your boyfriend! They have names for people like that, Allegra, and they aren't very flattering!*

Allegra cried. And then she bawled and hiccupped and sounded as if she were having an epileptic seizure. Eddie nearly handed the phone over and told her that everything was going to be okay and that he was just glad she was safe. After all, nobody was perfect, least of all him. But he recognized that one of the reasons Allegra had acted this way was because Eddie and Grace indulged her. It had to stop!

When Eddie woke up the next morning, it felt like his heart had been braised in a stew pot overnight. He couldn't move, could not rise or get dressed or brush his teeth or face down a

cup of coffee or imagine himself upright behind the wheel of his Cayenne. Even the name of his car inflamed his heart. Why had he ever bought it? Because it was a Porsche, because he wanted to impress his clients, because he wanted to give the impression of being hot.

He couldn't move from his supine position under the covers. He couldn't rise to relieve his bladder.

"Grace," he moaned. There was no answer.

Eddie closed his eyes and prayed for sleep. For the first time in forever, Eddie wasn't going to work.

When he awoke at noon, the house was quiet. Where was Grace? Had she come to check on him? There was no note, no glass of ice water, no new bottle of cherry Tums placed thoughtfully on his nightstand. Did she not find it unusual that Eddie had slept until noon? Was she not *worried*?

Miraculously, Eddie found he could stand, although he was shaky. He put on his oldest, softest khaki shorts and his T-shirt from Santos Rubbish Removal, and he crept out into the hallway. It had been so long since he'd been home in the middle of a weekday that he felt like a prowler. The doors to the twins' rooms were closed. Were they still sleeping? Hope had a job at the church rectory—she would most likely be there—but what about Allegra? Had she gotten up to go to her SAT prep course, or was that over? Eddie couldn't remember. He was a lazy-ass parent. He paid for Allegra's class, but when he remembered to ask her how it was going, he barely listened to her answer. And when the class was over, how did Allegra spend her days? Eddie had a vague idea that she went

to the beach with her friends. Where, he now suspected, she smoked weed and drank Wild Turkey. But that lifestyle was coming to a screaming halt. Eddie should bring Allegra into the office and make her file—but he was afraid she might develop a taste for the business, and he didn't want that. Real estate crapped upon the soul.

Allegra was probably asleep, he decided. He should wake her up and make her help Grace with the hens. He stared at her closed bedroom door, considering this—but he was in too much pain for a confrontation.

Eddie shuffled down the stairs to the kitchen. Grace had been to the henhouse already, probably twice. Seven dozen eggs waited in cartons on the counter. And there were fixings out for lunch; it looked as if Grace were making turkey club sandwiches. Eddie was starving, but he feared eating.

He poured himself a cold glass of milk. Through the open kitchen window, he heard Grace crying. Naturally, she would be upset about Allegra; she would be blaming herself. He heard her say, "I'm afraid of her. Isn't that the worst thing you've ever heard? I'm afraid of my own daughter."

It wasn't the worst thing Eddie had ever heard. He was a bit afraid of Allegra himself. She was so *confident,* so in charge of her world, that he sometimes forgot she had been alive for only sixteen years. Of course, Eddie wielded slightly more influence over their daughter because he controlled her spending power, but he agreed that Allegra was intimidating.

Whoever Grace was talking to murmured a response that Eddie didn't hear. Who was she with? But no sooner did he ask himself this than he realized Grace was confiding in the gardener. Benton Coe.

Don't you think it's weird that she took Benton as her date?

Eddie stepped out onto the deck. Grace and Benton were having what appeared to be a lovely little lunch, despite Grace's tears. Eddie bristled. While he was at work, toiling and sweating over their finances, Grace was at home picnicking with the person who was supposed to be working for them.

If Eddie were lucky enough to be reincarnated, he was coming back as Grace's gardener.

"Hey, there," Eddie said.

Benton was leaning back in his chair with his fingers laced behind his head. He looked a little more at ease at Grace's side than Eddie might have wanted him to, but there didn't appear to be anything *untoward* going on. It wasn't even like Grace was crying on his shoulder. She had her elbows on the table and was dabbing at her eyes with her lunch napkin. She and Benton were sitting next to each other, but not unreasonably close. And when Eddie stepped out, they didn't seem jumpy or alarmed. It didn't seem like they were *hiding* anything.

Benton got to his feet. "Hey, Eddie," he said. He shook Eddie's hand. "Grace was just telling me about your night."

Grace raised her weepy eyes. "How's your heartburn?"

"Never been worse," Eddie said.

"Can I get you some crackers and butter?" Grace said.

Eddie wasn't sure he could manage even that much, but it was embarrassing to be offered nursery food because he couldn't handle stuff like bacon and tomato — or even cucumber sticks and Grace's buttermilk-herb dressing.

"I'm fine," he said, in a way that made him sound like a pouting child.

Grace scooted her chair back and got to her feet. "I'll get the crackers."

Benton stood as well. "I should go. I have the lovely Mrs. Allemand waiting for me."

"Edith Allemand?" Eddie said.

Benton grinned. "The one and only."

Edith Allemand lived at 808 Main Street in a house that made Eddie salivate every time he drove past it. It was, possibly, the finest example of whaling-era money on Nantucket aside from the Hadwen House and the Three Bricks. Edith Allemand was about five hundred years old but still cogent and active. She was the kind of woman Grace had described her grandmother Sabine to be: impossibly refined and elegant. Otherwise, Eddie might have knocked on her door and begged her to let him list the house.

"Do you think she'll ever sell?" Eddie asked.

"Never," Benton said. "She's leaving the house to the Nantucket Historical Association."

Eddie's hopes deflated, even though he knew she would do something socially responsible with it like give it to the historians. "Perfectly good waste of a six-figure commission," Eddie said.

Benton threw his head back and laughed, and Eddie congratulated himself on being able to joke despite his excruciating pain. He liked Benton Coe, he decided. Nice guy, and clearly at the top of his professional game if Edith Allemand trusted him.

Benton waved. "Good to see you, Eddie. I'm sorry to hear about Allegra, but . . . this too shall pass."

"Oh, I know," Eddie said. "Thanks."

"Bye, Grace!" Benton called out. "Hang in there — I'll see you later!"

They could just barely hear Grace's voice from inside. "Thanks! Bye!"

MADELINE

She was awoken in the morning by a phone call from Trevor.

"You have to come home," he said. "We have a crisis on our hands."

Madeline didn't know why she felt surprised, but when Trevor showed her the photograph on Brick's phone, she gasped. Allegra was sitting on the hood of Ian Coburn's Camaro in pale, lacy underwear, and she was pinching a joint to her lips. Her long, dark hair was mussed, and her eyes held a faraway, dazed look. Ian Coburn was also in his underwear, a bottle of whiskey between his legs. It was disgusting, not so much because of what it showed but because of where it led the imagination.

"I guess they've been seeing each other on the sly for months," Trevor said.

"Oh my God," Madeline said. "How did you end up with his phone?"

"He threw it at the wall," Trevor said. "There's a hole in the plaster upstairs, but the phone survived." He minimized the screen so that Allegra and Ian Coburn disappeared. "Lifeproof case."

If only there were lifeproof cases available for humans, Madeline thought. Even from the kitchen, she could hear the sound of Brick crying—horrible, broken moans punctuated by shouted profanities.

Madeline climbed the stairs and stood outside the closed

door. She instantly flashed back to when Brick was a baby; she could never stand to listen to him cry. But hearing him cry as a sixteen-year-old was far, far worse. His pain was real, his heart was broken, he had believed in a girl, he had loved her, and she had deceived him. She had preferred another, she had carried on behind his back. She had humiliated him.

Trevor came quietly up the stairs. It sounded as if Brick were pounding on his mattress.

Madeline said, "What should we do for him?"

"What *can* we do?" Trevor said. "It's heartbreak. He has to work through it alone, just like the rest of us."

Madeline looked into her husband's green eyes. She said, "I am *not*, I repeat, *not* having an affair with Eddie Pancik."

Trevor said, "I'm glad you're home." And he gathered her up in his arms.

Madeline was weak with relief. She squeezed her husband as tightly as she could.

Brick cried out. "Why?"

Why? Madeline thought.

We won't get involved, she thought. Brick and Allegra were *kids*—this was their first time through all these confusing emotions. Allegra had strayed from the path of decent human behavior, but she was hardly the first person to do so.

We won't get involved.

They were kids.

The house phone rang. The caller ID said it was the Pancik house.

Trevor said, "That would be Allegra. She's been calling all morning."

"Has she?" Madeline said.

"He won't talk to her," Trevor said. "I've just been letting it ring."

Yes, Madeline thought. *Let it ring.*

We won't get involved.

But the anger in Madeline was its own beast. No mother should have to listen to her child cry like that.

She thought, *You wicked, wicked girl.*

Madeline picked up the phone. "Hello?"

"Madeline?"

It was Grace.

"Hey," Madeline said.

"I take it you heard?"

"I heard."

"The police called at ten after three," Grace said. "Eddie had to go to the station to get her."

Madeline was silent. *We won't get involved.* They had made that promise for a reason—but what was it?

Grace said, "There were a couple of seconds when I thought she was dead. Eddie is . . . God, he's just furious."

He's furious? Madeline thought.

"He stayed home from work," Grace said.

Well, even Madeline had to admit: this was surprising. Eddie went to work every day except for Christmas and Thanksgiving. He went to work on Easter, he went to work on Mother's Day, he went to work on New Year's Day—just in case someone's resolution was to buy a house on Nantucket. But, judging from Madeline's own dealings with Eddie, she gathered there was less going on for Eddie at work than Grace knew.

Grace said, "He came downstairs while Benton was here. I knew he was home, so obviously nothing was going on, but it still made me very uncomfortable to have them in the same place."

It was the mention of Benton that did it.

"Your daughter's behavior was despicable, Grace."

"Madeline, I'm sorry…"

"We all knew!" Madeline said. "That night when we came for dinner, Ian Coburn was texting her nonstop. And you and Eddie tolerated it."

"No," Grace said. "Eddie told her to turn her phone off."

"She was flaunting it in Brick's face!" Madeline said. "In front of all of us! As if daring us to notice what she was getting away with."

Grace whispered, "I saw her with him."

"What?" Madeline said.

"They were kissing in the car in the Stop and Shop parking lot," Grace said. "I saw them, but I told myself it wasn't Allegra. I told myself she wouldn't do that."

"What?" Madeline said. "How long ago was *this?*"

"Ten days?" Grace said. "Two weeks?"

"So you knew a week ago, and you didn't tell me? And you didn't say anything to Allegra?"

"I didn't want…"

"You didn't want what?" Madeline said. She carried the telephone into her bedroom and closed the door. "You didn't want to face what Allegra was doing to Brick because it's exactly the same thing you're doing to Eddie?"

"Madeline…"

"In this case, the apple hasn't fallen far from the tree," Madeline said. "Allegra is a cheater, and you, Grace, are a cheater."

There was silence on the other end, Grace no doubt stunned by Madeline's words. Madeline couldn't believe she'd said them out loud, but she was caught up in a swirling tornado of anger — not just about Allegra and Ian Coburn and the fact that Grace had apparently *known about it,* but also about Eddie and the fifty thousand dollars. Madeline wanted her money back! And, while she was at it, there were other things that ate away at Madeline but that she'd never bothered to bring up. Such as Grace's migraines. The whole world was supposed to stop and bow down to Grace's pain once a month, but when Madeline had had her third and worst miscarriage, Grace had attended five o'clock Mass rather than come straight to the hospital. Grace later explained that she was a Eucharistic minister and couldn't find a last-minute replacement, and she said she had prayed for Madeline and the soul of the baby — but, even so, Madeline had been hurt. Grace was her best friend and should have put *everything* on hold, especially since Grace alone knew how badly Madeline wanted another baby.

And then there was Madeline's suspicion that Grace hadn't actually finished reading her last book, *Islandia.* Madeline had seen it in Grace's beach bag the previous summer when Grace had announced that she had "made it" to page 150. And then, months later, Madeline saw the book on Grace's front hall table, and the bookmark remained at page 150. Had Grace simply stopped reading? Madeline had been too embarrassed to ask, but she had been pretty sure that her own best friend had never finished her book. This was maybe because . . . Grace's intellect was too lofty, because she had been a French-literature major at precious Mount Holyoke and read only things she considered "important" and "worthy."

Madeline couldn't remember ever being this angry before.

"You're right," Grace said softly.

"I know I'm right!" Madeline screamed. "And I want my money back!"

With that, she slammed down the phone and for one second felt *completely self-righteous!* She thought of her novel *B/G.* Maybe she *wouldn't* change any of the details! Maybe she would leave them all just as they were so Grace would know!

Trevor knocked on the door. "Honey, are you okay?" he asked. "Who were you talking to?"

"Grace," Madeline spat out. Then she started to cry.

NANTUCKET

Officer Curren Brancato texted his sister, Hollis, the picture of Allegra Pancik and Ian Coburn sitting on the hood of Ian's Camaro in their underwear. Underneath the photo, Curren wrote: *Your BFF is in BIG TRUBS.*

Hollis Brancato was no angel. Secretly, she had had *her* sights set on Ian Coburn. To learn that Allegra was hanging out with him at the same time that she was steadily dating Brick set her off like a fire alarm. She forwarded the photo to Kenzie and Bluto. *Allegra is a two-timer, and here's the proof.* She didn't use the phrase *two-timer,* however. She used other words, too profane to be repeated.

From Kenzie and Bluto, word spread to Hannah, and

Hannah felt compelled to tell the person who would be most affected, Brick Llewellyn, and then Hannah told Calgary and Taylor Rook and Parker Marz, and the rest of Brick's baseball team, so that he might have some brothers-in-arms.

By midafternoon on Friday, it was safe to say that every student at Nantucket High School had heard some version of what had happened to Allegra and Ian Coburn, and most of them had seen the photographic evidence. Some people said that Ian Coburn had been cuffed and thrown in jail; some said he was headed to Walpole. In truth, he had been given a slap on the wrist — the amount of cocaine found in his car was too small to charge him with intent to distribute — but his parents were concerned enough that they had already checked out several drug rehabilitation centers out West.

Worlds collided when Blond Sharon took her two ambiguously named children, Sterling and Colby, for their six-month cleaning appointment with Dr. Andy McMann. While other mothers sat in the waiting room and caught up, via *People* magazine, with Blake and Miranda and Kanye and Kim, Blond Sharon hung out in the exam room and chatted with Janice, the hygienist.

Janice said, "So, have you been out lately, Sharon?"

And Sharon said, "A few nights ago I went to the Sunset Soiree for the Nantucket Garden Club."

Janice mentally tuned Sharon out as she scraped away at the plaque on Colby's teeth with a vigor that made Colby wriggle. Colby was only seven. Janice had never *seen* so much

plaque on a seven-year-old, and she was about to tell Sharon so when Sharon said, "Grace Pancik was there with Benton Coe, her gardener."

"Really?" Janice said. "Were they *together* together?"

"Hard to say?" Sharon said. "I don't think officially? But Jody Rouisse and I found them sitting alone by this little pond, and Grace was crying."

Janice wondered if Grace had heard the rumor about Eddie and Madeline King. Maybe she was crying to Benton Coe about that? Janice almost asked Blond Sharon what she thought, but she wasn't sure if Blond Sharon had heard about Eddie and Madeline. Janice sneaked a quick glance at Sharon. She knew a lot—she always seemed to be in the right place at the right time—but maybe not everything.

Sharon said, "And then later I heard that Jean Burton thinks Grace is *pregnant*."

Whoa! This news startled Janice so badly that she accidentally poked poor Colby in the gum above her bicuspid, and Colby started to cry.

Janice said to Sharon, "Dr. Andy would *kill* me if he heard us gossiping about the Panciks. Eddie is our landlord."

"Okay, well," Blond Sharon said, "you didn't hear it from me."

The only person Janice felt safe repeating Blond Sharon's news to was Dr. Andy himself. Grace and Benton Coe, out together at the Sunset Soiree, Grace crying because she'd discovered she was pregnant.

"What?" Dr. Andy said. So few things pierced Andrew McMann's bubble of serenity—but this had done the trick. And *what* had Rachel told him recently about Madeline writing some sexy book, possibly based on her own experiences with Eddie Pancik?

On his lunch break, Dr. Andy called Rachel at the offices of Bayberry Properties. He said, "Janice told me Grace is having an affair with her gardener."

"Oh yes," Rachel said. "I've heard."

"Oh," Dr. Andy said. He felt a bit dejected. "Do you think maybe Madeline's book is about Grace and the gardener and not herself and Eddie? I mean, didn't you *tell* me the book was about a woman and her gardener?"

"Contractor," Rachel said. She lowered her voice to a whisper. "You just want to let Eddie off the hook because he's your *landlord.*"

Dr. Andy admitted to himself that this might be true. He held a delusion that if he kept in Eddie's good graces, Eddie would stop raising the rent; it had gone up twice in the last eighteen months. Dr. Andy had considered moving, but few people understood the logistical nightmare that moving a dental office entailed.

Rachel said, "The Pancik family is a mess. You do remember what I told you Calgary told me about Allegra?"

Dr. Andy made a noncommittal noise. When Rachel started talking about teenage drama, he tuned her out. His last memory of Allegra Pancik was as a pretty, friendly young woman with an impeccable smile and good flossing habits. And he preferred to keep it that way.

EDDIE

He was sinking.

The notice came from the bank, along with a stern phone call from Philip Meier, loan officer: numbers 9 and 11 Eagle Wing Lane were going to be repossessed unless Eddie could come up with the three months' back mortgage that he owed on each.

He was going to lose them. The time had come (said the newfound angler in Eddie) to "cut bait."

He went through the contacts on his phone once, twice, three times. Was there *anybody* else in his circle of acquaintances that he could ask? His buddy Lex from high school was now a slumlord in New Bedford. He was the only other person Eddie thought might have the cash and the interest (up his game a little, with two high-end projects on Nantucket)—but when Eddie called, an automated voice announced that Lex's number was out of service.

And so, Glenn Daley it was. Eddie didn't even bother with a phone call. The only way Glenn would realize that Eddie was dead-on balls serious was for Eddie to walk right into the office of Bayberry Properties.

This was exactly what Eddie did.

Rachel McMann, thankfully, was not at her desk. She was probably out trying to solicit clients off the tour buses.

Glenn tried not to show his surprise. "Edward!" he said, standing up. "To what do I owe this honor?"

The two men shook hands. Eddie nodded at the chair next to Glenn's desk, which was, blessedly, separated from the rest of the floor by three cubicle walls.

"By all means," Glenn said. "Sit."

It was hard to explain why Eddie hated Glenn Daley so much. He was a rotund, affable guy who was losing his hair and who wore slip-on shoes. He had a loud, cheerful voice and always knew who had won what game the night before and where the stock market closed, and he'd always just seen the movie everyone was talking about or just finished the book everyone was reading. The best way for Eddie to describe it was that Glenn had always been Eddie's rival, his adversary, the person he wanted to beat. This was probably borne out of their similarities—he and Eddie had started in the Nantucket real-estate business at the same time; they had started their own agencies at the same time—and the fact that Glenn was very good at what he did.

Glenn had been one of the cocaine abusers back in the nineties—rumor had it that an entire commission on a house on India Street had gone right up Glenn's nose—and then Glenn went through a high-profile divorce, which had reportedly cost him three hundred thousand dollars. Lots of people liked to claim that their ex-wife was psycho, but in Glenn's case, it was true. Ashland Daley had once chased Glenn through the Stop & Shop with a loaded pistol, and at the time, Eddie had remembered thinking it couldn't happen to a nicer guy.

But Glenn had proved to be like one of those stupid Weeble toys from Eddie's youth. *Weebles wobble, but they don't fall down.* Glenn quit the drug habit, Ashland moved to California, and Glenn started selling houses left and right, thanks to his happy-go-lucky personality and his desire for self-improvement.

Eddie sat down in Glenn's chair. And then, sotto voce, he

explained: design and build on Eagle Wing Lane, bit off more than he could chew, and did Glenn want to score an incredible deal and help Eddie out in the process by buying numbers 9 and 11? A million dollars for both. A total steal.

Glenn whistled. "A million dollars." He picked up a notepad and a pen. "How much did you pay for the land?"

Eddie considered lying, but Glenn could easily go down to the Registry of Deeds and check his work. "Buck fifty apiece," Eddie said.

"So three," Glenn said. He wrote *300* on the notepad. "And how much did you dump into them? Not three fifty apiece, no way, they're barely *framed,* Ed. I've driven past."

"About two apiece," Eddie said.

Glenn slammed his pen down. "Why come to me if you're just going to lie your ass off? I know Schuyler Pine designed all three for the price of one because you nominated him for commodore of the yacht club..."

"Wait a minute," Eddie said. "*How* do you know that?"

Glenn clammed up. Fiddled with the notepad, tore the top sheet off, and crumpled it up. He said, "Don't include number thirteen in your spiel to me, Eddie, if you're planning on keeping number thirteen for yourself. Divide everything by thirds, not halves. Two hundred on the land. And maybe, *maybe,* a buck fifty into each...but that's being generous. So that gives us five hundred. I don't see how you can come in here asking for a million dollars."

Eddie remembered now why he hated Glenn Daley: the guy was a douche bag! Obviously Eddie came in asking for a million so he could have enough money to finish number 13 and sell it!

Eddie said, "When you're finished, you can sell them *each*

for one point two. Each, Glenn. So two-four on a million-dollar investment, nearly a million and a half profit."

"I'll give you half a million," Glenn said. "I'll call Ben Winford, and I'll take them both off your hands *today* for half a million."

Eddie stared at the numbers on Glenn's notepad. Half a million was enough to make the mortgages go away and recoup about a quarter of his initial investment.

Then Eddie noticed the notepad itself. It was from the Four Seasons in Santa Barbara.

"Hey," Eddie said. He was trying to form a thought, but it wouldn't quite crystallize. When it did, Eddie swallowed. *No, he thought. No fucking way.* He pointed to the notepad. "Have you ever *stayed* at the Four Seasons in Santa Barbara? I hear it's really nice."

Glenn flipped the notepad over. "That's really none of your business, Eddie."

None of his business. *P* for *personal.* Barbie was sleeping with Glenn Daley! Sleeping, quite literally, with the enemy! She took trips with him to places like Santa Barbara, and she discussed business secrets like Eddie's deal with Schuyler Pine.

Eddie's scalp prickled. Had Barbie told Glenn what they were doing on Low Beach Road?

She wouldn't.

Or would she?

It might be good pillow talk. *Hey, guess what? Eddie and I are running a whorehouse.*

Eddie tried to think like his sister. They had been so close their whole lives, and yet a part of Barbie, in adulthood anyway, had remained inscrutable. *P* for *personal.* There were

things Barbie didn't want Eddie to know. Like…she was sleeping with big, fat, stupid, successful former druggie Glenn Daley.

Had she told him about the girls?

No, Eddie didn't think so, because something in Glenn's expression shifted, and Eddie thought, *He knows that I know.*

"Nine hundred," Eddie said.

"Six hundred," Glenn said.

"Seven hundred and you've got a deal," Eddie said, though seven hundred wasn't quite enough to get him where he wanted to be. But it was seven hundred more than he'd had fifteen minutes earlier, so why not call it a victory?

Eddie put on his Panama hat, the last one in his possession. He had wanted to replace the other two, but he didn't have the money for such an extravagance.

Seven hundred grand: pay the mortgages on his commercial properties, pay the remaining bills on number 13, pay the mortgages on his house (also a month or two in arrears), pay Hester Phan's stupid fucking "success bonus," pay for electricity and water and groceries and gas, like the rest of America. Maybe — *maybe* — there would be enough to get the floors and countertops installed at number 13, maybe talk to a drywall guy and painters so he would be that much closer to selling and be able to assure Madeline that her money would be coming along shortly.

"I'll have Ben draw up the papers," Glenn said.

Lawyers' fees. Seven hundred grand wasn't nearly enough. *P* for *personal.*

"Thanks, bro," Eddie said.

Glenn Daley raised an eyebrow, and Eddie strolled out of the office.

GRACE

The shift was minuscule, but Grace noticed it right away. Benton pulled away from their kiss a second sooner than he might have normally. He said he couldn't stay for lunch.

On the night of the Sunset Soiree, he had professed his love *in the middle of the street.* He had made love to Grace *in his own bed* (a welcome change from the garden shed). But now, he was acting strangely. Grace thought maybe he had been spooked on Friday morning, when she met his truck in the driveway and told him that Eddie hadn't gone to work, that he was still upstairs asleep, due to the fiasco with Allegra.

Or maybe Benton was just doing that thing that men did when they got close to a woman and the feelings got scary.

She wasn't sure, but Benton's timing couldn't have been worse. Grace *needed* him. She hadn't talked to Madeline in three days.

Have you and Madeline had a falling-out?

It was almost like Blond Sharon had predicted it. The only relationship Grace could *count on* had blown up. Madeline had been *so angry.* Grace hadn't even realized Madeline was capable of getting that angry. She was always so sunny and sweet, so California laid back. She took things in stride. She smiled, she listened, she excelled at understanding what she called "the three sides to every story."

Grace missed her so much. Fifty or sixty times a day, something would happen and Grace would think, *I have to tell Madeline.* But then she would look at the phone, and she would think of Madeline's words: *Allegra is a cheater, and you,*

Grace, are a cheater. And Grace would shudder. Madeline didn't want to hear from her. Madeline thought she was a common harlot.

It was *awful heartache,* fighting with her best friend. Madeline was probably hanging out at her apartment, breaking her writing discipline so she could meet Rachel McMann for lunch.

Eddie needed to pay Madeline back. Maybe if he did that, Madeline would be less angry, and Grace could call.

And now, on top of everything, Benton was acting funny.

Grace said, "Are you okay? You're acting funny."

"I'm not acting funny," Benton said. "I just can't stay for lunch today."

"Nobody else is home, if that's what you're worried about," Grace said. Eddie was back to work, Hope was at the rectory, and Allegra had gone into town to look for a volunteer job. She was to check in with either Eddie or Barbie *in person* at the office every hour. Neither Eddie nor Grace trusted that Allegra wouldn't simply slip off to the beach.

"I'm not worried about that at all," Benton said. He checked his phone. "I have to go."

"Go, then," Grace said. "You seem in a terrible hurry."

He sighed. "Grace."

"We only have two weeks until they come!" Grace said. She made a grand gesture with her hand. "Does this yard look ready to you?"

"Fifteen days," Benton said. "And, actually, yes, it does."

Grace couldn't figure out what was *happening* here. This *was* the same man who had spelled out his love for her, was it not? He had *said* he didn't care who heard him.

Then the worst came to mind.

"Is McGuvvy coming today?" Grace asked. "Is she flying in from California?"

"No, Grace," Benton said. "She is not flying in. I don't keep in touch with her—you know that."

"Right," Grace said. "I'm sorry. It's just that you seem distant, like you're pulling away."

Benton slid his phone into his pocket and faced Grace. "You should probably give your girls some attention."

"I'm sorry?" Grace said. "Are you telling me how to *parent?*"

"I had a conversation with Hope," Benton said. "It was no big deal, but even *she* told me Allegra was heading for trouble. I feel like I'm taking you away from your number-one responsibility."

"You...no, you're not," Grace said. "The girls are...well, they're *sixteen*. If I paid more attention to them, they would call me annoying and tell me to go away."

Benton sighed. "You're right. I have no business telling you how to parent."

"Is something else bothering you?" Grace asked. "Something you're afraid to tell me?"

Benton nodded slowly. "I think people are talking about us."

"Do you?"

"There's a woman named Donna who works for Mrs. Allemand, and she heard Madeline King was writing some sexy novel about a woman and her contractor. I guess people are saying it's based on you and me."

"Madeline?" Grace said. Madeline *was* writing a new novel, but Grace didn't know the subject.

"You haven't told Madeline about us, have you?" Benton asked.

"No," Grace said. She feared the tops of her ears would burst into flames, giving her away.

"I know she's your best friend," Benton said.

"*Was* my best friend," Grace said. "She isn't speaking to me right now because of this thing with Allegra."

"She's not writing this as some kind of revenge, then, is she?" Benton asked.

"No," Grace said, but her mind was racing to the night when Grace invited Madeline up to her study, and then all those phone calls. Madeline knew *every* detail. If she *were* writing a book...but no, Madeline wouldn't do that, not even as a revenge tactic.

Two of the women at this table will betray the person on their left.

Grace shook her head to clear it. "Who's Donna?" she said. "And where did she hear this rumor?"

"I guess she's friends with a girl named Greta, who's the nanny for that blond woman Sharon that we saw at the party."

"Oh God," Grace said. "Sharon is awful. Sharon makes stuff up all the time and tries to pass it off as the truth."

"Well, all I'm saying is what I heard."

"I thought you didn't *care* who knew," Grace said. "That's what you said the other night."

"I had been drinking."

"So you *do* care?"

"Well, I don't love being the subject of gossip. I have a business to run. I hate to generalize like this, but it's the women who hire me—however, it's the men who pay the

bills. But this all reflects much more poorly on you, Grace. I don't want anyone thinking badly of you."

Grace took a deep breath. "I'm ready to leave Eddie."

Benton raised his eyebrows in an expression of boyish hope. "Really?"

"Really," she said. Then she thought about the twins. Allegra was already such a mess, and Hope was fragile.

Benton read the doubt off her face, maybe, because he said, "Let's not get too far ahead of ourselves. Let's just work on the yard for the shoot for now."

Grace nodded. "Okay."

He said, "I'll stay for lunch tomorrow, Grace, I promise." He bent down and kissed her in a way that turned her inside out. "I love you."

"And I love you," Grace said.

Benton strode away, and a few seconds later, Grace heard the engine of his truck. She ran upstairs to her study and called Madeline.

Three rings, four rings, voice mail.

Grace said, "There's a rumor going around that you're writing your new novel about a woman having an affair with her contractor, and apparently some people think it's about me and Benton? This had better not be true, Madeline." Grace swallowed. "This had *better not* be true."

MADELINE

She hadn't held out much hope that Brick would want to ease his heartache by spending time with his mother, but Madeline offered, and Brick accepted. In the week following Allegra's deception, they hung out together. The first day, they grabbed sandwiches from Something Natural and drove out to Sesachacha Pond, where Madeline sat at the water's edge and Brick listened to music on his headphones. The second day it rained, so they went to the movies at the Dreamland Theatre, each with their own tub of popcorn and box of Milk Duds. The third day, they rode their bikes to Madaket and napped on the beach until the sun set in orange and pink streaks—then Trevor met them at Millie's for fish tacos.

The fourth day, Brick wanted to "stay home and chill," whatever that meant, so Madeline wrote in her apartment all day.

The fifth day, Brick asked Madeline if she wanted to join him and Parker Marz at Cisco Beach.

"Sure," Madeline said. Parker was smaller in stature than Brick's other friends, but he was smart and funny and related well to adults, and Madeline enjoyed his company.

When she pulled into the parking lot at Cisco, she said, "Are you sure you want me tagging along? I can just drop you guys and come back and pick you up later."

"You should definitely join us, Mrs. Llewellyn," Parker said. "Our social cred will skyrocket in the presence of a beautiful woman."

"Dude, chill," Brick said. He smiled for the first time in who knew how long. "It's my mom."

"Should I just drop you?" Madeline asked Brick.

"No, Mom, come with us. It's cool," Brick said.

Madeline followed the boys down to the beach and set up three chairs. Cisco was home to the Nantucket surf scene — young guys in wet suits standing possessively next to their boards, and the gorgeous, underfed girls who loved them. Madeline also recognized the elder statesmen of surf — men like Sultan Nash, the housepainter, and Thornton Bayle, paving king, who had ditched work for waves. Then there was a slew of aspirants — from kids Brick's age all the way down to fourth- and fifth-graders.

Brick charged into the water to bodysurf while Parker plopped into the chair next to Madeline.

"I think he's doing a little better each day," Parker said.

Madeline nearly laughed. "Do you?"

"He's my bro," Parker said. "And he got done wrong by that … well, excuse my French, Mrs. Llewellyn, but by that *bitch,* Pancik. That's the risk you take when you date a beautiful girl. Allegra is the most popular girl in school — well, her and Hollis; I mean, I have no prayer of scoring even one date with someone of their caliber, but the good thing" — Parker held an arm out to indicate Brick, floating alone over the swells — "is that I do not own a time share in Heartbreak City."

"You guys are all really young," Madeline said. "I think maybe Brick and Allegra were too immature for an exclusive relationship."

"It sounds like you're letting Allegra off the hook, Mrs. Llewellyn," Parker said. "And I hate to see you being a softie. Allegra had been cheating on him for a *while.* I saw her at the Cape Cod Mall with Ian back in April. They were at the

Chanel counter. I mean, come on, is it not *totally obvious* what game Allegra was playing? She picked an older guy with money. Brick never stood a chance!" Parker let out a weary sigh. "I just hope our boy bounces back."

Madeline reached over and squeezed Parker's arm. "He's lucky he has a good friend like you."

"I love that kid," Parker said. "He's my bro."

Madeline smiled, and then she brought her legal pad out of her book bag.

"Is that your new novel?" Parker asked. "My mom tells me it's a real doozy."

Madeline had received Grace's voice mail—*This had better not be true, Madeline. This had* better not *be true*—but it hadn't stopped Madeline's progress on the novel or even slowed her down. Madeline was going to write *B/G* until Eddie paid her back her money!

As soon as Madeline got home from the beach, her phone started to buzz. Rachel McMann. Madeline was tempted to let it go to voice mail, but, to be honest, she was starved for female interaction. She ached for Grace every second of every day.

"You're not going to believe this," Rachel said.

Madeline sniffed. She already didn't like the way this conversation was going.

"What?" she said.

"I heard?" Rachel said. "That Grace Pancik...?"

"Oh God," Madeline said.

"Took Benton Coe, her gardener, as her date to the Sunset Soiree, and now Jean Burton thinks she's pregnant."

"Pregnant?" Madeline said. "Grace?" This pierced her. She had tried and tried and *tried* to have another baby. If Grace had gotten *accidentally* pregnant by Benton Coe...

But no, uh-uh, no way, not possible. This was gossip at its most insidious.

"Rachel," Madeline said. "There is nothing going on between Grace and Benton Coe. Grace is happily, *happily* married to Eddie. So, please, Rachel...?"

"Yes?" Rachel said.

"Mind your own business," Madeline said.

EDDIE

He walked into the office with one thing on his mind. He had tried calling Barbie at home, and he'd left two messages on her cell—no response.

Eloise was in but on the phone. Eddie collapsed into Barbie's chair. She was wearing a red Diane von Furstenberg wrap dress and four-inch Manolos and the whopper pearl at her throat.

Eddie wondered if Glenn Daley had ever held that pearl between his teeth.

He said, "I'm selling numbers nine and eleven Eagle Wing Lane to Glenn Daley."

"Yes," she said, "I know."

"You know?" Eddie said.

"Someone in his office sent over the paperwork," Barbie

said. On her desk were two large coffees from the Handlebar Café, Barbie's new favorite place. She handed one to Eddie that was loaded with milk.

"Thank you," Eddie said. Barbie never brought him coffee. So this was a peace offering, or a please-don't-hate-me-for-sleeping-with-Glenn-Daley offering. Eddie was dying to address the issue, but he feared that to do so would be to embarrass them both. But he wanted her to know that he knew. He knew for sure.

"From now on," he said, "*I'm* going to schedule the girls."

Barbie shot a glance across the room at Eloise. She nodded. She was so damn insouciant that Eddie wanted to pick up her stapler and throw it across the office just to get a response.

"Okay?" he said.

"Okay," she said.

The next group in was Nightbill, a little more than two weeks hence. It was some kind of accounting or payroll firm from Kansas City. The contact person was a man named Bugsy Greer.

Bugsy? Eddie thought. He had checked the guy's photo out online. Quite frankly, he looked like someone from a horror show. He was completely bald, and there was something wrong with his teeth. Eddie had wondered which of the girls would have to have sex with Bugsy Greer, but then he shuddered and tried to think of something pleasant—hot-air balloons, Christmas trees.

He was *very nervous* as he prepared to make the phone

call. He left the office with his cell phone and loitered at the edge of the Nantucket Yacht Club parking lot. It was now summer, which meant that Eddie had to be more careful, or the attendant stationed at the guardhouse would tell Eddie to scram, or one of the old ladies carrying a Nantucket lightship basket would scold him.

He lingered on the far side of a brand-new Range Rover. He wished he'd listened more closely to Barbie when she was propositioning these groups.

Bugsy answered, "Hello?"

Eddie spoke so quickly, he tripped over his words. *Hey, there, Bugsy, this is Eddie Pancik, your real-estate agent on Nantucket? Excited about coming to the island? Need any dinner reservations? Pearl? Cru? Ventuno?*

And then Eddie said: *Listen, here's something for on the down low. We have a cleaning crew of five Russian girls who do more than just clean.*

"Really?" Bugsy said, his voice perking up.

"Really," Eddie said. "They can come back at night, if you'd like."

"We would like," Bugsy said.

"Would you?" Eddie said. He took some steady breaths. "You understand me, then?"

"I think so, yes," Bugsy said. "How much?"

"Twelve thousand a night," Eddie said. He felt both bad and good about raising the price. He was going to keep the extra two grand for himself.

Sleeping with Glenn Daley!

"That's fine," Bugsy said.

"Will you pay night by night or all at once?" Eddie asked. "Which do you prefer?"

"All at once," Eddie said. "If you can make that happen, Bugsy?"

"I can make that happen," Bugsy said. "Bugsy" was obviously some kind of nickname, and Eddie felt ridiculous using it. "I can make anything happen."

"I like the confidence of that statement," Eddie said.

A few days later, when Eddie checked his voice mail, there was a message from Madeline. He thought maybe she was calling to express her dismay or anger over Allegra's behavior, and Eddie was ready to list all the ways he'd punished his daughter: He'd taken away her phone, and she was grounded until further notice. No beach with friends, no parties, and she was never to see the Coburn kid again.

But it turned out that Madeline wasn't calling about Allegra.

The message said, *I've called Layton Gray, Eddie.*

Layton Gray was the Llewellyns' attorney, the very same attorney Eddie himself had recommended back when they needed someone to do their real-estate closing. *He's going to take action against you unless you pay us back by the end of next week. I'm being nice here, Eddie. You've got ten days.* Then she hung up.

"What?" Eddie said. "No good-bye?"

He was selling numbers 9 and 11 to Glenn Daley, and he would use some of the cash to pay Madeline and Trevor back. He would get out from under his debt, and he would live his life on the straight and narrow—as soon as he could.

He called home to check in with Grace and the girls. How

long had it been since he'd called just because? He would do it more often, he decided. He would do it every day.

Grace said, "Hi, there." She sounded perplexed. "Everything okay?"

"Just checking in!" Eddie said. "How's everything there? Are the girls home?"

"Yes," Grace said. "They're both here. Neither of them is working today, so the three of us are going to the Galley for lunch."

Eddie wondered if "grounding" Allegra could reasonably mean taking her to the Galley for lunch. But he knew how much Grace wanted special together times with the twins, and that would never happen unless Allegra were grounded— sad fact. Eddie himself loved the Galley for lunch or sunset cocktails, although he hadn't gone yet this summer. It was pricey. He wished Grace were tougher and had suggested Allegra take over mowing the lawn.

"Allegra seems . . . different," Grace said.

"In a good way or a bad way?" Eddie asked.

"Good way?" Grace said. "Like she might actually be contrite?"

"Yeah, well, she'd better be," Eddie said. He needed to hang up before his good mood evaporated completely. "Glad to hear things are headed in that direction. Have fun at lunch!"

"We will," Grace said.

HOPE

In a mere four days, Allegra's world had imploded like a dying star.

On the morning after, Hope had relented and allowed Allegra to use her phone to text Brick and Hollis and her other friends — but the results weren't pretty. Brick told her to never contact him again. He said she had made a joke of him. He had loved her as well as he knew how, but clearly it wasn't enough love or the right kind of love, which was fine, but he wasn't going to waste another second on her. *Good-bye and good luck,* he said.

The calm, firm words freaked Allegra out. Hope had never seen her sister lose her composure in this way. Allegra was *screaming,* her hair was wild, and she tore around Hope's bedroom as though looking for a way off the *Titanic.* She stared at Hope's phone, saying, "What do I tell him? How do I get him to forgive me?"

Hope sighed. She wished that she, like Cyrano de Bergerac, had magic words to offer her sister. But, even with as little experience as Hope had with relationships, she knew that Brick was beyond Allegra's reach at this point. He might forgive her in ten years or, more likely, twenty or thirty — when he was forty-six and possibly had a tempestuous sixteen-year-old daughter of his own.

"I don't know?" she said.

Allegra handed Hope the phone and said, "Here, you text him. He's always liked you. He *respects* you. Tell him I'm not doing well. Tell him to at least take my phone call."

"Okay," Hope said. She sent Brick a text that said: *Hot glass looks like cool glass.*

She waited. Surely he would respond to their secret code? Nothing.

She texted: *My sister isn't doing well. She's probably too selfish to actually kill herself, but high anxiety and depression are likely. Can you please just talk to her? Thanks. Your friend, Hope.*

Brick responded: *Please never contact me again.*

Hope texted: *It's me, Hope. Really. Hot glass looks like cool glass.*

Brick texted: *Yes, I know, Hope. Please never contact me again.*

Hope felt stung. This was not how it was supposed to go. Hope and Brick were supposed to forge a secret connection, a deep simpatico understanding that would lead to Brick falling in love with her. Brick was supposed to realize that Hope was everything Allegra was, only she was also good, nice, kind, and honest.

Hope threw the phone down on the bed. "He hates me, too, apparently."

Allegra started to wail. She picked the phone up to call him again, and that was when the screen started blowing up with texts from Hollis, Hannah, Kenzie, and Bluto. And none of them were very nice. Hope read the texts over Allegra's shoulder and cringed at the names her friends were calling her: *boozehound, pothead, anorexic slut.*

"Do I look anorexic?" Allegra asked, showing Hope the photo.

"Well, you don't look fat," Hope said, in a voice meant to point out a silver lining. In fact, despite the gruesome circum-

stances, the photo of Allegra was gorgeous in a way. Minus the booze and dope, Allegra and Ian might have been doing a shoot for fragrance. "Maybe the photo will go viral and someone at a modeling agency will see it?"

Allegra gave her sister a hopeful, watery gaze. "You think? Maybe?"

A text came in from Bluto: *Lying, cheating slut.*

"Maybe," Hope said.

Allegra put up a good fight. She had some choice words for Hollis and Kenzie, and she unleashed a mighty wrath on Bluto, calling him a lard-ass succubus. When she ran out of oomph, she fell back on the bed next to Hope.

She said, "I don't know what to do."

Hope said, "They'll come around."

"It doesn't matter. The toothpaste is out of the tube. You can't call someone a lying, cheating slut and then take it back. These are relationship destroyers. It's all Hollis's fault. She's been waiting for years to knock me down."

Hope had to concede that this might be true. Hollis and Allegra were pretty well matched, but Allegra had always been just a little bit luckier. Now that she had proved herself fallible, Hollis would solely retain the title of Queen Bee.

"This too shall pass away," Hope said.

"So what do I do until then?"

Hope didn't understand the question and said so.

"What do I *do* until it 'passes away'?" Allegra said. "I don't have a job, like you. Now I can't go to the beach. I'm forbidden

from leaving the house, for starters, but even if I weren't grounded, I couldn't go to the beach alone."

"Well," Hope said, "you could always read."

"Read?" Allegra said. Her tone of voice contained actual wonder, as if to say, *What?* As if to say, *Why would I do that?*

Hope tossed her sister the copy of *Lolita*. Hope had recently finished it and was thus able to claim personhood. The book had been excellent, thought provoking, original, and weird.

"Read this," Hope said. "There are some big words in it. It'll help you with your critical reading score."

Allegra studied the cover of the book skeptically. "*Lolita.* Vladimir Nabokov. Is it even in *English?*"

"Yes," Hope said. "It's about a grown man named Humbert Humbert, who abducts a thirteen-year-old girl and drives with her across America."

"Sick," Allegra said, but Hope could tell her interest was piqued.

Allegra had stayed in Hope's bedroom all of that first bad day, reading and napping, and Hope stayed in the room as well. She plowed through most of *House of Mirth,* and then she practiced her flute. She told herself she was staying in her room to watch over her sister so that she didn't do anything stupid, but really Hope was just enjoying their quiet camaraderie. When Hope finished playing a selection from Mozart's Flute Concerto in G, Allegra—who was lying on her back, staring at the ceiling, with *Lolita* splayed open on her chest—said, "You're really good. I wish I were good at something."

Hope said, "You're good at things."

"Like what?"

Hope took her flute apart and pulled felt through the mouthpiece. The things that Allegra was good at—being pretty, being popular—were pretty compromised at that moment.

"Like what, Hope?"

"Like lots of things," Hope said. "I'm not going to sit here and enumerate your many talents."

"Because you can't," Allegra said. "Because I don't have any talents. Because I'm a mean-hearted, cheating, lying tramp."

"Oh, stop it," Hope said. "You made a mistake, is all. We're young. We're supposed to make mistakes, learn from them, and move on."

"Tell me one good thing about myself," Allegra said. "Please? One thing."

"You have a great sense of style," Hope said.

Allegra was quiet. Her eyes closed. "You're right," she said. "I do."

Hope would have guessed that Allegra's newfound humility would be short lived and that by the end of the first day of shame, she would have tired of Hope's company. But on the second week, Allegra had managed to score a volunteer job at the Weezie Library for Children, shelving books part time. Their mother was so pleased that she suggested lunch at the Galley, just the three of them. Allegra not only agreed but actually seemed excited. Excited to be seen in public with

Grace and Hope? Well, it would get her out of the house — she would be relieved about that, maybe — and the Galley was fancy, so she would have a chance to dress up. Hope wore her strapless Lilly Pulitzer dress with the turquoise-and-white butterfly print. Allegra wore a jade-green patio dress from Tbags Los Angeles and a pair of Dolce Vita gladiator sandals. Hope had French braided her hair, but Allegra did some messy half-up, half-down style right out of *Vogue*.

"It's really not fair how beautiful you are," Hope said.

Allegra actually seemed embarrassed. "You look just like me," she said. "We're *identical twins*."

"Except you're Alice," Hope said, "and I'm the Dormouse."

"Stop," Allegra said. She lifted the end of Hope's braid and tickled Hope's nose with it. "We can both be Alice."

Lunch at the Galley was fun and special, despite Grace announcing every five minutes how fun and special it was. Grace took their picture at the entrance to the beautiful beachfront restaurant, and then, once they were all seated, she had their waiter take a photo of the three of them.

"These are my twin girls," Grace announced, loudly enough for half the restaurant to hear. "I can't believe how lucky I am today. This is so special."

Hope turned to Allegra to shoot an eye roll, but Allegra was smiling at their mother in earnest.

???? Hope thought. Allegra seemed *totally into* the mother-daughter-daughter luncheon. It was weird. A month ago, if Grace had suggested this outing, Allegra would have flat-out refused. Or if Grace had guilted or threatened her enough,

she would have sat sullenly at the table and texted the entire time.

Of course, now there was no phone and no one to text.

Grace ordered a glass of white wine, Allegra a Diet Coke, Hope an iced tea. They did a cheers. Grace said, "This is so fun! This is so, so special. Thank you for joining me."

"You don't have to thank us for coming to lunch with you," Allegra said. "You're our mother."

Maybe Allegra is being nice in an attempt to become ungrounded, Hope thought. She was doing such a good job, it might actually work.

Grace ordered the gazpacho and the Gruyère-and-spring-onion omelet. Allegra ordered the lobster salad. Hope ordered the mixed greens with blueberries and goat cheese, and a side of fries. They were seated with a view overlooking the white beach, the lifeguard stand, the blue, green, and yellow umbrellas of Cliffside, and the placid blue water of Nantucket Sound. Sailboats dotted the horizon, and the steamship cut its way over to Hyannis. A breeze lifted the lip of the awning.

"As I'm sure you probably know," Grace said, "the *Boston Globe* is coming to do a photo shoot and feature article on our garden next week. So Benton will be around a lot to help me get the garden ready."

Allegra said, "Benton who?"

"Mom's gardener," Hope said. "He's the one who gave me *Lolita.*"

"I really like that book," Allegra said. "I mean, it's disturbing, but it's holding my interest. What are you reading, Hope?"

Hope said, "*House of Mirth,* Edith Wharton."

Grace said, "I read that a million years ago, during my freshman year at Holyoke."

"Maybe I'll read that next," Allegra said.

Hope thought, *Where's my sister?*

They ordered a brownie sundae with three spoons, and Grace got a cappuccino and the check. As Grace paid the bill, Allegra nudged Hope under the table. Mrs. Kraft, their English teacher, was headed straight for them.

"Look at the lovely Pancik ladies lunching," Mrs. Kraft said. She beamed at the table.

Grace stood up and gave Mrs. Kraft an air kiss. "Hello, Ruth."

Hope wondered if she and Allegra would be expected to greet Mrs. Kraft in such a manner. Air kiss her English teacher? She couldn't bring herself to do anything but wave. Ruth Kraft—all the kids called her Ruthie behind her back— had a cumulus cloud of frizzy brown hair. She had been trained as an opera singer, and her classroom trademark was to belt out those phrases to which she wanted to give emphasis. Allegra, especially, liked to imitate her.

Shall I compare theeeeeeeeee to a summer's daaaaaaaaaay!

Mrs. Kraft had given Allegra a D, but there was Allegra, beaming an angelic smile anyway, saying, "Hiya, Mrs. Kraft!"

Mrs. Kraft said, "And how's our *summer* going?" Something about the way she sang it out made it sound like she was fishing for information. Was it possible that *Mrs. Kraft* had heard about Allegra getting caught drinking and smoking pot while modeling her underwear for Ian Coburn? If Mrs. Kraft knew, then it was official: *everyone* knew. Had Mrs. Kraft *seen the photo?* Hope felt seriously bad for her sister. News like

that would quickly make its way around the faculty room in the fall, and Allegra would have no one to ask for letters of recommendation. Last week, Hope would have found this gratifying. But now, she and Allegra were like the Corsican Brothers; someone kicked Allegra in the shin, and Hope felt the pain.

"The girls were just talking about all the books they've been reading," Grace said.

"Speaking of reading!" Mrs. Kraft said. She turned her attention now to Grace. "Have you heard about the new Madeline King novel? It's supposed to be quite scandalous."

"I haven't heard a thing," Grace said. And with a hand motion like the one Father Declan used at Mass, she indicated that the girls should both stand up. "I've been busy with the garden and the hens."

"I just figured you would know about it," Mrs. Kraft said. "Since you and Madeline are such close friends."

"Actually," Grace said, "Madeline and I aren't speaking at the moment."

This seemed to throw Mrs. Kraft for a loop-de-loop. She answered in a normal speaking voice. "Oh, I'm so sorry... open mouth, insert espadrille. I should never have brought it up."

Grace smiled ruefully and fiddled with the clasp of her purse. "Probably not."

Hope studied her mother. She wasn't *speaking* to Madeline? This was outrageous news, so outrageous that Hope thought her mother was lying—but then she realized that there *had* been an absence the past week or so; her mother hadn't been locked in her study on the phone with Madeline, like she usually was. Was it because of what had happened

between Allegra and Brick? Or was it because Grace was so engrossed by Benton and the garden? Every once in a while, it occurred to Hope that her mother was a human being with her own complicated set of emotions. She wondered if Grace and Madeline had had a fight, like Allegra and Hollis. But weren't Grace and Madeline too *old* for that kind of behavior?

Hope shifted her weight. She wanted to tell Mrs. Kraft to buzz off, go sing her arias or recite her sonnets, leave their mother alone. As if sharing this very same thought, Allegra spoke up.

"It was nice to see you, Mrs. Kraft. Enjoy your lunch."

"Oh," Mrs. Kraft said. She seemed so taken aback by this polite rebuff from her worst student that she wobbled on the wedge heels of her espadrilles. "Yes, thank you, I will."

Hope gave Mrs. Kraft a second little wave—this one of farewell—and followed her mother and sister out of the restaurant.

GRACE

Nantucket had a week of heat, and when Grace said *heat* she meant temperatures in the high eighties and low nineties. It was hot enough that the girls would come home from their volunteer jobs and jump right into the pool and Grace would stay inside with the central air-conditioning cranked unless she was tending the chickens or Benton was around.

Benton came only for a perfunctory hour, and he was all business. He couldn't stay for lunch or for any other reason. His other gardens were *in crisis,* he said.

Because of the heat.

Then the heat broke, and they got two and a half days of relentless, pounding rain.

On the first rainy day, Benton texted: *Not coming today. Staying home to catch up on paperwork.*

Grace curled up in bed and fought off a migraine. Was she really going to consider leaving Eddie for this man?

The second day, he texted, *Not coming today. Doing bills. BTW, I have a substantial one for Eddie, you might want to warn him?*

Migraine. Grace thought, *Not coming today to see the woman you love, or your pet project; sending Eddie a substantial bill,* which would send Eddie through the roof. He was still complaining about Hester Phan's fee, and when Grace had broached the matter of Madeline and Trevor's fifty thousand dollars, Eddie had glared at Grace and said, *Honestly, Grace, what do you think I do all day?*

Madeline hadn't responded to Grace's voice mail, and Grace began to worry that she'd done further damage to the relationship. She went back and forth between believing that Madeline *was* writing a novel about her and Benton — *Two of the women at this table will betray the person on their left* — and thinking that it was just a bad rumor cooked up by Blond Sharon.

But then Ruth Kraft mentioned Madeline's book, and Grace wondered how ditzy Ruth Kraft would have found out about it?

It must be true?

It couldn't be true. Madeline would never, *ever* do that, no matter how angry she was.

Would she?

If it were true, Grace would…she would…well, she would be so mad that she couldn't fathom *what* she would do. She had shared everything with Madeline in confidence! They had been friends for nearly twenty years!

Madeline would never, Grace decided. It was just a rumor.

Unless Madeline was exacting some kind of revenge.

Allegra is a cheater, and you, Grace, are a cheater.

What Madeline clearly didn't understand was that Grace was in *love*. There was *nothing* she could do about it!

The pain in her head descended, pressure like a lead helmet, squeezing, squeezing, crushing her skull. She was in love; she was dying to talk to Madeline and get the mess sorted out, but really, Grace wanted only Benton.

On a trip to the bathroom — the only reason she rose from bed — she stared out the window at her soggy backyard.

A garden was no good in the rain.

Happiness restored. The sun came out. Benton returned with a big smile and a ferocious appetite for Grace. He loved her again. The big day was nearly upon them.

Lawn mowed and trimmed, beds weeded, roses blooming, perennial bed freshly mulched, daylilies deadheaded, pool skimmed, chaises arranged with pillows plumped, grill scrubbed, deck swept, canvas umbrella cleaned, Adirondack chairs wiped down, hammock tightened. Together, Benton and Grace walked every inch of the property, clipping blos-

soms for an arrangement, smoothing imperfections in the white shell driveway, filling the bird feeders.

"It's ready," Benton said. He kissed Grace deeply up against the side of his truck. "I'll see you tomorrow."

Clara Teasdale, the *Boston Globe*'s home-and-garden editor, and Big George, a *Globe* staff photographer, arrived in a car driven by Bernie Wu. Bernie and Grace were friendly because Bernie Wu's daughter, Chloe, played the flute in the student orchestra with Hope. Apparently, Bernie felt comfortable enough in his friendship with Grace that he showed up forty-five minutes early and bypassed the front door. He walked Clara and Big George around the side of the house, to the backyard. He had stopped at the henhouse and pointed at each chicken, indiscriminately naming them, "Martha, Dolly, Eleanor, Ladybird, Hillary." Bernie Wu's wife was a big fan of Grace's eggs and was good for five dozen a month.

Clara laughed at the names. "First ladies," she said.

Grace and Benton were making fast, furious love in the garden shed, Grace clinging to Benton, wanting him farther and farther inside of her, wanting to become him. He thrilled her, he challenged her, he was her great big shining sun.

Grace heard what she thought were voices. Then, she clearly heard a female voice say, *First ladies.* She pulled away from Benton. "They're here."

"Already?" Benton said. He checked his watch. "Forty-five minutes early?"

Silently, they adjusted their clothes. Grace tried to smooth

the wrinkles out of her pale-pink linen shift. "You ready?" she asked.

Benton nodded, and Grace swung open the door to the shed and stepped out to greet their visitors. Grace noted the confused expression on Bernie's face when Benton followed her out. He was, at least, holding a rake and a clipboard.

Bernie then started speaking very quickly. Grace could tell he was nervous, but whether that was because he had over-stepped his bounds by barging into the backyard or because he realized he had interrupted something, she wasn't sure. Maybe he was just impressed by Clara and Big George and by the idea of Grace and Eddie's yard being featured in the *Boston Globe.* Grace hoped that was it, and she endeavored to set everything back to normal while continuously smoothing the front of her dress. She tried not to think of Benton's hands lifting it.

"Well, I'm off," Bernie said. "I'll be back here to pick you up at twelve thirty." He gave Grace a smile of what seemed like genuine good luck, and she waved. Big George was already at the far edge of the property, shooting a stream of photos of the Adirondack chairs and the placid blue surface of Polpis Harbor beyond, framed by Grace's blue lace hydrangeas.

Clara Teasdale was smitten with the yard and probably also with Benton, who was taking enormous pride in showing off his favorite features—the rocks of the streambed, the perennials, the roses, which were luscious enough to eat. The entire property was *showing off.* Benton lingered by the bench that held the potted ferns, and he described how he'd found the only Parisian antiques dealer wise enough to salvage the old benches from the Jardin des Tuileries.

Grace took over with Clara when it was time to talk about the hens. She even let Clara harvest half a dozen pale-blue eggs from the nesting boxes, despite the ladies' clucking disapproval at a stranger performing this task. Grace then threw open the door to the garden shed and listened to Clara *oooh* and *ahhh* over Grace's collection of watering cans and the high polish of the copper sink and the practicality yet allure of the soapstone countertop.

Big George snapped photos in a constant, clicking stream.

Grace showed off the riding mower in its alcove, then Big George asked Grace if she wouldn't mind bringing it out to the middle of the emerald-green grass and perching upon it in her pink linen sheath.

Clickclickclick.

As the hour wore on, there were suggestions of other fanciful photos—one of Benton amid the roses, brandishing the largest set of clippers, one of Grace standing ankle deep in the shallow end of her pool, and one of both Benton and Grace hanging from their arms from the branch of the big elm.

Then it was time for lunch. They hadn't discussed lunch as part of the shoot, but, nevertheless, Grace had gone all out. She'd made six kinds of tea sandwich—egg salad, naturally; cucumber and herbed cream cheese; radish and sweet butter; curried chicken salad; roast beef with horseradish mayo; and ham and baby Swiss. She had also bought three cartons of big, fat strawberries, and she'd made meringues and fresh lime curd.

Big George snapped photos of the food, and Grace was tickled.

She pulled a bottle of Schramsberg rosé sparkling wine

from Eddie's wine cellar, and, using Grace's ten-inch chef's knife, Benton sabered off the top. The cork landed in the day-lily bed, and everyone cheered. Grace, Benton, and Clara sat for the lunch, and they posed for Big George. Grace fed Benton a strawberry. Clara overfilled her champagne flute and drowned her ham and Swiss. Grace made Big George a plate piled high with sandwiches, and when he stopped to eat, Grace stole his camera and took pictures of him stuffing his face.

Benton said to George, "Are you a Stones fan, man?"

George said, "Isn't everybody?"

Benton plugged his phone into the outdoor speaker and played "Loving Cup." He poured the last of the sparkling wine between Grace's and Clara's glasses.

Benton said, "This has sort of been the theme song of our summer."

Clara said, "I can honestly say I've never had this much fun at a shoot before."

Grace agreed. It was *fun*. She envisioned life with Benton being this playful, this sensuous and carefree, every single day.

As Clara finished her wine, she ran through the notes she'd taken, aloud: *Benton, Ohio State grounds-crew work-study job; Surrey, England; passion for roses; Savannah, Oxford, the Nantucket Historical Association.*

Clara looked up and narrowed her eyes. "How did you find Grace?"

Benton gave Grace a look that could only be described as filled with love. "She found me," he said.

Clickclickclick.

NANTUCKET

Many of us knew the Pancik property would be featured in Sunday's *Boston Globe,* but others were taken by surprise as we stirred cream and sugar into our freshly brewed coffee and opened our newspapers. However, even those of us who knew to expect the article were astonished by what we saw. For starters, the article was entitled *Nantucket's Private Eden.* And the first photo—BAM! larger than life and in full color—was of Grace Pancik feeding Benton Coe a fat, delectable strawberry.

Whoa!

The caption read: *Homeowner Grace Pancik enjoys an alfresco luncheon with landscape architect Benton Coe, owner of Coe Designs.*

The article read: *Some matches are made in heaven, such as the one between Nantucket resident Grace Pancik and Benton Coe, the man she hired to design and execute the landscaping of her three-acre property in Wauwinet.*

Whoa!

Followed by a few paragraphs of background on Benton: impressive, but nothing we didn't already know.

Followed by a few paragraphs of background on Grace: *Mrs. Pancik was a French-literature major at Mount Holyoke College, which explains her fondness for the garden bench salvaged from the Jardin des Tuileries that is said to date back to the age of Louis XIV, Colbert, and the renowned Parisian landscape architect André Le Nôtre. This exact bench used to grace a long terrace, overlooking the Seine, called the Terrasse du*

Bord-de-l'Eau and most likely provided respite for the likes of Auguste Renoir and Claude Monet after a tiring visit to the nearby Louvre. Such vivid historical details thrill Mrs. Pancik and fuel her romantic imagination.

Mrs. Pancik is also passionate about her daylily bed, which she planted as a tribute to her beloved, now-deceased grandmother, Sabine Roddin-Baste, who kept an estate in Wayland with an apple orchard and a croquet lawn.

"My grandmother Sabine adored daylilies," Mrs. Pancik said. "She was the one who fostered my deep appreciation for green spaces."

Followed by a photo collage: Grace aboard a riding mower, looking not unlike a queen upon a throne; Grace and Benton hanging side by side from a branch like children on a playground; Grace drinking from a flute of champagne as Benton gazed upon her; Grace wading in the shallow end of her pool; Benton standing in the rose bed with a gargantuan pair of clippers; one of the hens—Martha or Dolly—strutting in the yard; and the inside of the garden shed, copper farmer's sink gleaming like a new penny. The sign above the sink read: *A garden is not a matter of life or death. It is far more important than that.*

Followed by paragraphs about how Grace and Benton collaborated on every aspect of the yard in their attempt to create different "moments." The pool and hot tub, tiled in bottle green and surrounded by antique pavers and real Nantucket cobblestones, made one feel that one had happened across a swimming hole in the woods. The rolling green lawn encouraged a stroll toward the Adirondack chairs, set where one could simultaneously hear the stream that ran

along the back of the Pancik property and see the sailboats on Polpis Harbor. Suspended between two-hundred-year-old elms was a hammock where Mrs. Pancik often relaxed as she read Victor Hugo and Alexandre Dumas within full view of the glorious rose bed, featuring twenty-two varieties of rose.

"But the essence of what we were trying to accomplish," Coe says, *"is embodied in the garden shed."*

Mrs. Pancik agrees. *"That's really our baby,"* she says.

Jody Rouisse called Susan Prendergast. "I, for one, think it's disgusting," she said. "I mean, is it not *obvious* to *everyone on earth* that those two are lovers? She was *feeding* him."

"Like Adam and Eve in the garden," Susan said. "Do you think the writer had inside information?"

"There was no mention of Eddie," Jody said. "I mean, they referred to her as Mrs. Pancik, but it was like Eddie and the twins didn't exist."

"I have to say, the way Benton is looking at her in that one photo is pretty hot," Susan said. "I wish someone would look at *me* like that."

"I thought the mention of the bench from the Tuileries was pretentious. And Grace reads Victor Hugo in the hammock?" Jody said. "It's probably more like *Cosmo*."

"She *was* a French-literature major," Susan said. "I hear her library is stacked with first editions."

"Well, what about Grace calling the garden shed their 'baby'?" Jody said. "You know, Jean Burton *thought* she

looked pregnant. I think there's a good chance that shed isn't the only baby."

"Her roses are absolutely incredible," Susan said. "You have to give her that."

"Fine," Jody said. "I'll give her that."

Dr. Andy McMann saw the paper first. Normally, he savored the solitude of his Sunday mornings. Calgary slept late, and Rachel slept even later. This allowed Dr. Andy to sit out on his deck, enjoy the sunshine and the breeze, drink his coffee, eat his lightly buttered rye toast and half a ripe avocado, listen to Schubert, and read the *Globe*. He usually skipped the Home & Garden section, but his eye happened to catch a glimpse of the word *Nantucket,* and he checked to see what it was all about.

Grace Pancik's yard. Some hotshot landscaper. Dr. Andy read the article and studied the pictures, and a feeling of distinct discomfort started at the base of his spine and traveled up to his neck. His landlord, Eddie Pancik, was being cuckolded by this Coe fellow—that much was obvious! Dr. Andy was hesitant to awaken Rachel for any reason, but this, he felt, couldn't wait. He carried the newspaper up to their bedroom.

Alicia Buckler, a title examiner for the Town of Nantucket, was reading the *Globe* while standing in line, waiting for a table at Black-Eyed Susan's, along with the rest of the world.

She turned to her wife Janice, and pointed at the photo of Grace and Benton hanging from the tree branch.

"I think we've both been working too hard," Alicia said. "We should take a vacation and goof off like these people."

Janice gasped. "That's Grace Pancik!" she said. "And Benton Coe."

Alicia thrust the paper at Janice in frustration. She was *sick and tired* of the way Janice seemed to know everyone on the island just because she cleaned their teeth. And she was fed up with their Sunday routine of eating at Black-Eyed Susan's. Every week, an hour of their day was wasted by waiting in line. Alicia pined for the olden days, when one could get breakfast at the Jared Coffin House, but if she brought this up, Janice would call her an old fuddy-duddy, and they would start to fight. Alicia was eight months older than Janice, and she was sensitive about it.

"Enjoy your tofu Benedict," Alicia said. "I'm going home."

But Janice didn't hear. She was too engrossed in the article.

Glenn Daley rolled over and nearly crushed Barbie. They were lying in bed, drinking mimosas and reading the paper. Glenn had been with a lot of women, but never had he enjoyed creature comforts like good champagne and five-hundred-thread-count sheets and fresh flowers by the bed the way he did with Barbie. And she smelled delicious, even when she first woke up. He didn't like to think that he was falling in love—his wife had ruined love for him forever—but he sure

as hell didn't want to be doing anything else or be with anyone else on this Sunday morning.

"Look at this," Glenn said, showing Barbie the paper.
"Your sister-in-law."

"Good God," Barbie said.

EDDIE

As the terrible old cliché goes: *When it rains, it pours.*

On Friday afternoon, Eddie received not one but two disturbing phone calls. One was from Madeline and Trevor's
attorney, Layton Gray, and one was from Philip Meier, at the
bank.

Layton was calling about the investment of fifty thousand
dollars. His clients were very upset, Layton said, and they
wanted their money back. Eddie and Layton had worked
together on countless real-estate deals. Eddie not only considered Layton a good guy; he considered him a sort-of friend,
and so what bothered Eddie most about the message was
Layton's tone of voice. It was litigious and smoothly distant,
with no hint that Layton even *knew* Eddie, much less had
thrown a few back with him at the bar at the Great Harbor
Yacht Club.

"Please call me to discuss," Layton said, "before I have to
take legal action."

Legal action? Eddie didn't think there were grounds for
legal action. It had been a good-faith investment. Madeline

and Trevor had written a check, and Eddie had promised them double back—a hundred grand—once he sold the houses. He had made a photocopy of the check and written across the bottom of the page, *Llewellyn investment in Eagle Wing Lane,* and then the three of them had signed the paper, which Eddie again copied, giving the original to Madeline and Trevor and keeping the copy for himself.

Nothing legal, nothing binding. A good-faith investment between friends.

And yet, the words *good faith* gnawed at him. He couldn't default on this. He had to keep up his end of the bargain. And he certainly didn't want Layton Gray to think that he, Eddie, had taken his friends' money and sunk it into a losing proposition. Layton did eight to ten real-estate closings a week; he dealt with every agency on Nantucket. If word about this got out...no, Eddie couldn't allow that to happen. He was *livid* that Madeline had called Layton; frankly, a part of him couldn't believe she'd actually done it. Lawyers cost money. If she had called, she was serious.

He tried to calculate a way to get Madeline and Trevor at least a portion of their investment back. Once he closed the deal with Glenn Daley (even thinking the man's name gave Eddie heartburn), he might be able to put aside ten thousand dollars for the Llewellyns.

Maybe?

Yes, he would do that.

Then, Philip Meier had called and told Eddie that he was ninety days behind on the mortgage for his house.

"Wait a minute," Eddie said. "That's not right...?"

"Ninety-two days, actually," Philip said. "You're in arrears twenty-seven thousand, eight hundred and ten dollars."

Eddie heart went up in flames, a sudden bonfire. "That can't be right!"

"It is right," Philip said. "We sent several notices to your office address."

Eddie eyed the pile of unopened envelopes on his desk — some new, some older, probably as old as three months.

"Am I going to lose the house?" he asked. He pictured Grace and the girls standing out on the front lawn in their pajamas while bank officials barred the front door.

"I need a check by Monday," Philip said.

Monday? Eddie thought. Where was he going to get twenty-seven large by Monday? Then he remembered that Nightbill was checking in on Monday and that Bugsy Greer had agreed to pay in full, in cash — eighty-four thousand dollars. Thirty-five of that would go to the girls, forty-nine of that would be split between him and Barbie. But Barbie didn't know that Eddie had upped the price, so he would have to cash her out at only seventeen-five, leaving him thirty-one-five!

Brilliant.

He said to Philip, "I can have it to you first thing Tuesday morning. In cash."

"Cash?" Philip said. "What are you planning on doing? Robbing a bank?"

They both laughed.

Philip said, "Tuesday morning is fine. Thanks, Eddie."

Eddie was buoyed by his victory, but he knew it was only a quick fix. He needed something big. He needed something

real. Where were all the buyers? Nadia had brought in the man she'd been sleeping with from Kasper Snacks, saying he was interested in buying a house. Eddie had nearly fainted with relief. Here was a benefit to the side business he hadn't anticipated—the girls would encourage buyers. But, as it had turned out, Nadia's special friend had been too midwestern, with no clue what investing in the Nantucket real-estate market would cost him. He'd taken one gander at the prices and decided to buy Nadia an ice cream instead.

Eddie spent Saturday in the office. There was nothing going on, and so he finished the paperwork for the deal with Glenn Daley. He stopped for a drink at Lola on the way home, despite the fact that martinis cost twenty bucks. He probably needed to be out more so he could meet people and hand out his business card, but being out cost money that he just didn't have. On the way home from Lola, he drove past the houses on Eagle Wing Lane. He could practically see himself, crushed like the Wicked Witch of the East, under the foundation of number 9. He couldn't bear to think of how happy and excited he'd been the day he'd closed on those three lots.

On Sunday morning, Grace was up and out of bed at six o'clock—off to the Hub to grab the Sunday *Boston Globe.* She was so excited to see the article that Eddie thought she might spontaneously combust. He tried to feel excited as well, but he was too consumed with worry that the beautiful property she loved so much might be repossessed.

He slept until nine thirty, a sure sign that he was depressed. When he woke up, the twins were out by the pool, reading.

"Where's Mommy?" Eddie said.

"Upstairs in her office," Hope said. "On the phone."

Eddie set about making scrambled eggs with dollops of cream cheese stirred in, the one breakfast dish that actually seemed to help his heartburn. He used nine fresh eggs, which was probably too many, but what the hell, the eggs were free.

Grace came down from her study, beaming. "Do you want to see the article?" she asked. "It's magnificent."

"Sure," Eddie said. "Since I paid for it."

"Okay," Grace said. "I tried to show it to the girls, but they weren't interested."

"Shocker," Eddie said.

Grace said, "The photographs were all staged, so don't get jealous."

"Jealous?" Eddie said.

"Of Benton, silly!" Grace said. She opened the newspaper flat across the sexiest countertop in the world to show the front-page photo of Grace feeding Benton a strawberry. NANTUCKET'S PRIVATE EDEN, the headline read.

"Nice," Eddie said. The photo was a tad suggestive of ... well, exactly *what,* Eddie wasn't sure. Maybe he *should* feel jealous? He looked at the other photos — Grace on the mower, Grace in the pool, Grace and Benton hanging from the elm tree like a couple of capuchin monkeys.

"Go ahead and read it," she said.

"I'll read it later," Eddie said. "I promise." The article was *long,* and Eddie didn't really have the attention span to delve into such an endeavor right then. His brain hurt. He was hungry for his eggs. He was happy that Grace was happy. She'd gotten what she'd wanted. The article was some kind of quest that she'd successfully completed. Eddie wished his life were like that. Instead, it felt as if he were standing nuts deep in icy

water, panning for nuggets of gold that he would either spend or lose, necessitating more panning. Endless panning.

He looked at the photograph of Grace feeding Benton again, but instead of feeling jealous, he merely felt intrigued. Benton Coe was a successful businessman. Did *he* have any money he would like to invest in number 13?

Eddie plated his pillowy, soft eggs and carried them out to the deck. With the first bite, he closed his eyes, and there he envisioned Benton Coe as some kind of prince who might save them all.

MADELINE

When Madeline saw the article in the *Boston Globe,* she thought to herself, almost involuntarily, *Grace and Benton look so happy.*

She wasn't sure if it was the article that inspired her, but for the first time in her writing career, Madeline didn't have a single hesitation when it came to ending her book. She felt like Gretchen Green, girl hero, swooping in to set things right. First, there was heightened drama and conflict: G's husband, Renfrew, discovers G's affair by checking her cell phone records. (As Madeline understood it, this was how most adulterers got caught, but she knew Grace would never get caught this way, because Grace barely used her cell phone.) When the affair is uncovered, G leaves her husband and runs away with B. They move to St. John, U.S. Virgin Islands, where B

has been commissioned to build an enormous compound of villas overlooking Honeymoon Beach. G takes up bird-watching, which aligns with her newfound sense of freedom. She feels like she has wings.

Madeline set down her pen and took a deep, cleansing breath. The book was done. Not only did Madeline know that Angie would love it—she knew that it was good.

EDDIE

When he walked into the office Monday morning, Barbie was already at her desk, with two coffees from the Handlebar Café and the newspaper open in front of her.

"Sit," she said.

He didn't like her telling him what to do, but something about her tone made him obey.

Maybe she was going to confess to her relationship with Glenn Daley.

She handed him his coffee, loaded with milk.

She nodded at the newspaper. "You see this?"

It was the article about the garden, open to the picture of Grace feeding Benton the strawberry.

"Yeah," Eddie said, shrugging. "Grace said the photographs were all staged."

"That's what Grace says," Barbie said. "But everyone else on this island says that you're paying this guy to screw your wife."

"Speaking of screwing," Eddie said, "how is Glenn?"

"Don't change the subject," Barbie said. "You need to get your house in order. I'm serious, Ed. You need to deal with this."

Eddie eyed his sister and saw the same girl with the bad perm and too much eyeliner fighting with Teresa Maniscalco outside the high school library because Teresa told everyone in school that the girls' locker room reeked like Barbie's vagina. Eddie could remember hearing the phrase *reeked like Barbie's vagina* and feeling mortified. He wanted to defend his sister's honor, but he'd never been good at facing up to his problems—he was too scrawny. He'd only ever been good at running away from them.

Barbie, afraid of no one, fought it out with Teresa Maniscalco, busted Teresa's lip open with one punch, and promptly took a three-day suspension. Eddie had walked past the main office, and he saw Barbie through the Plexiglas window, slumped in a chair, her arms crossed over her chest, glowering with pure steel resolve. He thought, *My sister is the toughest person in the world.* Way tougher than Eddie himself.

After that, nobody messed with Barbie. She worked her ass off and was accepted to Boston University, where she favored peasant blouses and learned to read tarot. After she graduated, she followed Eddie to Nantucket. Her first job was working as a personal assistant to a very wealthy woman with a summer estate on Abrams Point—and Barbie absorbed the lifestyle like a sponge. Which wine, which fork, which flowers. She learned about crystal and art dealers and the neighborhoods of Manhattan and Paris. Eddie could not *believe* her transformation. Maybe he didn't know shit from Shinola, but Barbie presented herself to the world as an

elegant and refined woman. And then, of course, she'd always had the sixth sense. That was the thing.

"Okay," he said. "Fine."

He reasoned with himself the whole way home. Grace was *not* having an affair with Benton Coe. It might have been a school-girl crush—Grace enjoyed having someone to talk to about her hens and her flowers—but Grace didn't have it *in* her to have an affair, Eddie didn't think. She was too programmed to be *good*—instilled in her from childhood by her grand-mother, her parents, her older brothers. Rebellion for her, Eddie knew, had been drinking tequila and smoking cigarettes—on the *same night,* on a *Tuesday!*—during her sophomore year at Holyoke. An affair in adulthood would be unthinkable.

Right?

Eddie's heartburn ratcheted up from the mellow 3 it had been that morning to a 7 and then an 8. And then, when he pulled into the driveway and saw Benton's big black pickup truck, it became a 9.

Eddie busted into the house. "Grace!" he called. He raced up the stairs two at a time—Fast Eddie—and barged into the master bedroom. Empty. Then he swung open the door of Grace's study without knocking—something he was forbid-den to do, because that study was her sanctuary, she said—but the study, too, was empty.

Eddie calmed down a bit. He had let Barbie poison his thoughts. Grace and Benton would be out in the garden, weeding and mulching and making plans to build an outdoor

shower with doors fashioned out of shutters salvaged from a French farmhouse. And climbing roses. Grace had forever wanted roses in her outdoor shower.

See? He did listen!

Eddie went through the kitchen and out onto the deck.

"Grace!" he called.

The backyard was uninhabited except by butterflies, bees, birds on the feeders. The garden was shimmering as if in some feverish utopian dream. Eddie walked out to the far edge of the property and plunked down in an Adirondack chair. The views across Polpis Harbor at this time of year were dazzling. He was a lucky man. Just like Barbie, he had come a long way since the days of Purchase Street in New Bedford.

He stood up. Where was Grace?

He wandered back over the rolling green lawn, past the hammock and the rose bed, past the swimming pool, past the perennials. He stopped at the five-foot angel statue and said, "Where's Grace?"

The statue didn't answer. It just stood there with the same inane, placid half-smile it always offered. Eddie had paid five figures for the statue. For that much money, it should respond when spoken to. He laughed at himself. Barbie was such a pill. She put thoughts into his head, and now he was losing his mind, talking to stone figures.

Then, Eddie saw the shed.

The garden shed.

He heard Barbie's voice: *You need to get your house in order.*

He tried the knob. Locked. Why would the door to the garden shed be *locked?* He pressed his ear to the door. He could hear noises—breathing, he thought, and movement.

He knocked on the door. "Benton, you're all done here, as of right now." He cleared his throat. "You're *done,* and I will not be paying your final bill. You've taken more from me than I owe you. Now, I'm leaving, and you will leave right after me, and you will never come back."

With that, Eddie turned and headed around the side of the house, into the driveway, past the black pickup, into his Cayenne. He felt preternaturally calm as well as proud of himself for his restraint. He had handled the situation admirably, he thought. Even Grace's grandmother Sabine might have approved. There was no messy confrontation, no fistfight; there were no screamed accusations or denials.

Down the road a couple hundred yards, Eddie pulled off into the parking lot of Polpis Harbor, and he waited. By the time he counted to ten, Benton's truck drove past. So Eddie was right. They had been in the locked garden shed together. They had been . . . Here, Eddie broke down. He didn't *cry,* exactly — he never cried — but his breathing changed. Grace, his Grace, whom he had first set eyes on as she served blueberry pancakes at the Morning Glory Café. She hadn't struck him as beautiful so much as wholesome. She had those big, brown, innocent eyes and a perfect smile. When she got embarrassed, the tops of her ears turned pink. She was the kind of girl Eddie had always wanted to marry, the kind who would put home and family first.

And she had. Until that summer. Or, possibly, last summer? How long had this thing with Benton been going on? Eddie couldn't bear to know. He realized he wasn't perfect, he realized he was so obsessed with making money that he'd let everything else fall to Grace. She did the housework and

prepared all the scrumptious meals, she did the shopping and took care of the girls. She'd gotten angry once and asked Eddie if he even knew what *grade* the twins were in. He had become indignant and said, *Of course I do, they're in third grade!* But the answer had been fourth grade, and Grace had said to him, *I'm never going to tell them you got it wrong, because they will be devastated. But really, Eddie, make an effort!*

He had tried harder after that. He showed up at Allegra's Thanksgiving play and Hope's flute concerts, even when it meant rescheduling an important showing. He had taken Allegra to New York City for the modeling interview, but Grace had been angry about that, too, saying that Eddie expended energy on the girls only when there was glory to be reflected upon him.

He knew that as a wife, Grace probably wasn't as happy or fulfilled as she might have been. For a long while, she compared herself and Eddie with Madeline and Trevor—a losing proposition every time. Trevor and Madeline held hands everywhere they went, Trevor bought Madeline flowers, Trevor always referred to Madeline as "my bride" instead of "my wife." Trevor watched romantic comedies with Madeline, and they had taken ballroom-dancing lessons together. Eddie had sneered at the dancing lessons, which had made Grace cry, presumably because Eddie had let her down in the ways she described, and in other ways he couldn't even imagine.

But what good would wallowing in his inadequacies do him?

Eddie collected himself, and then he drove back to work.

* * *

When he walked into the office, Barbie raised an eyebrow at him.

"Handled," he said.

Grace called the office an hour later. Eloise said, "Your wife is on line one."

Eddie said, "Put her through to my voice mail."

At three o'clock, Eloise approached his desk. Gone was her supersweet and helpful manner; that had vanished into thin air a few weeks earlier.

"Edward," she said, "I'd like my paycheck."

"What paycheck?" Eddie said. He paid Eloise every other Friday; she made twenty dollars an hour.

"For last week and this week," she said.

"It's only Monday," Eddie said. "I'll pay you Friday."

"I'd like my paycheck," Eloise said. She was wearing her no-nonsense expression, which scared Eddie a little bit. Eloise's husband was a Coffin; they had four children and thirteen grandchildren and were related to just about everyone. Eddie couldn't really afford to piss Eloise off, but he didn't have sixteen hundred dollars in the office account to give her.

"It's only Monday," Eddie said again. "Do you mind me asking why...?"

"I've gotten myself into a situation," Eloise said. "And I'd like the money today."

"I can give it to you tomorrow," Eddie said, thinking of Nightbill. "In cash."

"That won't work," Eloise said. "I need it now."

Eddie couldn't believe the way the women in his life were taking it to him today. It must have been Poop-on-Eddie Day, but nobody had bothered to warn him. He brought out the company checkbook and cut Eloise her check.

"Thank you," Eloise said crisply.

Eddie nodded. If she tried to deposit it today, it would most certainly bounce.

When both Eloise and Barbie were out for lunch, Eddie listened to Grace's voice mail. She said, *Hey, the girls are both home tonight, so I'm going to marinate some rib eyes and roast those fingerlings you like and shuck some corn. I was hoping we could have a nice family dinner…*

Then she dissolved into tears. She bleated out, *I'm so sorry,* and hung up.

Eddie worked until six, and then six became seven. Both Eloise and Barbie left for their lovely little lives outside of work. Eloise had her check tucked safely in her purse, no doubt, and was off to deal with her "situation."

At ten after seven, Eddie's cell phone rang, and he figured it would be Grace, asking when he would be home for dinner. As lovely as grilled steaks and corn and a good bottle of red wine and the company of his wife and daughters sounded, he

couldn't go that far. He would not be placated by fingerling potatoes when he'd caught his wife sleeping with the gardener! He couldn't just play through as though nothing had happened, as though nothing had changed.

He needed to talk to someone. He needed a friend. He pulled out his phone and dialed the Chief's supersecret cell phone number.

"Hey, Eddie," the Chief said. "How are you?"

"I'm *great,*" Eddie said, a little too enthusiastically. The Chief *had* said Eddie could call if he needed a hand. And Eddie needed one now. He didn't necessarily want to share what had happened; he just wanted another man to talk to. "Are you free tonight? I'd love to meet you somewhere for a drink. How about the Brant Point Grill in twenty minutes?"

"I have plans tonight, Eddie," the Chief said. "Sorry about that."

"You don't have to be *sorry,*" Eddie said. "It's really last minute. I've just had a day. Could you meet me later? Say, around ten?"

If the Chief could meet him at ten, Eddie could grab a burger from Lola and linger until nine fifteen, when he would slip out to 10 Low Beach Road to collect the cash — and then make it to the Brant Point Grill by ten.

"Ten?" the Chief said. "That would put me out past my bedtime. Sorry, Eddie."

"Are you *sure?*" Eddie said. "Nothing I can say to persuade you?" It was embarrassing, supplicating like this, but Eddie was near desperate to connect with someone who had nothing to do with his family or work or his diabolical side business.

"Maybe another time," the Chief said. His tone of voice

was verging on irritated, and Eddie didn't want to be an itch, so he said, "Okay, Chief, no problem." And hung up.

Eddie sat in the office until the sun went down and the room grew dark. Out on the street, Eddie watched people headed out for their delicious summer evenings. Groups of teenagers loped toward the Juice Bar for ice cream sundaes; parents pushed strollers to the playground at Children's Beach. Couples held hands on their way to dinner at Oran Mor or the Club Car. How Eddie would have loved to be picking up Grace and taking her to dinner at the Club Car. They could have ordered the caviar, which was served with an icy shot of vodka. Afterward, they could have sung at the piano bar. He would even have sprung for the twenty bucks it would have taken to get Ryan to sing "Tiny Dancer." He would have done it for Grace. She loved Elton John.

He was so…lonely. But he didn't have to be. He could go home for dinner. He could go next door to Lola, get himself a martini and a burger and maybe hand out some business cards.

In the dark, the office was downright gloomy. His depleted empire.

Eddie finally turned on a light. He forced himself to go through the pile of unpaid bills on his desk. There, on top, was a bill for twenty-four hundred dollars from Hester Phan. Her success bonus.

That did it. Eddie felt as if he were falling into a fiery pit of anger and indignation. Success bonus, his ass! He picked up the phone and made the call he'd been wanting to make all day.

*   *   *

After Benton left the office, Eddie drove out to Low Beach Road. He was still shaking. *Grace Grace Grace.* He'd come so close to losing her. Eddie tried not to regret what he'd just done, but a part of him wished he had just gone home. He thought about Grace coating the rib-eye steaks with her magic marinade. He pictured her drizzling the fingerling potatoes with olive oil, sprinkling them with sea salt and coarsely ground pepper, and shucking some Bartlett's Farm corn. Both Hope and Allegra would still be in bathing suits, lying in chaises side by side at the pool, reading. When Grace called them to set the table, they would dutifully rise to go help. They would even pick up their towels and deposit them in the outdoor hamper, where they belonged. Then Hope would go to the silverware drawer, and Allegra would pull out four plates. Together, they would head out to the deck.

Eddie would pull a great vintage of Ponzi pinot noir from his cellar. Grace would be so happy with his choice that she would raise her face to him for a kiss.

When he got home tonight, Eddie decided, he and Grace would have a talk. They would start fresh. No more Benton Coe. And, for his part, Eddie would give up 10 Low Beach Road. He couldn't ask Grace to end her affair until he cleaned up his own dirty mess. This week was it. The end. He would meet with his accountant, Frank, and they would decide which of Eddie's two commercial properties to put on the market. Even with the mortgages, he could probably still clear a decent profit.

Money couldn't buy happiness — except when it could.

He would figure it out. He just had to take care of this one last thing.

*   *   *

At ten minutes to ten, Eddie was sitting in his Cayenne outside 10 Low Beach Road. The air-conditioning in the car was on, but not the radio. Eddie had a cold bottle of water and a container of cherry Tums in the console. His hands were shaking.

A car pulled up behind his — Nadia's Jeep — and Nadia and the other girls climbed out. Their hair was piled into high confections, with curled tendrils framing their faces. Their makeup was thick and bright; it reminded Eddie of icing on a cake. They wore short skirts and teetered in stilettos. They were giggling and teasing one another in Russian. They seemed…happy, bordering on joyful, and Eddie tried to let the sound of their voices soothe his hot, aching conscience. These young women were here to prostitute themselves, but at least they seemed to be enjoying it. Or maybe what Eddie was witnessing was bravado or giddy anticipation of what they might consider "easy money." After all, it was better than cleaning toilets, right? Less demeaning? Eddie had no idea how the girls viewed it. In his heart, he knew this whole business was repugnant. Eddie's parents would be *so ashamed* that it pained Eddie to think of it. He wished Barbie had offered to come with him tonight. But she never offered. She just sat at her desk with her pens and notepads from the exotic hotels where she met Glenn Daley, and she waited for Eddie to hand over her portion of the cash.

"I'll leave my cell on," Barbie had said before she left work. "In case you need to call me."

"I don't see any reason why I would need to call you," Eddie had said. He wondered if Barbie had had a bad premonition about tonight or if she'd checked the tarot cards or tea

leaves or her goddamned crystal ball. But when he asked her, she said, "No, no, I'm saying, just *in case.*"

Whatever that meant.

When the girls saw Eddie, they erupted in cheerful greetings. *Eddie Eddie Eddie hi hi hi.* Nadia kissed him on the cheek, leaving, he was sure, fat, juicy lip prints. Elise and Gabrielle linked their arms through his, and, although he desperately wanted to disengage himself, he couldn't risk offending them or dampening their moods. He tried to tell himself that the girls were merely going to entertain the gentlemen in residence. Nadia would juggle; Julia would sing "Send in the Clowns"; Elise and Gabrielle would be a third and fourth in bridge.

Together, the six of them approached the side door of 10 Low Beach Road. The girls were quiet as Eddie knocked — two raps, then one.

A very tall, lean man with crooked teeth opened the door. This was Bugsy. He was wearing a blue T-shirt, jeans, and a Minnesota Twins baseball hat. He looked slightly less terrifying than he had on the Internet.

"Greetings!" he said. He opened the door wide and ushered them all inside.

Eddie let the girls precede him, and then he, too, entered. The side door led right into the humongous gourmet kitchen, which was lit only by ivory pillar candles. Set out on the Carrara marble countertops were a lavish spread of sushi and ice buckets holding bottles of Cristal champagne. The girls tried to contain their squeals of excitement. This was how it should be done — a proper wooing — although plenty of times this summer, they had walked in on pizza boxes and a tower of empty beer cans. And, one time, on a half-eaten chocolate

cake that had been crawling with ants. Nadia had confided that sometimes the mess was so bad, the girls became distracted because they knew they would be coming back in the morning to clean up.

It kill the mood, you know, Eddie? Nadia had said. *Thinking we the girlfriend tonight, but tomorrow, we the maid.*

Sushi was the girls' particular favorite, and they loved champagne. Bugsy said to Eddie, "Want to stay for a drink?"

"No, thank you," Eddie said. He wasn't comfortable being inside this house. He wanted to get the money and go.

"You wear that hat all the time?" Bugsy asked. "Even at night?"

Eddie nodded.

"You get it in Cuba?" Bugsy asked.

"Ecuador, actually," Eddie said. He was used to explaining that, although it was called a Panama hat, it was made in the town of Montecristi, Ecuador.

"You self-conscious because you're bald?" Bugsy asked. Bugsy was also bald. He touched the brim of his ball cap.

Eddie didn't want to discuss with Bugsy the things about himself that made him insecure, but he feared that to deny the statement would only invite a rebuttal.

"Yeah," Eddie said. "A little, I guess." He had started wearing the Panama hat in his late twenties, when his hair started to fall out.

Bugsy reached out to bump fists with Eddie. Then he put two fingers among his crooked, ruined teeth and gave a sharp whistle. Instantly, other men appeared in the kitchen, and within seconds, all of the girls were paired up—except for Nadia. Nadia, it seemed, belonged to Bugsy.

Eddie couldn't bear to watch this strange courtship ritual.

Already, Elise was kissing a man with black, slicked-back hair like a vampire's. Eddie turned to Bugsy but found himself unable to broach the matter of payment. It was Nadia who came to his rescue. She said, "Why don't you give Eddie money so he can vamoose?"

Bugsy tweaked Nadia's nose as if she were his precocious niece, and then he indicated that Eddie should follow him out the side door. Eddie was only too happy to leave. He waved at the girls and said, "I'll see you ladies tomorrow."

None of the girls responded. They were working. He had ceased to matter.

As soon as they stepped into the mild summer night air, Bugsy produced a padded envelope about the size of a feather pillow. So much money. Eddie did his best not to seem grabby.

"They'll come every night this week?" Bugsy asked.

"Yes," Eddie said.

"Well then," Bugsy said. "For services rendered." He presented the envelope to Eddie formally, with two hands.

"Thank you," Eddie said.

"Thank *you*," Bugsy said.

There was a sudden strong grip on Eddie's shoulder and a blinding light in his eyes.

"Whoa!" Eddie said. His Panama hat fell to the ground, and Eddie heard the unmistakable crunch of foot on straw, which made him wince. His third hat this summer. His final hat.

Inside, one of the girls screamed, and a second later, more girls were screaming. Eddie's hands were wrenched behind his back. He was being *cuffed*. A man with a salty South Boston accent read Eddie his Miranda rights. He was under arrest.

The girls were *screaming*. Were they being *hurt?* Eddie

wondered. Suddenly, Nadia popped out the side door and said, "Hello, Eddie, please, we need help inside." Her voice was calm and casual, as if they had blown a fuse or required his assistance in opening a jar of pickles.

"Miss?" the Southie accent said. "Stop right there, please. FBI."

FBI, Eddie thought. He wanted to run. He was Fast Eddie, the finest track star to come out of New Bedford High School in thirty-five years. If pressed, he knew, he could still sprint a quarter mile in under a minute. He could be halfway to Sankaty Head Lighthouse before anyone knew in which direction he'd gone. But then what? He lived on an island.

He closed his eyes and waited for the flames to start climbing the walls of his chest. He thought of Grace, asleep in their California king bed with the feather-top mattress. *Grace.* He pictured her washing the dinner dishes. He pictured lifting up her thick, dark hair and nuzzling the back of her neck, a move from early in their relationship that he had long ago abandoned.

He should have stayed home, eaten the steak and the fingerlings that she had made specially for him. He should have made love to his wife. Tried to make her laugh again. Tried to make her happy again.

But then he reminded himself that the only way he had ever known to make Grace happy was by giving her everything her heart desired.

"That's why I needed the money," Eddie said to the man behind him, whom he still could not see. "It was for my wife."

"Save it for the judge," the Southie accent said.

"If you let me go, I'll figure out something different to do for Grace," Eddie said. "Something better."

"You can figure it out in prison," the Southie accent said. "You'll have plenty of time."

The girls filed out of the house in a tight line, like they were being marched by Stalin. All of them were crying.

"Eddie!" Nadia cried out.

Instinctively, Eddie tried to free his hands.

"Easy, buddy," the Southie accent said. He led Eddie toward the back of a black Suburban. Eddie thought of the Chief turning him down for drinks. *I have plans tonight.* Did the Chief know about this sting? He must have. Eddie had thought they were *friends.*

You're a good guy, Eddie. A really good guy.

Realizing *just how untrue* this was broke Eddie's burning heart.

GRACE

Something about the article in the *Boston Globe* changed things for Grace. Seeing the photos of her and Benton and reading the text describing the wonderland they had created together had been so validating. It *was* a depiction of her private Eden. Grace knew it was crazy, but she felt as if she were the only woman on earth and Benton the only man. When

Benton came to the house on Monday, Grace was consumed with a crazy, searing desire. For the first time ever, she pulled *him* into the garden shed. She kissed him and said, "I'd really like to marry you."

"One little problem," Benton said. "You're already married."

"I don't care," Grace said.

Benton touched her face. "You can't just up and leave. What about the girls? They need you."

"This time next year, they'll be headed to college," Grace said.

"Yes, but a year is a long time," Benton said. "You're not seriously considering leaving Eddie *now*, are you?"

Was she? If she were in a position to talk it over with Madeline, Madeline would say, *You have two children, Grace, and a beautiful home. Are you prepared to give that up? Benton Coe is a talented man, but he has no roots here. He lives in an apartment above his office, he gallivants around the world all winter. He probably doesn't even have health insurance.*

I'm sure he has health insurance, Grace would retort.

She could now picture herself and Benton as a viable couple. Despite what everyone else thought, Grace didn't require much in the way of creature comforts; she could live out of a backpack. She could handle a winter in Morocco or Palm Beach, someplace warm and exotic, away from her endless responsibilities as a wife and mother.

"I'll do it," she said. "I'll leave at the end of the summer."

"You're talking crazy, Grace," Benton said. "But I like it." He growled and put his lips to the most sensitive part of her neck.

*   *   *

As they had so many times before, they were making love in the garden shed—until Grace heard Eddie's voice.

"Grace!"

It was all Grace could do not to shriek. She struggled to get back into her sundress and fix her hair while Benton pulled his shorts up, whispering profanities.

Grace put a finger to her lips. They needed to stay quiet. It sounded like Eddie was on the deck. When he went searching for her elsewhere, she and Benton could slip out. But Eddie wasn't stupid. Benton's truck was in the driveway, and Eddie had probably already checked the house, and—here was the worst thought—the gardening shed had four windows, although they were high up and Eddie would need a ladder. But if he got a ladder and peered in the window, he would see them. The longer Grace and Benton waited to open the door, the worse it would look. Every second they waited was bringing them closer to destruction. There wasn't even anything to busy themselves with in the shed. What would she and Benton say they'd been doing?

There was silence for a long moment, and Grace thought, *Open the door! No, keep it closed and locked!* Maybe Eddie would go back to work. What was he doing home, anyway? Benton was sweating buckets; he looked pale and nauseated, and Grace thought he might vomit in the copper sink. She needed him to be calm, take charge, tell her what to do.

Then there was a sharp knock on the door of the shed, and they both jumped. *Please, God!* Grace thought. She was an adulterer about to be caught—she had no business resorting to prayer, but that was what she did. She whispered a Hail Mary.

Eddie said, "Benton, you're all done here, as of right now. You're *done,* and I will not be paying your final bill. You've taken more from me than I owe you. Now, I'm leaving, and you will leave right after me, and you will never come back."

Benton nodded sharply. He was shaking. Why didn't he open the door and stand up to Eddie? Why didn't he say, *You just can't order me off this job, I've done* nothing wrong! Or, since that wasn't quite believable, why didn't he just tell Eddie the truth: *I'm in love with your wife! I'm going to marry her!*

Instead, Benton winced, and Grace actually thought he might cry. Then they heard Eddie retreat; they heard the engine of his car. He was leaving, just as he'd said.

Benton looked at Grace. "I'm going."

"But...?" Grace said. "I thought...?"

Benton said, "When word about this gets around, it is going to be so *bad,* Grace. Bad for you, but *really* bad for me. I could lose my business. I *will* lose my business, for sure. I can't stay here." He pulled at hanks of his ginger hair. "I can't believe I was so stupid! Jesus!"

Grace didn't like the way he was talking. She said, "Ten minutes ago you said you liked hearing how I would give everything up for you."

"Ten minutes ago we hadn't *gotten caught!*" Benton said. "And when I said you were talking crazy, I meant it. This is make-believe, Grace. I'm not saying it hasn't been wonderful. It was fun and exciting and sexy—just like a summer romance is supposed to be."

"It's more than a summer romance," Grace said. "I've already decided to leave."

"No, don't do that. Please." He opened the door to the

shed, and sweet, cool air filled the space, but Grace found she couldn't breathe. "I have to get out of here," Benton said, and he strode away, disappearing around the side of the house without a look back at Grace. A few seconds later, she heard the engine of his truck. She thought, *He's leaving me. He's leaving me.*

In the minutes that followed, Grace called Benton's cell phone seven times and left five voice mails. She sent him four text messages of varying lengths. In return, there was silence.

Grace called Eddie's office. She needed to tell him that, no matter how angry he was, he couldn't tell anyone about what he'd discovered. If he did, all of their lives would be ruined — his, hers, Benton's, and the twins'! But Eloise answered and delivered Grace's call to Eddie's voice mail. Grace was afraid that either Eloise or Barbie would listen to the message, and so she talked about dinner plans. Steaks. Potatoes and corn. Then she broke down and hung up.

Eddie wouldn't talk to her, and could she blame him?

Just then, a text came in from Benton. Grace was flooded with relief until she read it.

It said: *I'm leaving the island tomorrow. There's an opportunity in Detroit I've been considering for a while. I'm going to pursue it and let Donovan run the business here. We were careless and impetuous, Grace, and I accept 50 percent of the blame. I wish you well. You will always be my First Lady. XO B.*

Grace couldn't believe how *hurt* she was by his choice of words. He wished her *well*? He was moving to *Detroit*? They had been *careless* and *impetuous*? *XO*?

They had been in *love*—who cared about Benton's career or Grace's reputation? What did those things matter?

He accepted 50 percent of the blame. That was big of him.

Detroit? He had been "considering it for a while"—but this was the first Grace had heard about Detroit. Would McGuvvy meet him in Detroit? McGuvvy was from Ohio, right? And Ohio bordered Michigan, so, safe to say, McGuvvy would probably move to Detroit and teach sailing on the lake. Benton had probably been considering *going back to McGuvvy* for a while!

She would always be his First Lady, but what did that matter if she didn't end up with him?

Careless? He made it sound like they had forgotten to wind the garden hose or check the pool filters.

Impetuous? Grace knew what the word meant, but she looked it up anyway. *Acting or done quickly, without thought.* He couldn't have said anything that would have made her feel worse. He didn't love her; the shout-out on Lucretia Mott Lane had been a drunken lie and his subsequent declarations, further lies. He hadn't stood up to Eddie. He had acted *afraid* of Eddie, when he could have easily taken Eddie over his knee and spanked him.

He wished her well.

What ensued for Grace was nothing short of *total devastation*. She couldn't stand to look at the gardening shed. She would gladly hire someone to come knock it down. She wanted to pour gasoline over the roses and set them on fire. She wanted the whole yard to burn.

She climbed into her Range Rover and drove like a bat out of hell to Benton's office. It was still not quite noon, and all of the work trucks were gone, including Benton's black pickup.

Where was he? She just needed to see him, she needed a few calm moments to talk this through with him. Eddie wouldn't say anything to anyone; he didn't like sharing news that reflected poorly on him. No one would ever know what had happened. Benton could stay here. Or...Grace could go with him to Detroit.

No, she thought immediately. She couldn't leave the twins like that. There was just no way.

She parked the car haphazardly and raced up the steps to Benton's apartment. The door to his place opened, and a young, bearded man with glasses and a porkpie hat stepped out.

"Hi?" he said. "Can I *help* you?"

"I'm looking for Benton," Grace said. "Is he here?"

"He's out in the field, I do believe," the man said. "I'm Donovan, his manager. Do you have a question or a problem?"

"Both," Grace said honestly. Then she felt like a total fool. "I'm Grace Pancik."

"Oh, right!" Donovan said. "I thought you looked familiar. I saw the spread in the *Globe*. That was some great press. We've picked up three new clients from that already."

"Great," Grace said. She tried to smile, but her face would not obey. "Listen, I really need to get ahold of Benton..."

"Did you try his cell?" Donovan asked.

"I did," Grace said. She wanted to ask if she could sit in the apartment and wait for Benton to return, but it was also Donovan's apartment, and Leslie's, and Grace realized that her behavior now was bordering on psychotic. "Do you know *where* in the field he is? I really need to speak to him in person."

Donovan held out his palms as if checking for rain. "Benton is his own man," he said. "He doesn't share his schedule with me or anyone else."

Grace took a deep breath. "Okay."

"But you might check Edith Allemand's house," Donovan said. "He goes there Mondays and Fridays."

Edith Allemand's house — Main Street. "Thank you," Grace said. She hurried back down the stairs, but then she turned around.

"Donovan?" she said. "Do you know anything about Benton going to Detroit?"

Donovan said, "I knew he was considering it, but last I checked, he hadn't made a decision."

Grace climbed back into her Range Rover and drove toward Main Street. Sure enough, at number 808, Benton's truck was in the driveway. And right there in the front yard were Benton and the legendary Mrs. Allemand. Benton was holding both of Mrs. Allemand's hands, and Mrs. Allemand was talking. If Mrs. Allemand had been any younger than eighty-five years old, Grace would have felt jealous.

Grace pulled up in front of the house, chagrined at her own audacity (the voice of her grandmother Sabine begged her not to *make a scene*) — but there was nothing else she could do. She had to talk to him.

He noticed the car, and a concerned expression came over his face. He said something to Mrs. Allemand, then loped toward Grace's car. Grace loved the way he walked. She loved everything about him. She was a total goner.

He poked his head through the open passenger-side window. "Grace," he whispered. "What are you *doing* here?"

"I need to talk to you," she said.

"Do you understand how *inappropriate* this is?" he asked. "Do you know how this *looks?*"

"I don't care how it looks," Grace said. "And you used to not care. When you kissed me on Lucretia Mott Lane!"

"I have a business to run," Benton said. "And you have a family. Go be with your family, Grace. Take care of your daughters. Work things out with Eddie. Please, please don't make this any harder than it has to be. Please don't *stalk* me like this again, okay? It's making me a little nervous."

Stalking? Grace thought indignantly. She wasn't *stalking.*

But here she was, in front of Mrs. Allemand's house, and Donovan was sure to tell Benton that Grace had stormed the office.

Stalking.

"You still owe Hope that list of a hundred books," Grace said. "You can break my heart—that's fine—but don't disappoint a sixteen-year-old girl."

From the yard, Mrs. Allemand warbled out, "Is everything okay, Benton?"

Benton waved at Mrs. Allemand, then gave Grace one last look. "Please, Grace. Clean break, okay? You'll be fine. Now...good-bye."

Good-bye.

Grace drove off.

She wanted Madeline. Madeline was the only person who would understand.

The first thing Grace did when she got home was to resign as a member of the Nantucket Garden Club. In an e-mail to Jean

Burton, she cited "personal reasons." She didn't care what those personal reasons were interpreted to be. She didn't care about anything.

She opened her medicine cabinet. She took a Fioricet and tried to focus. Benton was gone—but what about Eddie? Could she still save her marriage? Did she *want* to save her marriage?

She would go out and get those steaks, she decided. She would light candles and pick a bouquet of fresh flowers, and she would try to set things right. In the meantime, maybe Benton would come to his senses.

Clean break, okay? Meaning what? Should she pretend as if the postcards from Morocco and the mint tea and the pistachio *macarons* and the ploughman's lunches and the slow dancing on the deck and the photo shoot with the *Boston Globe* and all their fiery lovemaking in the garden shed had never happened?

Detroit?

But Eddie didn't come home for dinner. He had to tend to the rental on Low Beach Road, he informed her in a terse text. Grace ate dinner in silence with the girls, who chattered with each other about the books they were reading. The food was delicious, but Grace couldn't force down a single bite. She had ruined everything. Her lover was gone, he had proved to be a coward—*Considering Detroit for a while now?*—and she had trashed her marriage. Just as Madeline had predicted. *How do you see this ending?*

Grace had four glasses of wine at dinner, then a fifth, because the girls were going to the movies together in town. Grace wandered upstairs in a bit of a stupor. She found her cell phone, read the text from Benton again. She needed Madeline. Could she call Madeline?

Allegra is a cheater, and you, Grace, are a cheater.

No, she could not call Madeline.

As Grace fell asleep, she tried to find a place of gratitude. Her girls were healthy and getting along. And she still had the most glorious property on Nantucket Island. Not to mention her Araucana chickens and a flourishing organic-egg business.

Exotic chickens and pale-blue eggs were all good and fine, but they were no substitute for love.

When Grace woke up at midnight, Eddie was still out. Still at the rental on Low Beach Road? Or possibly tying one on at a bar in town? Grace didn't even feel she could text and ask him. She crept down the hallway to her study and looked again at the article in the Sunday *Boston Globe.* There were her hydrangeas, her roses, her Adirondack chairs—all looking perfectly, professionally styled. There was the footbridge and the brook and Polpis Harbor beyond. There was the gardening shed and the copper farmer's sink, which she now wanted to tear out and deliver to the take-it-or-leave-it pile at the dump. And there were Grace and Benton, seated at the teak table in their accustomed places, raising their champagne glasses and smiling out at all the beauty they had created.

She texted Benton: *I miss you.*

Silence.

Eleven minutes later (she had meant to wait fifteen but couldn't), she texted: *I know you miss me.*

Silence.

There was nothing in the world, she decided, that wounded like silence.

*   *   *

Ever since the night of the séance, Grace had harbored mixed feelings about her sister-in-law, Barbie. *Two of the women at this table will betray the person on their left.* Eddie had been to Grace's left, Grace had been to Madeline's left, and Trevor had been to Barbie's left. Barbie would never be in a position to betray Trevor, and it was pretty clear Barbie wasn't referring to herself, anyway.

Grace would betray Eddie.

Madeline would betray Grace.

Barbie had been right: Grace had started her affair with Benton Coe six months later. *Did* Barbie have psychic powers? Or had Barbie's saying the words influenced Grace's behavior? Grace went back and forth on the question, but she had never viewed Barbie the same way since. And after the séance, Barbie had stopped joining Grace, Eddie, and the twins at the holidays. She claimed this was because she preferred traveling with one of her mystery men, but Grace always felt like Barbie had discovered something rotten about Grace and wanted to distance herself.

Besides, Barbie Pancik was, by nature, a very private person and hard to get close to. Her loyalties lay staunchly with Eddie and the business and, beyond that, with herself.

Imagine, then, Grace's surprise to find Barbie Pancik standing over her bed in the middle of the night, shaking Grace awake.

Grace cried out. It was a bad dream, Barbie looming over her, the black pearl swinging like a pendulum, her perfume suffusing the atmosphere of the bedroom.

"Grace, you have to wake up," Barbie said.

Bad dream. But no, not a dream. For some unfathomable reason, Barbie Pancik was in her bedroom. Bad something, something bad. Grace looked to her right—no Eddie. Eddie was dead. There was no other reason why Barbie Pancik would be here. Eddie had found out about Grace and Benton and had killed himself.

Grace clamped her hand over her mouth and shook her head.

Barbie lowered herself onto the mattress next to Grace and said, "You have to listen to me."

"No," Grace whispered. "Nonononono."

"Eddie is in trouble. There was a misunderstanding at the house on Low Beach Road, and the FBI have him in custody."

Grace went back to thinking, *Bad dream.* Because what Barbie was saying, even if she was real—which she did indeed seem to be—made no sense. FBI? What kind of *misunderstanding* could bring the FBI?

Barbie handed Grace a glass of water from the nightstand. "I want you to drink this, and then I'm going to tell you some things that you are never, ever to repeat. Do you understand me?"

Grace accepted the water and nodded. Barbie would have made a good mother, Grace decided.

Barbie said, "The FBI have Eddie because they suspect him of running a prostitution ring on Low Beach Road."

Grace blinked, then carefully set the water back down.

Barbie said, "Possibly, he's admitted to it. He didn't exactly tell me."

"Admitted to it," Grace said.

"Ben Winford is with him now, but I think he may have opened his mouth before Ben arrived. Apparently, Eddie hasn't watched as much *Law and Order* as I have."

"*Law and Order?*" Grace asked.

Barbie said, "I need you to get dressed. You're going down to the police station to bail him out."

"Me?" Grace said. "What about you? Are you coming?"

"No," Barbie said. "I need to distance myself from this. For business reasons."

"Is it true?" Grace asked.

"It doesn't matter," Barbie said. "Unless they can prove it."

For some reason, Nadia, one of Eddie's housecleaners, was at the police station. Grace blinked, thinking again, *Bad dream, nightmare,* the kind where people from different parts of her life showed up in places where they didn't belong. Why would Nadia be here? It was a mistake. But when Grace was ushered into the back of the station to post Eddie's bail, she saw Nadia, or a girl who looked exactly like Nadia, sitting in one of the interrogation rooms. Grace was so stunned that she took a step backward and peered in the room to make sure. Definitely Nadia. Grace heard her say, "I just clean the houses…" And then whoever else was in the room wisely closed the door.

Then Grace saw Eddie's other four cleaning girls sitting on folding chairs in front of the officer on duty. Grace had met them all en masse at one point, but she couldn't remember anyone's name except for Nadia's. The girls were in tube skirts, and they had all removed pairs of very high-heeled

shoes. One girl was rubbing her feet, one girl was softly crying. They smelled sharp and antiseptic, like hair spray and
cheap perfume. They looked...well, here Grace sighed. They
looked like hookers. Eddie had been using his cleaning crew
as prostitutes. Grace's stomach turned.

Grace said to the officer, a black woman striking enough
to be a supermodel, whose name tag read *Peters,* "I'm here to
post bail for Edward Pancik?"

There was much whispering from the girls. One piped
up and said, "You are Eddie's wife, yes?"

"No talking!" Officer Peters said.

Grace turned to face the girls. "Yes," she said.

At that second, the door down the hallway opened, and
Nadia came walking out, attended by a square-necked man
with a silver crew cut and a navy FBI windbreaker.

"Hello, Mrs. Pancik," Nadia said.

"What's happening, Nadia?" Grace asked. It could be a
mistake, right? It must have been a mistake. Grace could not
fathom that Eddie had actually taken these girls—none of
them over twenty-five, she didn't think—and turned them
into hookers.

But Nadia didn't seem capable of explaining. She turned
to the other girls and said something in Russian.

"Enough!" the silver crew cut barked out. "Kat, do you
have a place I can put Ms. Nadia here while I talk to the next
one? She should be isolated. They all should, really."

"We can't do what we can't do," Officer Peters said. She
smiled apologetically at Grace. "We just don't have enough
personnel when something like this happens."

Grace nodded, as if understanding what *this* meant. Officer Peters was talking to Grace as if they were in cahoots

somehow, and Grace decided to take advantage. She said, "I'd really like to see my husband. Can I see him?"

"Who's your husband?" the silver crew cut asked.

"Edward Pancik."

"Ha!" the silver crew cut said. "Better take a seat. It's gonna be a while."

"Let me see if I can find a room for Ms. Nadia," Officer Peters said.

Nadia said something to the other girls in Russian.

Grace wished she could understand! She said, "Are you... in trouble, Nadia?"

"Ma'am, please," the silver crew cut said. "I need her isolated! Jesus!"

Officer Peters disappeared down the hall. The silver crew cut eyeballed the five girls. He read names off a clipboard. *Elise Anoshkin, Julia Vlacic, Gabrielle Bylinkin, Nadia Roskilov, Tonya Yedemesky.* The girls raised their hands one by one.

The only good thing about finding out Eddie had gotten into this kind of heinous trouble was that it kept Grace from obsessing about Benton.

Grace had to triage.

And this was definitely worse.

At seven o'clock in the morning, a very weary version of Eddie's normally impeccably dressed attorney, Ben Winford, shook Grace awake in her chair.

Ben said, "Eddie's gotten himself into a real pickle this time." Ben stared up at the ceiling, which made Grace stare at

the ceiling. "Why don't my clients ever *call* me before they break the law? I'll tell them ten times out of ten, it's not a good idea. What did Richard Nixon teach us? What did the Boston bombers teach us? Criminals always get caught."

"Is he going to jail?" Grace asked. Her voice sounded like broken crackers after the Fioricet, the wine, and nearly no sleep. She thought of being in the garden shed with Benton. It had been the previous morning, less than twenty-four hours earlier, and yet it seemed like weeks ago.

"Oh, probably," Ben said wearily. He was, Grace realized, wearing his pajama top with his jeans. "This isn't exactly my specialty, but I know a guy in Boston who handles racketeering, prostitution, more Mob-type stuff. You know me—I'm basically a real estate–estate planning guy."

"Mob-type stuff?" Grace said. She felt as if she were going to faint.

Ben patted her knee. "The good news is, you'll get him out of here today."

Eddie was released three hours later, at ten o'clock. His bail was set at fifteen thousand dollars. Grace tried to pay using their platinum American Express, but it was denied, so she ended up writing a check. When they finally got out to the car and Grace told Eddie this, he laughed like an inmate at the asylum. He said, "The check will bounce, Grace. We're broke."

"What does that mean?"

Eddie shrugged. "I guess as soon as they figure out the check is no good, they'll come for me."

"No, what does it mean that we're broke?" Grace asked. "How can we be broke?"

She listened in silence as Eddie told her: the money was all gone. The spec houses were a financial noose around his neck. He'd sold two of the three to Glenn Daley, of all people, but that had only helped to pay Eddie's backed-up debts. Number 13 Eagle Wing Lane was still a hundred and fifty or two hundred thousand dollars away from completion, and Eddie had exhausted his options. He hadn't sold a house in nine months; the market was a wasteland. He had managed to keep corporate groups at 10 Low Beach Road, but that had only led him into this mess.

"Yes," Grace said. "Let's talk about *this mess*. What the hell is going on, Eddie? What have you *done?*"

"I can't tell you," Eddie said. "If I tell you, they might be able to get you for conspiracy."

"They will not get me for conspiracy," Grace said, "because I knew nothing about it. But you are going to tell me right now."

"I can't," Eddie said.

"Tell me!" Grace screamed.

Eddie held his face in his hands. Grace thought he might cry, and that would have frightened her, because Eddie never cried. He hadn't cried when either of his parents died, and he hadn't cried when Hope had been born blue. He hadn't cried over finding Grace with Benton in the garden shed yesterday morning. Would he cry now, at his own ruin?

No. He raised his head and said, "I needed money, and last year I had a client who had asked about the girls — could they come over and hang out with the guys? — and last year, I said no way."

"But then...?"

"Then, this year, I got in such deep water, Grace. I can't tell you how bad things got, moneywise, and I needed cash, and the guys who rent this house, baby, they are just loaded, so loaded that they pay ten grand *per night.*"

Grace gasped.

"A ton of jack, right? And I needed it, but I wouldn't have forced the girls. I asked them, just asked *what if?* And they were all *excited.* It's a lot of money for them."

"They're immigrant girls that you can exploit," Grace said. "What did you *expect* them to say? I think I'm going to be sick."

"The girls never complained," Eddie said. "I think they saw themselves as Julia Roberts in *Pretty Woman.* They loved the money. The money was *ridiculous*—for me and for Barbie, too.

"So Barbie *is* in on this?" Grace said.

"No."

"Eddie."

"Yes," Eddie said. "Yes, she's in on it. But the authorities don't know that, and they're not going to know it. I need Barbie to keep the business afloat while I'm..."

"In jail," Grace said. The words were incomprehensible, but she had to accept that they might be true. Eddie might be going to jail. Ben Winford had said, *Oh, probably.* Grace swallowed. Something else was nagging at her. "Did you...I mean, Eddie, did you...sleep with any of the girls?"

"No!" Eddie said. "God, no! I have never been unfaithful to you."

Grace nodded. She believed him.

"You're the unfaithful one! You were having an affair with Benton Coe *under my nose, in my own house.*"

Grace was quiet. "Well, he's gone. It's over."

"You sound sad about that," Eddie said. "Are you sad? Do you *love* him, Grace?"

She wanted to scream, *Yes, I love him! I love him more than I love breathing!*

But instead she said, "I can't even *think* about that right now, Eddie! We have bigger problems! We have *criminal charges!*"

"What do we tell the girls?" Eddie asked.

"We tell them nothing," Grace said. "They're children, Eddie. They do not need to know about the nefarious affairs of their parents."

"They're bound to find out," Eddie said, "the way this island talks."

"We'll shelter them as long as we can," Grace said. "Okay?"

"Okay," Eddie said.

When they got home, the girls were reading side by side in chaises by the pool, the two of them lithe and lovely in their bikinis, Allegra's red, Hope's black—no, wait, it was the other way around. Grace shook her head; it was the first time since they were infants, practically, that she'd gotten them mixed up. They were both wearing their hair down. Hope had fixed her hair to look like Allegra's, and it was really fetching. Here was a snapshot of the family life Grace had always wanted but had never quite been able to achieve—because of Allegra's tempestuous moods, because of Grace's wild and straying heart, because Eddie had always, always, *always* been working.

Grace called out, "Are you girls hungry for lunch?"

"Starved," Allegra said. "Where have you two *been?*"

"Out," Grace said.

"Out where?" Hope asked.

"Just out," Grace said.

"Wow," Allegra said. "You sound like me."

Grace made chicken-salad sandwiches, and she brought out a bunch of cold grapes from the fridge. She sliced some hothouse tomatoes, spread them with fresh pesto, then dotted them with tiny balls of mozzarella. She and the girls sat down at the outdoor table in the sun, but Eddie excused himself, saying he needed to sleep. He went up to the bedroom.

Hope said, "Is Dad okay?"

"Not really," Grace said. She cleared the girls' plates and stood up, not wanting to say anything else. Eddie was right: the girls needed to learn what was going on from Eddie and Grace before they heard it elsewhere — but she would let them have today.

MADELINE

Madeline read the completed first draft of *B/G* three times. It was good; it was *addictive*. The power and the urgency of the affair and the forbiddenness of it made it irresistible, but the genuine love between B and G made it luminous.

She wasn't going to publish it.

Oh, how she dreaded calling Angie. And yet, call Angie she must.

Angie's assistant, Marlo, answered. "She's at lunch."

"She is?" Madeline said. It was ten fifteen. No one ate lunch at ten fifteen, not even Angie Turner. Maybe "lunch" meant she was meeting her tile guy at a suite at the Warwick Hotel. Madeline decided to just tell Marlo, and Marlo could break the bad news to Angie. "Listen, Marlo, I'm not going to publish *B/G*. I have to pull it off the list."

"Please hold," Marlo said. "I'm putting you through to Angie."

"I thought she was at lunch."

"She just walked in," Marlo said.

"How's my favorite author?" Angie said when she came on the line. "How's the Next Big Thing? I'm just going to start calling you Number One, because that's where you're headed, Madeline. Straight to the top spot. The *New York Times,* the *Wall Street Journal, USA Today.*"

Marlo hadn't told her.

"Did Marlo tell you?" Madeline asked.

"Tell me what?" Angie said.

"I can't let you publish the book," Madeline said.

Silence.

Madeline waited. Maybe that was it. She had spoken the words. Could she just hang up?

But then Angie started to yell. Whippet-thin Angie, in her pencil skirts and Louboutin slingbacks, had an angry voice that nearly shattered Madeline's phone. Madeline couldn't

make out every word, but the gist was something like, *You can't just... The book, Madeline, you don't make those decisions, we do... Murder, bloody murder. This is going to be big, so big, so huge, you have no fucking idea how you're hurting yourself, might as well get a razor and slit your... How you're hurting me... I've bragged about this book to my friends, my actual friends... yoga... my son's soccer games...*

Then she took a breath. She said, "The marketing budget is *quadruple* what we gave you for *Islandia*. This is a whole new league for you. You will be right up there with your cousin Stephen."

Here, Madeline interjected. "He's not my cousin."

"You can't not publish it," Angie said. "That isn't a choice."

"It is, though," Madeline said. "It's my choice, and I'm sorry, Angie. I'm sorry I'm taking back the book, I'm sorry I'm disappointing you."

"You're *more* than disappointing me, Madeline," Angie said. "This isn't catching my fourteen-year-old daughter smoking on the corner of Bleecker and Sixth Avenue. *That* was disappointing. This is something far worse."

"I can't let you publish it," Madeline said. "I'm sorry I ever wrote it. I should never have let that story see the light of day."

Silence. It sounded as if Angie were lighting a cigarette of her own.

She said, "It's a good book, Madeline."

"But I don't feel good about it," Madeline said. "Listen, I don't want to keep you from your other work. Nothing you can say is going to change my mind."

"Oh, yeah?" Angie said. "How about this? You'll be hearing from our legal department."

And with that, she hung up.

*   *   *

An hour later, as Madeline was lying on the sofa of the apartment, reading the latest issue of the *New Yorker,* hoping for another great idea, her phone rang.

It was Redd Dreyfus.

Madeline sighed. He was calling to tell her…that she would have to pay her advance back? That he was firing her as a client? That her career as a novelist was over, and she might as well never traverse a bridge or tunnel to the borough of Manhattan again, because as far as the publishing world was concerned, she was dead?

Madeline steeled herself for the worst. "Hello?" she said.

"Madeline King," he said. "How are you, my darling?"

Redd sounded relaxed, but he also sounded old. He had been fiftyish when he signed Madeline as a client, which would make him seventyish now.

She said, "I'm so sorry, Redd." She swallowed. "I can't do it. The truth is, I blatantly used my best friend's affair as the basis for that novel. Not everything is the same, but the story is hers, not mine, and I can't let it see the light of day."

"Aha," Redd said. "You do realize it's not against the law to base your novel on true experiences, even if they belong to someone else, right? I mean, let's say your friend reads the book and feels you're trying to pass her real-life story off as fiction. Let's say she hires a lawyer. *Those* cases rarely see the light of day."

"It's not against the written law, maybe," Madeline said. "But it's against *my* law. The law I have with myself. I wrote the book because I was desperate for an idea, and then one fell into my lap. The timing was uncanny. I convinced myself that it was okay, that I would change the details and no one

would recognize it. But the essence of Grace's story is also the essence of my story, and it's not fair of me to use it. It's unethical."

"Well," Redd said. He took a long pause. "It sounds like this is the right decision for your soul. I applaud you for that."

"You do?" Madeline said.

"I do. I know Angie unleashed her holy wrath, but I got her calmed down."

"She said I'd be hearing from their legal department," Madeline said.

"She's trying to scare you. She's *desperate* to publish that book—it seems like a personal mission of hers—but it's *your* intellectual property. The thing that *matters* is that you wrote a really good book. And if you did it once, guess what?"

"What?" Madeline said.

"You can do it again," Redd said. "You'll come up with another idea, trust me."

Madeline said, "But what if Angie doesn't like it as much? Will I have to pay my advance back?"

"Hell no!" Redd said. "I mean, does Angie have to accept it? Hell yes. But I have full confidence that you'll deliver something even better, Madeline. If not on the next try, then on a subsequent try. And even if you don't *ever* deliver, it's very difficult for a publisher to get advance money back once it's been paid out. I've had authors who have been *ten years late* on delivery! I've had authors who *disappeared to South America!* I've had authors who *plagiarized the work of their teenage children!*" Redd's voice was growing animated. Madeline knew he had put on weight in recent years, and she

feared his having a heart attack right there at his desk. Thankfully, he calmed down. "My dear, I've seen it all. I know you feel like you're the only author who has ever used the travails of a close friend as fiction fodder, but, I assure you, you are not. What's the popular phrase? *Write what you know.* Authors do this kind of thing *all the time.* And I realize you feel like you're not going to be able to write something else, but, Madeline, I'm telling you, you are. You don't even have to believe in yourself. I'm your agent. I'll do the believing."

"Thank you," Madeline whispered.

"I'll handle Angie," Redd said. "After all, you don't just pay me to sit around my office and look handsome." He let out a great belly laugh. "Now, my darling, get to work."

Madeline hung up the phone and thought, *Yes!* She needed to stop worrying about Eddie and the fifty thousand dollars, and she needed to stop vilifying Allegra—she was a narcissistic sixteen-year-old girl—so what? Brick would get over her and move on, and his heart would be stronger in the place where it had been broken. But, most of all, Madeline had to stop missing Grace.

That was the toughest thing. She couldn't make herself stop missing Grace.

Maybe she could write a novel called *Missing Grace,* about a novelist who writes about her best friend's affair and then regrets it. It would be sort of like the woman on the cereal box eating from a box of cereal that has her own picture on it, and so forth infinitely.

Her brain hurt thinking about this.

She picked up her pen and a fresh legal pad.

Get to work!

*　　*　　*

A little while later, a phone call came to Madeline's cell phone from Rachel McMann. Madeline had decided to write not a sequel but a *prequel* to *Islandia*. She would tell the story of Nantucket before it became submerged under water. She would write a novel about the beginning of the end, her protagonists, Jack and Diane, still in their mothers' wombs. She would cast a foreboding shadow over everything; it would be psychologically terrifying because readers would know the water was coming.

Brilliant? Or potentially brilliant? Better than a sequel, anyway, Madeline thought.

Rachel McMann. *Now what?* Madeline thought. She had already had two long phone calls with Rachel about the Allegra–Ian Coburn–Brick situation; that topic was exhausted. And at the end of the second conversation, Madeline had let Rachel know that she was back to living at home. She and Trevor had worked things out. Moving on.

Madeline let Rachel's call go to voice mail. It was two o'clock—Madeline had only four hours left, and she was still working on an outline.

Rachel called again, and Madeline thought, *Really?* She picked up.

"Hello?" she said, allowing a tinge of impatience to creep into her voice.

"I need you to sit down," Rachel said.

"I am sitting down," Madeline said. "I'm working, Rachel."

"You aren't going to believe this," Rachel said.

Madeline sighed. *Gossip, gossip, gossip.* If she were smart, she would hang up now. But she wasn't strong enough.

"What?" she said.

"Grace Pancik was having an affair with Benton Coe," Rachel said. "Just as we suspected."

"I don't think we suspected that," Madeline said uneasily. "And I'm not sure what would make you think that was true."

"Oh, come on!" Rachel said. "When we all saw the article, we knew."

"The article doesn't prove anything," Madeline said.

"Okay, let's say, strictly speaking, the article *doesn't* prove anything. But . . . !"

"But *what?*" Madeline asked. She wanted to slam the phone down and never talk to Rachel again, but she had to know what Rachel was going to say. Who had found out about Grace and Benton for sure?

"Bernie Wu was the driver for the writer and the photographer of the article, and he said they arrived early, and it was *pretty clear* they'd interrupted something. Grace and Benton were locked in the garden shed, and they emerged looking very disheveled indeed."

Oh no, Madeline thought.

"You're gossiping, Rachel," Madeline said. "It's hearsay, and you should be ashamed of yourself for repeating it. It is *none* of your business."

"It sounds like you're taking the moral high ground," Rachel said. "Which is ironic, since we all know you're the one writing a book about it."

"I'm not writing a book about it," Madeline said. "I threw that book away."

Rachel gasped. "No!" she said. "Oh, Madeline." She sounded genuinely upset, like Madeline had told her she'd put her dog to sleep. "It was so good. I was *dying* to read it. In fact, I already posted about it in my Goodreads profile."

"I threw it away, deleted the file," Madeline said. "It was garbage."

There was a heavy silence on the other line, which was then replaced by Rachel's usual sparkly energy. "Well, the thing about Grace and Benton isn't the most scandalous thing I have to tell you, anyway. Because, did you hear what happened to *Eddie* Pancik?"

"No," Madeline said, exasperated. "I did not hear what happened to Eddie Pancik, and I don't want to hear." *Unless he won the lottery,* Madeline thought. *Or found a pot of gold sitting on the bottom of Miacomet Pond.*

"Eddie Pancik got arrested by the FBI last night," Rachel said. "He's been running a prostitution ring on Low Beach Road."

Madeline closed her eyes. She had several thoughts at once.

Poor Grace.

Eddie was far more desperate than I thought.

Poor Grace.

Madeline didn't trust any information coming from Rachel McMann. "That's absurd," she said.

"It's true," Rachel said. "I can't tell you how I know, but I know. Eddie Pancik has spent his summer pimping out a crew of five Russian housecleaners to his clients. His secretary overheard a conversation or two, I guess, between Eddie and his sister, and she put two and two together. She contacted the FBI."

"His secretary? You mean Eloise?"

"Yes, Eloise," Rachel said.

The thought of sweet seventy-year-old Eloise busting open a prostitution ring run by Eddie and Barbie was comical. And yet, Madeline could sort of see how it *might* be possible.

"Was *Grace* in on it?" she asked.

Rachel laughed, and Madeline vowed that this would be the last conversation—beyond polite small talk—that she would ever have with Rachel McMann. The woman was a pit viper. "Of course not!" Rachel said. "Grace was too busy screwing the gardener!"

"So Eddie's in jail, then?" Madeline said.

"Out on bail," Rachel said. "I guess the check Grace wrote bounced, so his sister and Glenn Daley had to come save the day. They're seeing each other, you know."

"Barbie and *Glenn?*" Madeline said. She had thought they were mortal enemies. "How do you know all this?"

"How does anyone know anything?" Rachel said. "I heard it on the street. People are talking."

Madeline hung up with Rachel, took ten breaths, walked to the window, and gazed down onto Centre Street. *People are talking.* Sure enough, there on the corner of India and Centre were Blond Sharon and Susan Prendergast, blabbering away.

Madeline wanted to call Trevor, but he would be in the air.

My fifty thousand dollars, gone, she thought. Really and truly *gone.* Madeline thought she would feel complete devastation, but instead she experienced a kind of relief. The money was gone, and so she was freed from worrying about it.

All she could think about was Grace. Poor Grace! Madeline decided the time had come to set aside her fear and pride.

She called Grace's cell phone. No answer, but Madeline wasn't surprised. She hung up without leaving a message.

Next, she called the house. Her heart was hammering, and her temples throbbed. She hadn't been this nervous since… she couldn't remember when. Maybe ever.

One of the twins answered. "Hello?" The voice sounded *very* curious; of course, Madeline's name would have popped up on the caller ID.

Madeline exhaled. It was Hope.

"Hi, Hope," Madeline said. She thought about identifying herself, but that seemed awkward and pointless. Hope knew who it was. "Is your mom there?"

"She's *here*," Hope said. "But she told us she doesn't want to talk to anyone on the phone."

"Okay," Madeline said. "Tell her I'm on my way over."

Grace was sitting on the front step when Madeline arrived. Madeline thought maybe she might be holding a shotgun to ward Madeline off, but she was holding something even more surprising. A cigarette. Grace was smoking.

"Don't look so shocked," Grace said. "I used to smoke in college."

"I didn't know that," Madeline said.

"See?" Grace said. "Still things to learn about your best friend."

The phrase *best friend* floated between them, a peace offering. Madeline took both of Grace's hands. "What's going on?" she said.

Grace stubbed her cigarette out on the front step. "Let's go upstairs," she said.

*   *   *

They assumed the same postures that they had weeks earlier, back when Grace had just kissed Benton for the first time. Madeline sat in the green leather chair, and Grace fell face first across the crushed-velvet sofa. Madeline recalled her words from that night. *I'll point out, Grace, because I'm your best friend and it's my job, that no good can come of this.*

No good.

Madeline thought that Grace might want to start with what had happened to Eddie, but instead, her lower lip wobbled, and she burst into tears. *I thought Benton and I were in love; I was making plans to leave Eddie, maybe as soon as the end of the summer. But then Benton and I were in the garden shed making love, and Eddie came home and found us. He didn't see anything, but he knew what was happening, obviously, and he told Benton to leave and never come back.* Grace swallowed. *And Benton left. I've been trying to get ahold of him, but he's shutting me out. He sent me a text saying he's moving to* Detroit!

Madeline sat on the floor next to the sofa and rubbed Grace's back while she cried. Madeline would never say so out loud, but this was probably all for the best.

Or maybe not. Maybe the best ending was the one Angie had described and the one Madeline had written. *I want an ending where the woman is happy instead of good.*

Madeline reached into her bag and pulled out her manuscript. She had planned on giving it to Grace as a symbolic gesture—Grace could shred it or burn it; Madeline didn't care.

But now she had a different idea.

"Listen," she said. "I did write a novel that was based on your relationship with Benton."

Grace raised her face. "You did *not!* I thought that was just a stupid rumor. I didn't think there was any way you would..."

"I did," Madeline said. "And here it is." She plopped the manuscript down on the side table. "But don't worry, I'm not going to publish it."

"You can't publish it, Madeline!" Grace said. "Especially not now!"

"I know, I know, Grace," Madeline said. "I told my publisher to pull it off the list."

Grace sat up, and her expression turned to one of rage. "I can't *believe* you! I told you about Benton because you are my friend! My best friend! And what? You used everything I told you? You promised you would never betray me, but you did. You did!"

"I'm sorry, Grace," Madeline said. "I wrote it out of desperation. I was so blocked. I spent the money on the stupid apartment, and then, when I sat down to write, the only story that came to mind was *yours*. I fought the urge for a while, but I was worried about money. I tried to get my fifty thousand back from Eddie, but I couldn't, and I was angry about that, and frustrated, and scared. But you're right. I had *no business* using your story. And that's why I told my editor I couldn't publish it. She was really, really pissed off. She *loved* it."

"She did?" Grace said.

"It's a good novel, Grace. It's a real love story. Maybe you should read it."

Grace regarded the manuscript skeptically. "I don't know about that," she said.

"I've missed you so much," Madeline said. "And, even though you're angry about my book, and even though I'm angry about what Allegra did to Brick, I am here with you in your study. I am *here*, Grace."

Grace looked at Madeline and dissolved into more tears. "What am I going to do now?" she said.

"Take a deep breath," Madeline said. "Tell me about Eddie."

"I'll tell you about Eddie," Grace said. "But now I don't trust you! You have to promise me you won't…"

"Grace," Madeline said. "I won't."

EDDIE

The most important person in his life now was his new attorney, Bridger Cleburne. Bridger worked at a very large, prestigious firm in Boston, but he hailed from Lubbock, Texas, where he had been the star pitcher on the baseball team that won the Little League World Series in 1984. Bridger used his childhood glory days as a point of commonality with Eddie, "Fast Eddie," the holder of so many track records at New Bedford High School.

Eddie didn't care about his track records or about Bridger's role in the Little League World Series. He needed Bridger to get him out of trouble.

But Eddie's "situation," as Bridger called it—a very long word, in his Lone Star State drawl—wasn't an easy fix. It

turned out that one of Eddie's cleaners—teeny, tiny Elise Anoshkin—was still a few months shy of her eighteenth birthday! A minor, an illegal minor! It was all looking dire for Eddie. The FBI had been watching the house since the second week of the "shenanigans"—another long word for Bridger—and a wiretap had been installed. The evidence was damning.

At first, Eddie thought he'd been turned in by Glenn Daley. He was sure Barbie had either knowingly confided in Glenn or had let some hint or clue slip during the heat of passion. Then, crazily, Eddie wondered if Benton Coe was to blame. Possibly, Benton had been looking for a way to get Eddie out of the picture so he could marry Grace. But Bridger had told Eddie that there were two informants, neither of them Glenn or Benton. One was Eloise, Eddie's secretary! Apparently, she had needed her paycheck so badly because her "situation" was that she had turned Eddie in: Eloise had overheard Barbie on the phone with one of the potential clients early on. Eloise had contacted her son-in-law's brother, Officer Dixon at the Nantucket Police Department, and the police had started watching the house.

The other, more dangerous informant was the thirty-year-old billionaire owner of the house. He had given the FBI full access to install surveillance equipment.

How had the *owner* found out? He had bumped into Ronan LNW from DeepWell at the bar at the Bellagio in Vegas. Ronan had been wearing, of all things, a Chicken Box hat, and when the owner asked Ronan about his connection to Nantucket, Ronan said that he rented an unbelievable house on Low Beach Road in Sconset. Imagine the owner's delighted surprise when he found out Ronan rented *his* house.

What were the chances? The owner bought Ronan a glass of twenty-five-year-old Laphroaig, and from there it wasn't hard to imagine that Ronan had leaked like a sieve and told the owner just *how much fun* he'd had in that house.

The owner wasn't angry about the *immorality* of the situation. But he was furious—being a cutthroat businessman himself—that Eddie hadn't given him a share in the profits.

Now, no matter how one looked at it, Eddie was going to jail. The feds had evidence on Barbie as well, but if Eddie made a deal, Barbie would be spared.

And so Eddie received a sentence of three to five years at MCI-Plymouth. Number 13 Eagle Wing Lane was repossessed by the bank, as were both of Eddie's commercial properties, including the offices of Dr. Andrew McMann, D.D.S.

The house was paid up until the end of the month, but Eddie was going to advise Grace to sell it. She could buy something smaller and use the difference to send the girls to college and pay back Madeline and Trevor.

These decisions were all made quickly, in a matter of days. Nadia and the other girls were on their way back to Kyrgyzstan.

It could have been worse, he supposed. Three to five years could become two years with good behavior. MCI-Plymouth was a far cry from the Plymouth County Correctional Facility. Eddie would have a TV in his cell, which would be a single, and the food was supposedly sourced from a nearby farm cooperative; there were barbecues held once a month in the state forest. There was a gym where Eddie could start an

exercise regimen, and an infirmary with a full-time nurse practitioner, who could, possibly, find a way to cure Eddie's chronic heartburn. Most important, there would be other white-collar criminals, whom he might, someday, sell houses to.

These things only slightly ameliorated the anguish caused by *going to jail*. The shame of it was enough to kill him. Now *everyone* knew that Eddie Pancik was an underworld king. He was a pimp. He could barely bring himself to look at the twins. What would their lives be like at school? What would the other kids say? Their senior year would be ruined, when it should have been the best year of their lives. Eddie decided the right thing to do as a father and a man was to formally apologize to them. He did this the morning of his sentencing, in the hours before he was to plead guilty to seventeen charges of sex trafficking, harboring illegal aliens, tax evasion, and corruption of a minor.

The girls were out by the pool, side by side, reading, as they often were now, despite the fact that Eddie had returned Allegra's cell phone, thereby restoring her access to her social life. Eddie strode out across the grass in his bare feet, head exposed to the sun now that all three of his Panama hats had bitten the dust. It was late July and one of the most glorious sunny days that God had to offer. The yard was blooming in forty different directions. It was so lush, so colorful, so aesthetically pleasing, that Eddie's overwhelming instinct was to get on his knees and pray—for forgiveness and in gratitude for the beauty of the world that he had taken for granted and that he would now be leaving behind.

He stood equidistantly between the foot of the girls' chaise

longues. His father had managed Ramos Dry Cleaners and had never made more than twenty-five thousand dollars a year, but Charles Pancik never had to prostrate himself in front of his children. He had been a man of honor. Eddie and Barbie still talked about him with reverence.

"Girls," Eddie said.

They set down their books and regarded him. They were wearing sunglasses, so it was hard to read their expressions. Since they had learned what had happened, they had treated him with a certain pity, almost as if he were terminally ill. But they must have been angry and disgusted with him, too. They must have been.

He said, "I owe you both an apology."

They stared at him.

"I did an inexcusable thing. I broke the law, and I engaged in a business arrangement that debased five young women, one of them only a year older than you. I used my position of power to make money from these girls selling their bodies. I was wrong, and I want you to know I'm very sorry."

Hope said, "It's okay, Daddy."

"No," he said. "It's not okay."

"It was a business arrangement," Allegra said. "You got paid, the girls got paid, the men got what they wanted. You didn't hurt anyone."

"You didn't kill anyone," Hope said.

"Well, that doesn't make it right," Eddie said, thinking, *Tax evasion, corruption of a minor, sex trafficking*—these would be words connected with his name for the rest of his life. "I've led by poor example, and as a result of my actions, I'm going to jail, and your mother is going to sell the house."

Hope shrugged. "It's just a house."

Allegra said, "I'd rather live in town, anyway."

"Okay," Eddie said. He couldn't understand why they were being so nice.

"Eddie!" Grace called from the porch. "We have to go!"

The girls stood to give Eddie a hug. "We love you, Daddy," Allegra said.

"We really love you," Hope said.

"And I love you both," Eddie said. "So much." He was overcome with emotion. "Take care of your mother. Please."

"We will," Hope said.

The ride from Polpis Road to the courthouse took twenty minutes, the last free minutes of Eddie's old life.

He said to Grace, "There's something I want to tell you."

"You slept with Nadia?" she said. She kept her eyes straight ahead, but her mouth was a grim, unattractive line. "I know it hardly matters in the scheme of things, but if you did, I want you to admit it."

"I did *not* sleep with Nadia," Eddie said. "What I want to tell you isn't about me. It's about you."

"You're going to tell me something about myself?" she said.

"It's about Benton," Eddie said.

Grace swerved the car at the mention of his name. It was probably the last thing she'd expected to talk about today, and yet Eddie had to get it off his chest before he left.

"What is it?" she said.

"I called him the other night," Eddie said. "Before I drove

out to Low Beach Road, I called him, and I asked him to stop by the office so we could have a man-to-man talk."

Grace gasped. "Did he *show?*"

"Yes," Eddie said. "I asked him what had been going on, and he told me he loved you. I honestly think he was asking me to step aside gracefully so you two could have a life together." Eddie cleared his throat. "But he was confused, too, maybe not as sure of himself as he thought. He was worried about the effect of such a scandal on his business. Nobody wants to hire a home wrecker. He was afraid for you and the girls. He enjoyed Hope and thought she was a great kid, but he had never even *met* Allegra. What happened within the confines of the garden shed might have looked a little different once it was brought out into the sun." Eddie had been struck, however, by Benton Coe's adoration of his wife. When Benton talked about Grace, Eddie could feel love coming off the man in waves. It had given Eddie pause. "I think he was willing to take the risk if it could be done with my blessing? My permission?" Eddie was pretty sure that was why Benton had agreed to come to the office—he thought Eddie was going to surrender. "But I wasn't about to just *hand you over.* You're my wife, my life, you're the mother of my children. I'm aware, Grace, that I haven't been the most attentive, nor the most loving, husband. I realize I didn't succeed at nurturing your interior life. Most days, I didn't ask what you were thinking or feeling. You had emotional needs that I was incapable of meeting, which was why I was glad you had Madeline. And, for a while, I was even glad you had Benton. I *knew* you liked him, I *knew* his friendship was important to you. I *knew* you enjoyed having someone to talk about flowers. But I'm not going to lose you to him. I told him, Grace, that if he ever

contacted you again, or if he even responded to a text or call that you made, I would have him killed."

"Killed?" Grace said. "Really?"

"Really," Eddie said. "I would have found someone to do it for money. I would have, Grace, and he knew it. Or maybe, let's say, I wouldn't have actually had him killed. But I would have ruined his life. I would have taken down his business, shredded his good name."

"He told you he loved me?" Grace said.

"He did," Eddie said. "And now, I think you should go with him, if that's what you want. Because I failed. I did this evil thing, and I let you down."

Grace didn't respond. Eddie had never been good at gauging her emotions, but if he tried now, he would say she seemed...overwhelmed. It was a lot to deal with—after all, in a few minutes, he would stand before the judge, he would plead guilty, he would be sentenced and would be taken into custody. Two law-enforcement agents would bring him via ferry to the mainland, where a van would meet them and transport Eddie to MCI-Plymouth. Eddie had a duffel bag in the back of the car, packed with sanctioned items. Grace would be able to visit in thirty days.

He was trying to think of it as going away to college, something he had never experienced. He toyed with this delusion—prison as an institute of higher learning—at least until he pulled up in front of the town building. FBI officers were outside, waiting, as was Eddie's lawyer, Bridger Cleburne, as was a photographer from the *Nantucket Standard,* as was...the chief of police.

Eddie groaned.

"Oh, Eddie," Grace said.

*   *   *

Eddie had mixed feelings about the Chief's role in all of this. The Chief hadn't known about the prostitution ring on Figawi weekend—no way—nor, probably, when they went out fishing. But at some point the Chief had found out what Eddie was doing, and he hadn't given Eddie any warning. By then, possibly, the FBI was involved, and the Chief's hands were tied. Eddie knew he couldn't have expected the chief of police to help; friends or not, there was the law to consider. Eddie hung his head as he walked up to the Chief.

"I'm so sorry, Ed..."

The Chief held up a hand. "Don't apologize to me. I told you I don't judge. But the court does, and I'm sad to see it go down this way."

Eddie stared at his feet and shook his head.

The Chief said, "You've always struck me as the kind of guy who can bounce back. Be careful in there, Eddie. Keep your nose clean, serve your time. We'll have that drink when you get back."

"We will?" Eddie asked. The road he had to travel between now and the time he would actually be a free man again, and able to sit on a bar stool next to the Chief, seemed infinitely long and arduous, but Eddie was heartened that the Chief thought he could do it.

"We will," the Chief said.

AUGUST

HOPE

As much as everything had changed, everything had stayed the same. Her father went to jail—he was gone—but he had never been around much before. Grace seemed subdued, but she got this way sometimes, especially when she had a migraine. She still did the gardening and cared for the hens, only now she gave Allegra and Hope chores. Allegra was to mow the grass every four days, and Hope was to skim the pool and deadhead the lilies each morning.

One day, Allegra asked Hope if she wanted to go to the beach.

Hope considered this. The beach. Could she and Allegra reasonably make an everyday summer outing to the *beach* when their father had just been sent to prison?

"Are you sure you want to go to the *beach?*" Hope said. She had envisioned sitting by the pool in a bubble of reclusive sadness all summer. She hoped that collective memory was short and that by the time their senior year started, people

would have forgotten about Allegra and Ian Coburn, and about their father, the pimp.

"I'm sure," Allegra said. "We can pack sandwiches, take our books, jump in the ocean."

It did sound appealing. Eddie was in jail, but *they* weren't. "Where are you thinking? Steps? Dionis? Sconset?"

"I was thinking Nobadeer," Allegra said.

"Nobadeer?" Hope said. Nobadeer was where the entire high school hung out. Allegra's former friends would be there. "Have you made up with Hollis, then?"

"God no," Allegra said. "But just because she might be there doesn't mean I can't be there. I like Nobadeer. It's my beach."

It was *your beach,* Hope thought. But the photo of Allegra in her underwear had knocked her name off the top of the Nobadeer masthead. Hope herself never hung out at Nobadeer—not because she didn't like it but because her sister and Hollis and their friends congregated there.

Hope said, "Let's try another beach for starters."

Allegra said, "Let's try Nobadeer for starters."

Hope sighed. They were still Alice and the Dormouse. She didn't have the energy to fight. She wondered if Allegra was planning on using Eddie's incarceration as some kind of social currency. Maybe she thought her old friends would find running a prostitution ring of illegal girls *cool,* or maybe Allegra thought they would feel sorry for her. Hope couldn't predict. Despite the fact that she was one, she did *not* understand teenagers.

Grace packed them sandwiches. She seemed happy they were getting out. "There's no reason to hide," she said. "Your

father made a bad decision, and now he's paying his dues. It doesn't reflect badly on the rest of us."

She sounded as if she were lying. Because she *was* lying. Eddie's downfall *did* reflect badly on the rest of them. Their lives—Allegra's Italian leather jacket, the red Jeep Wrangler, the chemicals that cleaned the pool, the groceries required to make beautiful sandwiches such as the ones Grace was now making—had been financed by a *prostitution ring*. Or at least partially so.

It *did* reflect badly.

Nonetheless, Allegra and Hope put on their bikinis and cover-ups and packed up towels and lotion, bottles of cold water and Diet Coke, and their most precious commodity— the novels they were reading—and accepted the picnic hamper from Grace.

They were off.

The day was bright and blue skied. Allegra insisted they take the top off the Jeep so that sun flooded the front seat as they drove down the sandy roads to the dunes of Nobadeer.

"I'm glad we're doing this," Allegra said. "This is a beach day. This is a gift from God—I mean, look at it."

They walked over the dunes, onto the golden sands of Nobadeer. The ocean seemed vaster here than anywhere else on the island. There were long breaking waves; the green-blue water sparkled. Tons of kids were surfing and boogie boarding and stand-up paddle boarding. The scene was picturesque, and for a second, Hope thought they were right to have come.

Elin Hilderbrand

Then she saw Bluto.

Bluto was impossible to miss. He weighed 250 pounds and was as pale as the moon. He wasn't ugly; he had the sweet, round, blue-eyed face of a baby and nice, thick light-brown hair. But he was crass, and he specialized in the mean exploitation of other people's worst flaws in order to keep people's attention off his own. Bluto was lying on a towel next to Hollis, Kenzie, and Calgary—and there, set a little bit apart, were Hannah and Brick. It was an all-star lineup of Allegra's worst enemies.

Hope turned to look at her sister. Allegra zoomed right for her former friends, beaming. She was wearing a straw hat, her Tom Ford sunglasses, a black bikini, and a black pareu around her hips. She was dazzling.

"Hey, guys!" she said.

Hollis snorted. Bluto said, in his high tenor voice, "Move along, Zippy."

"Zippy?" Allegra said.

"Your ankles are in different zip codes," Bluto said.

Calgary McMann laughed maniacally at this. Hope wanted to kick sand in his face. Her foot was less than a yard away from his towel. She then saw that Calgary and Kenzie had their legs entwined. Gross.

Allegra said, "You find that funny, Calgary? Have you told Kenzie how many times you've tried to kiss me?"

"That's not true," Calgary said.

With one finger, Allegra lowered her sunglasses. "The last time was when you waited for me outside the bathroom at your house earlier this summer. When I almost had to kick you in the nuts."

Kenzie stared at Calgary. Hope thought, *Yes.* Calgary had

356

pretended to like Hope, but only because Hope looked like Allegra. Hope thought Brick might be interested in this news, but he and Hannah were in a world of their own. They hadn't even seemed to notice Allegra and Hope. Brick looked as fit and tan as ever, and his hair was growing blonder. Hope's heart lurched in his direction, although she realized he and Hannah were having some kind of love conversation, and she also recognized that this was a positive thing. Hannah and Brick were a good match. Hannah was an A student, she played ice hockey, she had ambition: she wanted to play Division I in college and make the Olympic team. She wasn't as gorgeous as Allegra, but Brick was probably all finished with gorgeous.

Hope tore her attention away from Brick in time to see Kenzie jump up from her towel and lay into Calgary. "Did you try to kiss that slut? Did you?"

"Oh, please," Hollis said in her sly voice that always reminded Hope of the cobra Nag in *Rikki-Tikki-Tavi*. "This is hardly news. Everyone knows Calgary has had a hard-on for Allegra since the sixth grade."

"Shut up, Hollis!" Kenzie said.

Hollis rolled lazily onto her back. "Watch who you're speaking to like that."

Bluto said, "Leave it to Allegra to stir things up." He mugged up at them. "Just so you know, I'm not mad at you for screwing Ian Coburn. I think he's cute. I'm only *mad* because you didn't tell me."

"Well, I'm mad because you screwed him," Hollis said.

"Because you wanted to screw him yourself," Bluto said. "Admit it."

Hollis gave Bluto a withering look. "You're fat."

"And you're a bitch," Bluto said. "I'm *sorry* we're not friends with Allegra anymore, because I liked her better than I like you."

"I can't believe you just said that," Hollis said.

"And, you know, it was a really evil thing, you forwarding that photo," Bluto said. "You're a backstabber, Hollis Brancato. I'm sure you'll do it to me someday."

Allegra gently took Hope's arm and led her away from the squabble she'd created. No one had mentioned Eddie. Maybe they hadn't heard about what had happened. Or maybe they didn't care. Nobody their age noticed their own parents, much less other people's parents.

Allegra and Hope passed the towels of Brick and Hannah.

"Hi, Hannah. Hi, Brick," Allegra said. She smiled at them in a warm and genuine way but didn't break stride.

They looked up.

"Hi, Allegra," Hannah said. "Hi, Hope."

"Hey, Hope," Brick said. He paused. "Hey, Allegra."

Hope was too stunned to respond. Stunned at what, however, she wasn't quite sure. Maybe at the ability of people to be their normal selves, no matter what the circumstances. To *keep calm and carry on,* as the popular sentiment went.

When they were out of earshot, Allegra said, "They make a pretty cute couple." She linked her free arm through Hope's, and, despite every instinct that told Hope not to trust the friendly advances of her sister, she filled with a feeling of warm friendship and more—sisterhood, twinship. Her and Allegra, against the world, from birth until death.

"You think?" Hope said.

"Well," Allegra said. "Not as cute as us."

MADELINE

At ten o'clock in the morning, there was a knock on her apartment door. Madeline had just written the first page of her new novel, *The Before,* on her legal pad. Angie liked the new title and was encouraged by the premise of a prequel to *Islandia.* She wasn't quite as frantic as she had been about the popped bubble of *B/G.* If anything, she seemed almost exhilarated by having something to hold over Redd Dreyfus's head. "I've been indebted to him for so long," Angie said, "it was time for the tables to turn."

"Do you mind me asking?" Madeline said. "What *happened* between you two?"

"I'll tell you sometime," Angie had said.

Madeline didn't *want* to stand to open the door. The whole point of taking the apartment was to avoid random interruptions. But the knocking was insistent.

Who? Madeline thought.

If it was Rachel McMann "stopping by" to invite Madeline out for coffee, Madeline would lose her temper.

It might be Trevor. He was off today, working around the house and yard. He had threatened to come by and kidnap Madeline for a summertime adventure—a drive up to Great Point, lunch on the deck at Cru, a harbor sail on the *Endeavor. "Chim-chiminey, chim-chiminey, chim-chim-cheroo!"* Madeline would have a hard time turning her handsome husband down.

It might be Brick, with Hannah Dromanian. Brick and Hannah had started hanging out together in the aftermath of Allegra's deception. Madeline was worried Brick would fall right into another all-consuming relationship, but it did seem like the two were primarily friends. Hannah was one of those kids whom Madeline thought of as a natural-born achiever. She wanted to succeed, go places, see things, do things, and Madeline thought she might be a good influence on Brick.

Madeline was relieved to know it would not be Eddie Pancik at the door.

The knocking continued. Madeline's Mini Cooper was in the bricked spot. Whoever this was knew she was here, probably knew she was writing, and didn't care.

Grace?

The thought occurred to Madeline only as she pulled open the door. Madeline called Grace every day and had invited her ten or twenty times to come into town and see the apartment. But Grace said she felt safer at home. She didn't want to come into town and *bump into anyone*—and Madeline couldn't blame her.

Madeline would have expected that, with all Grace had been through, she would have looked haggard or wrung out, much as she used to after a three-day migraine. But Grace looked radiant. She was wearing white shorts and a blue gingham halter top; she was the picture of summertime. Her eyes were shining, her skin glowed, her smile was warm and peaceful.

Peaceful? Madeline thought. How was that possible?

"Hi?" Madeline said.

"You did it," Grace said.

"Did what?" Madeline said.

"You wrote this book about *me and Benton!*" Grace said. "It's all in there—the mint tea, the pistachio *macaron*s, the Rolling Stones singing '*Loving Cup.*'"

"I know, Grace. I'm so sorry," Madeline said. "I told you, I'm not going to publish it…"

Grace started shaking and crying, and Madeline thought, *She's going to sue me anyway.* Defamation of character. Libel. But then Grace took a step forward and wrapped her arms around Madeline.

"That was the ending I wanted," Grace said.

"Living in the Virgin Islands?" Madeline said. "Bird-watching?"

"Happiness," Grace said. "Peace."

EDDIE

He thought about feeling sorry for himself. He thought about falling into despair. He thought about crying. He thought about listing all the things he would miss about being free.

But what Eddie ended up thinking about on the drive to MCI-Plymouth, a drive that couldn't last long enough, as far as he was concerned, was the day the twins were born.

Allegra had popped out easily, as if from an ATM spitting out money. *Here you go, everything you asked for!*

Hope, however, had her umbilical cord wrapped around her neck, and before Eddie could process the arrival of his

first baby, Grace was being raced to the emergency room for a cesarean section. Eddie left Allegra with the nurses and followed, pulling on scrubs as he was directed, hurrying to keep up.

He couldn't watch the surgery—he didn't have the stomach for that, his head was down between his knees so he didn't faint—but he did remember seeing Hope's tiny light-blue body, covered in blood, and he remembered his terror, his naked screaming fear.

She's dead, he thought.

Grace called out in a voice he could barely stand to summon, *She's dead, Eddie, she's dead!*

She had a grip on his fingers—she was going to break them all cleanly in half—and he didn't care.

He wouldn't, he realized, care about his own self, his own person, ever again.

It turned out the baby wasn't dead. Somehow the doctors, the nurses, the wizards and angels, got Hope breathing—but she couldn't stay on Nantucket. She had to be MedFlighted to Boston, and Eddie was going with her. Eddie was in charge. Eddie was her *father.*

There was a lot of procedure that happened very quickly. Paramedics in blue jumpsuits, who struck Eddie as ridiculously calm and competent, strapped Hope onto a tiny stretcher. They applied heart monitors the size of dimes and an oxygen mask the size of an egg. Eddie went into the back of the helicopter with a human being small enough to nestle comfortably inside his Panama hat.

One of the paramedics was a woman with copper-colored corkscrew curls. Her name was Kristin, and she was stationed in the back to monitor Hope's vital signals. She handed Eddie

a pair of large over-the-ear headphones to muffle the noise of the chopper, and she put a miniature set of headphones, headphones for a doll, over Hope's delicate ears.

Before the world went at once loud and silent, Eddie said to Kristin, "Do people ever die in this helicopter?"

"Oh, sure," she said. "All the time." She smiled at him. "But your daughter is going to be fine."

The helicopter had lifted seconds later, and so had Eddie's spirit.

Kristin the MedFlight paramedic had been right: Hope was fine, better than fine. Occasionally over the years, Eddie would look at his slightly younger twin—when she licked her finger and turned the page of one of the books she was always reading (she was like Grace in this way), when she played the flute (how did she do it? Eddie had picked up the instrument once and had blown into the mouthpiece but had heard nothing but his own hot air)—and he would marvel at just how fine she had turned out to be, that small, pale-blue baby.

The last time Eddie had felt this way had been when he took Hope to the Summer House for dinner, just the two of them. He had been returning from the men's room to the table when he saw Hope lean over to taste his martini. His first instinct was to call out, *Hey, there, what are you doing, Hope? Come on.* But he stopped himself. He recognized Hope's natural curiosity about the adult world, beyond the edges of her own, and applauded her courage to explore it in a safe way. What he'd thought was, *Good for you, Hope. Good for you.*

* * *

These memories sustained Eddie all the way to exit 6 off Route 3 south, which was, unfortunately, Eddie's exit.

Eddie Pancik had never been much for self-reflection, but as the van pulled up in front of MCI-Plymouth, and as the uniformed guards stopped them at the gate to check Eddie's name off their list, Eddie tried to identify exactly how he was feeling.

The word that came to his mind was blessed.

NANTUCKET

There was so much chatter on Nantucket that we were surprised they couldn't hear us on Martha's Vineyard.

Russian prostitution ring, Low Beach Road, Edward Pancik arrested: this made the papers in Boston and beyond. We all had to suffer through people from off island asking us: *How could this happen on Nantucket?*

Nantucket was a place of men and women, of business and commerce, just like everywhere else. The more hard hearted and seasoned of us asked: *Do you not think there were prostitutes on Nantucket back in the whaling heyday?* It was the world's oldest profession. Eddie Pancik had hardly invented it.

Certain people benefited from the scandal. One was Eloise Coffin, Eddie's secretary. She had quit her job at Island Fog Realty—obviously—and was secretly hoping for a call from the local news station. One "investigative reporter" from an

Internet blog named *Jared's Apartment* called and asked to hear Eloise's story. And so Eloise told this reporter, Jared, about how she'd been placing her cartons of organic Greek yogurt in the office fridge when she overheard Barbara Pancik on the phone, proposing the unthinkable for their five Russian housecleaners. Eloise had been *completely aghast*—and *then* she caught wind of how much money Eddie, Barbie, and the girls would be making.

Eloise did *not* tell this Jared fellow that there had been a week or two when she had tried to get in on the action. She had been sweet and accommodating, she had bought Eddie a potted snapdragon with her own money, she had complimented Barbie on her green-and-white-print wrap dress, even though Eloise felt that kind of dress had gone out in the 1970s. She had tried to be one of the team, hoping that either Eddie or Barbie might confide in her and cut her into the profits.

But they had chosen to be selfish—the selfish, greedy Panciks—and Eloise had had no choice but to call her son-in-law at the Nantucket Police Department and tell him what she'd heard.

The "investigative reporter," Jared, never published the story anywhere that Eloise could find. She had her daughter-in-law, Patrice, check the Internet, but Patrice couldn't find a blog called *Jared's Apartment*. Eloise craved public acknowledgment of her do-gooding, and, falling short of that, she simply told her tale to anyone who would listen—friends, neighbors, her children and grandchildren, and her husband, Clarence.

But Clarence was six years older than Eloise, and he wore hearing aids that seemed to pick up sounds coming only from the television. Clarence had spent most of his retirement watching television—the Red Sox in summer and the Patriots

and Bruins in winter, and, if not sports, then the Food Network. Eloise knew that Clarence was secretly in love with Giada De Laurentiis.

Eloise said to Clarence, "I'm surprised more reporters aren't calling."

"It was the FBI who caught the guy, El, not you," Clarence said.

"Oh, I know," Eloise said. She had been a bit disappointed when she found out there was a second informant, one with more clout than Eloise. "But you'd think, I don't know, that they'd offer me some kind of reward."

"Reward?" Clarence said.

"Yes, you know—like money," Eloise said. "Or a plaque." Even a plaque would be fine, as long as it was presented to her on a stage, in front of an audience. Eloise would stand before photographers with the chief of the Nantucket police, each of them holding one side of the plaque, smiling for the cameras. That was sure to make the evening news: EMPLOYEE UNCOVERS PROSTITUTION RING.

But Clarence had stopped listening, and there was little hope of her getting his attention back. Giada De Laurentiis was on the tube, making homemade gnocchi with sage and brown butter.

Eloise sighed. *Reward*. Then she retreated to the kitchen table, where she would scour the classified ads. She needed another job.

The third house that Eddie Pancik was building on Eagle Wing Lane was bought immediately by Glenn Daley of Bay-

berry Properties, who, we later learned, had bought the other two spec houses from Eddie in a private deal. Rachel McMann begged Glenn for the first crack at selling the three houses once they were finished. But Glenn Daley had other ideas. He hired a new real-estate agent to join his agency—none other than Barbie Pancik! On the day that Barbie moved into her new desk—as it happened, the desk right next to Glenn's—Glenn pulled a diamond ring out of his drawer and proposed marriage.

"Will you be my wife?" he asked.

Barbie Pancik, too overcome for words, placed her perfectly manicured hand over her mouth and nodded an emphatic yes. All the other agents and associates in the office clapped and cheered, Rachel McMann a little less enthusiastically than some.

Grace Pancik put her Wauwinet Road house, "with three acres of gardens designed by renowned landscape architect Benton Coe," on the market for $3.5 million. In less than a week, Barbie Pancik (soon to be Barbie Pancik-Daley) had sold the place for full listing price. Grace and her two daughters moved into a charming cottage on Lily Street with a postage-stamp yard. It was hard to give up the hens, Grace said, but it would be nice to live in town and be able to walk to coffee, and to the post office to mail Eddie's care packages.

Jean Burton happened to see Grace at the Federal Street post office one morning, nestling a brand-new Panama hat in straw to send to Eddie, along with three bottles of cherry Tums and an index card with her lip prints on it.

"She's standing by her man," Jean said. "I really admire that."

We all agreed that it was laudable. What, after all, was to keep Grace from following Benton Coe to Detroit? The two of them had been madly in love. We had NOT been wrong about that.

Jody Rouisse said to Susan Prendergast, "Well, if she isn't going to Detroit to chase him, then I just might." But Jody Rouisse, as we knew, was all talk. The most she would ever do would be to follow Benton on Twitter, using the hashtag *#belleislepark*.

Speaking of Panama hats, rumor had it that Philip Meier, a longtime loan officer at Nantucket Bank, ordered a Panama hat online, a cheap imitation one that cost him $19.99. Philip then approached the bank employees who worked at the teller desk, all of them women.

He said, "I know it's only August, but how many of you want to dress up as prostitutes for Halloween and come with me to the Chicken Box? We're sure to win first prize. I'm going as Eddie Pancik."

The tellers laughed nervously. None of them wanted to go anywhere with Philip on Halloween. He was too touchy-feely; even the office holiday party was trying.

Finding he had no takers, Philip Meier went back to his computer and ordered an orange prison jumpsuit. He didn't need five girls; he could win Best Costume all by himself.

But still, it would be better with the girls.

He would work on them, he decided. He still had plenty of time.

Madeline King and Grace Pancik were back to being friends. We would see them side by side at Steps Beach; we could find the two of them, plus Trevor Llewellyn, out to dinner at Le Languedoc and the Straight Wharf on Saturday nights. We had all figured out by then that the "involvement" between Eddie and Madeline had been financial, not sexual, and we learned that Grace had paid Madeline and Trevor their fifty thousand dollars back only hours after she closed on her house.

It was rumored that the photograph of Allegra Pancik and Ian Coburn sitting on the hood of Ian's red Camaro in their underwear had gone viral and that both teenagers had been offered modeling contracts, with shoots in New York, London, and Hong Kong.

That rumor was quashed when Blond Sharon took her children to the Weezie Library and found Allegra shelving books from a cart among the babbling young children playing with wooden trucks on the braided rug, and mothers and caregivers reading in hushed tones. Allegra was certainly beautiful enough to be a model, Blond Sharon thought. Her long dark hair was loose over her shoulders, and her skin was a golden tan against the white eyelets of her sundress, which

was a more modest garment than Blond Sharon could ever remember seeing her wear.

"Allegra!" Blond Sharon said in surprise, her voice several decibels louder than was appropriate for a children's library. "What are you doing *here?* I thought you were on your way to fame and glory!"

"Fame?" Allegra said quizzically, as she slid *Bear Snores On* back into place on the shelf. "Glory?"

Blond Sharon blinked. Who had told her that Allegra Pancik was going to be a model for Lucky jeans, replacing Gisele Bündchen? Now she couldn't remember.

She left the Weezie library hand in hand with her two children, Sterling and Colby, who were late for their sailing lessons anyway. She felt a little deflated that the glamorous story she'd heard wasn't true.

But then she perked up. It was, after all, a beautiful day on Nantucket; the sun was shining, and Blond Sharon knew that it would be only a matter of time until this island gave her something else to talk about.

ACKNOWLEDGMENTS

As many of you are certainly aware, this novel was written while I was battling breast cancer. I have dedicated it to my surgeons, who are among the most brilliant, talented, professional human beings I have ever encountered. In addition, I would like to thank my medical oncologist, Steven Isakoff, for continuing to keep me in good health, and everyone else who treated me at Massachusetts General Hospital. A special thanks to the women in Dr. Colwell's office, most specifically Agnes Santomarco, Heather Parker, Amy Israelian, Kelly Hurley, and Mary Joyce.

I was buoyed by those of you who reached out to me, either on Facebook or in other ways—many of you are fighting or have fought this battle yourselves. Every word and thought and prayer was cherished.

I have to thank my family, my friends, my home team, too many people to name, who dropped off food and sent flowers, and people who stopped me in the street or in the aisles of the grocery store to let me know they were thinking of me. Of special note: my sorority sisters of Phi Mu at the Johns Hopkins University—amazing reach-out!—spearheaded by Sue Plano. And, in no particular order: my sister Heather Osteen Thorpe, my "person" Debbie Briggs, Charles and Margaret Marino, Rebecca Bartlett, Wendy Rouillard (iced tea delivery), Evelyn MacEachern (*macaron* delivery), Mary Haft (prayers galore), Wendy Hudson, Elizabeth Almodobar, Jill Roethke,

Acknowledgments

Jill Surprenant, Anne Gifford, Manda Riggs, my sister-in-law and fellow survivor, Lisa Hilderbrand, Helaina Jones, Heidi Holdgate (the pool is my happy place), Shelly Weedon, Holly McGowan, Melissa MacVicar, Stephanie McGrath, Laurie Richards, Mark and Eithne Yelle, Lori Snell, Logan O'Connor, Sheila Carroll, Jeanne and Richard Diamond, John and Martha Sargent—and my nanny, Erin Frawley, who managed to give my kids a normal, carefree summer at Nobadeer Beach, despite the big curveball.

Mark and Gwen Snider of the Nantucket Hotel—the club was my refuge, and much of this novel was composed poolside. Thank you for the sanctuary.

Michael Carlisle and David Forrer, there aren't words. You are simply sent from heaven.

Reagan Arthur, there really aren't words. You are to editing what Bruce Springsteen is to the rock anthem, what Mr. Blahnik is to the stiletto, what Bobby Flay is to the grill. You are the best in your field, and each year I stand more in awe of your talent and sensibility.

Last, I would like to thank my children, Maxwell, Dawson, and Shelby Cunningham. Having a mother who is writing two novels a year and battling cancer is kind of like having no mother at all, but the three of you managed to make me feel like I was doing something right each and every day just by listening to your voices and watching you grow. You are the reason I fight, you are the reason I write, you are what makes my life whole and complete, and I love you.

ABOUT THE AUTHOR

The following rumors about Elin Hilderbrand are true: she writes her novels longhand, she is a good cook and a terrible gardener, and she is fighting breast cancer. Everything else is up for speculation. *The Rumor* is her fifteenth novel.

ELIN HILDERBRAND

The Matchmaker

Dabney Kimball Beech, the 48-year-old Director of the Nantucket Chamber of Commerce and fifth generation Nantucketer, has had a lifelong gift of matchmaking (52 couples still together to her credit). But when Dabney discovers she is dying of pancreatic cancer, she sets out to find matches for a few people very close to home: her husband, John Boxmiller Beech, celebrated economist and Harvard professor; her lover, Clendenin Hughes, Pulitzer-winning journalist who lost his arm in Southeast Asia; and her daughter, Agnes, who is engaged to be married to the wrong man.

As time slips away from Dabney, she is determined to find matches for those she loves most – but at what cost to her own relationships?

The Matchmaker is the heartbreaking novel from Elin Hilderbrand about losing and finding love, even as you're running out of time.

Out now

HODDER

ELIN HILDERBRAND

Winter Street

Kelley Quinn is the owner of Nantucket's Winter Street Inn and the proud father of four – Patrick, Kevin, Ava and Bart, all of them grown and living in varying states of disarray.

As Christmas approaches, Kelley is looking forward to getting the family together for some quality time at the inn. But when he walks in on his wife Mitzi kissing Santa Claus – or the guy who's playing Santa at the inn's annual party – utter chaos descends. With the three older children each reeling in their own dramas and Bart (a Marine) unreachable in Afghanistan, it might be up to Kelley's ex-wife to save Christmas at the Winter Street Inn.

Before the mulled cider is gone, the delightfully dysfunctional Quinn family will survive a love triangle, an unplanned pregnancy, a federal crime, a small house fire, many shots of whiskey, and endless rounds of Christmas caroling, in this heart-warming novel about coming home for the holidays.

Out now

HODDER

ELIN HILDERBRAND

Beautiful Day

The Carmichaels and Grahams have gathered on Nantucket for a wedding. Plans are being made according to the wishes of the bride's late mother, who left behind The Notebook: specific instructions for every detail of her youngest daughter's future nuptials. Everything should be falling into place for the beautiful event – but in reality, things are far from perfect.

While the couple-to-be are quite happy, their loved ones find their own lives crumbling. In the days leading up to the wedding, love will be questioned, scandals will arise, and hearts will be broken . . .

In *Beautiful Day* Elin Hilderbrand takes readers on a journey into the heart of marriage, what it means to be faithful, and how we choose to honour our commitments.

Out now

HODDER